Praise for the Fatal Series
by *New York Times* bestselling author
Marie Force

"Force's skill is also evident in the way that she develops the characters, from the murdered and mutilated senator to the detective and chief of staff who are trying to solve the case. The heroine, Sam, is especially complex and her secrets add depth to this mystery... This novel is *The O.C.* does D.C., and you just can't get enough."

—*RT Book Reviews* on *Fatal Affair* (4.5 stars)

"Force pushes the boundaries by deftly using political issues like immigration to create an intricate mystery."
—*RT Book Reviews* on *Fatal Consequences* (4 stars)

"The romance, the mystery, the ongoing story lines... everything about these books has me sitting on the edge of my seat and begging for more. I am anxiously awaiting the next in the series. I give *Fatal Deception* an A."

—*TheBookPushers.com*

"The suspense is thick, the passion between Nick and Sam just keeps getting hotter and hotter."
—*Guilty Pleasures Book Reviews* on *Fatal Deception*

"Sam is a fun, strong character about whom readers will want to know more. Her relationship with Nick is spicy and realistic. The mystery is well constructed and forms a solid base around which all the other events revolve."

—*Library Journal Reviews* on *Fatal Jeopardy*

"The perfect mesh of mystery and romance."
—*Night Owl Reviews* on *Fatal Scandal* (5 stars)

The Fatal Series
by *New York Times* bestselling author Marie Force
Suggested reading order

And look for the next book in the Fatal Series from Marie Force, *Fatal Identity*

MARIE FORCE

Fatal
SCANDAL

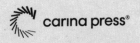

carına press®

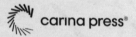 carina press®

ISBN-13: 978-0-373-00408-9

Fatal Scandal

Copyright © 2015 by HTJB, Inc.

Recycling programs for this product may not exist in your area.

www.CarinaPress.com

Printed in U.S.A.

ONE

THE DUAL SCANDAL ripped through the city with the power of a tsunami, flooding the airwaves with headlines that struck fear in Sam's heart. "Springer Alleges Farnsworth's Incompetence Caused Son's Death" and "Detective 'In Bed' with Judge on Custody Matter."

Sitting in front of the TV in the master bedroom, Sam hung on every word that was being said about her beloved chief of police, the man she'd known first as Uncle Joe. And her close friend, Detective Tommy "Gonzo" Gonzales, who'd been shot during the Springer investigation shortly after he'd been granted full and permanent custody of his young son Alex.

"Springer alleges that Farnsworth personally ordered the homicide investigation into the stabbing deaths of his younger son Hugo and eight of Hugo's friends be put on hold to allow for the conclusion of a six-month undercover narcotics investigation that had focused on Billy Springer and his associates." The talking head on CBC seemed to be taking great pleasure in reporting on the events that had led to Billy Springer's death at the hands of a Metro PD SWAT team.

"Are they going to mention how he shot at *us*?" Sam asked the TV. "Of course not. That won't be brought up."

"The department faces the secondary scandal surrounding Detective Sergeant Thomas Gonzales, who was shot in the neck by Springer during the confrontation at Springer's grandmother's house in Friendship Heights."

"Thank you!" Sam said. "Finally! Thanks for remembering Springer actually *shot* one of our people!"

"Gonzales's custody case was heard in the courtroom of Family Court Judge Leon Morton, the brother of Eva Morton, whose homicide case was investigated by none other than newly promoted Detective Thomas Gonzales. Neither the judge nor the detective disclosed their earlier connection, which is a conflict of interest, according to the attorney for the baby's mother, Lori Phillips."

"Oh my God, Gonzo," Sam whispered. She couldn't even think about what it would mean to Gonzo if he lost custody of the son he adored. "What a fucked-up mess."

"What's a fucked-up mess?" Sam's husband and the country's new vice president asked as he came into the bedroom where she sat at the end of the bed watching the news. It was one of two rooms in the house that wasn't being monitored by the Secret Service around the clock. The other was their loft on the top floor of the double-sized townhouse, the place they escaped to whenever they needed some time alone.

"Gonzo."

"What about him?" Nick asked.

"He failed to disclose an earlier connection to Judge Morton, who presided over Alex's custody hearing. He investigated the murder of Morton's sister years ago."

"Oh, damn."

"And now Lori and her lawyer are making a big stink out of the fact that they failed to disclose. She's taken her case to the media, and they're eating it up like the rabid dogs they are."

"Tommy must be freaking out."

"Yeah, I'm sure he is. And he's got enough on his mind with the wound taking forever to heal."

Sam blew out a deep breath to calm nerves that went

nuts every time she relived the way the Springer investigation had blown up in their faces and how they would've lost Gonzo without his partner's quick action.

Sensing her disquiet, Nick came to her and wrapped his arms around her, which calmed her like always. "He's fine, Sam. A little battered but fine. And this thing with the judge will blow over when something bigger happens. You know how the news cycle in this city works."

Sam looped her arms around his waist and breathed in the rich, masculine scent of home. He was so beautiful with his brown hair that curled at the ends, the dark olive complexion that made him look tan, even in the dead of winter, and the hazel eyes that saw her like no one else before him ever had. "And this thing with the chief. I'm worried about it."

"How come? Everyone knows Springer is just spouting off because he doesn't want to accept that one of his sons killed another of his sons—and a bunch of other kids too."

"I know, but what Springer is saying about Farnsworth. It's true. He did put the murder investigation on hold when it was zeroing in on Billy Springer because the narcs were completing a long-term undercover investigation and needed more time to sew it up."

"And that's unusual?"

"Nothing trumps murder. The whole thing was totally bizarre. We all thought so."

"Did he tell you why he made that call?"

"It was about money and the huge investment that'd already been made into the narcotics investigation. If nothing came of that outlay of cash, it would hurt us at budget time. Or something like that. And now it's coming back to bite him in the ass anyway."

"He's withstood worse. He'll get through this too."

Sam wanted to believe Nick was right, but she was

worried nonetheless. "Ever since the chief put the murder investigation on ice, I've had a bad feeling about how it could come back to haunt us."

"So you're saying Springer has good reason to be pissed?"

"Well, not necessarily. His son was, in fact, a murderer, and what father ever wants to admit that? But Billy might still be alive—and Gonzo never would've been shot— if we'd arrested Billy the night before the standoff with SWAT. And we'd all like to know how he found out we were focusing on him. The entire thing was a fucking disaster."

"Are you still up for going out tonight?" Nick asked.

Sam forced herself to rally for his sake. He needed this night out more than she did, and she needed it pretty damn badly. "Of course I am. I've been living for date night with my sexy husband."

He rolled his eyes at her as he always did when she commented on his supreme hotness.

"Besides, I know it's taken a tremendous amount of coordination to make it happen, so I wouldn't dream of backing out."

At the reminder of the restrictions that came with his new job, his smile faded. "Yeah, it did. It takes a freaking act of Congress for me to be able to walk out the goddamn door."

He'd known, of course, that round-the-clock Secret Service protection would be confining. But knowing it and living it were two very different things. He'd had protection at the end of his recent campaign for the Senate after Sam's family had been threatened. However, Nick was finding a huge difference between having a detail as a candidate and having one as vice president.

"Let me grab a quick shower and get changed," Sam said. "Where's Scotty?"

"He and Shelby are making pizza. Rumor has it her *boyfriend* will be joining them." FBI Special Agent Avery Hill was hardly her husband's favorite person, probably because of the not-so-secret crush he'd once had on her. "I'll be down in fifteen minutes."

"I'll be waiting." He left her with a kiss and headed downstairs to spend some time with Scotty before they left.

Sam rushed through a shower and changed into the sexy black cocktail dress she'd bought weeks ago with this evening in mind. It was their second New Year's Eve as a couple, and they were returning to the place where they'd gone last year to celebrate their new jobs—hers as the lieutenant in charge of the Metro Police Department's Homicide Division and his as a newly sworn-in senator, taking the place of his slain best friend, John O'Connor.

She smoothed Nick's favorite lavender- and vanilla-scented lotion onto her arms and legs as she thought about him and the changes they'd all endured since he accepted President Nelson's offer to become his new vice president. While her life had remained more or less the same, Nick's had changed dramatically, and she could see him chafing against some of the restrictions.

For one thing, the insomnia that had plagued him for most of his adult life had been relentless in the last couple of weeks. For another, the constant, intrusive presence of his Secret Service detail was driving them both to drink. The director of the Secret Service had given them special permission to remain in their own Capitol Hill home, but the officers assigned to protect Nick were clearly put out by the directive. Not that any of them had said as much to Nick, but it was obvious to both of them that the detail didn't approve.

They'd much rather have the family living at the Naval Observatory in the traditional home of the vice president. But with Sam's dad three doors down from them and still recovering from his recent surgery to remove a bullet from his spinal cord, there was no way she could move. Nick had known that and had made remaining in their own home a condition of accepting the president's offer.

Thank God he'd also negotiated for no Secret Service protection for her, which allowed her to continue in her role as the lieutenant in charge of the MPD's Homicide Division. The thought of being trailed by a detail gave Sam the heebie-jeebies. So while she retained the freedom to come and go as she pleased, Nick and Scotty were under lock and key, which had been an adjustment for all of them.

As the cold winter weather had set in, they'd been content to spend many an evening at home during the holiday season, watching movies and playing round after round of Monopoly with Scotty, who was shaping up to be a real estate shark in the making. He won every game. Sam couldn't help but wonder, however, what would happen when her guys began to chafe at being stuck at home so much of the time.

"We'll cross that bridge when we get to it," she decided. For now, she was thrilled to have a romantic evening ahead of her with the love of her life. She secured the diamond key necklace he'd given her as a wedding gift and slid on the gorgeous engagement ring she only wore when she wasn't working. He'd told her he liked seeing it on her hand, so she wore it for him as often as possible.

In the room that served as her closet, she found a black wool coat that she tossed over her arm before she headed downstairs wearing the four-inch black Louboutin stunners with the red bottoms that Nick had bought her for Christmas. Her husband knew the way to her heart was through her shoes, and she'd found one hell of a way to thank him. She smiled when she remembered dropping to her knees before him—while wearing only the shoes—and the way his eyes had widened with surprise and then pure desire when he'd realized her intention.

As she entered the living room, the doorbell rang and the Secret Service agent working the door admitted Avery Hill, who stopped to give Sam the head-to-toe once-over before he cleared his throat and said hello.

She really wished he'd quit looking at her that way before Nick ran a rusty steak knife through the guy's heart. Wouldn't that make for some memorable headlines—*Vice President Cappuano Charged with First-Degree, Premeditated Murder by Rusty Steak Knife of FBI Agent Who Lusted After His Wife. Story at eleven!*

The thing about it, though, was that Hill was a trusted and valued colleague on the job, and he had a relationship that was starting to be long-term going with their friend and personal assistant, Shelby Faircloth. Yet every so often, he still looked at Sam like he wanted to kidnap her and drag her out of her happy home to be his sex slave.

Whoa. Where the hell had the *sex slave* thought come from?

"Sam?" he asked, his brows furrowed. "Are you okay?"

"Yeah, sure. I'm fine. You?"

"Great. Good holiday?"

"Fantastic. You?"

"Very nice. The whole family was in Charleston for the first time in years."

Sam sucked at small talk, but she made an effort for Shelby's sake. She wanted Shelby to feel free to have any guest she wanted over to visit since she spent so much time at their house. Hill was at the top of Shelby's guest list, much to Nick's never-ending dismay.

Speak of the devil. He came into the room, and his amiable expression instantly hardened when he saw that Hill had arrived. Nick put his arm around her and kissed her temple. Not for the first time, she was grateful he didn't lift his leg and pee on her to mark his territory in front of the agent.

"What do you think of this shit with Farnsworth and Gonzo?" Hill asked, apparently oblivious, as usual, to the fact that Nick would prefer that Hill didn't speak to his wife—ever.

"I'm hoping it'll blow over when something bigger happens."

"Springer's out for blood. He's not going to be happy with anything less than Farnsworth's head on a stick."

Sam's stomach turned at the thought of anyone other than her beloved Uncle Joe as the chief of police.

"No sense speculating on what might happen," Nick said. "We've got somewhere to be. Are you ready, babe?" The Secret Service detail was hovering by the front door, waiting for the signal from Nick that they were set to go.

"Let me just say good-night to Scotty, and then I'll be ready."

"He's in the kitchen with Shelby."

Reluctant to leave Nick and Hill alone in a room together, she took hold of her husband's hand and tugged him along with her to the kitchen, where Scotty was making pizza with Shelby. At times like this, Sam felt like a total loser as a mother because it would never occur to her to make pizza from scratch when there were perfectly good take-out numbers to call. Fortunately, Scotty didn't seem to realize he'd landed a dud for a mother. He lit up at the sight of her and Nick the way he always did.

"Sam! Check it out! I tossed my own crust just like that chef guy on TV does it." He'd recently turned thirteen and had grown at least two inches since he came to live with them over the summer. A member of Scotty's Secret Service detail sat at the table reading the paper, sticking out despite his effort to be unobtrusive. They were all obtrusive, and Sam hated having them in her house. But the alternative of having Nick and Scotty unprotected was unthinkable.

"Looking good, buddy. If I tried that, the crust would be stuck to the ceiling."

Nick patted her shoulder. "It's best that you have your pizza delivered."

How did he always know what she was thinking? That was one of her life's most enduring mysteries.

"We're heading out," Nick said. "Are you guys all set with everything?"

"We're good," Shelby said, smiling at Hill, who hovered in the doorway.

Scotty nodded in agreement. "Yep."

"Give me a hug," Sam said.

"My hands are all dirty, and you look really nice," Scotty said.

"I'll risk it."

He held his hands up and away from her while she gave him a squeeze and a kiss on the cheek. "Be good for Shelby."

"Duh, I'm always good."

And wasn't that the truth? He was a good and decent boy, and they were blessed to have him in their lives. If only they could get his adoption finalized, everything would be perfect. As required by the courts, they had a private investigator looking for Scotty's biological father, but so far their efforts hadn't yielded any results.

"Shelby said we can have champagne at midnight."

The tiny blonde Sam called Tinker Bell balked. "I said no such thing! Don't get me in trouble."

Scotty laughed at her outrage.

"I said you could stay *up* until midnight, but if you get me in trouble, it's off to bed with you right now."

"I'll behave," Scotty said gravely, a devilish glint in his eyes.

"Happy New Year," Nick said.

"Same to you," Shelby said. "Have a good time, and don't worry about anything here."

"Thanks, Shelby." With a hand placed possessively on her lower back, Nick ushered Sam from the kitchen.

Hill ducked out of the way to let them pass. "Happy New Year," he said.

"Same to you," Sam said while Nick remained stubbornly silent.

As they stepped into the living room, the Secret Service agents sprung into action, talking on radios and doing all the stuff they did every time Nick dared to leave the house. Before her eyes, his entire body went tense, letting her know how much he detested all the hoopla.

Brant, the lead agent on his detail, waited by the front door. "Mr. Vice President, Mrs. Cappuano, we're ready for you."

After Nick held her coat for her, Sam squeezed his arm and smiled up at him, hoping to defuse some of his tension by reminding him that at the end of the day, it was still about the two of them. "Let's go have some fun."

He returned her smile and seemed to relax ever so slightly. "Let's do it."

TWO

NICK HAD SECURED the same K Street lounge where they'd held their promotion party last year. Except this time, it was just the two of them and his detail rather than the raucous crowd of friends and family that had joined them a year ago.

"Are they closed tonight?" Sam asked.

Nick gestured to a candlelit table set for two in the middle of the big room that usually served as a bustling nightclub. "For a private party of two."

"My husband must have some kind of cache to be able to shut down a hot spot like this on New Year's Eve."

"Yes, he's very powerful and influential," he said with the self-deprecating grin she loved so much. "In truth, the only way the Secret Service would go for it was if we had the place to ourselves." He shrugged. "So we have the place to ourselves."

She ran her hand down the length of his red silk tie and hooked her index finger under his belt. "Having the place completely to ourselves doesn't totally suck."

"Don't get any ideas. We're not alone."

Though his detail had faded into the background, they were always there and always watching. Determined to ensure he had a good time tonight despite the prying eyes around them, Sam walked over to the table. He was right behind her, holding the chair for her. The moment they were seated, a waiter emerged from the kitchen.

"Mr. Vice President, Mrs. Cappuano, it is indeed an

honor to have you here tonight. I'm Mario, and I'll be your waiter."

"Thank you, Mario," Nick said. "I believe we need some champagne."

Sam nodded in agreement, and the waiter hustled off to get it. "Champagne makes me silly and uninhibited," Sam reminded her husband.

"Does it? I'd forgotten that."

Since he never forgot anything where she was concerned, she rolled her eyes to let him know she wasn't buying it. "I think you're just trying to make sure you get lucky later."

"Do I ever have any problem getting lucky?"

"Are you calling me easy, Mr. VP?"

"If the Louboutin fits…"

Laughing, Sam said, "I can't even deny these accusations."

"I love that you're easy." He kissed the back of her hand, sending shivers of sensation darting up her arm and straight to her nipples, which stood at attention. Naturally, he noticed, his hazel eyes heating with pleasure at the way she reacted to him. "You have no idea how much I count on the one thing in my life that's always easy and effortless."

"You're the only one who's ever said that dealing with me is effortless."

"I love *dealing* with you, as you well know."

She loved when he looked at her the way he was now, as if the sun, the moon and the stars rose and set with her.

The moment ended when Mario returned with their champagne, which was presented with flourish. "Please enjoy," he said when he'd filled two crystal flutes. "I'll be back with your appetizers momentarily."

"So we don't have to order?" Sam asked when they were alone again.

"All taken care of."

In her past life, before him, it would've made her crazy to have a man order for her. But when he did it, she felt cared for and maybe a bit coddled. Not that she'd ever admit as much to him. She had a reputation to maintain, after all.

"I can see the gerbils working overtime on the treadmill as you try to convince yourself to let go and roll with it," he said, amusement dancing in his eyes.

"You can see no such thing."

"Whatever you say, babe. Any minute now there'll be smoke pouring out your ears."

He knew her better than anyone ever had—better than anyone ever would. Her inclination at first had been to fight that, to preserve a piece of herself so she'd survive if things between them didn't work out. Now, after a year with him, she had faith it would work out and knew for certain she'd never survive without him.

"Now what're you thinking?"

"You tell me. You're the one with ESP."

He studied her intently, making her squirm ever so slightly in her chair. "You're thinking that you love me so much it's not even funny, and you can't wait until we get home to the one place where there're no prying eyes so you can have your wicked way with me. Am I close?"

"If you hadn't already told me how easy I am, I'd tell you you're delusional. But we know better, don't we?"

"Yes, we do." Smiling, he raised his glass to her. "To my gorgeous, sexy, exasperating, *easy* wife, I love you more than anything, and I can't wait to see what our second year together will entail."

Charmed and touched by his sweet words, she touched her glass to his and took a sip of the dry, chilled bubbly. "Mmm, that's good."

"Drink up. I've got plans for later, and I need you un-inhibited." He waggled his brows suggestively, which had her squirming in her chair for a whole other reason.

Sam glanced toward the far side of the large room where four Secret Service agents were seated at a table talking quietly and pretending they weren't watching them. She knew others were positioned outside, creating a perimeter of protection all around them. If she allowed herself to think too much about being surrounded every time she was with her husband, she'd lose her mind. So she chose not to think about it—most of the time.

"Pretend they're not here," Nick said. "Focus on me."

Focusing on his exquisitely handsome face was certainly no hardship. Mario plied them with four courses of delicious food and wine and more champagne before he carried out a flaming soufflé for dessert.

"So, are you going to tell me how the deposition went today?" he asked as they dug into the soufflé with two spoons.

"How do you think it went? I had to relive the nightmare day when Melissa came into our house with a bomb strapped to her chest."

"Did it take all day?"

"Yep. Her lawyers were nothing if not thorough."

"And I'm sure you were unrepentant."

"You're damn right I was. I don't regret anything I did that day. She can sue us all she wants, but I did my job and I have no doubt that Freddie and I saved all our lives that day."

"I was there. I can attest to that. What happens now?"

"Who knows? They take my deposition, and the whole thing goes away until it rears its ugly head again. I'm not giving it another thought until I have to." Eager to change the subject, Sam said, "You know what the good thing is about your detail?"

"Is there a good thing?"

"Yep. We can get totally hammered, and they have to drive us home."

"That isn't a bad thing. Are you totally hammered?"

"I think I might be. Are you?"

"Nope. I paced myself."

"Always in control, aren't you?"

He gazed at her meaningfully. "Not always."

Sam's bite of soufflé got stuck in her throat. The reminder that she was the one person who could break his legendary control made her want to go home immediately. "Is it time to go?"

"Not quite yet." He fed her another bite. "Want to dance?"

Sam looked over at the Secret Service detail. The three men and one woman were done eating and were monitoring them without actually looking at them. "I'd prefer to dance at home without an audience."

"We can do that." He checked his watch. "It's almost midnight."

"Are they going to let us go up to watch the fireworks?" It went against everything she believed in to ask anyone for permission to do anything, but she didn't want to make his life any more complicated than it already was by constantly clashing with his detail.

Nodding, he said, "That was my primary request for this evening. I had a promise to my wife that needed to be kept."

Last year, they'd stood on the rooftop of this very building, newly in love, newly back together six years after an unforgettable one-night stand. They'd promised to come back to that spot to see in every New Year together. She'd wondered if they'd get to do it in light of his new security constraints.

"Did you doubt that I'd remember?"

"Oh, I knew you'd remember. I've learned not to question such things. Your memory is freakishly good. I just wasn't sure if they'd allow it."

"Apparently, there'll be sharpshooters on adjacent buildings keeping an eye on us, so no sudden moves."

She rested her hand on his leg and ran it slowly up to cup him intimately. "So nothing like this?" she asked as he hardened under her hand.

"That's absolutely allowed."

Sam laughed at the lusty look he sent her way as he covered her hand with his to keep her from getting away. "How about you save that for when we get home?"

"There's plenty more where that came from."

"There's so much I could say to that."

Nick put his free arm around her and pulled her and her chair closer to him. With his lips close to her ear, he said, "I know it sucks balls to be constantly under surveillance, babe, but I just want you to know... That we can still be us in the midst of it is the only thing saving my sanity right now."

"We'll always be us, no matter where we are or who is watching." She stroked her hand up and down his length, loving the way he throbbed under her palm. "Speaking of sucking balls, I have a hankering—"

He kissed her before she could finish the sentence. "Don't say it, or I'll drag you out of here without keeping my promise."

Sam happened to glance over at the table full of agents, all of whom were face-first in their phones, except for Melinda, who was watching them. The tall, frosty blonde seemed to enjoy her job a little too much if you asked

Sam. "Tell Secret Service Barbie to quit looking at my hot husband."

"Um, she's sort of paid to look at me."

"I don't like her."

"Oh, Jesus. Why not? What've you got against her?"

"I don't like the way she looks at you."

"Samantha," he said, "are you being serious right now?"

"Dead serious. There's something about her that bugs me."

"Just like there's something about Avery Hill that bugs me?"

"Something like that."

Nick busted up laughing, which had Sam removing her hand from his crotch. If he was going to laugh at her, he didn't deserve a hand job. A buzzing noise from under the table interrupted the snappy retort she was working up.

"Saved by the phone," he said, aware that he'd gotten himself into trouble.

"I know I should ignore it, but what if it's Scotty?"

"Go ahead and check it. You won't relax knowing there's an unread text on your phone."

And wasn't that the truth? She retrieved her phone from her purse and flipped it open to find a text from Gonzo.

Shit is hitting the fan. Need to talk to you. Call if you can.

"Crap, it's Gonzo. He says the shit's hitting the fan. He wants me to call him."

"Go ahead. We have time before midnight."

"They're supposed to be celebrating their anniversary tonight." Gonzo had met Christina, Nick's former chief of staff, at their party here last year and they were now engaged. Sam placed the call and waited for Gonzo to pick up.

Nick put his arm around her and kept her close while he took advantage of the opportunity to check his own phone. Sam had learned to hate that phone, which often rang in the middle of the night, with Terry passing on information he thought Nick needed to know. It had been bad enough when only her phone did that. Now they had two of them that went off at all hours.

Gonzo picked up on the sixth ring. "Hey, sorry. I was on the other line with Andy." Nick's lawyer friend had spear-headed Gonzo's efforts to get custody of his son. "Lori's lawyer filed an injunction to overturn the ruling that gave me full custody."

"Shit. What did Andy say about that?"

"That they've got a case, and I should be worried. Lori also went to the fucking media, and now it's a total shit-storm."

"I saw some of that earlier."

"I don't know what to do, Sam. Part of me wants to pack up Alex and run. The other half of me wants to pretend this isn't happening. And then there's the part that wants to wrap my hands around her fucking neck and squeeze the life out of her."

"Please don't do that. And it won't help anything if you run away. You'll have to come back eventually and face the music." She leaned into Nick's embrace. "Just remember that everyone felt you were the better parent. If they reopen the case, another judge isn't going to necessarily see it differently."

"I can't believe I might have to go through that hell all over again. I wish she'd just go away. She doesn't even want him."

Sam didn't know what to say to that. From everything she'd heard, Lori Phillips had gone to tremendous lengths to clean up her life in an effort to get custody of her son.

But that wasn't what Gonzo needed to hear right now. "I know this has to be really stressful, but there's nothing you can do on a holiday weekend. Try to relax until you know more. And don't do anything stupid that'll make your case more complicated—or mess up your recovery. We need you back at work."

"I know. I just feel like… God, Sam, I'm *losing* it over here."

"Do you need me to come over there and keep you from doing something stupid?"

"No, Chris is here, and she's doing what she can. The thought of losing Alex… I can't lose him. I'd never survive it."

"Do you promise you'll stay calm and let the process work the way it's supposed to?"

After an uncomfortably long silence, Gonzo said, "Yeah."

"Gonzo, seriously. Don't do anything you'll regret. Think about your hard-won career and the family that needs you. Stay calm."

"Thanks, Sam. Chris told me to call you. She said I'd feel better after I talked to you, and I do."

"Anytime."

"Sorry to interrupt your evening. I know you guys had plans."

"No worries. You know you can always call me. I'll check in with you tomorrow."

"Sounds good," he said. "Happy New Year."

"Same to you, and happy anniversary too. It'll be a happy New Year for all of us. I know it will."

"I hope you're right."

"Um, when have you ever known me not to be right?"

Her husband and friend groaned in stereo.

"On that note, I'll let you go."

"Take care." Sam closed the phone and blew out a deep breath. "He's freaking out."

"I heard," Nick said.

"And blaming himself."

"I wonder how Lori found out about his connection to Morton."

"Her lawyers must've done some digging around."

"You know I'm always on Gonzo's side," Nick said tentatively. "He's become my friend as much as he's yours."

"But?"

"He fucked up by not disclosing his past relationship with Morton. I'd be surprised if the whole case isn't tossed. The bar will probably have something to say about Morton not disclosing it either."

"Damn. What a mess. Poor Gonzo. He thought he was home free with permanent custody of Alex, and now this."

Nick consulted the silver TAG Heuer watch she'd given him for Christmas, much to his surprise. "May I be selfish for a minute here?"

"But of course."

"Before we start another crazy year, I need a few minutes alone with my wife on the roof."

"Your wife is always happy to give you a few minutes."

He got up and helped her out of her chair and into the coat that magically appeared, brought by a member of the attentive restaurant staff. With the coat in place, he gathered her long hair and let it slide through his fingers in a move reminiscent of when they first reconnected after John O'Connor's murder. He'd been combing his fingers through her hair as often as he could ever since.

Hand in hand, they followed two of his agents up the stairs to the roof while two others followed behind them. Their city stretched out before them, from the Capitol to the Washington Monument to Lincoln to the right and Jefferson to the left. In the middle sat the White House, where Nick now had an office in the West Wing that he would report to for the first time the day after tomorrow. When they'd stood here a year ago, they never could've imagined that particular development transpiring the way it had.

"We've got you set up over here, sir." Brant gestured to a protected corner of the roof that left only two sides open. A small sofa had been placed on the roof along with a blanket.

"Thanks, Brant." With his hand on her back, Nick guided Sam to the appointed spot.

"Much more cozy than last year," Sam said.

"And far less private." The agents had faded into the darkness, but they—and others—were watching closely. They'd been told to tell no one of their plans for New Year's Eve. If no one knew where they were, the chances of any sort of incident were minimized.

Sam snuggled up to him. "We'll make the most of it."

He put his arms around her and tossed the blanket over them. "I remember how cold you were last year even though you pretended otherwise."

"How could I be cold when you were holding me and making me hot for you the way I always am?"

"Mmm," he said in a low growl that sent shivers dancing down her spine. "I love that you're always hot for me. This, right here…" He hugged her in closer to him. "The best thing in my life, hands down."

"And the boy."

"And the boy," he said. "Thank you for the most amazing year of my life. A year ago tonight, if I'd employed my wildest imagination, I never could've conjured up the year we've spent together. Just when I think I love you as much as a man can possibly love a woman, I find out there's more."

Sam sighed with pleasure and delight at the magic she found in his arms. "I keep waiting for it to get real, you know?"

"How do you mean?"

"The blush has to wear off the rose eventually, doesn't it?"

Chuckling, he said, "I don't think that's going to happen to us, babe. It keeps getting better all the time. Especially lately. Living in the bubble like we are, the time we spend by ourselves out of the spotlight is even more important than it used to be."

"My New Year's resolution is to spend as much time completely alone with my husband as I possibly can."

"Your husband wholeheartedly approves of that resolution."

"What's yours?"

"To continue to love my wife and son with everything I have to give them." He sealed his resolution with a kiss that ended when the first of the fireworks erupted over the city, casting the landmarks in vivid blues and reds.

Sam appreciated the way he used his muscular frame to shield them from the watchful eyes of his detail. She caressed his face, dragging her index finger over his lower lip that was still damp from their kisses. "Same time and place next year?"

"I wouldn't miss it for the world."

THREE

THEY ARRIVED HOME to Shelby asleep on the couch, wrapped up in Avery's arms. The agent was awake, watching the New Year's festivities in Times Square on TV. Nick hated having that guy in his house, but Hill's attentions were now focused on Shelby rather than Sam. At least he hoped so.

Every so often he caught him looking at Sam with something way outside the bounds of friendship, and at those times, Nick wondered if he'd really moved on or if he was merely using their wonderful personal assistant to stay close to Sam. If Nick ever discovered that to be true, he'd have the agent transferred to an outpost in Siberia so fast his head would spin.

He'd like to think he was above using his position for his own agenda, but in the case of the FBI agent who had a "thing" for his wife, he wouldn't hesitate to have him removed from her orbit if it came to that. So he kept a close eye on the guy who seemed to be around their house more and more often lately. With all the women in the District he could be dating, why their personal assistant?

Not that Shelby wasn't fabulous—she was. Any guy would be lucky to date her. But Nick found the situation curious at best, fishy at worse. So while Sam talked to Hill, Nick went through the motions of hanging their coats in the front hall closet. He hoped Hill would get the hint and go home so Nick could take his wife to bed.

What if he said that? "Hill, could you please leave? I need to make mad, passionate love to my wife, and you're screwing things up just by being here." Nick smiled to himself as he imagined the look of utter scorn he'd receive from Sam if he said it, but damn, he wanted to. Rather than get himself in trouble when he was planning to get very lucky, he went into the kitchen to fix himself a nightcap from the bottle of bourbon Graham O'Connor had given him on the one-year anniversary of John's death.

Rather than wallow in their ongoing grief, they'd chosen to toast their son and best friend with drinks and cigars that had left Nick feeling rather sick at the end of the evening. But they'd gotten Graham and his wife, Laine, through the day, and that was all that mattered. One year. How was it possible that John had already been gone a year? He'd never believe the changes to all their lives since then, most particularly Nick, who'd gone from John's chief of staff to the Senate to vice president of the United States in one short dizzying year. He'd also gone from single to married to fatherhood in the same year.

The best part, by far, had been reconnecting with Sam in the wake of John's murder. That something so amazing and life-changing could've come from the worst day of his life was nothing short of a miracle. She was a miracle. His miracle.

She came into the kitchen looking gorgeous in the clingy, sexy black dress, her cheeks still red from the cold, her blue eyes sparkling with amusement. "Hiding out?"

"Nothing of the sort." He held up his glass. "Having a nightcap. Join me?"

"I'll have what you're having."

"Feeling risky tonight, are you?" Bourbon wasn't usually her drink of choice, but he poured her a couple of fingers nonetheless. "Is he gone?"

"They both are, so you can come out of hiding. I'm proud of you, though, for leaving me alone with him."

She patted his face indulgently. "My little boy might be growing up."

Amused, he took a sip of his drink. "Does thinking about how quickly I could have him transferred to Siberia count as growing up?"

"Nick…"

"What? I didn't say I was doing it. I simply said I'd *thought* about it."

She shook her head and grinned at him. "Want to know what I was thinking about?"

"Always."

"You'll have to come upstairs to find out." Taking her drink with her, she left the kitchen and headed for the stairs.

Curious and aroused and amused, he went after her, watching the gentle sway of her exceptional ass on the way up. That she put a little extra swing in her step for his benefit wasn't lost on him. His detail had disappeared into what used to be his study and now served as command central. The loss of the office space was a small price to pay for being allowed to remain in their home. He had no idea what the agents did all night while he slept, and he honestly didn't care.

Before the new job, Nick had craved the time alone with Sam at the end of every long day. Now he absolutely lived for it. From the moment their bedroom door closed behind them, they were completely alone until seven the next morning, at which time he was required to check in with the detail—five days a week. On weekends, they gave him until nine. In private, he and Sam referred to it as his "prison schedule."

In the hallway outside Scotty's room, Darcy, one of the agents assigned to his son's detail, stood when she saw them approach.

"Good evening, Mr. Vice President, Mrs. Cappuano, and Happy New Year."

"Same to you, Darcy." He gestured to Scotty's door. "May we?"

"Of course."

By now, Scotty's detail was accustomed to the fact that they never went to bed without checking one last time on their sleeping son. After being away from him, even for a few hours, they needed to lay eyes on him.

Nick followed Sam into the room that was tricked out in Red Sox and superhero decorations and smelled like the Hatchet cologne he'd recently begun wearing much to their dismay. Sam had tried to tell him that no girl— ever—would be attracted to a guy who smelled like that stuff. She'd bought him some Lacoste cologne for Christmas, and they were hoping he'd take to it—soon.

Sam leaned over the bed, brushed dark hair from Scotty's forehead and kissed him. Nick followed suit, running his fingers through the hair that was so much like his he might've been the boy's biological father. But he wasn't. Some other guy had fathered him, and they were making the required effort to find him so they could finalize the adoption. Nick might actually sleep at night once that was done.

He shared a smile with Sam, then followed her from the room.

"Good night," they said to Darcy.

"Good night. Sleep well."

In their room, Nick closed the door and locked it. None of the agents would dare step foot in there unless the house were on fire or the country under attack, but Nick always locked the door anyway, needing the assurance that for these few hours anyway, they'd be completely alone. If Scotty needed them, he would knock on the door.

He stripped off his tie and shirt, tossing them over a chair in his haste to be free of the dress clothes he spent far too much time in these days. Watching Sam's contorted effort to reach the zipper of her dress had him crossing the room to assist.

"Oh, please," he said. "Allow me." Moving her hair to the side, he punctuated his words with kisses to the back of her neck that had her sighing and leaning against him. "I can't get to the zipper with you snuggled up against me." He slid his arms around her.

"I needed this first."

"Anytime."

"Thank you for a lovely evening."

"It was entirely my pleasure, as is any time I get to spend with you." He peppered her neck with kisses, making her moan when he latched on to her earlobe. "Let me get that zipper for you. I want to see what's under this number."

"There wasn't room for much, so don't get too excited."

He pressed his erection into the cleft between her buttocks. "Too late." Her girlish giggle, the one she saved only for him, was music to his ears. He released her only enough to access the zipper. With it unfastened, she shimmied out of the dress, sending his arousal into the red zone as he watched her hips slide from side to side. "Could I get that on video sometime?"

"In your dreams."

"That was so hot, babe."

"What was? All I did was take off my dress."

He took hold of her hand and pressed it against his erection. "And look what happened when you did."

"Mmm, that feels pretty serious. We should do something about that." She turned to him, her breasts barely contained by a sheer strapless bra. His gaze wandered down to the scrap of thong that covered her.

He licked lips that had gone dry with lust. "And you said I shouldn't get too excited. Look at you."

She pulled his T-shirt up and over his head and then went to work on his belt and pants. "I'd so much rather look at you." When he sprang free of his boxers, she took him in hand and then dropped to her knees before him.

Oh, Christ. "Sam, I don't know if I can take that tonight."

"Since when are you good for only once? It's a holiday. We've got all night, and we even get to sleep in." As she spoke, she let her lips vibrate against his shaft as she stroked him. The combination was overwhelming, and she'd barely touched him. Then she opened her mouth and drew him in, sucking and licking her way down his length.

"God, Samantha." When his legs began to tremble, she cupped his balls, sliding her fingers back and forth until he could no longer control the need to pump his hips.

She took most of him, letting him slide into her throat and then swallowing, which finished him right off.

Fisting her hair, he let go of all his thoughts and cares and worries, giving everything he had to her in wave after wave of pleasure. She brought him down slowly, gently licking and touching him until he nearly had to beg for mercy. She kissed her way up to his belly and then to his chest, tonguing his nipples and then his lips.

"Come with me." She grabbed the comforter and two pillows off the bed and brought them to the floor in front of the gas fireplace, which she lit with the press of a button. "Remember last year?"

"I remember." He joined her on the floor, wrapping his arms around her as she arranged the comforter over them. "The first night we spent in this house." Behind her back, he unhooked her bra and moved it out of the way, loving the feel of her breasts against his chest. Then he pushed the thong down her legs, and slid his leg between hers.

"In case I never told you," she said, "I really love this house. I love that it's right near my dad's. I love that you live here and that Scotty lives here now and that we got to stay here after your promotion."

Laughing, he said, "Is that what we're calling the mess I've made of our lives?"

"Uh-huh. I love that I got a whole room for a closet, and you *know* how much I love our loft."

"The loft is a personal favorite of mine too." As he kissed her, he moved so he was on top, poised between her legs while gazing down at her. "But having you here with me is the best part. You and Scotty. You guys are all I need to be happy."

Based on the fact that he hadn't heard a word from his new boss or the new boss's staff since the day he was sworn in, Nick had a sneaking suspicion that Nelson had used him to boost sagging approval ratings. The president had been reelected by one of the narrowest margins in history, and the Democrats had lost control of the House. The president's second term promised to be contentious and polarizing, so a popular vice president wouldn't hurt anything.

"What're you thinking about?" she asked him.

He realized that he'd punched out on her, which he never did when she was naked beneath him. "How good you feel." More than anything, Nick hated having to hide his worries from Sam, who'd been so supportive and un-derstanding as the Secret Service invaded their lives and their home.

"You know how you can make me really happy right now?" she asked with the coy smile he adored.

"How?"

She took him in hand, stroked him until he was harder than he'd been before she made him come, and guided him home.

As he slid into her, his mind cleared of anything that didn't involve her. Encased in her tight heat, he had no choice but to give her his full attention. As long as he had this, as long as he had her, he'd be okay. That was all he knew for sure. Then she wrapped her arms and legs around him, and his heart overflowed with love for her. She gave him everything, even things she didn't know he needed.

"Samantha." His lips found hers in a hungry, devouring kiss. He was still kissing her when he felt her tighten around him, a sign that she was close. She who'd had trouble achieving climax in past relationships came every time with him, which was another thing to love about what they had together. He gave it to her hard and fast, which always triggered her release. This time was no different.

He kissed her again, to smother the sound of her cries, and went with her, surging into her until they were both depleted and breathing hard. "Love you," he whispered.

"Love you too. Happy New Year."

"Same to you, baby." Though he expected the New Year to be lousy on many fronts, he'd do everything he could to make sure it was a happy year for her and Scotty. Their happiness and safety were the only things that truly mattered to him.

A RINGING PHONE woke them early the next morning. Sam groaned when she realized it was hers. She checked the caller ID and saw it was Dispatch. "Motherfucker."

"Good morning to you too, love," Nick said as he yawned.

"It's work."

"Shit."

She sat up in bed and let the covers fall to her waist. "Holland."

"Lieutenant, we've got a homicide on Constitution Ave near West Potomac Park. The victim is located inside a parked vehicle."

"I'm on my way. Call Cruz."

"Yes, ma'am."

"Shit, fuck, damn, hell," Sam said as she got out of bed and headed for the shower. So much for a holiday weekend off duty.

Nick laughed at her string of swears. "Sorry, babe."

"Don't the fucking murderers know it's my weekend off?"

"They're very inconsiderate that way."

Over her shoulder, she said, "Shower. Now." She loved the way his eyes widened with surprise at her command. The sound of his footsteps behind her made her heart beat faster with anticipation. She stepped into the shower and turned up the heat, filling the stall with steam as she quickly washed her hair.

He came in behind her, his arm encircling her waist. "Allow me," he said, taking the bottle of conditioner from her and working it through her long hair.

Sam pushed her rear against his erection, which earned her a sharp slap on the ass that made her cry out with surprise and shocking desire. She'd never forget the first time he'd done that or how much she'd liked it.

He did it again, on the other side this time, before bending her at the waist and taking her hard and fast from behind. It was over almost before it began, but every inch of her body tingled with aftershocks as he washed between her legs and sent her on her way with yet another well-placed spank. "Be careful out there, babe."

"Always am."

"Let me know what's going on when you can."

"Will do. Thanks for the morning wake-up call."

"Anytime."

Sam kissed him and left him to finish his shower. She put on a robe to walk across the hall to get dressed, trying to ignore the agent who was positioned outside Scotty's room as he made an equal effort to ignore her. How long would it take before she became accustomed to having people crawling all over her house?

She threw on jeans, a heavy sweater and the fleece-lined snow boots that Nick had given her for Christmas. Her wet hair would make her cold on the crime scene, so she put on a knit hat and wrapped a scarf around her neck. She went downstairs, grabbed an apple and a bottle of water before bolting past the agent at the door and stomping down the ramp, checking the time on her phone as she went.

Twelve minutes from phone call to car with shower sex. Not bad.

As she drove, she ate the apple and yawned her head off, jonesing for the diet cola she'd been forced to give up when her stomach revolted against the acid in the soda. While she wouldn't have traded a minute of the evening she'd spent wrapped up in her gorgeous husband, she wished now that she'd spent a tiny bit more of it actually sleeping.

She parked illegally on Constitution Avenue and stepped under the yellow crime scene tape that a patrolman held up for her. "What've we got?" she asked Officer Beckett, who stood next to the car.

"Female vic, approximately thirty years old. Waiting for Dispatch to get me the details on the car."

"Have you touched anything?"

"I gloved up to open the car door and check for a pulse.

I also checked the glove box for a registration, but it wasn't in there. That's as far as I went on my own."

"Good job."

She pulled latex gloves from her coat pocket and snapped them on before leaning into the car for a closer look. The woman had long brown hair and pale skin. Sam noted bruising around her neck and throat, indication that she'd been manually strangled. She reached across the front seat for the purse that sat on the passenger seat and went through it looking for a wallet, which was at the bottom.

Sam pulled it out and stood upright, relying on the first light of day to get a read of the name and address on the Maryland license. Lori Phillips. A bolt of shock traveled through Sam, drawing a gasp from her tightly clenched lips as she took a second look at the woman and recognized her as the mother of Gonzo's son—the same woman he'd faced off against in court, the same one he'd said he wanted to strangle.

"Fuck," Sam whispered.

"What's got you swearing before the sun is even up?" her partner, Detective Freddie Cruz, asked as he joined her.

Sam turned to him, not surprised to see him bed-headed and rumpled as he always was when he responded to calls late at night or first thing in the morning. "It's Lori Phillips."

Freddie's mouth opened and then closed. "As in *Gonzo's* Lori Phillips?" he asked in nearly a whisper.

"One and the same."

"Shit."

"Thus the swearing." Sam didn't tell him—and wouldn't tell anyone—what Gonzo had said to her the night before. But she'd be having a conversation with her detective sergeant the second she could break free from the crime scene.

Freddie zipped his coat all the way to the top. A whipping wind made it that much colder than it already was. "How do we play this?"

"I don't know. I just got here myself. I need a minute to think." Sam took Lori's phone out of her purse and handed it to Freddie. "How do we see what's on this?"

Freddie took it from her and pushed some buttons. "It's password protected. We'll need to get it to Archie for a dump." He glanced at something over her shoulder. "Here comes the ME." Then he looked down at her, concern etched into his handsome face. "You don't think—"

"No! I don't think that. And neither do you."

"Right. Of course I don't think that." After a long pause, he said, "But everyone else will."

"Shit, fuck, damn, hell," she muttered, staring down at Lori and thinking of the shitstorm that would erupt when the media caught wind of the fact that she'd been murdered. In any homicide investigation, Sam's first thoughts were always for her victim and getting justice for both the victim and the victim's family. In this case, however, she couldn't help but think of her close friend and how this particular homicide would turn his life upside down.

"What you said." As a rule, Freddie left the swearing to her, but even he was known to break loose in the most extreme situations, and this certainly counted as extreme. "What's the plan?"

"Work the scene and keep a lid on our vic's identity until I can get my head around this. Don't tell anyone her name. See about getting video surveillance footage from around here. Surely we have cameras in the area. And the minute you can, get that phone to Archie at HQ." Sam dropped Lori's wallet into her coat pocket. "Beckett!"

The patrolman came over to them. "Yes, ma'am?"

"You hear back from Dispatch on the car?"

"Just now." He handed her a slip of paper on which he'd written, George Phillips with an address in Bowie, Maryland.

"Thanks. I'm putting a gag order on every detail of this investigation. Got me?"

"Yes, ma'am. No one will hear anything from me."

"Good. Where's Crime Scene?" she asked of the detectives who would go through the vehicle with a fine-tooth comb.

"On their way."

"Thanks, Beckett." After she and Freddie did a visual search of the car and found nothing obvious to aid in the investigation, Sam waved for Lindsey McNamara, the District's chief medical examiner, to come forward. "All yours, Doc."

"Do we know who she is?"

"We do."

Lindsey secured her long red hair into a ponytail. "And?"

"For right now she's a thirty-one-year-old Jane Doe. Got me?"

"Okay."

"I'll brief you as soon as I can." To Freddie, she said, "Keep an eye on things, get Patrol to begin a canvas of the area and keep me posted on anything that transpires. As soon as you can, get the phone to HQ."

"Got it. Where are you going?"

"To Gonzo's."

"Sam. You gotta know, he would never…"

"We'd both like to think that, Freddie, but honestly, you never know what someone will do when they feel desperate and pushed to the brink."

Freddie blanched. "You said you weren't thinking that."

"I gotta go. Keep the scene under control."

"I will."

As Sam took off toward her car, she ducked under the yellow tape and felt sick to her stomach. No, she didn't actually think her close friend and colleague was capable of murder. However, Gonzo had been under a tremendous amount of stress as he recovered from the gunshot wound and also dealt with the media circus over his connection to the judge.

And now Lori was dead, and everyone would be looking to him. The first thing they did in any homicide investigation was investigate motive. And who had the greatest motivation to get Lori out of the picture?

Detective Sergeant Thomas Gonzales.

FOUR

RIDDLED WITH ANXIETY, Sam drove across the city to the apartment Gonzo shared with Christina and Alex. She'd give just about anything not to have to do what she was about to do. His words from the night before echoed through her mind, making her wonder if someone she thought she knew as well as anyone was capable—

"No," she said out loud. "Don't even think it. He's not capable." But she couldn't get past the awful stress Gonzo had been under since he'd been shot shortly after being given full custody of Alex. Sam couldn't forget the way Lori had appeared at the hospital while they waited to hear if Gonzo would survive and demanded they turn over Alex to her while he was incapacitated.

Sam had wanted to kill the woman herself that day. She could only imagine how Gonzo had felt when he learned that Lori's lawyers had dug into his life and uncovered the connection between him and Judge Morton. One of them should've disclosed it, but neither had and now...

"Now she's dead, and the media will go crazy pointing the finger at him." She pounded her hand on the steering wheel. "Fuck, fuck, *fuck*!" Her phone rang, interrupting her plan to do more swearing. "Holland."

"Please hold for Chief Farnsworth." The phone clicked and he came on the line. "Holland?"

"Yes, sir."

"Sorry to bother you on a holiday."

"I've already been bothered by Dispatch."

"What've you got?"

Sam swallowed hard. She should tell him. She absolutely should tell him. But she couldn't—not before she had a chance to talk to Gonzo. "Female vic strangled. Found in a car on Constitution by West Potomac Park. Early stages."

"Keep me posted," he said with less interest than he'd normally give a homicide. Nothing about what was going on with him right now was normal.

"I will."

"I'm calling a commander's meeting at noon. I'd like you there."

"Of course."

"Again, I apologize for interrupting the holiday. It's just… Well, I need…" He cleared his throat. "I'll see you at noon?"

Sam hated the uncertainty she heard in his usually assertive voice. More than that, she hated the pang of fear that struck in the vicinity of her heart when she realized he sounded scared. Her uncle Joe—her chief—never sounded scared. "I'll be there."

"Thank you. See you then."

Sam stowed the phone in her coat pocket as she pulled up to the curb outside Gonzo's building. She thought of the last time she'd been here, for a Christmas get-together Christina had put together to bolster Gonzo's flagging spirits.

His recovery was taking longer than he would've liked, and he'd been chafing to get back to work. The time with his squad and other friends had done him good, and she'd left the party feeling hopeful that he'd be back where he belonged before too much longer.

Now this.

Sam got out of the car and trudged up the two flights of stairs to Gonzo's apartment where she knocked on the door. Since he often mentioned Alex's early wake-ups, she was confident they'd be up.

He came to the door with the baby in his arms. The smiling dark-haired boy was a mirror image of his father, right down to the dimple in his adorable little chin. "Hey," Gonzo said, clearly surprised to find her on his doorstep. "What're you doing out so early on a holiday?"

"Can I come in for a sec?"

His brows narrowed with questions he didn't ask. "Sure." He stepped aside to let her in and put Alex down. The baby toddled off to the corner of the living room where his toys were kept. "What's up, Sam?"

Sam forced herself to look at him, to make eye contact. "Is Christina here?"

"She's in the shower."

Sam's stomach ached the way it used to when she'd been strung out on diet cola. She rubbed a hand over it, trying to figure out how she should play this as she tried not to notice the still raw-looking wound on his neck. "So, um, after we talked last night, did you go anywhere?"

"No. I was here all night. I did what you said and tried to stay focused on Chris and our anniversary. We had a good night, all things considered. Why?"

"You wouldn't lie to me, would you?"

He tipped his head quizzically. "*Lie* to you? No, I wouldn't lie to you. Why would you ask me such a thing?"

Sam sighed. "Lori was found murdered this morning in a parked car downtown. She'd been manually strangled."

All the color seemed to leach from his face as he processed what she'd said. "And you thought, because of what I said last night…"

"No, I didn't really think that. I didn't *want* to think it."

"Sam, come on! This is *me*. You can't possibly think that I'd actually *harm* her. Sure, I wanted her to go away and leave us alone, but not like this. Never like this." He glanced over to where his little boy was playing with trucks. "She's his *mother*, Sam," he whispered. "I wouldn't. I *couldn't*. Even if I said I wanted to. You have to believe me."

"I do. I believe you, and I believe in you. But you have to know, this is going to blow up big-time, and all eyes will be on you until we figure out what happened."

He ran both hands through his hair as the impact of what she'd said seemed to settle in on him. "This is a fucking nightmare. This whole thing, from the second she first called to tell me… Except for him. He's the blessing in all of it, but what if he thinks, someday… That I could've…"

"Gonzo." Sam rested her hand on his arm and squeezed. "Take a breath."

He did as she directed and then glanced at her, seeming devastated. "She's really dead? You saw her with your own eyes?"

"I did and she is."

"Who else knows it's her?"

"Right now only Cruz, but I won't be able to sit on this for long. Farnsworth already knows we've caught a new case. He's going to have questions."

"Goddamn. I don't even know what to do. What should I do?"

"Hey, Sam." Christina came into the room wearing yoga pants and a tank top. Her shoulder-length blond hair was still damp from the shower. "You're out early."

"Baby." Gonzo held out his hand to her, and she grasped it, letting him draw her into his embrace.

"What wrong, Tommy? You're scaring me."

"It's Lori," he said softly. "Someone killed her."

"*What?* When?"

"We got the call early this morning," Sam said.

"Oh my God." And then her face went slack with horror and understanding. "You aren't here because you think he had something to do with it, are you? Because he didn't! He was right here with us all night! I'll make a statement. What do I have to do?"

Gonzo rubbed his hand over her back. "Calm down, honey."

No doubt sensing their dismay, Alex toddled over to them and tugged on Christina's pants. She bent to pick him up, wiping tears from her face as she did. "He had nothing to do with this, Sam. You know that as well as I do."

"Mama," Alex said, tearing up.

Christina held him close, encouraging him to snuggle into her embrace.

Watching Christina with the baby gave Sam a pang of longing. She'd been trying to have a baby for most of her adult life with no luck, and when Alex had dropped into Gonzo's life out of the blue she'd been filled with unreasonable jealousy.

"Can we make a statement?" Christina switched into professional mode as the initial shock passed. "If we come out ahead of the story, then they can't drag us through the mud."

"I wouldn't recommend that," Sam said. "Here's the bottom line—you both have motive, and you're each other's alibi."

"How can you say that?" Christina asked angrily. "You're our *friend*. You know us! You can't honestly think we'd be capable of *killing* someone."

"Babe." The calm tone of Gonzo's voice belied the panic Sam still saw in his eyes as well as the grim set of his mouth. "Sam's right. She's playing devil's advocate. It doesn't matter what we know to be true. What matters is what everyone else will believe and say."

"There has to be something we can do. We never left this apartment from the time we got home from the grocery store yesterday afternoon."

"Does the building have security cameras?" Sam asked.

"I think it does," Gonzo said, brightening.

"I'll get a warrant." Sam pulled her phone from her pocket and placed a call to Captain Malone, her mentor and boss.

"Happy New Year," he said. "To what do I owe the pleasure?"

"I need a warrant," Sam said without preamble.

"For?"

"The apartment building where Detective Sergeant Gonzales and his fiancée live with his son." Sam gave him the address. "I need the security footage."

"Um, do you mind if I ask *why*?"

"The mother of his son was found murdered this morning. We're seeking to prove that neither he nor his fiancée left the house from the time they arrived home yesterday afternoon to the present time."

"Holy Christ," Malone said in barely more than a whisper.

"Warrant? Yes?"

"Yeah, I'm on it. I'll be back to you ASAP."

"Thanks. We haven't told anyone who our vic is yet. I'd appreciate you keeping the lid on it until we figure out a plan."

"Done. Will you be at the noon meeting?"

"I'll be there."

"See you then."

"What did he say?" Gonzo asked the second Sam ended the call.

"He's getting the warrant. Does the building have a super or a manager?"

Gonzo nodded. "He's on the first floor. A guy named Tony. I can't remember his last name."

"He's in 1A," Christina added.

"I'm going down to talk to him," Sam said. "Sit tight and try not to worry. If you didn't do anything, you have nothing to worry about."

"*If?*" Christina asked, incredulous. "You really don't believe us when we say we had nothing to do with this, do you?"

"I do believe you. But I need to prove that as fast as I possibly can so no one has a chance to ruin your lives with innuendo."

"Go ahead, Sam," Gonzo said, sounding resigned. "We'll stay here."

"Don't talk to anyone. Don't take any calls. Don't make any. Got me?"

"Yeah," he said. "I got you."

She certainly didn't have to tell him how important the next few hours would be to maintaining control of this situation. She went down the stairs to find the super, stopping short at the sight of several men working on something inside the main door. "Is one of you Tony?"

"That'd be me," a tall, muscular black man said. "What can I do for you?"

Sam flashed her badge. "Lieutenant Holland, Metro PD."

"Ahhh, the VP's wife," Tony said, smiling. "We got a celebrity in our midst, fellas."

The men with him stopped what they were doing to take a good long look at her, which made her skin crawl. She hated when people brought up her personal life when she was on the job. Why did everyone have to make such a BFD out of who she was married to? What did it matter?

"Right now I'm a cop, and I have questions," she said brusquely.

"What can I do for you?"

"The building has security cameras?"

He gestured to the other men. "It does. They're fixing them as we speak. Why?"

Sam's stomach sank at that news. "How long have they been broken?"

"Since about noon yesterday. I noticed it this morning. That one there?" He pointed to the camera that monitored the vestibule. "It was hanging from its wires when I came home from my girl's place. I called these guys in and paid extra since it's a holiday. We take security seriously around here." He paused, glancing up the stairs. "One of your guys lives here."

"That's right." If she could get a look at who disabled the system, it might help. "I've requested a warrant for the security footage."

"How come?" he asked, suspicious now.

"It's part of an ongoing investigation. I'm not at liberty to discuss the details. Am I going to have to wait for the warrant to receive your cooperation or can you help me?"

"I'm not really sure I'm allowed to just hand over the video. I'd need to check with my boss."

"Can you do that now?"

"Sure." He stepped into his apartment and closed the door behind him.

"What happened to the cameras?" Sam asked the workers.

"Someone unscrewed it from its anchor and left it to dangle," one of them said. "The only footage you're gonna get is of the floor."

And of course they'd had their hands all over it as they fixed it, wiping away any prints that might've been left behind. Sam felt increasingly queasy as the implications set in. Without the camera, they'd have no way to prove that Gonzo and Christina never left the building last night.

Sam's phone rang and she took the call from Freddie while she waited for Tony to return. "What's up?"

"Lindsey is about to transport the vic to the morgue. Crime Scene is here, and they're looking for the okay to take the car back to the lab."

Stepping out of earshot of the workers, Sam said, "Let them take it. We need a thread to pull. I'll take whatever I can get."

"You talked to him?"

Sam appreciated that he didn't name names. "Yeah, he's shaken but adamant. Neither of them left the apartment from the time they got home from the grocery store yesterday afternoon."

"Good," Freddie said with an audible sigh of relief. "That's really good."

"Except we can't prove it." She told him about the disabled camera in the building's vestibule.

"Oh, crap. So what now?"

"I don't know yet. I'm waiting to hear if the super is going to be able to get me the video they do have. If we can get an image of someone disabling the camera, that would at least give us something to go on. Malone is getting a warrant, but I've asked the super to cooperate. He's calling the building owner."

"Sam…"

"I know. Believe me. I know."

"What can I do?"

"Rip her life apart. Find me someone else who had motive, and do it as fast as you can. I want the whole squad on this one. Call everyone in, tell them the order is from me."

"Okay." His relief at having something to do was conveyed with the single word. Gonzo was one of his closest friends, as well as his colleague, and he'd want to do anything he could to help him.

"Work fast. This investigation will probably be taken out of our hands the minute the brass finds out who our vic is."

"Got it. I'm all over it."

"Keep me posted. I have a meeting with the chief at noon, and then I'll find you."

"Assume it's okay to share what we know so far with the rest of the squad?"

"Yes." Sam agreed reluctantly. The more people who knew, the more likely they were to have a leak, not that any of her people would breathe a word without her approval. Still, if she had her way, no one would know who their vic was until they'd found someone else who'd wanted her dead.

Tony emerged from his apartment.

"I've got to go. Talk to you shortly." She closed the phone and returned it to her pocket. "What's the verdict?"

"He said to give you the video now, but he wants a copy of the warrant on file. Just in case."

Under normal circumstances, Sam would ask just in case of what. But these were not normal circumstances, and she'd take the cooperation where she could get it. "I'll get it to you as soon as I have it."

"Come into the office." He led her to the back of the building where a hole-in-the-wall served as the "office." From a machine located in the back corner, he removed a CD that he placed into a case and handed over to her. "The last twenty-four hours," he said, as he placed a new recordable CD into the machine.

"Would you mind signing something to indicate that you turned it over to me?"

"Um, sure, I guess."

"I'm not going to haul your ass into court or anything."

"So you say now."

Sam shrugged to concede the point. For all she knew, her entire case could hinge on him, and she had no right making promises she might not be able to keep. From her back pocket she pulled out the notebook she carried with her at all times and scratched out a handwritten chain-of-custody note that she asked him to sign. "Print your name and phone number under your signature and date it for me if you would."

He did as she asked and handed the notebook back to her. "Is your guy upstairs in trouble?"

"I don't think so." She stashed the notebook back in her pocket. "Thanks for your help."

Tony handed her his business card. "Send me that warrant when you have it. Email is on the card."

"I will. Thanks again."

"I like him," Tony said. "He's a good guy and a great father to that little boy."

"I couldn't agree more." Sam left the office and went back upstairs to speak to Gonzo.

He must've heard her coming, because the door flew open. "What the hell took so long?"

"Good news, bad news. Which do you want first?"

His jaw clenched. "Bad."

Sam would've made the same choice in his situation. "Someone disabled the security camera yesterday."

"Fuck," he said in a low growl. "So what's the good news?"

"The super gave me the video." She held up the CD. "We might be able to see who did it."

"But there's no proof I never left the building last night except for my word and Christina's."

"At the moment, no." Before he could flip out, she added, "We're on it. Freddie and the rest of the squad are ripping up the rest of her life. If there's someone else with motive, we'll find them."

"And what am I supposed to do in the meantime? Any second now it's going to get out that she's dead, and the media will be on me like white on rice."

"Which is why you're getting out of here while the getting is still good. Go to your parents' place or to Christina's family. Go somewhere else until this dies down."

"And that won't look like I'm running away?"

"It's a holiday, for Christ's sake. People have plans on holidays. Go have dinner with your parents and act like everything is normal. If you stay here, you're going to get stuck here when the story hits the news."

"My parents invited us home for the weekend, but we wanted to spend our anniversary alone," he said grimly. "I can't tell you how much I wish I'd gone."

"I wish you had too."

FIVE

GONZO WENT INTO the bedroom he shared with Christina and began throwing clothes into a duffel bag he'd pulled from under the bed. He'd heard the saying "coming out of your skin" throughout his life, but he'd never experienced the sensation himself until now. He literally felt like he was going to implode.

"Tommy." The sound of his name coming from the woman he loved had him spinning around to face her. "Take a minute. Try to calm down."

"Where's Alex?"

"I put him down for a nap."

"We don't have time for a nap."

She came to him, resting her hands on his chest where she could no doubt feel his heart racing. "Breathe."

"I can't."

"Try. For me."

He drew in a rattling deep breath and released it.

"Do it again."

"Chris—"

"Do it again."

Resigned, he did as she asked.

"You didn't do anything wrong. You didn't kill Lori."

"Everyone will think I did."

"Let them think what they will. We know the truth. We *know* it, Tommy."

"I wanted to."

"You wanted to what?"

"Kill her. When I found out she had her lawyers looking into me, investigating me, looking for something she could use against me. Then when she discovered my connection to Morton and went to the media with it, I wanted to kill her."

"Thinking that doesn't make you a murderer."

"I told Sam, last night when she called… I told her I wanted to wrap my hands around Lori's neck and squeeze the life out of her."

Christina gasped. "You said that *out loud*? To *Sam*?"

"Yeah." A wave of nausea had him swallowing repeatedly. "I was blowing off steam. How could I know that someone was going to actually *do* that to her?"

"Oh my God, Tommy. No wonder she came here thinking it was possible."

"She knows I didn't actually do it, Christina! *You* know I didn't!"

"What if she tells someone you said that?"

"She won't."

"How do you know that for sure?"

"I know it. I know her. She's not going to tell anyone."

"If it's her ass in the sling, she'll protect herself before she'll protect you."

He shook his head. "If you think that, you don't know her at all. She always protects her team before herself. Always. I'm not worried about her telling anyone. She's one of the few people in this world I trust completely." He kissed her forehead and held her close for a minute he didn't have to spare. "We gotta get out of here. Sam's right about what'll happen when they release Lori's name to the media."

Her hands trembled as she gathered her hair into a ponytail. He hated that he'd caused her such distress. "We'll be okay, babe," he said with more confidence than he had. "As long as we stick together, it'll be okay."

"I'll pack for Alex." She turned and left the room, crossing the hall to the baby's room.

Gonzo sat on the bed and dropped his head into his hands. How in the hell had everything gotten so fucked up so fast? He should've disclosed the connection to Judge Morton. He knew that. But he'd been so desperate to gain custody of Alex he'd kept his mouth shut, taking any advantage he could get. And now it had blown up in his face in every possible way.

Lori was *dead*. Jesus. After all she'd done to clean up her life in the last year, who would want to kill her? Was it someone from her past life as an addict? Had she met someone new and ended up in an abusive relationship? It was time to stop being freaked out and start acting like the detective he was.

His phone rang and he withdrew it from his pocket. He didn't recognize the Virginia number, but he took the call anyway, despite the pang of fear that struck him at the possibility of more bad news. "Gonzales."

"It's Leon Morton."

Gonzo automatically sat up straighter. "Oh, Your Honor."

"I'm sorry to disturb you on a holiday."

He didn't mention that he'd already been thoroughly disturbed. "No problem."

"I wanted to get in touch to apologize." The judge's speech was halting, as if he were pained. "I hate that this has happened, that you're in such a tough spot."

He had no idea how tough that spot had become overnight. "Thank you, sir, but it's not your fault. I should've said something."

"One of us should have. I was naïve to think it wouldn't come out."

"As was I," Gonzo said.

"I wouldn't change a thing about the outcome. Custody was granted to the right parent."

"Thank you for that."

"As you can imagine, the scrutiny has been damaging. I've decided to retire to prevent it from going any further."

Gonzo felt sick again. With Morton out of the picture, all the scrutiny would be on him, which it would be anyway now that Lori was dead. "That's probably for the best."

"I just want to say, despite all this, I appreciate, we *all* appreciate, what you did for our family so long ago. My parents were able to rest in peace knowing Eva's killer had been brought to justice, and for that I'll be eternally grateful. I'm sorry it's come back to haunt you in this way."

"It's not your fault, so please don't sweat it. We'll figure it out." He hated to think about Lori's murder in terms of the upside—the end of the custody battle. That is, if he wasn't arrested for her murder.

"Well, I won't keep you any longer. My best to your fiancée and Happy New Year to you both."

"Same to you. Thanks for calling."

"Least I could do."

"Take care." Gonzo ended the call and sat staring at the floor, thinking about what the judge had said.

"Who was that?" Christina asked as she came back into the room, carrying the monogrammed backpack her parents had given Alex for Christmas.

"Judge Morton."

"Seriously? What did he say?"

"That he's sorry about what's happened but still grateful for what I did for his family years ago."

She sat next to him on the bed. "That's nice of him."

"It was."

"Did you tell him about Lori?"

"I didn't see any reason to. He'll find out soon enough. The whole world will." He put his arm around her and kissed her cheek. "Let's finish packing and get the hell out of here before the shit hits the fan."

AT HQ, SAM went directly to the morgue where Lindsey McNamara had begun the autopsy on Lori Phillips. "What've you got for me, Doc?" Sam asked as she stepped into the cold, antiseptic-smelling space that always gave her the creeps.

"Nothing much so far. I just started."

"Tell me you've got fingerprints on her neck. Tell me this was an act of rage and not something premeditated enough that our perp gloved up."

Lindsey glanced at her. "Are you going to tell me who she is?"

"If I do, you've got to help me keep it quiet for a while."

"How come?"

Sam blew out a deep breath. "She's Gonzo's baby mama."

Lindsey's green eyes widened with shock. "The stuff in the news, about his connection to the judge…"

"It's a shitstorm that's about to get a whole lot shittier."

"Does he know?"

Sam nodded. "I saw him earlier. He's a fucking mess."

"But he didn't… Well, of course he didn't. But he probably wanted to, and the press will be all over him."

"Which is why the rest of my squad is currently digging into Lori's life, looking for motive somewhere else."

"Damn." Lindsey gazed down at the naked woman with the visible bruising on her neck and the stretch marks on her abdomen that indicated she'd once carried a child.

Was it weird that Sam was envious of stretch marks on a dead woman? Yeah, it was very weird, but she'd become accustomed to the odd longings that went along with her infertility. They struck at the strangest times.

"First he gets shot and now this," Lindsey said with the empathy Sam had come to expect of her friend and colleague. That empathy was one of the reasons she was such a first-rate medical examiner. "The poor guy is having a hell of a run of bad luck."

"I know. He was already down before this with the wound taking so long to heal." Sam was worried about how much lower Gonzo could get before he'd hit rock bottom. "Anyway," she said, shaking off those glum thoughts, "how was the anniversary celebration?"

Before her eyes, Lindsey blushed like a schoolgirl. "Great." She, too, had met her boyfriend, Terry O'Connor, at Sam and Nick's promotion party the previous New Year's Eve. Terry was now Nick's chief of staff, since Christina stepped down after the campaign to spend more time with Alex and Gonzo.

"That's it? That's all I'm getting?"

"There is one thing I could tell you."

"I'm listening."

"We got engaged."

"That's huge news! Congratulations. I'm so happy for you guys."

"You've come a long way from the days of 'Why does Nick's world and my world have to collide?'" Lindsey said drolly.

"I like to think I'm maturing in my old age."

Lindsey snorted with laughter. "That'll be the day."

"So how did he ask?"

"He kept it very simple and sweet. We went to dinner and then came home, and he asked me there."

"So where's the ring?"

"At home where it belongs, same place yours is when you're working."

"What's it look like?"

"It's gorgeous. A big solitaire surrounded by smaller diamonds and a diamond band. I love it."

"Were you totally surprised?"

"Not totally. We've talked about it a few times, but I didn't know last night was the night. I cried my eyes out when he asked, and he did too when I said yes. It was very… It was lovely."

"I'm feeling a little misty myself just hearing about it."

Lindsey cocked an eyebrow at Sam. "You? Misty?"

"I know! Don't tell anyone."

"Your secret is safe with me."

Sam looked down at the waxy remains of Lori Phillips. "Are we weird to be standing here having this conversation with a dead body laid out in front of us?"

"Most people would probably think so, but this is what we do and who we are. If we couldn't be normal in the midst of all this senseless death, we'd probably be locked up in a loony bin by now."

"True."

"And I have no doubt whatsoever that you'll get justice for this poor girl. No matter what she was putting our friend through, she didn't deserve this."

"No," Sam said with a sigh, "she didn't. Let me know when you've got your report done."

"Don't I always?"

"Thanks, Doc." Sam left the morgue and headed for the stairwell to the second floor. Coming down the stairs as she went up was Sergeant Ramsey from the Special Victims Unit. He scowled at her as she went past him. "Always nice to see you too, Sergeant."

"Fuck off."

Sam spun around. "Excuse me?"

He kept going down the stairs. "You heard me."

Sam stormed up the remaining stairs and took a left to go to SVU when she'd planned to go to IT. She walked through the rows of cubicles, drawing the attention of every detective she passed as she made her way to the lieutenant's office in the back.

Without knocking, she strolled into the office of SVU Lieutenant Davidson and slammed the door.

"Help you with something, Lieutenant?" Davidson asked without looking up from what he was doing.

Sam refused to talk to the top of his dark head, so she waited until he finally looked up at her. "Ramsey."

"What about him?"

"He just told a superior officer to fuck off."

"Did he?"

"He did."

"Okay."

"What do you plan to do about it?"

"I'll talk to him."

"See that you do."

"Um, yeah, I said I would. Anything else?"

Sam knew she ought to quit while she was ahead, but what fun was that? "You know what they say about tone at the top?"

"What about it?"

"You might want to let your people know that insubordination is unacceptable around here and isn't good for their career development."

"*You* might want to get your own house in order before you start butting into mine."

"My house is in fine order, thank you very much. Yours, on the other hand, could use some work." Satisfied to have the last word, Sam opened the door and went back the way she came.

Detective Erica Lucas raised a brow in Sam's direction as she passed Erica's cubicle.

"Lieutenant," Erica said.

"Detective. Nice to see you."

"You too. How's your niece doing?"

"Much better. She's going back to school in Virginia to finish up her senior year."

"Glad to hear it."

"Thank you again for your sensitivity with her."

"No problem." She glanced at the lieutenant's office. "Everything all right?"

Sam lowered her voice so they wouldn't be overheard. "Just another run-in with my good friend Ramsey."

Erica rolled her eyes. "Watch out for him. He hates your guts."

"Any idea why?"

"I have my theories." Erica's gaze darted around nervously. "Let's grab a coffee off campus sometime soon."

"We'll do that."

Nodding, Erica said, "I haven't seen you since your husband's promotion. Congratulations."

"Thank you. I think."

Erica laughed and shook her head. "I can't imagine."

"Neither did we."

"I'd love to hear all about it."

"I'll call you about that coffee."

"Sounds good." Sam left SVU and headed for IT where she received a much friendlier reception from Lieutenant Archelotta, the one fellow officer who'd seen her naked during their brief fling several years ago.

"Hey, Sam. What brings you up to my neck of the woods?"

She produced the CD from Gonzo's building. "Could you take a look at this for me and see if you can isolate the person or persons who disabled the security camera in an apartment building?"

"Sure, I'll put one of my guys right on it."

"How'd you end up working on the holiday?"

"Nothing better to do," he said with a sheepish grin. "You?"

"Caught a homicide first thing."

"Oh, damn. So, I haven't seen you since everything happened." He stretched to look around her. "Where's your Secret Service detail?"

"No detail for me. Just him and the boy."

"How'd you pull that off?"

"He made it a condition," she said with a shrug. "They wanted him badly enough to give him what he wanted."

"That's very cool. I can't believe your husband is the VP."

"Neither can he."

Archie laughed. "So business as usual for you, then?"

"That's the goal."

He held up the CD case. "I'll get something ASAP for you on this and the phone Cruz brought in."

"Thanks, Archie." Keeping an eye out for Ramsey, Sam went downstairs to the detectives' pit where most of her team had assembled. Freddie was on the phone so she gestured to her office. He held up his index finger as he nodded.

Sam sat behind her mess of a desk and corralled her still-damp hair into a clip. Her brain was whirling with disturbing thoughts and implications. A knock on the door preceded Captain Malone stepping into her office.

He shut the door behind him.

"Captain."

"Lieutenant." He was in jeans and a sweater today, his service weapon holstered to his hip and his badge clipped to the front pocket of his pants. Though he was approaching his late forties, he was still a badass in her eyes. "Tell me what we know about the Phillips homicide."

"She was found early this morning in a car parked on Constitution Ave near West Potomac Park. She'd been manually strangled."

"She was in the driver's seat of the car?"

"Yes."

"Was it her car?"

Sam shook her head. "It was registered to a George Phillips of Bowie."

"Let's get someone up there to talk to him."

"It's on the to-do list. I need to get with my team and figure out our next move."

"And Detective Gonzales?"

"I spoke with him earlier. He and his fiancée were home all evening, celebrating their first anniversary. They arrived home yesterday afternoon and hadn't yet left the apartment when I saw them."

"And they can prove that?"

"Not exactly." She filled him in on the situation with the security cameras in Gonzo's building. "The super said the cameras were working fine yesterday. Archie has the footage and he's checking to see if we can figure out who disarmed them."

"I'm getting a bad feeling about this."

"You and me both."

"If someone wanted to off her, who better to frame than someone who's been locked in a custody battle with her?" Malone asked.

"I've had the same thought."

"Where is he?"

"I suggested he visit his parents in West Virginia today." She paused before she added, "As planned."

"Good thinking."

"How do we handle the brass on this? The minute we announce the name of our vic, the media will be all over us—and all over Gonzo. We know he didn't do it, Cap."

"You know that, and I know that, but we also know he had motive. As did Christina."

"They didn't do it."

"We're going to need to prove it. You got that, right?"

"Yeah," Sam said with a sigh.

"And we're going to have conflict of interest issues working a case in which one of our guys had a strong motivation to see this woman dead."

"So what are you saying?"

"The chief will want to call in outside reinforcements."

Sam bent her head, which had begun to pulse with the early signs of a migraine. "What kind of outside reinforcements?"

"You know exactly what kind."

The FBI. Avery Hill. "I'm getting tired of having him underfoot in every investigation, as if we can't function on our own."

"We function just fine on our own, but sometimes we need help. Such as when he cut through miles of red tape and got a search warrant for your niece's dorm room or when he pushed the bullet through the lab after your dad's surgery."

"For all the good that did us."

"It's more information than we had before."

The National Integrated Ballistics Information Network had come back with no match to the nine-millimeter bullet that had been retrieved from her father's neck.

"If the person who fired that shot screws up again, we'll

have him—or her," Malone reminded her. "Your dad's bullet is now in the system. The case can break wide open at any time."

Malone wasn't telling Sam anything she didn't know, but her high hopes for an immediate break had been dashed.

"How's he doing anyway?"

"Terrible. The pain is bad. The doctors say it'll get better, but it's been more than a month, and it's not improving at all. They've got him so hopped up on morphine that he's out of it most of the time. Just when I thought his situation couldn't get worse, it did."

"I'm so sorry, Sam. I know it's rough. Hell, it's hard on us to see him like that, and we're just his friends."

"You're much more than that to him. To all of us."

"Let me know if there's anything I can do, okay?"

She nodded. "The visits from you—all of you—have sustained him."

"We love him," Malone said simply.

Sam needed to change the subject before she broke down in front of her boss. "We've got a meeting to get to."

"Yes, we do. Speaking of shitshows."

"I'll meet you there in a minute."

"See you then."

Before she left her desk, Sam downed two of the prescription pills that kept the migraines under control. Freddie appeared at the doorway, and Sam waved him in as she chased the pills with water.

"Everything okay?" her partner asked. "You look weird in the eyes."

"Gee, thanks. Trying to fend off a migraine."

"Just what you don't need today."

"Or any day. Where are we?"

"McBride and Tyrone have gone to Lori's apartment

to interview the neighbors. I've got Archie's team dumping her phone, and Arnold is trying to figure out where she worked."

Sam withdrew Lori's wallet from her pocket and handed it to him. "Have Arnold go through it and catalog everything in it. You may find some employer info in there."

"Got it. Will do."

"I have a commander's meeting at noon. After that, we're going to Bowie."

"Right."

"Sorry if this is fucking up your holiday plans."

"It's not. Elin had to work today anyway. New Year's Day is huge at the gym with all the resolutions."

"Why in the hell do people do stupid things like suddenly decide to start working out just because it's January first?"

Freddie laughed at the question and walked away shaking his head. "Don't knock it till you try it."

"That'll be the day."

SIX

WITH THE THOUGHT of working out at a gym giving her the willies, Sam called Nick before she left for the chief's meeting.

"How's it going, babe?"

"Shitty." She brought him up to speed on what her morning had entailed.

"Holy fuck," he said in a soft whisper. "Gonzo, he's…"

"Innocent. We all know that. Now we've just got to prove it. Can you give me Andy's number? He might have some information about Lori after overseeing Gonzo's end of the custody case."

"Sure." He recited the number for her.

Sam wrote it down. "Thanks."

"Gonna be a long day, huh?"

"Looks that way."

"I'll see you when you get home. Love you."

"Love you too."

She left a message for Andy and then headed for the chief's suite, where she was stopped by his admin. Sam never could remember the mousy woman's name.

"Could I speak to you for a moment, Lieutenant?" she asked so softly Sam almost couldn't hear her. Her brown eyes darted nervously toward the chief's closed door.

"What's up?"

"I know you're close to the chief on a personal level."

"So what about it?" Sam asked, immediately on edge. She hated being reminded of her personal connections to the brass. So her dad had been a big deal in the department. She'd clawed her way to her current rank all on her own. Well, that wasn't entirely true, but she tried not to think about the discretion the chief had used in making her a lieutenant after learning about her decades-long battle with dyslexia.

"I'm worried about him. He's not himself, and his face…"

"What's wrong with his face?"

"It's sort of gray and unhealthy looking."

Sam was ashamed to say that she hadn't paid much attention to how the chief was holding up under Springer's intense campaign to discredit him. "I'll talk to him after the meeting."

"Thank you," she said, releasing a deep breath. "I'm sorry to bother you."

"You didn't. Thanks for bringing it to my attention."

She glanced again at the closed door. "He listens to you."

Sam nodded. "We go way back." He'd been a huge part of her life growing up, as an adopted uncle. The chief and his wife had been unable to have children of their own. Sam and her sisters, among others, had helped to fill the void for them. Since she joined the department almost fourteen years ago, the two of them had worked hard to maintain a professional relationship in addition to the personal one.

Sam knocked on the door and entered to find the chief along with Deputy Chief Conklin, Captain Malone and all the lieutenants. Wow, he'd called in the troops. She nodded to Archie and Higgins from the Bomb Squad. When had he made lieutenant? She scowled at Davidson and ended up in a seat next to Vice Squad Lieutenant Cole McDonald. Awesome.

She and McDonald had locked horns at the end of the Springer case when his compromised narc investigation had fucked up her homicide investigation.

"Is everyone here?" Farnsworth asked Conklin, who took a look around the assembled group and then nodded. "Thank you all for coming in on a holiday. I appreciate it very much. As you know, the department—and me in particular—is under fire for our handling of the Springer case. Bill Springer is channeling his grief over losing two sons into a witch hunt aimed squarely at this department and this office."

As Farnsworth spoke, McDonald looked down at his hands, which were twitching on his lap.

He ought to be twitching. His fuckup had led to a nightmare for the department and the chief. Well, if she were being entirely fair rather than only outraged, he was probably as upset about it as anyone. Sam raised her hand.

"Holland."

"I'm wondering if we have any more information about how the narc investigation was compromised."

Beside her McDonald froze, his discomfort and anger palpable.

Sam knew she was an asshole for blindsiding her fellow lieutenant with the question, but one of her best officers had nearly died because of his team's screwup, and she wanted answers.

"McDonald?" the chief said. "What've you got?"

"We're continuing our internal investigation. I've spoken with every member of the undercover team in-depth, and no one had contact with Springer or any of our other marks the night before the shoot-out in Friendship Heights."

"So we still don't know how he found out we were focused on him for the homicides?" Sam asked.

"No." McDonald spoke through gritted teeth. "We don't."

"It's been six weeks—"

"I know how fucking long it's been," McDonald lashed back at her. "Do you think this isn't on my mind every fucking minute of every fucking day?"

"McDonald," Malone said. "Take a goddamn breath."

"I'm breathing just fine, Captain. We're doing everything we can to get to the bottom of what happened that night, but I don't yet have the answers we all want and need. I wish I did." He paused before he added, "You should know, myself and a couple of my guys have been receiving death threats. We suspect they're coming from the other members of Springer's posse who're still in the wind after the investigation went to shit."

Farnsworth's face looked like it had been carved from stone as everyone waited to hear what he would say. "How long have you been receiving death threats?"

"Almost from the beginning."

"And you're just now mentioning them?"

"We know how to take care of ourselves, Chief. We're not looking to make it into a bigger deal than it already is. These guys aren't going to show their faces in this city again anytime soon. They know we're looking for them."

"I want a full report, with details and specifics, about each of the death threats, as well as who has received them, by the end of the day," Conklin said.

"Yes, sir," McDonald replied.

Despite her antagonism, Sam felt for the guy. She'd had a long-term undercover investigation go south on her once. Sometimes she still had nightmares about Marquis Johnson's agonizing screams after his young son Quentin was shot during a raid she'd led at a crack house. Quentin wasn't supposed to be there. The fact he was there that night still weighed on Sam more than a year later.

"I think you ought to make a statement," Sam said to the chief, surprising herself as much as the others. "You need to come clean about what happened that night and why, let them know we're continuing our internal investigation and we understand and sympathize with Mr. Springer's grief over the loss of his sons. You could update the press on Detective Gonzales's condition as he continues to recover from the shot to his neck by Billy Springer, who was implicated in the murders of his brother and eight other teenagers, which would be a great way to remind them that a decorated officer was nearly killed by Mr. Springer's sainted son." When she realized all eyes were on her, Sam swallowed hard before continuing. "We haven't said a word about what happened that day since that day. It might be time for an update. Sir."

After a long pause, Farnsworth said, "What does everyone think?"

"I agree with Lieutenant Holland," Malone said. "Springer has had the microphone and the spotlight on him for weeks now. Let's retake control of the story. You could do the press conference and go on some of the radio and TV talk shows and just be honest. Tell them we're investigating what went wrong and hoping to provide some answers for the Springer family, as well as the community as a whole."

"I'd want to consult with Public Affairs," Farnsworth said.

"I'll get someone down here." Conklin got up and left the room.

"I also need to clear it with the mayor. She's been on my ass over this for weeks now."

"Why don't you see if she'd be willing to attend the

press briefing?" Sam said. "To show her support for her embattled police chief."

"I'll ask her." He seemed less than thrilled with the idea, but Sam couldn't blame him.

Conklin returned. "Captain Norris will be down momentarily. I asked him to come personally."

"Thank you. Does anyone else have any thoughts to add?" Hearing none, Farnsworth dismissed the other officers. "Conklin, Holland and Malone, please stay."

Malone glanced at Sam, his brow raised in question.

Sam knew what he was asking her and nodded reluctantly. As soon as the room cleared of the other officers, Sam moved to a seat closer to the chief's desk. "We have another situation you should be aware of," she said, noting the ashen color of his skin. His admin was right that he looked like shit.

"What's that?"

It pained her greatly to have to add to his worries and to give voice to her concern about Gonzo. "The mother of Detective Sergeant Gonzales's son was found murdered in a parked car this morning. She'd been manually strangled."

Farnsworth stared back at her, his eyes flat and blank. "This would be the same woman who recently exposed his earlier connection to the judge that heard their custody case?"

"Yes," Sam said.

The chief's deep sigh spoke for him.

"Tell me he has an alibi for last night," Conklin said.

"He and his fiancée were home all night with their son, celebrating the first anniversary of the night they met. I talked to him around eleven o'clock, and he expressed dismay about the story hitting the media and the possible implications for the custody matter. He was upset but under control."

"He never mentioned the child's mother?" Conklin asked.

And then there's the part that wants to wrap my hands around her fucking neck and squeeze the life out of her.

"No," Sam said without blinking. "Sir."

"So he and the fiancée who also loves the kid are each other's alibi?" Farnsworth asked.

"Yes." Sam told them about the situation with the security cameras in Gonzo's building and the video she'd delivered to Archie earlier, hoping for a lead as to who disabled the cameras. "We're also digging into Lori's life. She was a recovering addict who'd recently lost custody of the child for whom she'd turned her life around. We're hoping to find motive elsewhere before we release the victim's name."

"You'll have until tomorrow before they'll be demanding we release the name of the victim," Conklin reminded her.

"Yes, sir. I've called in my entire squad to work the case today. I assumed the overtime would be approved."

"What choice do we have?" Farnsworth asked. "I can't afford any more shit raining down on this department, and the murder of this woman who was connected by controversy to Sergeant Gonzales is going to be a shitstorm of epic proportions."

"Are we looking at conflict-of-interest trouble with this one?" Malone asked.

"That was my next question," Conklin said.

Farnsworth stroked the stubble on his chin as he thought it over. "I'd like to call in Hill to consult so we can defer to him if it leads back to Sergeant Gonzales."

"It's not going to!" Sam said. "He's not a murderer. He's a decorated Homicide detective."

"I'm well aware of his qualifications as well as his impeccable record, Lieutenant," the chief said. "However, he's also a father who'd do anything to protect his child."

"Anything except murder," Sam said. "I know him as well as I know anyone, and I'd bet my badge and my career on his innocence. Besides, one of the reasons he's still out of work is that the strength in his arm has yet to return. I doubt he'd be physically capable of manually strangling anyone."

"He's been under a lot of pressure lately," Conklin said, apparently dismissing her argument, "between the wound that's taking a long time to heal and the revelations about his connection to the judge. People have done crazier things than commit murder when they're under that kind of strain."

"What's crazier than murder?" Sam asked, adding, "sir," as an afterthought.

"Deputy Chief Conklin's point is well taken," Farnsworth said.

By whom? Sam wanted to ask, but didn't. "We're running the risk of the FBI and others thinking we can't handle our own cases. We've called them in on the last few."

"As I recall," Conklin said, "you were more than happy to have Agent Hill's help in your niece's case."

"That was different," Sam said.

"How so?" Conklin asked. "Because it was personal? This one is personal to Gonzales. He had a child with the woman, and she's been making very public trouble for him. Now she's dead, and his alibi is his fiancée. You know as well as I do how this will play in the press, Lieutenant. Bringing in the FBI to consult covers our asses, which are already on the line right now."

It was somewhat out of character for Conklin to raise his voice, which told Sam the strain was wearing on him too. "Fine, if you all think we need the Feds, call the Feds. But this investigation will not lead to Sergeant Gonzales."

"If there is even the slightest hint of his involvement, we're out of it," Farnsworth said. "Do I make myself clear?"

"Crystal. May I get back to work?"

"Go ahead," Farnsworth said.

Sam left the office and ran square into the inquiring gaze of the chief's admin. "I didn't get a chance to talk to him one-on-one, but I will as soon as I can. I agree he looks a little gray."

"He's not himself."

"He's under an awful lot of pressure right now. Try not to worry too much. He always comes through." The thought of him not coming through was something Sam couldn't accommodate in her already overloaded brain.

The admin nodded, but she didn't seem reassured.

"I've got to get back to work. I'll check in with him later."

"Okay, thanks."

Sam left the chief's suite and headed for the pit, crossing the lobby with a growing feeling of anxiety. Her phone rang and she took a call from inside HQ. "Holland."

"This is Haggerty."

"What've you got?" she asked the Crime Scene Unit's lieutenant in charge.

"Any idea why there'd be a slip of paper with Sergeant Gonzales's home address under the floor mat in our vic's car?"

Sam felt like she'd been gut-punched. "I have some idea, but I can't get into it at the moment. Add it to the evidence list. Anything else of interest in the car?"

"Nothing yet. I'll have the report to you by tomorrow morning."

"I'll take it sooner if you can do it."

"We'll try. I'd rather be thorough than fast."

Sam held back the snapping retort that lingered on the tip of her tongue and slapped her phone closed. "What the fuck?" she muttered under her breath as she went into her office and closed the door to call Gonzo.

He answered on the first ring. "What's up?"

"Tell me something."

"Sure."

"Have you had any contact with Lori since that day in court when you won custody?"

"I've left her a couple of messages about seeing Alex, but she never called me back. I was trying, you know?"

"Yeah."

"Why do you ask?"

"Crime Scene found a slip of paper with your name and address under the floor mat of the car."

He was silent as he processed the new information.

"You gotta help me out here, Gonzo. Who else would have motive to kill her?"

"How the hell should I know? I barely knew her!"

"Think, Gonzo. Think long and hard. Give me a thread to pull." She could almost hear him thinking over the phone.

"Rex Connolly. He's the dude she was with when I first found out about Alex. Supposedly she's not with him anymore, but he might know something about her life. He's in the system—drugs, B&E, sealed juvie record if I'm remembering correctly. Lori was in the system too. Drug charges."

"This is good."

"The social worker who oversaw the custody case, Justine Travers. She recently got married, and that's her new last name. She works for the courts and spent a lot of time with Lori during the case. And my friend, Mark Angelo. He was with me the night I met her, and he knew her before. His sister, Sara, was close with Lori. I could give him a call."

"No, you won't. I'll call him. Text me the number."

"All right."

"This helps a lot. It gives us somewhere to start."

"When are you going public with Lori's name?"

"Not until we absolutely have to. Where are you?"

"Almost to my parents' place in Harper's Ferry."

"Stay there until you hear from me. You understand? Do not move from there."

"I won't."

"We're going to figure this out. I promise."

"I'm counting on that."

"I'll call you later." Sam stashed the phone in her pocket, grabbed her keys and coat and headed for the pit. "Cruz! With me."

"Coming."

"McBride!"

Jeannie McBride popped up from her cubicle. "Yes, ma'am?"

"Find me Rex Connolly." She passed along the information Gonzo had given her about Rex's record. "Text me a current address."

"I'm on it," Jeannie said.

"Everyone else, report in to Cruz in the next fifteen minutes with where you are."

Murmured replies of "Yes, ma'am" and "Got it, LT," from the subdued group followed her command.

SEVEN

FREDDIE DONNED HIS ever-present trench coat and ran after her, his mouth full of something. His mouth was always full of something, usually donuts or other junk that never added a single pound to his lean physique. "Where we going?"

"Don't talk with your mouth full. It's gross."

"If I didn't talk with my mouth full, I'd never talk."

Sam snorted out a laugh at that truth. "We're going to Bowie to talk to George Phillips, owner of the car that Lori was driving."

"Are we going to tell him she's dead?"

"I want to know who he is to her before I tell him anything."

"Does the brass know who the vic is to Gonzo?"

"Yep and they're bringing in the Feds to babysit us to make sure we don't step over any lines."

"I feel like the Feds are underfoot a lot lately."

"So do I, and I said as much to them, but I was overruled."

With Sam at the wheel and Freddie punching the address into the GPS on his phone, they headed out of the parking lot and into midday traffic in the District. "Why can't we do something about the gridlock in this city?" Sam asked.

"Is that a rhetorical question?"

"No, I'm serious. If we can put men on the moon, why

can't we figure out an efficient way to move cars through a modern, cosmopolitan city?"

"You raise a good question."

"Why is it even like this today? It's a freaking holiday."

"Caps are playing at home this afternoon."

"Awesome. It's going to take us an hour at this rate to get to Route 50. While we're stopping and going, see if you can track down a social worker named Justine Travers. She works for the District Court. Try Faith Miller. She'll know how to reach her."

"You do remember it's a holiday, right?"

"Of course I do. I'm supposed to still be in bed with my husband right now."

"Ew."

"Oh my God! Like you're one to talk, Mr. All-Sex-All-The-Time."

Snorting with laughter, he said, "It's not *all* the time."

"Whatever you say."

While she dealt with the aggravation of trying to get anywhere in D.C., he took to the phone, working their network to locate Ms. Travers.

"Hi, Faith, sorry to bother you. This is Freddie Cruz. Do you have a second?" After a pause, he said, "We're trying to get in touch with a social worker named Justine Travers. Do you have a number for her?" Another pause and then he began writing. "Thank you so much. Sorry again to bother you."

After he ended the call, Sam said, "She didn't ask you why you wanted to know?"

"I think she was going to, but I bailed out before she could."

"Good job. Call the social worker."

"That's what I was doing before you started quizzing me."

Sam took her eyes off the road long enough to glower at him. "You got any more of those donuts?"

While he waited for Justine to answer the phone, he pulled an unopened pack of white-powdered donuts from his coat pocket and handed it to her.

"I hate you for this."

"You don't hate me. You love me."

"Right now, I hate you."

"Saint John said, 'Whoever says he is in the light and hates his brother is still in darkness.'"

"That's me. Empress of the dark. I do my best work in the dark."

He rolled his eyes at her. "Hi, Justine? This is Detective Cruz from the Metro PD. I wondered if you might be available this afternoon to answer a few questions about one of your clients?"

Sam held her breath while she waited to hear what Justine had to say.

"Lori Phillips," Freddie said. "Yes, I understand that her custody battle was with one of my colleagues. It's important or I wouldn't have bothered you on a holiday." He glanced at Sam. "We'll get a warrant. I'll call you back when we have it."

Before he'd ended his call, she was on the phone with Malone to get the warrant moving. "This might be a tough sell," Malone said.

"She has more information about Lori's life today than probably anyone else. We need her, Cap."

"I'll do what I can."

"Let me know."

Forty-five minutes after they left HQ, they finally took the exit for Route 50, heading east toward the Baltimore-Washington Parkway. They arrived in Bowie twenty-five minutes later. "Who has ninety fucking minutes to spend battling traffic so they can do their goddamn job?" Sam asked as she pulled up to George Phillips's residence.

"Language, Lieutenant," her Bible-thumping partner said disapprovingly.

"I agree that *traffic* is a dirty word."

"That's not the dirty word I was referring to, as you well know."

"*Job*. That's another dirty word on a holiday that I was supposed to be spending with my goddamn family."

"Sam! Come on."

"Oh, sorry," she said. "I got carried away."

They headed for the front door of the white ranch house. Sam rang the bell. "I hope he's home after we came all this way." She pounded on the glass storm door.

The inside door swung open, and the man went from annoyed to pissed off when they showed their gold badges. "What do you want?" he asked through the door.

"A few minutes of your time," Sam said.

"I ain't got a few minutes. I gotta go to work."

"We can take you into custody, which would ensure you'd miss work."

He gave her one of those looks that would be deadly if looks could kill. She got a lot of them during a good day on the job. The door was pushed open, narrowly missing Sam's face. "Hurry up about it."

"Are you George Phillips?"

"Yeah, so?" His greasy hair was combed over his mostly bald head and tattoos covered his forearms. He looked like he hadn't shaved in days, and the house smelled stale and musty.

"I'm Lieutenant Holland, and this is my partner, Detective Cruz. Metro PD."

"You're the vice president's old lady."

Freddie snorted and then covered it with a cough.

George looked around them, trying to see outside. "Where's your Secret Service?"

Sam gritted her teeth and pressed on. "How're you related to Lori Phillips?"

"Is she in trouble again? I told her after the last time not to call me. I'm through with her and her nonstop drama."

"Answer the question."

"She's my sister. My younger sister."

"When was the last time you saw or talked to her?"

"She was at my ma's house on Christmas. But I didn't really talk to her. She was all pissed off about losing custody of her kid, so I kept my distance. Why? What's she done now?"

"Can you tell me how she happened to be in possession of a car you own?"

"What'd she do to my car? I swear to God—"

"She's dead, Mr. Phillips. She was found strangled in your car this morning."

"W-what? She's *dead*? Lori's dead."

"Yes. I'm sorry to have to tell you the bad news."

He seemed to stagger backward before he recovered his bearings and moved to a sofa in the front room. With his head in his hands, he said, "How?"

"She was manually strangled."

"Who would've done that? What about that cop she was battling with over the kid?"

"He has an alibi."

"Of course he does. That guy hates her guts. Who else would benefit from her being dead more than him?"

"That's what we'd like to know."

"It's him! It has to be him! She was making trouble for him! It was all over the news. He was in bed with that judge, and he cheated her out of her baby."

"Mr. Phillips, Detective Sergeant Gonzales is a decorated police officer. We have no reason whatsoever to suspect him."

"Sure, you don't," he said bitterly. "My sister never had a chance against that decorated police officer who used his connections to steal her baby away from her."

Sam glanced at Freddie, who gave her a look that told her his thinking matched hers—they were wasting their time here.

"I'd like to know who else Lori had problems with."

He shook his head. "No one that I know of."

"Would your mother know?"

Shrugging, he said, "Doubtful. Lori didn't air out her troubles with us. We went for months without even knowing where she was. Turns out she was in rehab."

"Why did she have your car?"

"I let her borrow it while hers was in the shop. I have a truck from work, so it was no problem to let her have it for a few days."

"We'll need someone to identify and claim the body after the autopsy is completed. Would you be able to do that?"

"Yeah, I guess so," he said with a sigh. "Better me than my ma."

Sam handed him the notebook she carried with her. "Can you write down your phone number so we can notify you?"

He took the notebook from her, wrote the number and handed it back to her. "Did she suffer?"

Sam hated that question and never knew exactly how to answer it—truth, partial truth or outright lie? Of course she'd suffered. She'd been murdered. "Some, maybe, but we can hope it was over quickly."

He nodded, seeming somewhat satisfied with that. "I hate to ask about my car..."

"It'll be released to you as soon as it's been fully processed."

"Thank you."

Sam handed him her card. "Please call me if you think
of anything else that might be relevant to our investigation."

"I will."

"The first few hours of a homicide investigation are
extremely critical, so we ask that you refrain from speaking publicly about your sister's murder until we release
her name."

"I assume I can tell my ma?"

"Yes, but please ask her to refrain from any public state-
ments, as well."

"Yeah, okay."

Sam and Freddie left the house and returned to the car.

"You think they'll keep a lid on it?" Freddie asked.

"I certainly hope so. The longer we can keep the media
out of this, the better our chances of figuring out who
killed her before the press ruins Gonzo's life." Sam's phone
rang with a 202 number she didn't recognize. "Holland."

"Mrs. Cappuano?"

Sam winced at the rarely used salutation. "That's me."

"This is Lilia Van Nostrand."

"*Who?*"

"Your chief of staff, ma'am."

She sent a baffled glance to Freddie. "My chief of
what?"

"Staff. At the White House?"

"*Oh.* Yeah. That." After a long, uncomfortable pause,
Sam said, "What can I do for you?"

"I'm calling about our staff meeting tomorrow at nine
a.m."

"We have a staff meeting tomorrow at nine a.m.?"

"Yes, I left a message last week about it."

"Sorry, I didn't get it." She grimaced at Freddie, who hid a smile behind his hand.

"Can you make the meeting?"

"No, I'm sorry I can't. I'll be working at nine tomorrow morning on a homicide investigation." In other words, *important* stuff, Sam thought.

"Oh, well, this is a dilemma indeed. Your staff is looking forward to meeting you and receiving direction from you."

"How did I end up with a 'staff' anyway?"

"We worked for Mrs. Gooding, and Mrs. Nelson assumed you'd appreciate the guidance of a seasoned second lady staff."

Mrs. Nelson assumed, did she? "Could I call you back? I'm right in the middle of something at the moment."

"Yes, of course. I'll look forward to hearing from you."

"Right. Okay. Bye then." She slapped the phone closed. "Oh my freaking *God*."

"Sam."

"What? Mentioning the name God is not taking His name in vain. That was my *chief of staff* at the freaking *White House* wanting to know if I'll be at the nine a.m. *staff meeting* in the morning. I have a freaking *staff*."

"Don't you mean another freaking staff?" Freddie asked, pointing to himself.

"This is not a joking matter."

"Oh, but it is. It really, *really* is."

Glaring at him, she said, "Shut up." She opened the phone and hit the name of the person who was usually number one on her list of favorites.

Nick answered on the third ring, sounding out of breath. "Hey, babe."

"What're you doing that has you breathing hard?"

"Working out," he said with a laugh, "so get your mind out of the gutter."

"My mind is nowhere near the gutter. It's actually at the White House."

"Huh?"

"I just got a call from a fancy-sounding dame with a fancy-sounding name who claims to be my 'chief of staff.' Know anything about that?"

"I heard they were retaining Mrs. Gooding's staff for you in case you wanted an experienced team. I told you that."

"Um, *when* did you tell me that?"

"I don't know the exact date and time, but we had a conversation about this."

"Was I asleep? Unconscious? In a sex-induced coma perhaps?"

"Ugh, jeez," Freddie mumbled. "Young ears."

Sam made a face at him while Nick laughed at her question. "You were wide awake and appeared to be listening."

"Well, I wasn't! And now I've got Lilly Von Noodle calling me about meetings at the White House! I don't want to go to meetings at the White House!"

"That's not her name, is it?"

"How the hell do I know what her name is? I've never heard of her until she called to tell me she's my so-called chief of staff. Joe Farnsworth is my chief of staff—the only one I need."

"Samantha, take a breath, will you please?"

"Don't use that tone with me. I'm not a child."

"Okay, don't breathe then, but don't call me when you pass out."

"Nick, this isn't funny! These people expect me to come to a meeting to give them 'direction.' What direction am I supposed to give them? And hello, I have a job and a homicide to contend with that indirectly involves one of my closest colleagues while my actual chief is fighting for his career. *I don't have time for this!*"

"I'll talk to Nelson's people and see what we can do, okay?"

"Yes, okay, as long as you get me out of any meetings over there."

"I'll do what I can, but we did talk about you taking on a minor role as second lady before we agreed to accept Nelson's offer."

"A minor role doesn't include staff, Nick!"

"Yes, it does," he said with a low chuckle that infuriated her even further if that was possible. "Who do you think will do all the work?"

"What *work* is involved in a *minor* role?"

"Babe, can we talk about this when you get home?"

"There's that tone again."

"What? All I'm saying is I'd rather talk to my wife in person than on the phone when she is upset and yelling at me. How is that a tone?"

"All right, fine. I'll talk to you when I get home."

"Great, I'll look forward to it."

"I will not."

"I thought you always looked forward to talking to me."

"Not about this crap."

"We'll figure it out. Don't worry."

"I'm supposed to call the Von Noodle lady back. What do I do about that?"

"I'll take care of it."

"No meeting tomorrow."

"Got it."

"Are you patronizing me?" she asked.

"Would I dare do that to my lovely wife who comes packing heat?"

At that, Sam finally cracked a grin and gave a small snort of laughter.

"Are you better now?" he asked.

She was always better after she talked to him, but no way was she going to tell him that when she was still pissed about getting calls from the White House. The *freaking* White House!

"Samantha? Are you still there?"

"I'm here."

"Are you plotting my death by rusty steak knife?"

"Not currently, but I reserve the right to break out my steak knife later."

"Duly noted. I'll see you tonight?"

"Yeah, you will."

"Love you, babe. Be careful out there."

"Always am. You too, on the other thing."

"The *other* thing," he said, ending the call laughing.

Sam was also smiling when she stashed her phone.

"Did he talk you down off the cliff?"

"You're being very sassy today, Detective. Is that your New Year's resolution? To sass your superior officer as much as possible?"

"No, actually it was to sass my friend Sam as often as possible."

"I liked you better when you were afraid of me."

"And when was that exactly?"

When Sam's phone rang again, she looked at the caller ID with trepidation and was relieved to see a number she recognized. She took the call on speaker so Freddie could hear too. "Speak to me."

"Got the tox screen back on Lori Phillips," Lindsey said. "Her BAC was 0.18 and we found traces of cocaine in her nose and in the blood work."

Sam let out a low whistle. "So much for rehab."

"We also found signs of recent sexual activity."

"DNA?"

"Running it now."

"Do you suspect rape?"

"There was no trauma, so it's possible it was consensual."

"I really want to know where our girl was yesterday. Thanks, Lindsey. Let me know when the DNA is in."

"Will do."

Sam hung up with Lindsey and called Archie. "Where are we with the dump on the phone Cruz brought in this morning?"

"Smartphones take about eight hours, which of course you know."

"I need text data as soon as you have it. I'm trying to figure out where my vic spent her final hours."

"Will get it to you as soon as I have it."

"Thanks, Archie."

"While I have you, I need to schedule a time to get your squad trained on the new tablet system we'll be implementing this month."

"What tablet system?"

"Do you read your email, Sam?" he asked with a laugh.

The men in her life were amusing themselves at her expense today. "Occasionally."

"I sent an email weeks ago to all the squad commanders asking them to schedule their training. I just noticed that you haven't scheduled yours yet."

"We don't need tablets. We're good with what we've got."

"It's mandatory, Sam. We all have to do it."

"Why are we being forced to take on something new that we don't need?"

"You're going to love it once you get used to it."

"No, I won't. I still have a flip phone, and I like it that way."

"Ouch," Archie said with an audible wince. "Take it up with the brass. Until then, email me a couple of dates to get with your squad. I need about four hours."

"Four *hours*?"

"Gotta go. I'm watching your security film."

"Fine."

"Email the times. By tomorrow."

Sighing, Sam closed her phone and juggled it between her hands. "Did you know they're making us use tablets in the field now?"

"I can't wait. We'll be able to file reports from anywhere, access the system from anywhere, run prints. It's going to be awesome."

An absolutely brilliant idea occurred to Sam. People were always telling her to delegate. Normally, she'd push this dreaded task off on Gonzo as her second in command, but since he was out of commission, Freddie was the next best thing. "I'm putting you in charge of working with Archie to get our squad trained on the stupid things."

He blanched. "Does that mean I have to deal with getting *you* trained too?"

She graced him with her most charming smile. "Yep. Not that I expect to ever use it since my partner is so *excited* about it."

"Oh my God."

"Freddie! The Lord's name! How dare you?"

"You drive me to it."

"You'll get with Archie by tomorrow to set it up. Yes?"

"Yes," he said through gritted teeth.

"Excellent."

EIGHT

SAM CALLED JEANNIE MCBRIDE. "Where are we with Rex Connolly?"

"There were several of them in the system. I just tracked down the one you need. He lives in Laurel."

Sam wrote down the address. "Thanks, Jeannie." She handed her notebook to Freddie. "Put this in the GPS," she said, reminding him she still hadn't bothered to figure out that device either. Why should she when he was around to do everything for her? Sam had learned a long time ago that the more she knew, the more she was expected to do. As technology had overtaken their workplace, their workload had tripled, which was why simpler was better as far as she was concerned.

They left Bowie and drove north to Laurel on the parkway. Rex Connolly lived in a run-down row of townhouses that sat so close to the parkway you could hear the roar of traffic from the parking lot.

"What possesses people to want to live right on top of a major roadway?" Sam asked Freddie.

"All they can afford?"

"I guess." She rapped on the glass storm door outside the house. "We're kinda lucky this happened on a holiday."

"How so?"

"People we need to talk to are more likely to be home and press corps probably has the second string working on a day like this."

"True."

The door swung open to reveal a tall, bald, muscular dude with tattoos covering his huge arms, barrel chest and even his face. Sam shuddered. How anyone could do *that* to themselves she'd never understand. He wore only a pair of sweatpants that rode low on narrow hips. "Mr. Connolly?" she asked through the door as she and Freddie showed their badges.

"Yeah. What do you want?"

"We need a few minutes of your time. May we come in?"

"Not without a warrant."

"You got something to hide in there?"

"Nope, but I got rights, and you ain't comin' in my house."

A naked woman appeared in the front hall behind him. "What's going on?"

"Nothin', babe. Go back to bed. I'll be right there."

The woman walked away as nonchalantly as she'd appeared, as if it was a regular routine for her to walk around naked in front of strangers. Maybe it was.

"Let us in, Mr. Connolly, or we'll take you downtown to chat. Your call."

With a growl that Sam could hear through the glass, he pushed open the door and then walked away.

Sam and Freddie followed him into a dirty, messy space that smelled of stale cigarettes and beer.

In the kitchen, he lit up a cigarette and blew the smoke in their direction. "Not sure what you're after," he said, "but I didn't do it. I been right here fucking my girl for the last twenty hours, and I got the used condoms to prove it."

"As delightful as that sounds, we're looking for information about an old friend of yours."

"What old friend?"

"Lori Phillips."

He let out a harsh laugh. "Ah, good old Lori who found religion and decided she was too good for the likes of me after I took care of her and her brat? That Lori? Why you sniffing around her? 'Cuz she's making trouble for your boy Gonzales?"

"That's not why. We're wondering when you last spoke to her."

He thought about that. "Saw her at a party over the holidays. She wanted to talk, but I got something new going on, so I said hi and that's it. Lori made her bed with me. She wanted to live clean and sober, and I wasn't part of that."

"You know anything about who her dealer might've been when she was using?" Sam asked.

"Right. I give you that info, and next thing I know you're arresting me for using. What, do you think I'm stupid or somethin'?"

"We have no interest in arresting you, Mr. Connolly," Sam said. "We're looking for information about Lori. Only."

"What's she done?" he asked as he raised the cigarette.

"She's been murdered."

His hand froze halfway to his mouth. *Murdered? How? When?* He seemed genuinely surprised—and dismayed—to hear the news.

"We don't have all the details yet, but we're working on that."

"I bet your buddy Gonzales knows what happened to her. She was making all sorts of shit for him."

"We're not looking at him for this."

"'Course you aren't," he said with a bitter chuckle.

"What can you tell us about her friends, associates, dealers? Anything you can give us would be helpful."

"She doesn't associate with the people she knew when she was with me anymore. She's gone clean."

"We have reason to believe she was off the wagon when she died."

"Really? Aw, shit. Kid worked really hard to straighten things out. She loved that little boy. Wanted to be better for him. I thought she was making a go of it."

"Who were some of her friends, Mr. Connolly?"

"Sara Angelo was her best friend."

"Do you know where we can find her?"

"She actually lives two blocks that way." He rattled off the street name. "Don't know the number though. Saw her at the 7-Eleven a couple weeks ago, otherwise I wouldn't have known she was so close."

"Who's Lori's dealer?"

He shook his head. "You're gonna have to find that out for yourselves. I know you're standing here in my house telling me it ain't gonna come back to bite me in the ass, but you'll have to excuse me if I'm not buyin' that. Been burned too many times already by your kind."

"How about the names of any friends from her partying days?"

Rex shook his head. "Can't help you there, either. I start sending cops to those guys, and I'll be in the morgue next to Lori."

"We could take you downtown until you feel more compelled to cooperate."

"And I'd be sprung before your tour ends, and you know it. I'm not giving you those names." He crossed his arms over his broad chest. "Arrest me if you want to. Won't get you anywhere."

Sam tried to stare him down, but he never blinked.

"I'd like to help you get whoever did this to her," Rex said. "She was a nice girl and we had good times together, but I'm not risking my own neck for someone who's dead. Not happening."

Sam handed him her card. "If you think of anything that might help and you're willing to share, my number's on there."

He nodded.

She tipped her head to tell Freddie to move toward the door. As they went out, he was busy on his phone.

"Got the address for Sara Angelo."

Perhaps there was something to be said for owning a smartphone, Sam thought, but as long as he had one at work and Nick had one at home, she didn't need one of her own.

They got back in the car, and Freddie directed her for several blocks until they arrived at another nondescript row of townhouses.

"Every one of them exactly the same," Sam said as she took in the community. "How many times do you think I'd try to get into the wrong door if I lived here?"

"Daily?"

"Perhaps even hourly." Sam glanced at him as she rang the doorbell. "Why don't you take the lead here?"

"Oh, um, okay." After a pause, he said, "Is this punishment? For busting your chops?"

"That would make me vindictive and mean, and I'm neither of those things. It's about training, about bringing you along, about—" Her string of bullshit was interrupted when the door was opened by a flushed-looking woman with dark hair and eyes.

"Sorry," she said, "I was working out."

Sam and Freddie showed their badges.

"Detective Cruz and Lieutenant Holland, Metro PD," Freddie said. "Could we have a few minutes of your time?"

"Oh, um, sure." She stepped back to allow them to enter

her well-kept home. After the last two they'd visited, hers was a refreshing breath of fresh air—literally. "What's this about?"

"You're friends with Lori Phillips?" Freddie asked.

"Yes," she said hesitantly. "What about her?"

"When was the last time you saw or talked to her?"

"We were at a Christmas party together in early December. We text pretty regularly, though. Why? Is she in trouble? She's worked so hard to turn her life around. So hard."

"I'm sorry to have to tell you that she was found murdered this morning."

Sara's mouth opened and then closed when nothing came out. Her eyes filled with tears. "*Murdered?*" Her voice was barely more than a whisper. "Who would want to hurt her? She was the sweetest person." And then her expression hardened. "The baby's father. She was making trouble for him. I bet it was him."

Freddie maintained his composure when he said, "It wasn't him."

"You have to say that! He's a cop! Of course he didn't do it. But who else could it be?"

"That's what we'd like to know too."

She swiped angrily at the tears on her cheeks. "Have you even *considered* that it might be him?"

"He has an alibi."

"Right. Whatever. People like Lori, they don't matter to you as much as another cop does. I get it."

"That's not true," Sam said. "We want justice for her as much as you do."

"Somehow I doubt that. She's been my best friend since we were in high school. I bet I want justice for her more than you do."

"Fair enough," Sam conceded. "All I'm saying is that we care about every murder victim equally. We want justice for all of them. Can you tell us who else might've had a beef with Lori? Was she dating anyone that you know of?"

Sara was quiet for several minutes while she continued to wipe away tears. "There was this one guy she talked about a couple of times."

"Do you know his name?" Freddie asked.

"Liam Hughes."

"How did they meet?"

"Online a couple of months ago. She really liked him."

"Do you know which online service she went through?" Freddie asked.

"I think she met him through a site called DateFinder."

"Where does he live?"

"In Baltimore, I think."

Sam wanted to moan at the thought of going all the way to Baltimore. "Do you know if she was with him yesterday or last night?" Sam asked.

"I really don't know. I was away for much of the last week skiing with some friends in Colorado. I hadn't talked to her since I got home. I was planning to call her today to check in." Her shoulders sagged as the realization seemed to hit her all at once that she'd never speak to her friend again. "What happened to her?"

"She was manually strangled," Freddie said. They'd learned from experience that it was better to just say it than to sugarcoat the truth.

"God," Sara said with a sigh. "I don't know anything about murder, but that sounds rather personal. You're sure the baby's father didn't do it? It'd be awfully convenient for him to have her out of the picture, especially when she was making trouble for him."

"It wasn't him," Freddie said bluntly.

Heartbreak turned to anger in a flash. "*How do you know that?*"

"We know *him*," Freddie said. "We've known him for years. We know what's inside of him and what's not. He loves that baby, and he'd never do anything to cause him harm, including murdering his mother."

Sam wanted to tell her partner he'd said that well, but she held her tongue. No need to pile on the platitudes. They weren't going to convince this woman who'd never met Gonzo that he wasn't capable of murder.

"Ms. Angelo," Sam said in the softest tone she possessed, "one thing I've learned after many years on this job is to refrain from leaping to obvious conclusions until we have all the facts. That's what we're doing now—collecting the facts. And you've been very helpful. You've given us a direction we didn't have before, and we appreciate that." She handed over her card. "If you think of anything else that might be helpful to our investigation, please give me a call."

Sara took the card from her.

"We've yet to contact all of her family," Sam said, "so if we could ask for your discretion in the meantime, we'd appreciate it."

"I'm not going to call the TV stations, if that's what you're insinuating."

"It's not, but we appreciate your discretion just the same."

"I'm sorry," Sara said. "I'm upset. She was my friend for a long time. We drifted apart during the years she was off the rails with that dirtbag Rex, but we've come back to each other recently." Her voice broke and new tears tumbled down her cheeks.

"We're very sorry for your loss," Freddie said.

"Thank you."

As they left the house, Freddie shook his head. "That never gets any easier."

"Never will."

"So I guess we're going to Baltimore?"

"If we can track down Hughes." In the car, she waited for Freddie to find the guy on his phone. "Can you explain the appeal of online dating to me? I mean how does anyone trust that they haven't agreed to a date with a serial killer?"

"It's possible your perspective on the issue may be somewhat skewed by your profession."

"I hate to admit you're right about anything, but…"

He laughed. "Painful for you, is it?"

"Excruciating. Still, I can't imagine hooking up with a guy I met on the Internet." She shuddered. "Super creepy."

"I hate to remind you that you found a creep in your own apartment."

Thinking about her ex-roommate, who was now her psychotic ex-husband, made Sam shudder. Four years of her life she'd never get back. "Damn, you're on a roll of rightness today."

"I love that. I'm going to let it go straight to my head."

"Don't injure yourself," Sam said.

"I can't hear you. I'm busy enjoying how right I am."

"Get over yourself and find this guy she was cyber-romancing." Sam took advantage of the opportunity to place a call to Archie. "Did Crime Scene bring in our vic's computer from her house?" she asked when he answered.

"Not yet."

"Apparently she had something going with a guy she met on DateFinder. I'd like access to that account ASAP."

"I'll let you know as soon as it's in the house."

"Thanks. Anything on the video?"

"Nothing but darkness and shoes. I'm taking screen-shots for you. Whoever disabled the cameras knew how to dodge them so he or she wouldn't be seen."

"Great." There went that lead up in smoke. "I'll hit you up when I get back from Baltimore."

"Baltimore? WTF?"

"Following the leads."

"Ugh, better you than me."

"Thanks, you're a pal." She hung up to the sound of Archie's laughter. "Everyone's a comedian today."

"You bring it out in us."

"Did you find our guy?"

"I think so. Head north up the parkway."

"I'd like to be on record as saying I'm doing this under extreme duress. Metro police do not go willingly to Baltimore for any reason other than good Italian food."

"Unless potential murder suspects live there."

"What you said."

"Perhaps a delicious Italian lunch might be in our future?" he asked hopefully.

"You just ate breakfast."

"That was hours ago, and I'm a growing boy."

"While you're busy growing, give our friends in the Baltimore PD a heads-up that we're coming. See if our guy Hughes has a history with them and let them know we'd appreciate their backup."

"But we don't need their backup."

"You know that, and I know that, but we still have to suck their dicks."

"Ugh, Sam! For crap's sake."

"What'd I say?" The traffic came to a complete stop around the Route 32 exit for the National Security Agency. "Why? Why, why, *why*? Are the Caps playing up here too?"

He consulted his ever-present link to the outside world. "Nope, but the Ravens are playing at home today."

"Motherfucker. I hate this day with the fiery passion of a thousand hemorrhoids."

Freddie squirmed in his seat. "Ouch. That burns."

Sam's phone rang and she took the call because it gave her something to do besides ruminate on the wonders of traffic and hemorrhoids. "Holland."

"Happy New Year, Mrs. Vice President."

Sam nearly groaned out loud when she realized it was Darren Tabor from the *Washington Star*. Make that a million hemorrhoids. "What'd you want, Darren? I'm busy."

"I heard. Caught a homicide this morning. Hell of a way to start the new year."

"Just another day in paradise for us."

"Also heard an interesting thing about the possibility of an inside job on this one?"

"What? What're you talking about?"

"A source told me you're looking at Gonzales in the murder of his baby mama."

Sam almost drove off the road. "*What?* That is not true. Do you hear me, Darren? It's categorically *untrue*. Gonzo is *not* a suspect."

"Is it true your vic is his baby mama?"

"No comment."

"Come *on*, Sam. You gotta give me something."

"No, I don't, and if you run with Gonzo as a suspect, I'll sue your ass off and make sure he does too."

"My source is solid on this."

"More solid than I am as the commander in charge of the investigation of which you speak? And who is this so-called source of yours anyway?"

"You know I can't tell you that."

"Listen to me, Darren. Believe it or not, I think of you as one of the good guys in your field. If you print anything that even *hints* of Gonzo's involvement in a homicide, I'll make sure you never get another quote from any member of the Metro PD or any member of the vice president's team. Am I clear on that? And if you think I can't do it—"

"Ease up, Sam. I'm not going to run with it. For now anyway."

"You better not run with it ever. You'll be ruining the career and the life of a man who deserves better after taking a bullet in the line of duty and nearly dying a very short time ago. Remember that?"

"Yeah, I do."

"And do you remember how I got you the very first exclusive interview with him after he was out of danger?"

"Yeah, yeah."

"You want those sorts of favors to dry up faster than a virgin's vagina?"

"Oh my hell, Sam," Freddie said with a groan that matched Darren's on the other end of the phone. "That's disgusting."

"Did it get the point across?" she asked Darren while looking at Freddie, who scowled at her.

"You're a piece of work, Mrs. Cappuano," Darren said.

"I also better not see any mention of the VP's wife talking about virgin's vaginas in the paper."

"And here I thought I was getting hungry for lunch," Darren said. "Thanks for ruining my appetite and my story."

"Happy to be of service. Don't screw me over on this one, Darren. I've got a very long memory when it comes to people dicking with my team."

"This is going to seem like a hideously horrible segue, but how's Jeannie holding up with the trial coming soon?"

"That's the worst segue in the history of bad segues, and I'm going to forget you asked it like that when I tell you she's holding up fine, and she'll hold up fine all the way through to sentencing for that son of a bitch who attacked her."

"The trial's gonna be a circus."

"We're fully aware of that."

"When she's ready to talk, you know how to find me."

"I'll keep you in mind, provided you stick to our deal on the Gonzo thing."

"Will you call me when you're ready to release the vic's name?"

"If I can, I will. That's all I'm giving you."

"Good enough for now. Anything you want to say about the situation with the chief?"

Sam laughed and laughed and then laughed some more. "Behave yourself, Darren."

"Yeah, yeah. You're worse than my mom."

"On that note…" Sam slapped the phone shut. "Who in the hell is calling the fucking *press* and telling them we've got an inside job with *Gonzo* as our chief suspect in a *murder*?"

"What the hell is right."

"Could you maybe, just this once, consider an actual swear word?"

"I just did."

"*Hell* is not a swear!" Sam dialed HQ. "This is Lieutenant Holland. Put me through to the pit, please."

"The what?"

"The Homicide Detectives' Division," Sam said sweetly, though she was seething on the inside.

"One moment, please."

"Who trains these imbeciles who answer the phones?"

"Obviously not you."

"Right? Because if I did at least they'd speak MPD basics."

"Among other things."

"What was that, Detective?"

"I was just saying how right you are, Lieutenant."

"Thought so. Why isn't anyone answering the goddamn phone?" She hung up and redialed. "Chief Farnsworth, please."

"Who's calling, please?"

"Lieutenant Holland."

"Oh, yes, of course. Let me put you right through. And may I say congrat—"

"If you want to keep your job, don't say it."

"Yes, ma'am."

"Is this what the new year is going to be like? Because I gotta say, I'm not digging it so far." The line clicked before the chief came on the line. "Holland?"

"Yes, sir. I got a curious call from Darren Tabor, who seemed to know an awful lot about who our victim is and how she was related to Gonzo. In fact, he said Gonzo is rumored to be our top suspect when that is not at all true."

"How the hell did he get all that?"

"That's what I'd like to know. He said it came from inside MPD."

"After what went down with Stahl, no way is anyone here going to be stupid enough to use our phones to make calls to the media."

"He didn't say the call came from inside HQ. He said the source was from inside."

"Any thoughts on who it might be?"

"Normally I'd say Stahl, but he's been on best behavior since he somehow managed to post bond to get out of lockup until his trial. And I'd still like to know how he got the dough for that."

"As would I."

"Ramsey in SVU has something up his ass with my name on it."

"That's a lovely visual, Lieutenant."

"He told me to fuck off just this morning, in fact. I reported it to Davidson, not that he'll do anything about it."

"He really told you to fuck off? Over what?"

"I believe I said good morning to him. It was an unprovoked attack."

"What've you done in the past to warrant his enmity?"

"I've been my usual charming self with him. I had a minute with Erica Lucas after I talked to Davidson, and she inferred there's some info to be had there. We're going to do coffee."

"While you do coffee, I'll have a word with Ramsey and see if he's our leaker."

"Don't let on that I told you anything."

"Wouldn't dream of it."

"How's it going with Public Affairs?"

"Like having a root canal without the drugs."

Sam grimaced at the exhaustion she heard in his voice. "Listen, your little mouse outside the door, what's her name?"

"Do you mean Helen, my admin?"

Helen! That was it. "Yeah, her."

"And you wonder why you're always pissing people off."

"I don't actually wonder."

He grunted out a laugh. "What about her?"

"She's worried about you. Doesn't like your color. Gotta say I agree with her. You're looking a little gray around the edges."

"Got a few things on my mind."

"Look, I know you're a big boy and can take care of yourself, but you'll be no good to us if you go down physically over this. First of all, that scumbag Springer isn't worth risking your health, and second of all, well, I don't have a second of all other than we all need you healthy. Will you see someone? Please?"

"Marti has been after me about the same thing," he said of his wife. "I'll make an appointment."

"You'll do it now? After we hang up?"

"Yes, Sam! I said I'd do it. Now, where are you?"

"Sitting in bumper-to-bumper traffic on the way to Baltimore, of all places."

"What the hell for?"

"A lead on the Phillips case. She met a guy online who lives there. We're trying to piece together her final days without cell or computer data to work from yet."

"All right. Keep me posted. Have you heard from Hill yet?"

"No. Should I have?"

"He's been called in. Expect a call from him."

"Oh, joy. This day just gets better all the time."

Freddie's phone rang, and he took the call after glancing at the caller ID.

"I gotta get back to the meeting with Public Affairs," Farnsworth said. "In case I forgot to tell you, good thinking earlier on getting out there with our side of the story. I've been in hunker-down mode, but you're right that the public needs to hear from me."

"I'm usually right. That's what Nick says."

"Jesus. I walked right into that one. Keep me in the loop on Phillips."

"I will. Call the doctor. Bye." Satisfied she'd made her point and kept her promise to Helen, she slapped the phone closed. See, that right there was why she'd never get a smartphone. You couldn't slap them closed.

NINE

"WHAT DO YOU mean he *hit* you?" Freddie was saying, his voice tense. He remained rigidly still as he listened. "So he just punched you? For no reason?" After some more listening, he said, "Call it into MPD or I'll do it for you. Want me to do it?" A short pause. "Yes, Elin! It's a crime when someone punches you in the face. And you also need to be seen at the ER. Can someone take you?"

Sam gave him a questioning look.

"She broke up a fight at the gym, and some guy punched her."

"I can call it in."

He held up a finger, telling her to wait a minute. "Did someone call the cops and rescue?" he asked. "All right. I'll be there as soon as I can. I'm outside of Baltimore right now, so it'll be a little while. You're sure you're okay?" He rested his head on his hand, which was propped on the car door. "Yeah, baby. I love you. Sorry you got hurt. I'll get there soon." He ended the call and held the phone in a tight grip.

"She's okay?"

"She says she is, but I can tell she's been crying."

"I'll get you to her as soon as possible."

Nodding, he stared out the window at the sea of traffic standing between them and the city.

"Did you get through to Baltimore PD?"

"Yeah, they've had eyes on the guy's place for a while now. They aren't sure if he's into drugs or hookers."

"Fabulous. Warrant?"

"They're willing to get it for us if they can have in on the search."

"Of course they want in."

"We would too."

"Does that wonder phone of yours know any back routes into the city?"

He seemed relieved to have something to do besides worry about his injured girlfriend. After a couple of minutes of intense typing, he instructed her to take the next exit. Twenty anxious minutes later, they pulled onto Hughes's street in the Fells Point section of Baltimore, where they spent ten more minutes looking for a place to park.

"I used to love to come drinking up here in the summer," Sam said. "One of my college friends was from here. Those were some good times."

Freddie took a look around at the quaint area. "I don't think I've ever been here before."

"Not much of a party animal, are you?" she asked as they got out of the car.

"Not then and not now."

"You ever just want to bust loose and go wild?"

"How do you know I don't?" he asked.

"Right. Your idea of wild is sex after church." His usual snappy comeback was stifled by his worries over Elin. "She's going to be all right, you know. She was talking and crying and mad. Those are all good things."

"I hate that I'm all the way up here when she needs me."

"You'll be with her soon enough." Sam wrapped her scarf around her neck. "How is it colder up here than it is in D.C.?"

"We're right by the Inner Harbor. Wind is colder off the water."

Different shades of brick distinguished the townhouses where Liam Hughes lived. "I wouldn't get lost as easily here."

Rather than run with the softball she tossed him, Freddie only nodded. His mind was elsewhere, but Sam didn't blame him for that. She'd be freaking out if Nick had gotten hurt when she couldn't get to him.

They knocked on the door several times, but no one answered.

"Great," Freddie said. "We came all the way up here for nothing."

"Let's check with the neighbors to see if they know where he is."

Sam took the unit on the left side of Liam's while Freddie took the right. A young woman with a baby on her hip came to the door. Sam showed her badge. "Wondering if you can tell us where your neighbor might be—Liam Hughes?"

"Who knows? He keeps strange hours. He's up all night with music thumping and then he sleeps all day. We had to move the baby's room to the other side of the house because his music was waking her up."

"So you've had words with him?"

"As few as possible. We're not exactly what you'd call friends. He's got people—women mostly—in and out of there at all times of the day and night. My husband thinks he's a pimp. We love to speculate on what goes on in there."

"Would you mind if I wrote down your name and number in case I have follow-up questions?"

"Sure, no problem."

Sam met Freddie back out on the street, where he had a similar report from the neighbor on the other side—lots of parties, lots of women and loud music. "The guy sounds like a tool." She glanced at her partner. "I know you want to get back to the District, but I'd like to hang out for a short time to see if he comes back."

"What's a short time?"

"An hour max?"

Freddie grimaced but then nodded. "Okay."

"Sorry."

"Not your fault." He glanced at his phone as they returned to the car. "Hey, what do you know? We've got a warrant out for Hughes. Nonpayment of child support."

"Excellent. Let's hope little daddy comes home so we can arrest his ass for that and then ask him some questions about his friend Lori."

"I need some food." Freddie gestured to a sub shop at the other end of the block. "You care if I run down there really quick?"

She pulled a ten from her wallet. "Get me a veggie something or other and a water."

"Got it. Be right back." He jogged off down the street while Sam got comfortable in the driver's seat of her car.

She fired off a text to Nick. Well here I am spending New Year's Day on a stakeout in Baltimore. Didn't see my year starting this way.

He wrote right back. What're you doing way up there?

Freddie had a hankering for Italian—ha! Following a lead, what else? Did you deal with my "situation" yet?

Making some calls. Don't worry about it. I got you covered.

Thank you. Sorry to be a lousy second lady.

As long as you continue to put out on a regular basis, you're the best second lady ever.

Ha-ha, sex fiend. What if the Secret Service is monitoring your texts?

They're only monitoring my official phone. This one is personal. Did you see the shit on the news about Gonzo being a suspect?

WHAT?!?

It was all over CBC. You didn't know?

NO!!! OMG! Gotta go deal with this. TTYL

Sorry, babe. Hang in there. Love you.

Love you too.

Sam placed a call to HQ, asked for the chief and was told he was in a meeting. "Helen, it's Lieutenant Holland. I need to speak to him right now. It's urgent."

"Please hold."

Sam was forced to listen to the ridiculous light rock that served as the hold music. Nothing said badass cop shop quite like a little light rock. They needed Bon Jovi to liven things up. She'd bring that up at the next department meeting. As she waited for the chief, a man came walking down the street from the far corner. His eyes darted nervously around as he headed for the door she was watching.

She threw down the phone and got out of the car, crossing the street so she would meet him at the stairs that led to his townhouse. She flashed her badge. "Mr. Hughes? Lieutenant Holland, Metro PD, Washington, D.C. I have a few questions I'd like to ask you."

At the sight of her badge, he turned and bolted back the way he'd come.

Swearing under her breath, Sam took off after him. Didn't these idiots know that nothing said, "I'm guilty of something," quite like running from cops? She dug in and caught up to him two blocks from where they'd started. Grabbing the hood of his sweatshirt, she pulled hard and brought him down onto the sidewalk. She went down with him, landing hard on her right knee.

She planted her left knee in his back and had him cuffed within seconds.

"What the fuck? I didn't do anything! You can't just tackle me like that and arrest me."

"Oh no? Looks like I just did. And if you didn't do anything, why'd you run?"

Freddie came around the corner a minute later, looking slightly undone by the sight of her on the ground with their guy. "I leave you for ten minutes, and you manage to find trouble."

"Trouble finds me. Detective Cruz, meet Liam Hughes."

"I'd say pleased to meet you," Freddie said, "but you don't seem too pleased."

"I'm going to sue your asses off for this," Hughes said, straining against the cuffs.

"Then I ought to tell you that you have the right to remain silent," Sam said. "Anything you say can and will be used against you in a court of law." After she'd recited the Miranda warning, Freddie dragged Hughes up off the sidewalk and escorted him to the car. "And PS, dirtbag, you can't sue our asses off when you're wanted for failure to pay child support."

"I don't owe that bitch nothing. That kid ain't mine."

"Tell it to the judge."

Sam limped along behind him, her knee throbbing from

the direct hit to the sidewalk. Every muscle in her body was on fire from the sprint, proof that the gym might actually be a resolution worth making before she lost her edge. At thirty-five, the old gray mare wasn't what she used to be.

After Freddie had tossed Hughes into the back of the car, he turned to her. "Are you okay?"

"Yeah, smacked my knee and wore myself out, but otherwise, I'm fine."

"Want me to drive?"

She tossed him the keys. "I won't say no to that." On the passenger seat, she found the bag of food he'd left there before coming after her. "Glad to see you protected the food."

"Of course I did. God knows when you'll give me another chance to eat."

"So when faced with the dilemma of going after your partner who was possibly in over her head, you saw to the sandwiches first? Good to know where I rate."

"This can't possibly be news to you after all this time."

"I want a lawyer," Hughes said from the backseat.

"Shut the fuck up," Sam said as she took a huge bite of her sandwich, wishing it was full of meatballs rather than vegetables. "We should check in with Baltimore so they don't get pissy with us for making a grab in their city."

"I'll do it." Somehow he managed to eat, drive and make the call to the Baltimore PD's Homicide Division to let them know an investigation had led to an arrest in their city.

Professional courtesy and all that happy horseshit. Sam got sick and tired of playing nicey-nice with all the fragile egos involved in police work. God forbid they should step foot in someone else's turf without letting them know. Then she remembered the call she'd been on when she saw Hughes coming and the reason for it.

"They're going to give us a heads-up when the warrant

comes through. They're trying to track down a judge. Holiday," he said over a mouthful of sandwich.

"We got trouble," she told him. "CBC is reporting Gonzo is our chief suspect in the murder of his baby mama."

"What? What the hell?"

"*Fuck* is the word you're looking for there. Who knows? Apparently our leaker didn't just go to Darren, and now he'll be pissed with me because someone else scooped him." So many egos, so little time. She placed another call to the chief.

"I was able to interrupt him once," Helen said in a testy tone. "But I can't do it again."

"I was off chasing down a suspect in a homicide investigation."

"Homicide!" Hughes said from the backseat. "*What the fuck?* I didn't kill no one."

Sam ignored him. "I really need to talk to the chief. It's a life-and-death situation." While that might not be entirely true, Gonzo's life and career were certainly on the line and well worth fighting for.

"Please hold, and please be there when he comes on the line."

As soon as the line clicked over to hold, Sam said, "Gee, Helen, I thought we were pals. I'm feeling hurt by your attitude."

"You did not say that to her," Freddie said, his mouth full of what might've been chicken parm. Sam's mouth watered at the thought of it.

"Nope. I said it to the hideous light rock that serves as hold music at our workplace."

"That stuff is pretty bad."

"I've got someone wailing about endless love in my ear as we speak."

"Damn, Gonzo must be flipping out."

"Maybe he doesn't know yet." As she said the words, her phone rang with another call. A check of the caller ID revealed Gonzo's number. "He knows. Call him, will you? Tell him we're doing what we can to contain this shit." Sam knew as well as Gonzo would that the accusation alone would be enough to damage his sterling reputation and possibly ruin his career. Naturally, that was the goal of whoever had the audacity to leak lies about the investigation.

"Holland?" the chief barked when he came on the line. "Are you there this time?"

"Sorry about before. I was apprehending a suspect in the Phillips case."

"What Phillips case?" Hughes asked. "Are you talking about Lori? I barely know her! What's she done?"

Sam nodded to Freddie, who took a turn telling Hughes to shut up.

"We've got a problem. CBC is broadcasting that Gonzo is our suspect."

"Motherfucker," Farnsworth muttered, echoing Sam's thoughts.

"Our leaker has been busy. Any leads yet on who it might be?"

As they drove through the congested city, Sam could hear Freddie trying to talk Gonzo off a cliff.

"Conklin is up talking to Ramsey now. Haven't heard anything yet though. I'm stuck in this meeting with the Public Affairs hacks who think they know better than I do about how to represent this department."

"Can't you fire them and get new hacks?"

"I wish it were that easy," he said with a bitter chuckle. "I'd better get back in there. We're making plans for a big blitz starting tomorrow morning."

"Anything I can do? You know I hate every single thing about the notoriety, but if it'll help, I'd gladly go out there with you to show my support."

"Interesting that you should offer. The PAO said I should ask you, and I refused to."

"How come?"

"Just like you don't embrace the notoriety, I don't embrace the idea of asking you to use it on my behalf."

"It may as well be good for something other than a total pain in my ass."

Farnsworth laughed at her choice of words. "How do you feel about being on TV at seven in the morning?"

"I feel good about it. Great, in fact. Let me know where to be, and I'm all yours."

"The only reason I'm allowing this is because you were the lead detective on Springer. Not because you're the VP's wife."

"Thank you for saying wife. I've already been called his old lady today. And yes, it's okay to laugh."

It was good to hear him laugh. There hadn't been much for him to laugh about lately. "That's hilarious. Does the person who said that still have all his teeth?"

"Only because I needed info from him."

"He's a lucky man. He has no idea how lucky."

"No, he doesn't. Hang in there, sir. I'll see you in the morning."

"Thank you, Sam. I can't tell you how much I appreciate the support."

"Least I can do for driving you crazy all these years." Smiling, Sam closed the phone and returned it to her pocket.

"Did you really just *volunteer* to go on TV?" Freddie asked her. "Have you lost what's left of your mind?"

"Probably, but if it helps him, I'll do it and it'll give

me a chance to say publicly that Gonzo is not a suspect. Speaking of him… Is he freaking out?"

"What's the next step past freaking out? The worst part is he thought it was actually coming from us."

"I hope you set him straight."

"As much as I could, but the poor guy is going nuts. His phone is ringing off the hook with calls from all the same reporters who made him out to be a hero after the shooting, wanting to know if he's a murderer now."

"We gotta get ahead of this somehow." She pulled out her phone again and called Malone. When he answered, she said, "We've got a big problem."

WHILE SCOTTY VISITED with Skip and Celia, Nick spent the holiday on the phone, first with his chief of staff, Terry O'Connor, who'd been working over the last few weeks to pull together their new team. Nick was set to officially begin his new role as vice president tomorrow, with a greatly expanded staff that included his own national security advisors. Imagine that.

Though Terry had overseen the compilation of what he called their dream team, Nick had consulted at every turn, approving all of Terry's choices. His chief of staff's inside-the-Beltway connections were coming in handy during this time of transition. Terry's father, Graham, who was Nick's adopted father and political mentor, had also weighed in on his son's choices, and Nick wouldn't have it any other way.

The retired Senator O'Connor was far more excited about Nick's big promotion than anyone else was, and it pleased Nick to see the older man smiling and fully engaged in the political process that he loved so much.

His phone rang for the twentieth time that day with a

call from Derek Kavanaugh, White House deputy chief
of staff.

"Sorry to keep you waiting for a return call, Mr. Vice
President," Derek said when Nick answered.

"Can the bullshit, Derek." The two men had been
friends for fifteen years, since both were junior staffers
to congressional members and new to Washington.

Derek laughed. "Just following protocol, sir."

"Derek…"

"Sorry, *Nick*. How's it going?"

"Okay so far if you count being surrounded by security
okay. Takes some getting used to."

"It's not your first rodeo with the Secret Service. I'd
think you'd be used to it after the campaign."

"This is a whole other level. I have to say it makes me
a bit nuts to have to ask their permission to take a walk
over to my father-in-law's house, and I'm sure the neighbors love the way they've got Ninth Street barricaded."

"It's awesome they let you stay in your own house."

"I didn't give them much choice, and while Ambrose
was all for it," he said of the Secret Service director, "I get
the distinct feeling that my detail isn't so thrilled."

"They'll get used to it, and so will you."

"I guess." Nick couldn't imagine ever becoming accustomed to feeling like a goldfish inside a small bowl with
all eyes on him. "The reason for this latest call is I could
use some advice about navigating the White House staff
when it comes to Sam's role."

"Sam has a role?"

"I know—it's funny to us too. But here's the thing, they
want her in there at meetings and whatnot, and we all know
that's not going to happen. So how do I get around this in a
way that keeps my wife happy and gets the job done too?"

"Hmm, that's a tall order, especially since Gooding's

wife was extremely hands-on and very well regarded around here."

"Sam is going to be extremely hands-off."

Derek laughed again, which was actually good to hear. He hadn't had much to laugh about since his wife was murdered and a huge conspiracy uncovered in the aftermath of her death. "Surely you told them that before you took the job."

"I did, but she's getting calls from a Lily someone who wants her there in the morning for a staff meeting that's not going to happen."

"Lilia Van Nostrand," Derek said. "She's well regarded here too. A real go-getter."

"If that's the case, I have a feeling she's going to dislike my wife rather intensely."

Derek made a sound that might've been a laugh that turned into a cough. "Perhaps it might make sense for you to meet with her and explain Sam's…limitations."

"*Limitations*," Nick said, laughing. "That's a good word for it. And it's a great idea to meet with her. I'll ask Terry to set something up. I don't want to get off on the wrong foot over there, but I made promises to Sam when I took this job. Chief among them was that her life would remain relatively similar to what it was before."

"That might be a hard promise to keep. There'll be times when they'll want both of you at events."

"*They* have been told there'll be times when they might get only me."

"Personally, I think it's really cool that she's doing something no other second lady has ever done—that I know of. No security and still working the streets as a cop. It's awesome."

"It gives me angina to think about her running around

with no security and a big target on her back because of who she's married to."

"If there's one thing I know about Sam, it's that she can more than take care of herself."

"True. Besides, if someone ever decided to take her, they'd probably give her back within thirty minutes." Nick made light of it, but the thought of her being taken terrified him.

This time Derek made no attempt to conceal his laughter. "You said that, not me."

"You were thinking it."

"You'll never get me to admit that."

"I really appreciate your help in navigating all this stuff. You've been a tremendous asset to Terry and to me." Nick had decided to refrain from asking Derek about the odd radio silence from the West Wing over the last few weeks. Not wanting to take advantage of their friendship, he'd save that card for if or when he really needed it.

"My pleasure. Looking forward to having you around the West Wing, *sir*."

"Shut up, Derek."

"Yes, sir. See you tomorrow."

"Hey, Derek?"

"Yeah?"

"You doing all right?"

A deep sigh came through the phone loud and clear. "As well as can be expected, I guess. We got through the holidays. That's something anyway. Thank goodness for my family and Maeve," he said of his young daughter. "She gives me a reason to get up every day and keep pushing forward."

"You're surrounded by a lot of people who care about both of you. I hope you know that."

"I do, and it's gotten me through. Thanks for all you've done. You and Sam have been incredible friends to us."

"We wish we could do more."

"I'm told time helps. I certainly hope so."

"I'm here if you need me. All kidding aside, the new job doesn't change a thing. I hope you know that."

"I do know, and I appreciate it, *sir*."

Nick appreciated his attempt at levity. "I'll let you get away with that crap now, but no more of it. See you tomorrow."

"See you then—and thanks for asking, Nick."

"Take care." He ended the call and sat for a long time thinking about Derek, his gorgeous wife Victoria and the sinister plot Arnie Patterson had engaged in to get close to President Nelson's inner circle.

Months later, the whole thing still made Nick feel sick and disgusted over the tactics Patterson and his sons had employed to try to win the election for president. Their new address was a long way from 1600 Pennsylvania Avenue. The three of them and several of their flunkies were in federal prison awaiting trial on murder and conspiracy charges.

Nick was about to move on to some of the briefing books Terry had brought him to prepare for his new job, when a knock sounded on the door. "Come on in," he called, expecting to see Scotty, not Shelby. "Hey there. What're you doing here today? Even a sweatshop like this allows for holidays off."

Grinning, the petite blonde came into the room and left the door propped open behind her. "I was texting with Scotty and heard Sam got called out on a case. I thought this might be a good chance to speak to you privately about something."

"Sure." Nick gestured to the second chair in his makeshift home office in one of the spare bedrooms on the second floor. He missed his den downstairs that was now command central for the Secret Service. "What's up?" he asked when she was seated and fidgeting nervously with her fluffy pink scarf. "Please don't tell me you're quitting. We'll die without you."

"No, no, definitely not quitting the best job I've ever had."

"Better than running your own business?"

"Much better and far less stressful."

"So what's on your mind?"

"Well, you knew when we first talked about the job that I'd been pursuing a rather personal project on the side."

At first he didn't know what she was talking about, but then he remembered. "Oh, right." Did he ask how it was going? Or did he wait for her to offer the information?

"I wanted to tell you that my project has been successful." She glanced at him with eyes bright with tears. "I'm pregnant."

For a brief second, Nick's brain froze as he considered how this news would affect Sam, and then he realized Shelby was waiting for him to say something. "That's fantastic news, Shelby. I'm really happy for you. When are you due?"

"Around the Fourth of July. I didn't want to say anything until I was past that critical three-month mark, but so far so good despite my advanced years."

She was forty-two and had told them she was running out of time so she'd sought out fertility help.

"That baby is going to be very lucky to have such a terrific mom."

Shelby dabbed at her eyes. "That's very sweet of you to say. I've been stressing out about telling you guys. I know this is a tough subject for Sam—and for you. I don't want you to think—"

"Shelby, all we'd ever be is happy for you and delighted to know there'll be a baby around next summer."

"Oh, I won't bring him or her to work. That would be too disruptive."

"Why wouldn't you bring the baby to work? There's no reason you couldn't have him or her here with you."

She began to cry in earnest. "God, Nick, I mean Mr. Vice President, you kill me."

"I'll kill you if you call me that," he said teasingly. "I'm Nick to you, and I always will be, and of course you'll bring your child to work with you. There's nothing you have to do for us that couldn't include your baby."

Shelby shook her head as she mopped up the tears. "You really are the nicest guy ever. Thank you so much. You and Sam and Scotty—you have no idea how much I love this job and my new life. And all of you. You're like family to me."

"We feel the same way."

"I have to find a way to tell Sam this news. I want to be sensitive to what she's been through…"

"I'll take care of telling her. She'll be thrilled for you."

"You think so?"

Truthfully, he had no idea how she'd react, but Shelby didn't need to know that. "I really do. Don't worry about a thing. Just take care of you and the baby."

"Do you mind if I tell Scotty?"

"Of course not. He'll be so excited for you."

"I know he will. He's such a great kid. I want mine to be just like him. I'll wait to tell him until after Sam knows, though."

"Sure, whatever you want."

"Well, I'll let you get back to work. If I don't see you

before you leave tomorrow, I hope your first day at the White House is awesome. We haven't known each other long, but I'm so proud to be working for the vice president of the United States who also happens to be my very good friend."

Nick stood and hugged her. "Thank you for that and for all you do for us. Sam and I say all the time that we'd never survive without you."

"Thank you—for everything. I'll see you tomorrow."

"See you then."

After she left, Nick stared at the door for a long moment pondering how this news would go over with Sam. Sure, she'd be thrilled for Shelby the way she was for her sister Angela, who'd recently had baby Ella. Sam doted on her new niece and her other nieces and nephews. But that didn't mean she wasn't heartbroken on the inside.

Despite their frequent efforts over the last few months, they'd had no luck conceiving again. Sam's thirty-fifth birthday in October had been overshadowed by the realization that time was getting away from her. He'd broached the subject of seeking out fertility treatment, but she'd been through that once before when she was married to Peter and wasn't at all interested in doing it again. Her feeling was that it had happened naturally for them once before. Maybe it would again.

Nick would give up everything he owned and every ounce of success he'd experienced in his career if he could just give her that one thing she wanted more than anything else. Since Scotty had come to live with them, the topic had seemed less raw and fraught with peril. Scotty more than filled the void for her—for both of them. However, though she rarely spoke of it, he knew Sam still wanted the experience of being pregnant and giving birth.

He would have to find a way to tell her Shelby's news

and hope it didn't gut her too badly to hear that yet another woman close to them was going to have the experience Sam had thus far been denied. She'd be thrilled for Shelby. Nick was certain of that, but inside she would ache for what might never happen for her. He was equally certain of that.

TEN

SHELBY LEFT SAM and Nick's home, feeling as if a huge weight had been lifted off her shoulders. Nick had been nothing but supportive and happy for her. Knowing what Sam had been through with her history of miscarriages, Shelby had dreaded telling them about her baby. Thinking about how and when to tell them had taken some of the excitement out of it for her.

Now she felt like she had permission to wallow in the joy that had filled her from the moment she first heard the incredible news from the fertility doctor she'd been working with for more than a year now. With Nick taking care of telling Sam, Shelby had one more person she needed to tell, and she was equally anxious about how her news would go over with Avery Hill.

The sexy FBI agent was a big part of her exciting new life as the personal assistant to the vice president and his amazing and accomplished wife. She'd met Avery through Sam and had been immediately attracted to him. Thinking about the day he'd come to interview her fertility doctor as part of a homicide investigation and found her in the waiting room could still make Shelby cringe all this time later.

The way she'd gone after him and asked him out for coffee was mortifying. She'd blamed it then on the hormones and the emotional wallop of pursuing her goal of having a baby for the out-of-character pursuit of a man who seemed well out of her league. Or so she'd thought until she got to know him better and found that he suited her in many of the most important ways.

He'd known from that day forward that she was trying to have a baby. They'd talked infrequently about her side "project" while they continued to spend more and more time together, so she honestly had no idea what to expect from him when she finally shared her news.

She drove to the Adams Morgan neighborhood where he lived and spent fifteen minutes trying to find a parking space. Everyone was home today with it being a holiday, and parking spots were in short supply. Luckily, her tiny pink Mini Cooper fit into the one spot she was able to find. The three-block walk to Avery's place gave her time to collect herself and prepare for whatever might happen during this long overdue conversation.

Since she'd texted him to ask if it was okay to stop by, she wasn't surprised when the door swung open as she came up the stone steps to his townhouse.

"Come in." He swooped her into the heated warmth of his gorgeous home. Everything about this guy reeked of style and class, two things Shelby appreciated tremendously. "What're you doing out in this freezing cold weather?"

"Coming to see you," she said, smiling at him even as her nerves went wild when she thought about what she'd come to tell him. At some point over the last few months, she'd become rather attached to the sexy devil and would hate to lose him. Shelby followed him into the cozy den where he spent most of his time at home. She went straight to the fireplace to warm her hands over the flame. "I love this room."

"So do I. The rest of the house is sort of wasted space. As you know, I use this, the bedroom, kitchen and bathroom. That's about it."

"Still, it was a good investment that you'll never regret." She'd helped him shop for a place to live when he'd been made the director of the FBI's Criminal Investigation Unit. This had been their favorite of all the places they'd looked at.

"Come sit," he said, extending his hand to her.

Shelby crossed the room to join him on the soft leather sofa that she'd also helped him to pick out. His e-reader sat on the coffee table, open to the biography on J. Edgar Hoover that he'd been reading lately.

He put his arm around her and brought her in for a lingering kiss. "Hi there," he said.

"Hey there." She never got tired of looking at that face with the amazing cheekbones, the sensual lips, the golden eyes. Don't even get her started on that South Carolina accent.

"This is a nice surprise."

"I'm glad you think so." She'd wanted some time to herself so she'd gone home after their midnight celebration last night, and they hadn't made plans for today. "You're enjoying your day off?"

"For the moment. I'm waiting for a call from our favorite lieutenant to consult on a case, but as usual, she's dragging her feet where I'm concerned."

"You'll hear from her if she's supposed to call you."

"I'm sure I'm dead last on her to-do list, but she's got a hot one that's getting hotter by the minute."

"What happened?"

"The mother of Gonzo's child was murdered."

"Oh my God. They don't think he had anything to do with it, do they?"

"No, but the media is reporting that he's the primary suspect and quoting MPD sources."

"Come on," Shelby said. "They can't honestly think he'd do that."

"They don't, but a 'well-placed MPD source' apparently does."

"Wow. That's crazy. Sam must be furious."

"I can only imagine, but something tells me you didn't come here to talk about Sam."

"No, not really."

"Is something wrong, Shelby?"

"Not at all. Something is actually really right, and I'm so excited to tell you about it."

"What is it?"

"You know that 'project' I've been working on since we met?"

"The baby project?"

"That's the one. It seems that it's been successful."

"You're pregnant?"

"I'm pregnant."

"That's great news. Congratulations. I know how much you've wanted that."

"What does this mean for us, Avery?"

"I don't know. What do you think it means?"

"I fear that it means you'll be running for the hills, since you didn't sign on for a package deal."

"Didn't I?"

"What do you mean?"

"Didn't I know from the beginning that this was a possibility?"

"Well, yeah, I guess so, but that doesn't mean I expect you to be part of it. Unless you want to be, that is."

"Is there any chance this baby is mine, Shelby?"

"I… I suppose there's a chance."

"Then I'd say I'm part of it."

"And if it isn't yours?"

"I'm still part of it if you want me to be."

"I don't want you to feel obligated."

"I don't feel obligated. I feel…sort of excited actually."

"You do?" Despite her fervent desire to get through this without them, tears filled her eyes anyway. "You're not just saying that?"

"Shelby," he said with a chuckle as he drew her in closer to him, "I'm not just saying that." With his lips close to her ear, he said, "Every time we made love without protection, I knew what could happen. I've known all along what you wanted, and I hoped maybe I could be the one to give it to you."

She rested her hand on her chest. "I think my heart just stopped for a second there."

"What do you think this has been about all this time?"

"I wasn't sure. We don't really talk about it."

"No," he said with a sigh, "we don't, and that's my fault mostly."

"How so?"

He hesitated, sighed and sat up straighter. "If I tell you, you might not want to be with me anymore."

"I'll still want to be with you."

"You should wait until you hear what I have to say."

"Are you married? Gay? Really a woman?"

He laughed and shook his head. "No to all of the above."

"Then what could be so bad?"

After another long pause during which she wanted to beg him to just tell her what was on his mind so they could move forward, he said, "Long before I ever met you and before I knew she was married, I sort of had a thing for Sam."

"Sam, *my* Sam?"

"Yeah."

Shelby pulled back from him as a thousand disturbing

thoughts riffled through her mind one right after the other. "Is that why you started seeing me? To stay close to her?"

"Had nothing to do with it. I just happened to meet you through her. That was the full extent of it." He took hold of her hand. "Think about all the time we've spent alone together. Think about the hours we've spent in bed together, the nights you've slept in my arms, the time we've spent watching TV, making dinner, hanging with Scotty. What did any of that have to do with her?"

"Were you ever going to tell me you'd had feelings for her?"

"I'm telling you now."

Filled with disbelief, Shelby blew out a breath. "Now, months after this started, you tell me you had a thing for my boss and close friend. That's kind of a sin of omission, Avery."

"When would've been a good time to tell you? When could I have told you when you wouldn't have thought exactly what you're thinking right now, that I used you to get closer to her?"

"Did you?"

"No! You and I have nothing to do with her other than the fact that we both work with her."

"This is why Nick doesn't like you." So many things came into sharp focus in the span of a few seconds. "They know, don't they? They both know this, and no one told me. God, how big of a fool could I possibly be?" She pulled free of his grasp and got up, her legs wobbling under her until she recovered her bearings. "I... I have to go."

"Shelby, come on. Stay here and let's talk about this." As he spoke, his phone rang. He glanced at the caller ID and swore under his breath. "Please don't go."

"Take the call. I can see myself out."

"Shelby, honey, *please*. Stay and talk to me."

She wanted to tell him not to call her that, but the words got stuck on the huge lump in her throat. Blinded by tears, she rushed out of his house and tripped on the last stair, falling to her hands and knees on the sidewalk.

The impact took her breath away as searing pain from her knees and palms tore sobs from her chest.

Avery came running down the stairs. "Shelby! Are you okay?"

She wanted to fight him off, to tell him to go to hell, but he scooped her up as if she were weightless and carried her back into the house. "God, honey, you're bleeding."

She was also crying too hard to speak. Her heart ached almost as badly as her knees did.

Avery deposited her on one of the stools in his kitchen, carefully placing her legs on the next stool. "Hang on just a second. Let me get the first aid kit." He went into another room and when he returned, he was on the phone, speaking in a clipped tone.

"Get to HQ and see what's needed." After a pause he said, "I was going to handle it, but now I can't. I'm giving you an order, George." He put his phone on the counter and got busy cleaning up her cuts. Of all days to wear a skirt with her favorite pale pink tights. They were now a shredded mess, just like her knees.

The pain was ridiculous and reminded her of the time she'd fallen on the street in front of her house when she and her sister were trying out Rollerblades they'd gotten for Christmas. She'd never gone near the Rollerblades again.

He dabbed antibiotic ointment on the wounds, and Shelby gasped from the shocking pain.

"Sorry, honey."

His use of that word caused shocking pain in the vicinity of her heart. She'd *loved* the way that endearment had sounded coming from him. "Don't call me that. I'm not your honey. Not anymore."

"Yes, you are."

She pushed his hand away from her leg. "No, I'm not. You lied to me and used me and God knows what else."

"I didn't do any of those things."

"You wanted my friend and settled for second best when she wouldn't have you."

"That's not true." He took her by the chin and forced her to meet the steely gaze he directed her way. As always those honey-golden eyes made her melt until she remembered why she was so upset. "Nothing about you is second best. You're first-class all the way, and every minute I've spent with *you* was because of you and no one else but you."

"I don't believe you. The only reason you're saying those things is because I might be carrying your baby." She wiped angrily at the tears that continued to fall from her eyes even though she'd moved from hurt to fury. "I wish I'd never told you that."

"Well, you did, and now I know." His movements were jerky as he cleaned up her other knee. "I'm taking you to the ER to make sure you didn't hurt more than your knees when you fell. After that, we're coming back here and we're going to talk this through."

"I'm not going to the ER and I'm done talking."

"You *are* going to the ER, and we've only begun to talk."

"I don't want to be with you."

"Okay." As if she hadn't said a word, he grabbed his keys, pulled on a coat, picked her up and carried her to his car in the garage.

Knowing she was no match for him, Shelby went along with it. But the minute she could, she would break free of him. Permanently.

GONZO FELT LIKE he was having a heart attack as he watched the news unfolding in the city. A police source had named him as the chief suspect in the murder of his son's mother. The talking heads rehashed the custody battle he'd waged with Lori, picking apart every detail and obsessing about the fact that he hadn't disclosed his previous connection to the judge.

"Attorneys for Lori Phillips broke the news of the connection between Gonzales and Judge Leon Morton three days ago, and now she's dead," the CBC talking head said almost gleefully. "Coincidence or is the man recently hailed a hero actually a cold-blooded killer?"

"Oh my God," he said as the shock ricocheted through his body, leaving him reeling. Didn't all his years of impeccable service count for anything?

Christina came into the room.

"Where's Alex?"

"With your mom. She's reading him a story and trying to get him to nap."

"This is totally out of control, Chris. They're having a field day at my expense. I'm never going to be able to work again in that city if someone doesn't fix this quickly."

"We need a lawyer, and we need one now."

"I've tried to call Andy."

"We need a criminal lawyer. I want to call my brother."

"I didn't do anything!"

"Tommy, babe, I know that. You know that. We need to make sure you don't get railroaded for something you didn't do."

"How can this be happening? The cops investigating this case are my friends. They're like family to me. Why aren't they saying it's not true?"

"They probably haven't had the chance because they're

trying to figure out who really killed her. Let me call Carson."

"If I bring in a big-time criminal lawyer like him, I may as well declare my guilt at the same time."

"You need to protect yourself."

"If I lawyer up, Christina, everyone will think I'm guilty."

"Baby, they already do! My phone is ringing off the hook."

"Fuck. This is a motherfucking nightmare. And why the hell isn't Sam returning my calls?"

"I'm sure she's doing what she can… Oh, look! She's making a statement outside HQ."

Gonzo spun around and nearly fainted from the relief of seeing his boss and friend approaching the microphone.

"I have just a brief statement. This morning, the body of Lori Phillips was found in a parked car near West Potomac Park. Ms. Phillips had been strangled. You are correct in reporting that she is the mother of MPD Detective Sergeant Thomas Gonzales's young son. You are *incorrect* in reporting that he is a suspect. I will repeat myself to ensure that you hear me. Thomas Gonzales is *not* a suspect in the murder of Lori Phillips. Whatever information you may have received from a so-called police source was erroneous. The only police source with credibility on this case is me."

A bottle blonde from one of the local TV stations asked, "How can you investigate a case that involves one of your own people?"

"Did you just hear me say this case does *not* include one of my own people?"

"How was Detective Sergeant Gonzales eliminated as a suspect?"

"He has an alibi and is a decorated police officer who

was recently grievously injured in the line of duty. In addition, we have a person of interest currently in custody and will have more information in the next few days. In the meantime, if you continue to broadcast and publish Sergeant Gonzales's name in connection to this case, you'll be opening yourself to civil litigation. I wouldn't blame him for suing your asses off. That'll be it."

"When does your husband begin work at the White House?"

Sam rolled her eyes at the reporter who'd asked the question and turned away from the reporters to go back inside.

"There," Christina said. "Do you feel better now?"

Thanks to Sam's statement he was now able to get air to his lungs. "Yeah. But I won't really feel better until they catch whoever actually killed her."

Christina stepped closer to him and wrapped her arms around his waist. "Hold on to me, baby. Just hold on to me."

Her nearness, her affection and her support calmed him. He put his arms around her and did as she requested. She was the only thing holding him together and the only thing he couldn't live without.

"How will I ever be able to do my job again with people thinking I'm capable of killing someone? I've spent my career tracking down killers, and now they think I am one?"

"Let me tell you something I know for sure. The news cycle has a limited lifespan. In a day or two, something else will happen and people will forget all about this."

"That might be true, but I'll never forget." And he'd sure as hell find out which one of his brothers or sisters in the police department had seen fit to point the finger at him.

WHILE FREDDIE TOOK Hughes to Central Processing, Sam headed for the detectives' pit to check in with the rest of her team. The first one she ran into was Gonzo's partner, Detective Arnold. The young officer approached her tentatively. "It's not true, is it, Lieutenant? He didn't kill her, did he?"

"No, he didn't kill her, but someone wants us to think he did. And I'm starting to think that someone is in this building."

"Seriously?"

"How else would the press be hearing from a 'police source' with information about the investigation?" She released the clip that held her hair, ran her fingers through the length and then resecured it. "Where is everyone?"

"Jeannie and Tyrone tracked down some of Lori's coworkers, and they went to interview them. Carlucci and Dominguez are with Crime Scene at Lori's place."

"Warrant?"

"Yes, ma'am. Captain Malone was able to secure it for them."

"Excellent."

"I'm working the phones trying to track down the social worker who oversaw Gonzo's case. She's out of town for the holidays, but I left several messages on her phone."

"Good work. Thanks for the update and keep me posted." Sam went into her office and did a quick scan of her email, where she found a report from Lindsey detailing the findings of the autopsy. Lori had been manually strangled, but there were no usable prints on her neck. "Of course there weren't," Sam muttered. The semen found in Lori's vagina had been sent out for DNA analysis that would take about forty-eight hours, and Lindsey had included detailed information about the drugs and alcohol found in Lori's system. No defensive wounds to the victim's hands, indicating that the fatal attack had possibly taken her by surprise. "Someone she trusted," Sam deduced. "We need to get closer to her inner circle."

"Talking to yourself, Lieutenant?" Captain Malone asked as he came into her office.

"Working the case, Captain."

"What've you got?"

"A woman who worked hard to turn her life around found strangled in a parked car belonging to her brother. She had an elevated blood alcohol count and traces of cocaine in her system."

"So she was off the wagon."

"Seems that way. And all of this is happening days after she went public about Gonzo's previous connection to the judge who heard their custody case. What I want to know is what 'police source' is telling the media he's our prime suspect."

"We're looking into that."

"What did Conklin find out when he talked to Ramsey?"

"Ramsey said he didn't do it."

"I don't believe him. I saw him on the stairs this morning, and he told me to fuck off when I said hello to him. I reported it to Davidson, for all the good that'll do."

"What beef does Ramsey have with you?"

"Who knows? I worked with him on the Kavanaugh investigation and have had a couple of other brushes with him, but nothing that would cause him to do something like this. And I don't believe for a second he had nothing to do with it. We had words this morning, I complained about him to his lieutenant and a couple of hours later my second in command is being accused of murder by an 'inside source'? You do the math on that one."

"It does smell fishy. We'll stay on it. In the meantime, where are we with figuring out who really did it?"

"We've got a guy in custody I'm going to talk to as soon

as Cruz gets him through Central Booking." She told him about Hughes, the outstanding warrant on child support charges and the new warrant being processed to search his house for evidence in the Phillips case.

"You're working with Baltimore on that?"

She nodded. "They're getting the warrant and are aware that we arrested him."

"Excellent. I'll be sure to include 'plays well with others' on your evaluation. Speaking of playing well with others, Hill's Deputy Agent Terrell is here to consult on the case."

"Why not Hill?"

"Apparently, he had a personal matter to attend to today and was unavailable."

"Huh, interesting." Since the only personal life Hill had, that Sam knew of, involved her assistant, she was immediately curious. And then she told herself that *his* personal business was certainly none of *her* business. "Where is Terrell?"

"I put him in the conference room until you got back."

"I'll bring him up to speed on what we've got so far."

"Thank you for that and for what you're doing for the chief in the morning."

Sam almost asked him what he meant and then she remembered promising to make the rounds on TV with the chief. The thought of it made her stomach quiver with nerves. But she'd do it for him. "The bullshit may as well be good for something, right?"

Cruz came to the door. "Hughes has been processed. He's in Interrogation Two with Beckett watching him."

"Go see to Elin."

"Are you sure? I can wait until after we talk to him."

"Arnold is here and the FBI dude. We got it covered."

To Malone, Sam said, "Detective Cruz's girlfriend was assaulted this morning at her place of employment."

"The gym on Sixteenth?" Malone asked.

"Yes, sir."

"Heard about that. Word is she took one hell of a hit. We got the guy in custody. He's cooling off downstairs."

"Go, Cruz. Report in later and let me know how she is."

"I will, thank you."

"She's okay, right?" Sam asked Malone.

"I think so. Officer Andrews is the one who said she took a bad hit, but that's all he said."

In a day full of things to worry about, Sam thought, now there was something else.

ELEVEN

FREDDIE RUSHED OUT of HQ, pushing through the scrum of reporters still lingering in the courtyard on his way to the parking lot. He wasted no time pulling out of the lot and into traffic on his way to the George Washington Hospital emergency room. On the way, he tried to call Elin, but the call went straight to her voice mail, indicating her phone was probably off or dead.

She was forever forgetting to charge it. He'd bought her a charging case for Christmas, not that she ever used it. The woman drove him crazy in more ways than one, but he loved her anyway. And the thought of her hurt, assaulted… He gripped the wheel tighter in response to the flash of rage that seized him.

It took twenty painful minutes to get to the hospital. He ran into the ER and up to the desk. "Detective Cruz, Metro PD." He flashed his badge to the receptionist. "My girlfriend, Elin Svendsen, was brought in by EMS."

"Let me check with the nurses to see where she is. Have a seat, and I'll let you know."

"I'm not going to have a seat. I want to see her. She wants me with her."

"Hang on just a minute, Detective."

Sam had taught him to dislike receptionists, but he'd never disliked one more than the woman who stood between him and Elin. He shot off a text to Elin. I'm out here. Tell them to let me in.

He had no idea if she'd get the text or if her phone was even on.

While he paced in front of the reception desk, waiting for permission to go to Elin, he was stunned to see Avery Hill and Shelby Faircloth emerge from the treatment area.

"Hey," he said to Hill, who seemed distracted and maybe upset about something.

"Oh, hi," Hill said. "What're you doing here? Did Sam get hurt again?"

"No, my girlfriend, Elin, took a hit to the face at work today."

"Is she okay?" Shelby asked.

"I think so. I haven't seen her yet." In a quick glance, Freddie noted Shelby's red, puffy eyes, the torn tights and bandaged knees. "Are you okay?"

"I will be. Took a fall on the sidewalk and messed up my knees."

"Sorry to hear that," Freddie said, surprised to hear that skinned knees had brought her to the ER.

"I'm going to get Shelby home," Hill said.

"I hope you feel better," Freddie said.

"Thanks," Shelby said with a small smile that didn't reach her eyes. Something was definitely amiss.

They walked away—slowly—and disappeared through the automatic doors. Freddie pulled out his phone and dashed off a quick text to Sam. Just saw Hill and Shelby at GW ER. She said she fell and busted up her knees. Seemed like maybe something more going on, but they didn't say. Thought you'd want to know.

Sam wrote right back. Thanks. How's Elin?

Still waiting to be allowed back. About to flip out on receptionist.

That's my boy. Go get em tiger. Let me know how she is later.

Will do.

The harried receptionist came back out. "Right this way, Detective."

Freddie stashed the phone and followed the woman, his heart beating fast as he prepared himself to see Elin and her injuries. But all the preparation in the world couldn't have readied him for the sight of her swollen face, the huge bruises, the cut and swollen lip. She was attached to an IV and several monitors. Blinking back tears, he rushed to her side. "Baby, I'm here," he said as he kissed her forehead.

She came awake slowly, moaning as she tried to find a comfortable position.

"Don't try to move."

"Freddie…"

"Yeah, honey, it's me. I'm right here. Sorry it took me so long to get here."

She reached for his hand and held on tight. "S'okay. You were working."

"What're the doctors saying?"

"I have broken bones in my face. They want to keep me overnight. They're waiting for a room upstairs."

Freddie's entire body went rigid with rage at the words *broken bones*. "Who did this to you?"

"There was a fight at the gym."

"Did you know the guy who hit you?"

She looked up at him with those iridescent blue eyes that had slayed him from the first time he ever saw her during the O'Connor investigation. "Yeah, I know him."

"Do you feel up to telling me what happened?"

"You're going to be mad at me," she said, her eyes filling with tears.

Freddie brushed the white-blond hair back from her forehead. "I won't be mad."

"Yes, you will."

"Baby, I love you. There's nothing you could tell me that would change that." Though he said what she needed to hear, he was deeply fearful of what she had to tell him. Had she been unfaithful? He could handle just about anything except for that. That... That would kill him.

She began to cry in earnest, tears spilling down her cheeks. "I thought I could handle it on my own."

"Handle what?"

"This guy at the gym who was hassling me."

"A guy at the gym was hassling you." It took every bit of self-control Freddie could muster to keep from losing his shit at that news. "For how long?"

"Awhile now."

"And you never told your boyfriend, who happens to be a cop, about this?"

"I was handling it."

"Elin..." Freddie took her into his arms—carefully, so as not to hurt her. "Why would you try to handle something like this on your own when you don't have to anymore?" He wanted to weep at the thought of her being so deeply troubled by something and not asking for his help. "Don't you know you've got your own personal cop in your bed who would do anything for you?"

She was sobbing now, the tears leaving wet spots on her hospital gown.

Freddie took a tissue from a box on a table next to the bed and worked carefully to dry her face. "Tell me everything. Don't leave anything out."

"I'm afraid to."

"Why, honey?"

"I don't want you to go after him and get yourself in trouble. That's why I didn't tell you. I was afraid for you."

"I won't get in trouble. I promise. Now tell me."

She let out a sigh and settled into her pillow, wincing at the small movement. "His name is Andre and he joined the gym about a month ago."

"This has been going on for *a month*?"

"It's only been bad for the last week or so."

"Bad how?"

"He keeps trying to get me to talk to him, to go out with him, to train him. I've told him I'm living with someone, and I'm happy and to leave me alone."

"And he didn't?"

"No, he… The other night when I was leaving work, he was waiting for me when I got to my car. It was the first time he really scared me. I pulled out the pepper spray you gave me and told him I'd use it if he touched me. He backed off, and I got in the car and drove away."

"This was the night you said you couldn't get warm after you got home, wasn't it?"

"Yes," she said softly.

"God, Elin, why didn't you tell me?"

"I told Glen the next day," she said, referring to the gym manager. "They suspended his privileges at the gym."

"And you didn't think that would piss him off?"

"Freddie… I'm sorry. Don't be mad with me. I was trying to handle it on my own."

"I'm sorry, baby. I'm not mad at you. I'm mad that this guy hassled you, and I had no idea you were going through something like this. How could I not know you were so upset and stressed out?"

"I didn't want you to know. It's not your fault."

It bothered him greatly that she'd felt the need to keep

something so huge from him, but he'd deal with that part of it later—after he heard the rest of the story.

"Anyway," she said with another sigh, "Andre came into the gym today looking for me and Glen stopped him from coming in. Andre is a lot bigger than Glen, and I was afraid he was going to hurt him, so I tried to help him."

Freddie had to bite his tongue to keep from asking why she'd had to be the one to protect Glen.

"It turned into a big melee with other staff and members getting involved."

"How did you get hit?"

"I don't think he meant to hit me…"

"Who hit you? Was it Andre?"

She gave a tiny nod that seemed to cost her. "He whirled around and connected with my face. It all happened so fast… I hit the back of my head on the desk. And then I was sort of out of it for a while. Next thing I knew the police were there, and they were arresting him."

"You said Andre is bigger than Glen, and Glen is huge. Andre could've killed with one hit. You know that, don't you?"

"I know that now, but I really wasn't afraid of him hurting me."

"You pulled pepper spray on him," Freddie reminded her, making an effort to keep his voice down. "You must've felt threatened to do that."

"I wanted him to know I could and would defend myself. That was all." She glanced up at him. "I knew you'd be mad with me."

"I'm not mad. I'm sad that this happened to you, and that you felt you couldn't come to me about it. That makes me really sad."

"I'm sorry. I should've told you."

"Don't be sorry. Nothing about this is your fault. You're

the victim here, and you're going to pursue charges against this guy, you got me?"

"Yes, I will. I want him to leave me alone."

"We'll see about getting a restraining order too," Freddie said, even though he was far too aware of how often restraining orders were violated.

Her eyes fluttered closed. "Tired, Freddie. So tired."

"Get some rest." He kissed her forehead. "I'll be right here."

"Love you."

"Love you too, baby." He'd never loved her more than he did right then. Seeing her bruised and beaten had sparked a primal need to protect her. That she'd kept such an important thing from him in order to protect him was something they'd have to talk more about later. And he'd also be having a conversation with this guy Andre as soon as he could get back to HQ.

SAM AND ARNOLD entered the interrogation room while Terrell headed for observation. She'd suggested it might be better to keep the FBI out of the room for the moment, and he'd agreed. He was much more malleable than his superior, that was for sure. Hill would've demanded entry into the interrogation room, even if it made sense to take a softer approach at the outset.

Bringing the FBI acronym into an investigation changed the game. She wanted Hughes to talk to them, not clam up.

The minute they walked into the room, he surged to his feet. "I want a lawyer." His shoulder-length brown hair had been tied back into a ponytail, and his jeans and hoodie had been switched out for an orange jumpsuit. "They fucking strip-searched me!"

The strip search tended to humble even the most obnoxious of collars. "Routine part of processing," Sam said. "Who do you want us to call for you?"

"How the hell do I know? I've never needed a lawyer before."

"Not even when you were taken to court for failure to pay child support?"

"Is that the kind of lawyer I need now?"

"Not exactly. Can you afford to pay for a lawyer or would you like us to call the public defender?"

"How much does a lawyer cost?"

"Don't exactly know the going rate, but I suspect they aren't cheap. All that schooling goes to their heads."

"Fine, then call the public defender."

"You know they're closed today because it's a holiday, right?"

"So what does that mean?"

"A sleepover," Sam said, gratified to watch some of the starch go out of him as he began to realize his predicament. "Of course if you rescind your request for a lawyer, we can have our chat today and maybe get you home before bedtime." She shrugged, as if it didn't matter at all to her what he decided. "Up to you."

"What do you want to know?" he asked tentatively.

"I can't talk to you with your request for a lawyer on the record."

"Fine! No lawyer, for now anyway."

"Detective Arnold, please record our conversation with Mr. Hughes."

Arnold moved from his post at the doorway and turned on the recorder, noting the date, time and parties present.

"Mr. Hughes," Sam said, "have you rescinded your earlier request for an attorney?"

"Yeah," he said.

"I can't hear you."

"Yes, I've rescinded my request for an attorney. Can we get on with it?"

"Let's talk about Lori Phillips."

He paled at the mention of Lori's name. "I thought this was about outstanding child support?"

"We'll get to that. I want to start with Lori."

He eyed her tentatively. "What about her?"

"How do you know her?"

"We went out a couple of times. No big deal."

"How long have you known her?"

"I don't know. A few months maybe?"

"How did you meet her?"

"An online dating thing. I meet a lot of girls that way."

"When was the last time you saw her?"

He squirmed in his seat and fidgeted with his hands. "I don't know."

"I think you do know. I think you know exactly when you last saw her."

"We hooked up yesterday. So what?"

"Tell me what happened yesterday, and don't leave anything out."

He looked down at the table, seemingly trying to decide what he should say. Then he looked up at her, and Sam detected the first hint of fear. All the cockiness was gone. "She hit me up with a text in the morning, telling me she was going to be in the city and wanted to get together. So I told her to stop by."

"Did she?"

"Yeah, she did. We hung out for a couple of hours, and then she left to go do something with one of her friends for New Year's. I was going to a party. It was all good."

"Can you give me a list of people who were at that party who can confirm you were there?"

"Yeah, sure."

Sam slid her notebook across the table. "Give me at least three people." While he got busy writing, she said, "What went on while she was at your house?"

"We hung out. And stuff."

"What stuff?"

"We fucked. Is that what you want to know?"

"Yeah, it is. How many times did you fuck?"

A bead of sweat appeared on his forehead, which gave Sam a queer sense of accomplishment. "Like, you want a number?"

"That'd be good."

"Twice. And she blew me too. Satisfied?"

"Sounds like you were. So it was probably your semen that was found inside her vagina after she was murdered?"

His face got even paler than it already was at the mention of murder. "I didn't kill her. She left my house around two, and I haven't seen or talked to her since."

"How come you didn't glove up when you had sex with her?"

"She's on the pill."

"That doesn't protect you against diseases."

He shrugged that off as if it wasn't something he worried about.

"Did she tell you where she was going when she left your place?"

"Nope and I didn't ask."

Sam tended to believe him when he said he didn't kill her, but she was still going to request the DNA to make the connection to the semen. "I'm going to need you to provide a DNA sample."

"Why, so you can build a murder case against me?" More beads of sweat joined the others at his hairline.

"If you didn't kill her, you've got nothing to worry about."

"Right. I know how you people work. You'll tie me to her through my spunk, and next thing you know, I'm a murderer. I take it back. I want a lawyer. I'm not saying another word until I have one."

"Sure thing. I'll make the call, and I'm requesting a warrant for your DNA. If that comes through, you'll have no choice but to comply or risk additional charges. Right now, you're only facing charges on the child support thing and resisting arrest. This could get a whole lot worse for you short of murder if you don't cooperate."

He gave her a mulish look and crossed his arms, sending the signal that their conversation was over.

She got up and pushed in her chair. "Detective Arnold, please take Mr. Hughes downstairs."

"Yes, ma'am."

Sam walked out of the interrogation room and ran into Terrell as he and Malone came out of observation.

"I'm thinking he's not our guy," Terrell said.

"Your thinking matches mine. I tend to believe him when he said she left at two. It would be easy enough to prove he was elsewhere without her last night. I'll call the people he listed to confirm he was at the party."

"I'll get the warrant for the DNA," Malone said.

"We may as well close that loop." Sam unclipped her hair and let it fall down her back, rubbing her fingertips over her scalp. "We're right back to square one with figuring out who killed her. I'd really like to know where she went after she left his house."

Archie came down the corridor toward where they were gathered. "There you are," he said to Sam. "I've been looking for you."

"What've you got?"

He handed her a thick pile of papers. "The dump on

Lori Phillips's phone. I've got something else that might interest you too."

"What's that?"

"The vic was found in a car parked near West Potomac Park, but the nine-one-one call reporting the body in the car came from ten blocks away." He showed her an address that had Sam's heart sinking. It was right near Gonzo's place. Son of a bitch. "I listened to the recording of the call. It was a man, he was out of breath, said he'd been running and saw a body in a car. He wouldn't give us his name or any other info."

"Interesting. Thanks, Archie."

"I did a quick look at the text messages and there's some other stuff in there that might help. She did a lot of texting yesterday."

"Just what I needed to put together her day. Appreciate this."

"Sure, no problem." He withdrew a flash drive from his pocket and gave that to her too. "The nine-one-one call is on here. Let me know if I can do anything else to help."

"You've already done a lot, thanks again." After Archie walked away, she said to Terrell and Malone, "Let's get everyone into the conference room to see where we are."

"You're going to need to head home soon to get your beauty sleep for your TV appearances tomorrow," Malone said with a teasing grin.

The reminder of her promise to appear with the chief made her groan. "No one said I had to be beautiful."

Malone laughed. "Your public has big expectations. You wouldn't want to let them down, would you?"

"Ugh, shut up."

"See how she talks to her superior officers?" Malone said to Terrell, who chuckled.

"Her reputation does precede her," Terrell said, his

brown eyes twinkling. The good-looking dark-haired agent wore an expensive suit. That must be a thing with FBI agents—he who has the best suit wins.

"I'm sure you've heard nothing but how charming I am."

"Yes, indeed," he said. "That's exactly what I've heard."

"I like this guy," Sam said. "He rolls with me."

"She likes you," Malone said. "Consider yourself fortunate."

"I am indeed blessed," Terrell replied drolly.

"And he's sarcastic too." Sam wanted to add that he also didn't stare at her the way his superior officer did. "It doesn't get any better than this."

"I aim to please," Terrell said with a grin.

They returned to the pit, where most of Sam's team had gathered. "Everyone in the conference room. Ten minutes." She took the printout Archie had given her into her office and shut the door. The first thing she did was plug the flash drive into her computer and call up the nine-one-one call.

"Nine-one-one, please state your emergency."

"There's a lady in a car," a man said between heavy breaths. "I was running and saw her."

"Where is the car located?" the operator asked.

"Near West Potomac Park. Constitution side."

The voice sounded muffled as if the caller was holding something over the mouthpiece. Between that and the heavy breathing, it was difficult to get a read on whether she recognized the voice. She listened to it three more times, thinking of all the people who'd like to screw her and her team: Lieutenant Stahl, Detective Ramsey, her ex-husband, Peter Gibson… Not to mention the litany of criminals that had come through their doors.

Someone had gone to a lot of trouble to make it seem possible that Gonzo could be at fault. Who would want to do that? She listened to the recording three more times and still had no more information than she'd had before. Ejecting the flash drive from her computer, she added it to her pile for the meeting, hoping someone else might hear something she'd missed.

Then she took a few minutes to go through the text messages downloaded from Lori's phone. Archie had taken the extra step of cross-referencing the calls to names and numbers from Lori's list of contacts. Sam appreciated that tremendously and planned to tell him so the next time she had the chance.

She gathered all her materials, tugged her ever-present notebook from her back pocket, grabbed her phone and a pen and headed for the conference room where her team had gathered, less Cruz and Gonzo. She'd never admit to feeling somewhat hobbled without them, but they were the two detectives she relied most heavily upon.

She had no choice but to press on without them. However, their absence made her more acutely aware of how valuable they were to her. Not that she'd ever tell them that.

TWELVE

"NOT SURE EVERYONE has met FBI Agent George Terrell," Sam said when she took a seat at the head of the table. Chief Farnsworth and Captain Malone were standing in their usual positions in the back of the room. "He's helping us out on this case since it involves someone connected to a member of our team."

After a series of murmured hellos and nice to meet yous, Sam said, "Cruz is with Elin at the hospital. Apparently she was injured at work today."

"Is she okay?" Arnold asked.

"She was talking and pissed, so I assume so. Who's got an update on the case for me?"

"I'll go," Jeannie said. "Tyrone and I were able to track down the dentist Lori worked for. He said she was a good worker, prompt, professional and reliable—until a little over a month ago. After she lost the custody hearing, she seemed to lose interest in the job and everything else. She called in sick more often than she showed up and one of the other women in the office had suggested that she was on something. The dentist was planning to speak to her tomorrow and they were going to let her go. He said, and I'm quoting here, 'We all felt for her after the custody hearing didn't go her way, but the recent spiral was obvious to all of us, and something had to be done.'"

"Did he give you the sense that she knew her job was in jeopardy?" Sam asked.

"We got the feeling that if she knew, she wouldn't have cared all that much."

"The autopsy indicated an elevated BAC, as well as cocaine in her system, so the dentist and his staff were right that she was using again," Sam said. She divided the stack of paper containing Lori's text messages and handed some to each of her detectives. "Let's track down these individuals and see what they know about her movements yesterday. I want a report on each person and what you find out about them. Shoot it to my email. Have we heard anything from Crime Scene's search of her house?"

"Nothing yet," Tyrone reported, "but I'll stay on top of them."

"Thank you. We appreciate all of you giving up your holiday to come in today."

"Murder happens," Arnold said.

"Yes, it does," Sam said. "I have a theory I want to run by you. First, I want you to hear the nine-one-one call, which was made about ten blocks from where the body was discovered, conveniently close to Gonzo's place." She made use of the computer workstation in the conference room to play the recording for her team. "Listen again," she said after the first time. "Do any of you recognize the voice?"

"It's sort of hard to say when it was so muffled," Carlucci said.

"That's what I thought too," Sam said. "Someone was making an effort to disguise their voice, so they were worried we would recognize it. Which leads to my theory that we need to look at people who had it in for *us* as a team and as individuals. Who would want to cause trouble for our squad, our department or any of us personally?"

"Do you have people in mind, Lieutenant?" Farnsworth asked.

"A long list," Sam said. "Starting with Stahl, Ramsey and Gibson, not to mention the wide array of people we've arrested, who're currently suing us, like Melissa Woodmansee, or after us for other things, such as Bill Springer."

"So you're suggesting someone killed the mother of Gonzo's child in order to make trouble for us?" Malone asked. "Kind of far-fetched, Lieutenant."

"I know it is, but we've all seen crazier things on this job than someone killing someone else to forward their own agenda."

"I think it bears looking into," Farnsworth said. "We've made our share of enemies over the years, and any one of them would be thrilled to see us defending ourselves or one of our top officers against a murder charge."

"Someone has gone to a lot of trouble to point the finger at Gonzo," Sam said. "The security cameras in his building were disabled, making it impossible for us to prove he never left the building after he got home yesterday afternoon. His name and address were found on a slip of paper underneath the floor mat in the car Lori was found in. The nine-one-one call was made from his block. Whoever killed her wants us to think it was him."

"But we know it wasn't," Arnold said. "We *know* he didn't do it."

"We do know that," Sam said, "but the problem is we can't prove it. We have his word and Christina's that neither of them went out after they got home yesterday afternoon, but we can't prove that either. And with the custody ruling in jeopardy thanks to Lori taking her case to the media, they both had motive."

Arnold stared at her, his anger palpable. "He's your friend. You can't honestly believe—"

"I don't believe that, Arnold. I'm just pointing out the fact that we can't actually *prove* he didn't do it."

The young detective slumped down in his chair, anger replaced by fear. "We have to do something."

"Tell me what we can do. I'm all ears."

"I don't know, but there has to be something."

"The one way to definitively prove Gonzo's innocence is to build a case against someone else—a case that will hold up all the way through a trial."

"I did a search for Lori," Jeannie said. "I found something interesting. She was on the board of directors for a church in Bowie that's been tied to controversy. They protest at funerals for service members, among other distasteful things."

"I've heard of that church," Tyrone said. "They showed up at Bobby's funeral. People were furious."

Sam remembered that funeral for one of Tyrone's friends from the police academy who'd been hit by a car during a routine traffic stop—and she remembered the controversy that had swirled when the church protestors chose to attend and make it about them.

"Bobby's folks have never gotten over that," Tyrone said. "That people who call themselves God-fearing types would turn a police officer's funeral into such a circus... It was sickening."

"This is a really good lead." Sam gestured to McBride and Tyrone. "I want you two to follow up on it in the morning."

"Will do," Jeannie said.

Sam looked to her third-shift detectives. "Carlucci and Dominguez, dig into Lori's financials overnight and have a report for me in the morning. You can work from home since you were here all day."

"Yes, ma'am," Carlucci said.

"I don't like to be dramatic about these things, but Gonzo is counting on us to take the heat off him. Let's keep him foremost in our minds as we go forward, and let's remember that someone has gone to a lot of trouble to make it seem like he did it. We know better. Now all we have to do is prove it. I'm going to work on the vengeance angle by paying each of my enemies a visit. Call me if anything breaks on the text messages. Otherwise, I'll see you all in the morning."

The somber detectives filed out of the room, their marching orders in hand. Most of them would probably work all night if it would help to clear Gonzo.

Farnsworth and Malone remained behind.

"What's your plan for these vengeance visits?" Farnsworth asked.

"I'm going to hunt down each of them and ask them where they were yesterday," Sam said.

"You are not doing that alone," Farnsworth said.

"I'll go with her," Malone said.

Sam glanced at him. "I'll do the talking."

"Of course, Lieutenant. Wouldn't have it any other way."

"Let's start up at SVU and see where our friend Ramsey spent New Year's Eve."

"I'm with you," Malone said.

"Keep me posted on what you find out," Farnsworth said. "I swear to God, if this leads back to Stahl, I'll kill him with my own hands."

Sam swallowed hard as she recalled the last time a fellow officer had said those words to her and what had happened shortly afterward. "You've got enough on your plate. Leave the scumbags to us."

"Helen emailed you the info you need for the morning," he said. "You're sure you're still good with doing this? I wouldn't blame you—"

"I'm fine with it."

"Is Nick? Have you asked him?"

"Um, no, and I don't plan to 'ask' him. I plan to 'tell' him I'm doing it, but he won't have a problem with it."

"Are you sure? We're basically taking advantage of the fact that you're married to the VP to deal with the media on this. We should make sure he's on board."

"Let me worry about him. I can assure you he'd want me to do anything I could to help you out."

"Close the door," Farnsworth said.

Malone, who was closest, did as he asked.

"I've been thinking…"

A trickle of fear worked its way down Sam's spine. "About?"

"Maybe I should just resign. Might be best for the department—"

"No," she said emphatically. "That would *not* be best for the department. *You* are what's best for the department. If you quit, you basically hand Springer and all the other loudmouths an easy victory. I know it's hard. I know it's awful to be caught in the crosshairs with the media. I was there myself not all that long ago after Johnson blew up in my face, and it's no fun at all when you're in the thick of it. As hard as it is when it's happening, it passes. They move on to something else, and they forget about you. It'll happen this time too."

"You're right, and I've certainly seen it happen enough times. But Springer is determined. I fear he's not going to be happy with anything less than my head on a stake."

"So you're just going to hand it to him? Sir."

Farnsworth laughed. "Don't you love how she tacks on that 'sir' at the end when she remembers who she's talking to?"

"I find that equally endearing when she does it to me," Malone replied.

"Have your fun at my expense, boys, but you know I'm

right. This too shall pass, and when it does, you'll be right where you belong—leading this department. *Sir*."

"As much as I hate to admit she's right," Malone said. "She's right."

"Say it again," Sam said. "I didn't hear you the first two times."

Both men laughed—as she hoped they would—and the tension marking the chief's face seemed to ease ever so slightly.

"We've all got your back, Chief," Sam said. "Please don't give up."

"I appreciate the pep talk. Hopefully tomorrow will take some of the heat off."

"How do you plan to explain where it all went wrong?" Sam asked.

"I'm going to tell the truth. We had built a strong narcotics case against Billy Springer and his associates, and I allowed Vice the time to finish their case before we charged Billy in the murders of his brother and his brother's friends. It was my call. It was the right call at the moment, but our narcotics investigation was compromised, which led to the events at Billy's grandmother's home in Friendship Heights."

"And when they ask how the investigation was compromised?"

"I'm going to say we are conducting an internal inquiry to determine how that happened, but we don't know yet. And believe me, I want to know as badly as Bill Springer does."

Sam thought about it for a long moment. "It might just work. The public will appreciate your honesty."

"I guess we'll find out soon enough, won't we?"

"We will," Sam said. "No matter what, we've got your back."

"And I appreciate that more than you know. I'll let you get going so you can go home at some point."

"I'll see you in the morning."

"Bright and early," he said with a grimace as he left them.

"He's taking this hard," Sam said, filled with concern as she watched the chief walk away.

"It's because he knows he fucked up. He never should've put the homicide investigation on hold for the narcs. It shouldn't have happened. We told him so at the time."

"Do you think he should resign?"

"Absolutely not. Billy Springer was a murdering, drug-dealing douche bag who got exactly what he had coming to him. The only one who can't seem to get his head around that is his father."

"The guy's got a big bully pulpit."

Malone grinned at her. "Ours is bigger. He's about to find out how much bigger it is. Now let's go track down some scumbags and call it a day."

"WHAT SHOULD WE have for dinner?" Nick asked Scotty, who was playing a game on his Xbox, which had been moved upstairs from the den to the room Nick was now using as an office.

"Whatever you want is fine with me."

"What's the matter?"

"Nothing."

The one-word answer surprised him. He'd been warned that the teenage years would bring about a child he barely recognized, but he'd refused to believe Scotty would ever be "typical." So while his better judgment told him to leave it alone, his intuition told him to dig deeper.

Moving from the doorway to the sofa they'd hauled up the stairs together, Nick sat next to him. "Hey, buddy?"

"Yeah?"

"Pause the game for a second, will you?"

Always obedient, Scotty did as he was told.

"Tell me what's wrong."

"Nothing's wrong."

"Are you bummed you have to go back to school to-morrow?"

"Totally bummed. I love vacation."

"So here's the thing… From the minute you came home earlier, I could tell something was off. I'm still new to this fatherhood gig, but I'd like to think I know you pretty well by now. Is it just the end of vacation that's got you down?"

Scotty fiddled with the game controller, and when he looked up at Nick, his eyes were bright with unshed tears. "Isn't there *anything* that can be done for Skip?" he asked softly. "I hate seeing him in bed all the time and in pain. I don't want to ask Sam about it because I know she's upset too."

Touched by his concern for his new grandfather, Nick said, "They're talking to the doctors about it, and they're hoping he's going to improve with time."

"I miss him," Scotty said, wiping away a tear. "He's always asleep when I go over there now."

"That's because of the medicine they're giving him."

"That's what Celia said too."

"I know it's upsetting. It is for all of us, but they're doing everything they can for him, and we have to hope he's going to get better with time. His body is very frag-ile. It has been since the shooting, but it's more so now since the surgery."

"I hate that he's in pain."

"I do too, but the pain could turn out to be a good thing."

"How is that possible?"

"It could be a sign that he's getting back function in his extremities since the bullet was removed."

"Does that mean he'll walk again?"

"I don't think he'll recover to that point, but I've learned not to rule anything out where he's concerned. He's tough as nails. He should've died the day he was shot, but look how far he's come since then."

"I barely remember my own grandpa because he died when I was so young. Being around Skip... I like having a grandpa again."

"I know, buddy. He's the best. I'll tell you what... Tomorrow when I get to work, I'll make some calls. I bet there's someone somewhere who knows something we don't know."

"Like in the government?"

Nick shrugged. "Maybe. There's all sorts of stuff going on and maybe someone is working on something that will help him."

"That'd be awesome."

"Do me a favor, and don't tell anyone. I don't want to get the family's hopes up if there's nothing we can do, okay?"

Scotty nodded. "Okay. Thanks, Nick."

"You know you can come to me with anything, right? Anything at all."

"I know, but you're starting your new job and you're busy—"

"I'm never too busy for you. Ever. When you're forty and have your own kids, I'll still be right here."

"I'm still getting used to that." He looked down at the floor before glancing up at Nick, tentatively. "Do you think, at some point—not now—but maybe someday, it would be okay if I called you Dad?"

Moved to tears and stunned speechless by the emotional gut punch, Nick stared at him.

"It's okay if you don't want me to—"

Nick put his arm around Scotty and drew him into a hug. "I want you to," he said gruffly. "Right now, today, tomorrow, whenever you want to. It would be the greatest honor of my life to be called Dad by you."

"You're the vice president of the whole country," Scotty said dryly. "You've had greater honors."

"No, I haven't."

"Thanks," Scotty said. "You know… For everything."

"You don't need to thank me. Sam and I are so happy to have you as part of our family. The day you told us you wanted to stay for good—best day of our lives." Nick's ringing phone ended the moment. "This might be Sam." He smiled at Scotty as he released him and pulled his phone out of his pocket, seeing his friend Andy's number on the caller ID. "I gotta grab this."

"Go ahead," Scotty said.

"Hey, Andy."

"Mr. Vice President. How goes it?"

"It's Nick, and it's going fine. You?"

"Good. I actually had a night away with Elsa for New Year's Eve while her parents had the baby. We just got back and I saw that I missed a call from Sam. I tried to call her, but got her voice mail, so I figured I'd try you." Nick got up from the sofa. "Be right back," he said to Scotty. He went into the hallway. "Did you hear the news about Lori Phillips?"

"What news?"

Nick filled him in on what had happened.

"Oh my God. That must be why Gonzo has called me four times too. Tell me he didn't have anything to do with it."

"Sam says he's not a suspect, but the media isn't buying. They're crucifying him."

"Holy shit. Do you know why Sam called me?"

"I don't, but she might be looking for info about the custody case."

"There's not much I can really tell her in light of my confidentiality requirements."

"I doubt she'd be looking to you to violate confidentiality."

"I left her a message. Tell her I'm around all night if she wants to call me. I'll help if I can."

"I'll tell her."

"I'm also calling because I heard from the investigator who's looking for Scotty's father. He thinks he might've found him."

Nick walked into his bedroom and closed the door. "Where is he?"

"In New Jersey. Working on the boardwalk on the Jersey Shore."

"How do you know it's him?"

"I don't have all the details yet, but my investigator is good. If he wasn't sure it was him, he wouldn't have called me."

"What's the next step?"

"I fly up there to talk to him."

"Shouldn't I do that?"

"Definitely not. I want to see if we can get around telling him who you are. Let me get a sense of what we're dealing with and see if I can get him to sign away his rights without bringing you into it."

"How soon will you go?"

"I'm trying to clear my schedule for the day after tomorrow."

Nick sat on the bed and ran his fingers through his hair. "Why am I totally panicking right now?"

"Don't panic. I'll do my best to get this sewed up quickly for you."

"You know what we were talking about when you called? He asked if it's okay to call me Dad." Nick's voice broke. "This can't go bad, Andy. It just can't."

"It's not going to. You've got Scotty's age on your side. He's able to say what he wants, and it's obvious to me and everyone who knows you all that he's exactly where he wants to be."

"Able to say to who?"

"A judge, but I don't see it coming to that. I'm much more concerned about the father wanting money from you."

"I'll give it to him. Whatever he wants."

Andy's low chuckle echoed through the phone. "Nick, seriously. If you happen to meet the guy, don't say that, okay?"

"Let's hope it doesn't come to that."

"What about Scotty?"

"What about him?"

"Will you tell him we've located his biological father?"

"I haven't given that a thought. I was hoping you wouldn't find him."

"You probably ought to think about it. If it's him, and we're almost entirely sure it is, Scotty has a right to know we've located him."

"I'll talk to Sam. We'll figure out what to do."

"Good enough."

"Andy... No matter what, we can't lose him. It would kill Sam."

"Not to mention what it would do to you."

"Not to mention."

"We'll get it taken care of. Try not to worry."

"Right... Will do."

"I'll be in touch."

"Thanks, Andy." Nick ended the call and sat perfectly still for several minutes as an array of troubling thoughts rendered him incapable of moving or thinking about anything other than what could go wrong. A knock on the door snapped him out of the stupor. "Yeah."

The door opened and Scotty stuck his head in. "About that dinner…"

Nick forced himself to put his worries aside so he could focus on the boy who meant the world to him. "What do you feel like?"

"Spaghetti?"

"You always say that."

"I always like that."

"You got it. Come help me."

"Are you okay?"

"Yeah sure. Why?"

"Your hair is standing up straight. It does that when you're worried about something and run your fingers through it."

"Is that right?" Nick hooked his arm around Scotty's neck and messed up his hair. "There. Now we match." He walked toward the stairs, bringing Scotty with him.

Scotty's belly laugh went a long way toward assuaging Nick's worries. But they stayed with him while they made dinner together. How would he ever tell Sam about this?

THIRTEEN

"I CAN'T BELIEVE I'm actually going to this guy's house voluntarily," Sam said as they approached the building where Lieutenant Stahl lived.

Malone followed her up the stairs. "Me either."

"Has anyone talked to him since he got out?"

"Not that I know of. Ever since he attacked you, everyone has kept their distance. Cops don't rub elbows with felons if they want to continue to be cops."

"To be fair, he's not a convicted felon. Yet."

"True. Only a matter of time, though."

"So how are we approaching this?" Sam asked.

"We're establishing his whereabouts on the thirty-first."

"What do we say when he asks why we want to know?"

"He'll know why we want to know. He's heard by now that Gonzo's baby mama was murdered. If I know him at all, and I know him way better than I ever wanted to, he's enjoying the speculation pointing to Gonzo."

"How does a career cop get to a place where he's gleeful to see one of his brothers being falsely accused of murder?"

"He gets there when his career doesn't go as planned," Malone said, "and he gets to watch others who started long after him reach heights he never could've dreamed of. He starts to get bitter, and the bitterness festers."

On the third floor, they rapped on his door and waited.

"Open up, Stahl." Malone knocked again. When there was no answer, Malone looked behind them, scanning the parking lot below. "He couldn't have gone far. The terms of his bail made it so he can't leave the area."

"Is anyone checking on him?"

"Nope. You know how bail works. They only check on him if he misses a court date." Malone looked down at her. "You want to wait awhile?"

Sam checked her watch. It was already almost seven. She'd been at it for thirteen hours and was running low on gas. "Let's see if we can find Peter and then I'll call it a day."

Malone followed her to the Capitol Hill neighborhood where she lived and unfortunately, Peter did too. The captain parked behind her on Seventh Street. Sam's stomach hurt at the thought of seeing her ex-husband, but if it helped Gonzo, she'd do it willingly. She'd eliminate Peter as a suspect and go home to her wonderful second husband. Thinking of Nick and Scotty waiting for her at home helped to propel Sam up another flight of stairs with Malone right behind her.

"I got this," he said, nodding for her to stand off to the side. Before she could protest or tell him he didn't need to mollycoddle her, he was pounding on the door. "Police, open up."

The door across the hall opened and a woman looked out at them. "There's no one there. He moved and the new people haven't moved in yet."

"Do you know where he went?" Sam asked with a growing sense of unease.

"No idea. We weren't friends. I just knew him to say hello to. Seemed like a nice enough guy. What'd he do?"

So many things, Sam thought. Too many to count, beginning with his failure to give her some critical messages from Nick while pretending to be her friend.

"We just wanted to talk to him," Malone said. "Does the super live on the property?"

She shook her head. "I can get you his number."

"That'd be great," Malone said. While she went to get the number, Malone glanced at Sam. "We'll find him. Don't worry."

They should've been visiting him in prison where he belonged for attempting to kill her and Nick with crude bombs attached to their cars.

The neighbor returned with the number and handed the piece of paper to Malone. "Thanks very much for your help."

"Is he in trouble?"

"Not that we know of," Malone said, "but he has been in the past."

"Wow, I never would've guessed that. He seemed so… normal."

"I thought so too," Sam said, pleased to know she wasn't the only one who'd been taken in by his false charm. "Thanks again for the help."

"I'll get on this tonight," Malone said. "I'll find him."

"Thanks. I'm sure he hasn't gone far. He won't be able to stalk me if he's not close by."

"When was the last time you saw him?"

"I guess it was when I came by to see if he was dicking with me after the wedding by sending the threatening cards."

"That was almost a year ago."

"Time flies when you're finally happily married."

"Didn't Nick have a guy on him?"

"For a while, but he called him off when I told him he was wasting his money." Back at her car, she turned to the captain. "It makes me nervous that we don't know where either of them are. I'm picturing them in a bunker together trying to figure out ways to ruin my life and the lives of everyone I care about while Ramsey delivers Chinese food to them."

He grunted out a laugh. "Go give that overactive imagination of yours a rest for a few hours. I'll see you on TV."

"Yeah, yeah, stop enjoying that so much."

"I'm going to enjoy watching you seethe when they ask you personal questions."

"I need to think of something wildly inappropriate that I can say if they ask me personal crap."

"I'm no politician, but something tells me Nick won't approve of that."

"I know," she said glumly. "He ruins all my fun."

Suddenly exhausted as the adrenaline of the day drained from her system, Sam pushed herself off the car. "I'll see you tomorrow. Call me if anything pops."

"Will do."

Sam drove the two blocks to her home on Ninth Street, where she had to show ID to park in front of her own house. Thankfully, the neighbors had been cool about the increased security, mostly because they all loved Skip and knew how much he liked having Sam and her family nearby.

Everyone loved Skip, but no one more so than her, or so she thought. Sam got out of her car, took a longing glance at her own home and headed for her dad's house, entering with a quick knock to the front door.

Celia was on the sofa, a glass of white wine in hand and the TV on. "Hey," she said when Sam came in. "Just getting home?"

"Yep. Happy New Year to me. Lori, the mother of Gonzo's son, was found dead in a car this morning."

"I heard about that on the news. Tell me there's no truth to him being a suspect."

"No truth whatsoever, but why should the press let the truth get in the way of a good story?"

Celia shook her head in dismay. "I couldn't believe what I was hearing earlier."

"I think someone has gone to some effort to make it look like he could've done it."

"He must be beside himself."

"He is," Sam said, as she added a call to her friend and colleague to her before-bed to-do list. "How's our patient?"

"Sleeping comfortably after a rough day." Celia raised the wineglass. "Now I'm medicating myself." Celia snickered at her own joke. The laugh turned into a sob almost instantaneously. "Sorry." She covered her mouth. "It's just...hard. It's really hard to see him this way. I don't know how much more he can take."

Sam reached for her stepmother and hugged her.

"Sorry to be so maudlin. I think I might be a little drunk."

Laughing, Sam pulled back so she could see Celia's face. "Can't say I blame you for that."

"I was so hoping we might get some sort of miracle from the surgery. I'm ashamed to admit I had all my eggs in that basket when I certainly knew the realities. I just never imagined this scenario."

"None of us did."

"He asked me about the pills in the safe-deposit box."

Sam went cold all over at the thought of those pills and what they were for. "No. We're not there yet."

"He is, honey. His quality of life has gone from bad to awful, and the more time he spends in bed, the greater the risk of secondary infection." Leaning her head back against the sofa, she looked at Sam. "I'm not going to let this go on indefinitely. I made promises to him that I intend to keep."

Celia's words struck terror in Sam's heart, but she didn't fault her stepmother. She didn't want her father to live in agony either. "I'm going to talk to the doctors again tomorrow. There's got to be something they can do that's not been tried yet."

"I appreciate your help the same way I have since the surgery."

"Just give me a couple of days, okay?"

Celia reached out to brush the tears off Sam's face. "Okay."

Sam hugged her again. "I'm going to kiss him goodnight." She got up and cut through the kitchen to get to her father's bedroom in what used to be the dining room. A hallway light lit her way into the room, where she bent over the hospital bed to kiss his forehead. The one improvement since the surgery was that he no longer required the respirator while in bed. Under normal circumstances, that would've been hailed as a major victory.

His eyes fluttered open. "Hey, baby girl."

"Hey, Skippy. Didn't mean to wake you. Just wanted to say good night."

"Glad you did. Long day, huh?"

"No worse than usual."

"Heard the shit on the news about Gonzo."

"It's total shit and not true."

"Figured as much."

"We've got a few threads to pull tomorrow. We'll figure it out."

"You always do. Saw your boy earlier. Love that kid."

Sam rested her hand on his shoulder and brushed the hair back from his forehead, which felt warm to the touch. Another pang of fear assailed her when she tried to conceive of life without him at the center of it where he belonged. "He loves you too."

"You should get home to your boys and get some rest while you can."

"Will you be able to sleep?"

"Yeah, don't worry about me."

"Right…" She leaned over to kiss him. "Love you, Skippy."

"Love you too, baby girl."

Sam left him to sleep and went back to the living room. "He's awake and feeling a bit feverish if you ask me."

"I'll check on him."

"You'll let me know if you need me, right? Anytime—day or night."

"I know where to find you. Thanks, honey. You girls and your families have been a godsend to both of us. You should see the way your dad lights up when Scotty comes to visit."

"Scotty adores him." She leaned over to kiss Celia. "Hang in there. I'll check in tomorrow."

"See you then."

Her heart heavy and burdened by her father's deteriorating health, Sam left his house and headed down the ramp. In the three years since he'd been shot, their lives had been a roller-coaster ride with more downs than ups, especially lately. They'd known, of course, that they were living on borrowed time. The surgery had given them hope that had been dashed in the weeks since. Things weren't getting better. They were getting worse by the day.

As she trudged up the ramp to her house, she was further disturbed by the unsettling thought that if her father died, they wouldn't need the ramp anymore. "No," she said out loud. "He's not going to die. That's not going to happen."

The agent working the door opened it for her. "Good evening, Mrs. Cappuano."

"Hi." As she wondered if he'd heard her talking to herself, she took off her coat and laid it over the sofa.

Nick came out of the kitchen wearing an apron and looking positively adorable in the new Harvard T-shirt she'd bought him for Christmas and the worn, faded jeans she loved on him. Sexiest vice president in the history of the universe. "Hey, babe."

Sam wanted to shake off her worries to focus only on him and Scotty, but the sight of his handsome face broke the grip she'd had on her emotions.

Fortunately, he realized right away and took her by the hand to tow her to the kitchen. "Could we have the room, please?" he asked the agent, who was sitting at the table reading the paper.

"Of course." The agent got up and left the room.

Nick put his arms around her. "What's wrong?"

"Where's Scotty?"

"He went upstairs as soon as there were dishes to be done. Talk to me, babe."

"My dad… I just saw him and Celia. It's bad and getting worse."

"I know. Scotty was upset about it earlier too. He asked why there's nothing we can do. I told him I'd make some calls tomorrow."

"Like official calls?"

"Are there any other kind from the White House?"

"Can't you get in trouble for that?"

"For reaching out to some of the best doctors in our country who might be able to help my father-in-law, a high-ranking police officer who was shot in the line of duty? Let them make a thing of that for all I care."

Sam tightened her hold on him and breathed in his familiar scent. His nearness calmed her in a way that nothing else could. "You should care. This is a whole new ball game for you."

"Trust me when I tell you I don't care. If it blows up into a huge scandal but we find some help for him, I still won't care."

"Thank you. I'm not even going to argue with you because I feel so desperate."

"I'll do whatever I can for him—and for you." He held her for a long time, until she was finally able to relax into his embrace. Running his hand up and down her back, he said, "You must be hungry."

"I could eat."

"Scotty and I made sauce."

"From scratch?"

"Uh-huh."

"Show-off."

"I learned a few things growing up with an Italian grandmother. Want me to make you a plate?"

"In a minute," she said. "I need a little more of this first."

"As much as you want whenever you want it."

"All the time. What did I ever do before I had you to come home to?"

He released the clip that held up her hair and combed his fingers through the unruly curls that fell below her shoulders. "I love when you come home to me. Every night, when you come in, I realize I've been holding my breath all day waiting to see you, to know you're safe…"

She raised her head and looked up at him.

He framed her face and gazed into her eyes as he kissed her softly and sweetly. Then he leaned his forehead against hers. "We need a date in the loft tonight."

"Yes, please."

"First, let me feed you."

Reluctantly, Sam released her hold on him and took a seat at the table. He poured a glass of the chardonnay she loved and then brought her a plate of pasta with the sauce he and Scotty had made. "Smells amazing."

"It tastes pretty damn good, if I do say so myself."

"So many talents," she said, waggling her brows.

He opened a beer for himself and joined her at the table. "What went on around here today?"

"A few things." The words were spoken casually, but his lips tightened with tension that she noticed right away.

"What things?"

"Andy called looking for you and said he'll be home all night if you want to call him back."

"Oh, good. I need to get the lowdown on Lori's attorney for the custody case as well as the social worker."

Fiddling with the bottle cap, he said, "He also told me they think they've found Scotty's father in New Jersey."

The bite of delicious pasta got stuck in her throat. When she finally managed to get it down, she took a sip of her wine. "They actually found him."

"Yes."

"So what now?" The question belied the bolt of terror that seized her at the thought of anything messing with their plan to adopt Scotty.

"Now Andy goes there and has a conversation with him."

"What if he wants him? What do we do then?"

Nick reached for her free hand. "Even if it were to go to court—"

"*Court?* It could come to that?"

"Purely speculation on Andy's part, but even if it came to that, Scotty is old enough now to say what he wants, and we know what he wants. I felt better when Andy put it like that."

"So what's the worst-case scenario with the father?"

"Andy thinks he'll want money if he finds out who we are, so he's going to try to get this done without him finding out."

"That's a long shot."

"Agreed, but he figures it's worth a try. He's going up there to see him this week."

Sam put down her fork and rested her free hand on her stomach. "And we're supposed to function while this is going on?"

"I know. But the good news of the day is that Scotty asked me if it would be okay—at some point—to call me Dad."

"Oh, wow," she said softly. "That must've been a moment and a half."

"It was."

She squeezed his hand. "I want this done. I want him to be ours forever."

"We're working on it. We have to be patient and dot all the Is and cross the Ts."

"I hate Is and Ts. All those dots and crosses drive me nuts."

Nick laughed and bent his head to kiss her hand. "Let's keep this between us for now. I don't see any need to worry him until we know what we're dealing with."

"Totally agree."

"Finish your dinner."

"I'm not hungry anymore."

"Samantha… Clean your plate or no dessert."

"Are we talking dessert or *dessert*?"

"The good kind. The loft kind."

"In that case…" She twirled another forkful of pasta. "This sauce is amazing. I'm truly impressed."

"Scotty said it was better than the stuff in the jar."

"High praise coming from him."

"So there's this thing at work tomorrow night."

"What thing?"

"The West Wing staff is having a reception to welcome us to the team. They invited you and Scotty to come too. If you want to."

"Oh."

"It's at the White House." He watched her closely as she absorbed that news, amusement dancing in his gorgeous hazel eyes.

"You want me to go to the White House for a…thing… tomorrow night with no time to prepare myself for this?"

"Only if you want to."

She scowled at him. "Don't do that."

"What am I doing?"

"Letting me off the hook when you shouldn't let me off the hook. I'm your wife. I should be there when you celebrate your new job. At the freaking White House."

He rolled his lips together to keep from laughing.

"Don't you dare laugh at me."

"I wouldn't do that."

"Yes, you would!"

"Not when I want to get really, really lucky tonight."

She rolled her eyes at him. "You get really, really lucky most nights, even when you laugh at me."

"Have I mentioned lately how much I love you?"

"Don't do that either!"

"I'm not allowed to tell you I love you?"

"Not when you're trying to coerce me."

"I love to coerce you. It's one of my favorite things to do, but since it's making you cranky, tell me how the case is going."

"It's going," she said with a sigh. "We've got a few leads

that we'll dig into tomorrow. The faster we get this sewn up, the faster Gonzo's life can get back to normal."

"I can't believe they're actually trying to pin it on him. They were giving him the hero's treatment a few short weeks ago."

"The thing is, we can't prove he didn't do it. Someone dicked with the security cameras in his building, his name and address were found under the floor mat in the car Lori was in and he and Christina are each other's alibi. They both love Alex, and Lori was making trouble for them."

"So you're saying the only way to completely take the heat off them is to find the person who actually did it?"

"Yep. We're doing everything we can, but so far we've yet to find anyone who had more of a motive than they do. It's early in the investigation though." She took another sip of her wine and smiled when he topped off her glass. "So Freddie was at the ER at GW with Elin, who took a hit to the face at work today."

"Is she okay?"

"I guess so. I don't really know the details yet, but she was able to call him. She said she saw Shelby there. With Hill."

"What? How come?"

"Apparently she'd fallen on the sidewalk and cut up her knees."

"Huh." Nick scratched at the stubble on his unshaven jaw. "I hope that's all it was."

"What else would it be?"

He glanced at her tentatively.

"What?"

"She came by earlier today to share some news with me. It's news you might find upsetting, and she wanted me to decide how best to tell you."

"She's pregnant."

"Yes."

"Well, you're just full of all kinds of information tonight."

He scooted his chair closer to hers and took hold of both her hands. "It's okay to feel a little undone by this news. I did too."

"I'm happy for her. I am."

"I know you are. And I know your heart breaks a little more every time someone around us gets the one thing you want more than anything."

She shrugged off his concern even as her heart did in fact break. His sweetness and understanding went a long way toward soothing the ache. "So if she was at the ER, it might be more serious than skinned knees."

"Jeez, I hope not." He released her hands to pull his phone from his back pocket.

As Sam watched him dash off a quick text, she stared at the platinum band he wore on his left hand. She loved seeing that ring on his finger and knowing he belonged only to her for the rest of their lives. At times like this, when her world was in chaos, the sight of that thin band of metal calmed and grounded her.

He put down the phone and took hold of her hands again. "Talk to me. Tell me what you're thinking."

"I'm happy for her. Truly happy for her and Angela and Gonzo and Derek and everyone else we know who has kids. It's just that sometimes I wonder if it's going to happen again for us."

"I've been thinking about that today since Shelby was here and how we haven't done everything we could do to make it happen."

She was shaking her head before he finished speaking. "I've been through fertility treatment before. It's hideous. I said I'd never do it again. You think I'm crazy now. You ought to see me when I'm hopped up on hormones. Plus you'd have to give me shots, which would make me hate you." She shook her head. "I can't do that again. I just can't."

"Totally up to you, but I wanted you to know I'm willing."

She raised a brow and tipped her head. "And you know what would be required of you?"

"Umm, no, not really."

Sam covered her mouth but was unable to suppress her laughter.

"What's so funny?"

She was laughing so hard she could barely breathe, let alone speak. "Suffice to say it would involve your hand and lots of porn."

"Jesus, Sam."

"What? I speak the truth."

"Whatever. Have your laughs. I'd do it for you if you wanted me to."

She moved from her chair into his lap. "And I love you for that. I really do, but I can't go through that again. It was a nightmare the other two times, and it was all for nothing. I say we keep doing what we're doing, and if it happens, it happens. If not, I'll find a way to live with the many blessings we already have."

"Nothing has to be decided right here and now. If you want to think about it—"

She kissed him. "Nothing to think about. That's not something I'm willing to put myself through again, and it would take all the romance out of a pretty good marriage."

"A *pretty* good marriage?"

"An above-average marriage."

"Above average?"

"A spectacular, amazing, fantastic, wonderful, beyond-all-expectations marriage. Better?"

"Much."

"Why would we mess with that?"

"To give you what you want most in the world?"

"I already have more than I ever dreamed possible with you and Scotty. I promise that's enough for me. Anything more would be frosting on an already amazing cake."

"It is pretty good cake."

"Just *pretty* good?"

"Astonishing, delicious, delectable, mouthwatering. Best cake I ever had. Better?"

She smiled and then kissed him again. "So much better."

FOURTEEN

STRETCHED OUT ON Avery's sofa, Shelby eyed her phone on the coffee table but made no move to reach for it even though she'd heard it chime with a new text. She who never let a text go unanswered couldn't be bothered to even read this one. What did it matter?

He'd refused to take her home because he wanted to take care of her.

She'd lacked the wherewithal to fight with him.

Hindsight, she'd discovered this afternoon and evening, was an interesting perspective. So many things made sense now that she knew the truth. She thought about the time Avery had brought Sam home after Willie Vasquez's murder. Nick had arrived while she talked to Avery outside Sam and Nick's house. After Avery left, she'd talked to Nick about her desire to date the FBI agent. Nick had been all for it. Now she knew why. It wasn't because he thought she and Avery would make for a good couple. It was because Nick wanted Avery to date someone else, so he wouldn't pose a threat to Nick's marriage.

More than anything she felt like a fool. Three people she was close to had kept the truth from her for months. They'd let her get invested in her relationship with Avery. They'd let her think that maybe this time, finally, she'd get her happy ending. But all the while they knew who Avery really wanted and couldn't have.

She recalled how she'd asked Nick if he'd mind if she went out with Hill. "Hell, no," he'd said. "Go. Have a great time. By all means." She'd found that odd at the time because she'd already picked up on the fact that Nick didn't like Avery—and Nick seemed to like everyone.

"So stupid," she whispered.

Avery came into the room carrying a steaming mug of the tea he kept on hand for her.

Shelby had once been charmed when she realized he'd gotten her favorite tea. Now, like everything else about him, the hot tea left her cold.

With his offering in hand, he sat on the coffee table and held it out to her.

Shelby forced herself to sit up, to take the mug, to take a sip and to not look at him.

"I'm sorry, Shelby. I can only imagine what you must be thinking, but I promise you that what has happened between us had nothing to do with anyone but you and me."

"So the fact that you were in love with my friend and employer had nothing at all to do with us?"

"I'm not in love with her. I was never in love with her. I was…infatuated."

"Infatuated. How nice. And while you were infatuated with my friend, you decided to go out with me so you could stay close to her."

"That's not true. I see her at work all the time. I didn't need to go out with you to stay close to her. Nothing ever happened between us. It was just a one-sided thing that is now in the past."

"All this time, I couldn't figure out why Nick Cappuano, who likes everyone, doesn't like you. I mean, on paper, you're his kind of guy—accomplished, athletic, charming. The two of you should've been the best of friends and yet you aren't. I couldn't figure out why. But now it all makes sense. He hates you because you want his wife."

"I don't want his wife. I like her. I admire her. I understand that she's extremely married, and I'd never get in the way of that or cause trouble for either of them. It was a crush. Past tense." He placed a cashmere throw over her lap and tucked her hair behind her ear.

She ought to tell him to stop touching her, but she liked when he touched her.

"The crush I have on you, on the other hand, is very much present tense."

Shelby shook her head. "Don't say that stuff."

"Why not? It's the truth. Do you think I would spend most nights with you if I didn't care about you? Do you think I'd tag along on your dates with Scotty if I didn't really enjoy both of you?" He leaned in to kiss her forehead and then her cheek. "Do you think I'd make love to you every chance I got if I didn't truly want to?"

"I honestly don't know what to think. I'm confused."

"Nothing to be confused about. You and I are together, and we have been for a while now. She and I are colleagues. That's all we've ever been, and all we'll ever be."

"Hypothetically, if she weren't married anymore, would you still be interested in me?"

"Yes, I would. Do you think I've just been killing time with you while waiting for a perfectly healthy young guy to kick the bucket so I could move in on his wife?"

That glorious South Carolinian accent, those golden eyes, the cheekbones... She was crazy about him. Or she had been until she found out he was crazy about Sam.

"You're blowing this way out of proportion, you know," he said.

"How am I doing that? Three people I care about and trust have kept a very big piece of information from me for a very long time. I feel like a fool." She felt like an even bigger fool when her eyes filled with tears. Again.

"I'm so, so sorry. I never wanted you to know that I used

to have feelings for her, but I felt like I was lying to you by not telling you, and I didn't like that either. My feelings for her were silly feelings compared to what I feel for you. Those are real feelings. She was a fantasy. *You* are real and amazing and funny and formidable and adorable and—"

"Don't say cute. Don't even think about it."

"I wouldn't dare. I know better by now." He caressed her face and disposed of her tears with a minimum of fuss. "I want to watch your belly get all big and round. I want to be there when you bring this little person into the world. I want to sleep with you every night and laugh with you and put up with you imitating my accent—badly, I might add."

"I do a great Avery Hill."

"Keep telling yourself that, darlin'. I want you to remember something else too."

"What's that?"

"I changed my opinion of the color pink for you."

Shelby didn't want to laugh, but a gurgle escaped nonetheless. He had, in fact, come around on the pink issue.

With a finger to her chin, he compelled her to meet the sexy golden gaze that had made her want to drool from the first time she ever laid eyes on him. "You forgive me?"

"I want to, and I hate myself for that."

"Why do you hate yourself?"

"Because. This is the best relationship I've ever had, and I don't want it to end. But I also want to be able to respect myself. You kept something big from me—something I had a right to know. That doesn't happen again."

"It won't."

"This isn't the FBI, Avery. If you want me, really want me, I won't put up with secrets and intrigue. That's not what *I* want. I'd rather be alone than be with someone I can't trust. I deserve better, and not just from you but from two people I consider my friends as well as my employers."

"You're right, I was wrong, and I'm sorry. I'm truly sorry you were hurt because of me. Your knees and your heart."

"It's very evolved of you to actually use the word 'sorry'. That right there makes this different from any relationship I've ever been in."

"I promise I'm not just telling you what you want to hear, Shelby." He leaned in slowly, his eyes open and fixed on her, and kissed her. "Kiss me back."

"I'm not ready to."

"When will you be ready?"

"I'll let you know."

Oh, that smile did crazy things to his sexy face. She was powerless against that smile.

He kept kissing her, subtle brushes of his lips over hers, teasing her with far less than he was capable of. "How's it going?"

"Fine."

"How do the knees feel?"

"Not so good."

He took hold of her hands, which were also bruised and scraped. Then he pressed gentle kisses to each palm. "I called in to work. I'm staying home tomorrow to take care of you."

"That's not necessary."

"It is to me."

"I have to work tomorrow."

"You're going to call them and tell them you got hurt and that you need to take a sick day. And then you're going to stay here with me, snuggled under this blanket my sister got me for Christmas. Then you're going to let me make it up to you by torturing me with a full day of your favorite chick flicks."

"You have no idea what you're in for. Do the words *Legally Blonde* mean anything at all to you?"

"Not yet, but after tomorrow I'm sure I'll be fully indoctrinated."

He put his arms around her and Shelby leaned her head against his chest. After all these years of navigating the dating game, you'd think she'd have a better handle on whether or not she should give him another chance. That he'd sincerely apologized and assured her that whatever he'd felt for Sam was in the past now went a long way toward soothing the ache inside her.

But she'd have to talk to Sam and Nick about this situation at some point, and the thought of that made her feel sick. She loved them both. That they could've kept something like this from her surprised and hurt her.

"Let's go to bed, darlin'," Avery said.

When he slid his arms under her, intending to carry her upstairs to his bedroom, Shelby looped hers around his neck. She'd deal with her employers tomorrow.

BECAUSE THE PUNCH had broken bones in her face and around her eye, doctors decided to keep Elin in the hospital overnight. They gave her something to help her sleep and after she was settled in a room upstairs, she conked out. Freddie sat by her bedside, staring at her bruised and swollen face, seething over how it had come to be that way.

That she had kept something so important from him for a month made him crazy. A guy had been hassling her, and she didn't think he needed to know? Just when he thought he had this relationship thing figured out, something happened to remind him he was in way over his head with her and had been from the beginning.

He could still remember the first time he'd laid eyes on her during the O'Connor investigation when he'd had to listen to her describe the kind of wild sex she'd had with the dead senator. He'd wanted her madly then and nothing had changed in the year since.

It was exactly a year today since he went to find her at the gym, thinking of New Year's resolutions that had nothing to do with working out and everything to do with getting the incredibly sexy Elin Svendsen into his life and his bed. No one had been more surprised than he was that she was equally attracted to him. This woman who could have anyone actually wanted him.

A lifetime of abstinence had melted away in one lifechanging night with her. He'd put everything on the line for her—his faith, his close relationship with the single mother who'd raised him and most important, his heart. It had been totally and absolutely worth it. Now they lived in an apartment they'd chosen together.

Freddie loved coming home to her every night. He loved sleeping with her and weekends with her and making love with her. So it killed him to know she'd been troubled and bothered by someone and hadn't told her boyfriend the cop. What did it mean for them that she could've kept something like that from him for so long?

While she'd been getting a CT scan earlier, he'd called HQ to find out the status of the man who'd hit her. He was in the cooler awaiting arraignment in the morning. Freddie kept telling himself his place was at the hospital with her and that he shouldn't leave her for any reason.

But as her face continued to swell and the bruises turned a dark, vicious purple that matched the rage that had been festering inside him all night, he knew he couldn't sit idly by and do nothing. Bending over the bed, he kissed her lips and waited to see if she would wake up. She never stirred.

"I'll be right back," he whispered as he kissed her again. "I love you." After leaving her room, he stopped at the nurses' station, where he recognized several of the women who'd cared for Sam after a car accident last winter. "I have to step out for a short time. If my girlfriend, Elin Svendsen, wakes up, can you please tell her I'll be right back?"

"She shouldn't wake up for a while," one of them said. "We'll keep an eye on her. Don't worry."

"Thanks a lot. I'll be right back."

"We'll be here."

"Thanks." He headed for the elevators and cut through the emergency department to get to his car. The temperature had dropped significantly during the hours he had spent inside, so he zipped his sweatshirt and ran for his car, anxious to take care of what needed taking care of and to return to Elin. He ought to call Sam, but she'd talk him out of what he was about to do. He couldn't let that happen, he decided as he reached his car.

The old Mustang fought back, and for a second he didn't think it would start. But then it roared to life, backfiring as he punched the accelerator. A few minutes later, he pulled into the parking lot at HQ, parked in one of the spots reserved for visitors outside the main door and jogged inside. He nodded to the sergeant working the main desk and headed for the detectives' pit, which was deserted.

Since officers never took weapons into the cell block out of fear of being overpowered, Freddie locked his gun into his desk drawer and then took the stairs down two floors to the cells where people were held while awaiting arraignment.

"Hey, Cruz." Sergeant Delany was on duty. "You're working late."

"Yeah, it's one of those days."

"What can I do for you?"

"The guy who was brought in from the 16th Street gym…"

"Andre Elliott. He's in number six."

Freddie looked the sergeant in the eye. "He put my girl-friend in the hospital. I'd like to have a chat with him."

After a long pause, during which Freddie never blinked, Delany said, "Go ahead." He handed Freddie the key to the cell.

"Thanks."

Delany nodded.

Freddie unzipped his hoodie and removed it before using the key to open the cell door.

Elliott was stretched out on the narrow cot, but sat up when Freddie came in. "Who are you?"

Raising the hoodie so it covered his face, Freddie hung it over the camera that was trained on Elliott. He was tall and muscular with a complexion that indicated mixed-race lin-eage. He had a jagged scar on his bicep and sleeve tattoos. The knuckles on his right hand were bruised and swollen.

"I'm Detective Cruz." With his hands propped on his hips, his gold shield was visible to the other man.

"What'd you want?"

"The woman you hit at the gym today…"

"What about her?"

"She's mine. She says you've been hassling her for a while now."

"She lies."

"No, she doesn't." Freddie took a step closer. Even though the guy was bigger than him and probably a whole lot meaner, Freddie was running on adrenaline and rage. He felt like he could kick the shit out of a raging bull if he had to. "Let me make myself really clear. Stay the fuck away from her, or you'll be dealing with me."

"You think I'm afraid of you?"

Freddie moved so fast Elliott never saw the knee to the groin coming. He cried out in pain as he went down hard.

Without giving him time to recover, Freddie punched him in the face, in the same area where Elin had been hit. Then he took a handful of Elliot's hair and forced him to look up.

Freddie brought his face down close to Elliott's. "Stay the fuck away from her, or I swear to God I'll fuck you up. Are we clear?"

"I'll have your badge for this."

"No, you won't. We don't think much of scumbags who hit women around here." He pulled hard on the handful of hair. "*Are we clear?*"

"Yeah."

"I didn't hear you."

"We're clear."

Freddie released his hold on Elliott's hair and pushed him aside, leaving the man slumped on the floor, cupping his injured testicles. On the way out of the cell, Freddie walked past the camera before he pulled his hoodie off it.

At the desk, he handed the key to the Delany.

"Everything all right?" Delany asked.

"It is now. If you could forget I stopped by, I'd consider it a personal favor."

"Never saw you here."

"Thanks, Sarge. Happy New Year."

"Same to you."

Freddie went up the stairs two at a time, propelled by the same surge of adrenaline that had brought him here. He retrieved his weapon from his desk and was on his way to the hospital five minutes later. Only when he was back in Elin's room, his hand swelling from the impact to Elliott's face, did the adrenaline leach from his body, leaving him cold and shaky as he leaned over the bed to kiss her forehead.

Sagging into the chair next to the bed, he accepted that

he'd risked his hard-won career by going to the jail. But he'd do it again to protect the woman he loved.

SAM AND NICK waited an hour after Scotty went to bed before heading up to their loft on the third floor. On the way up, Nick went into Scotty's room to check on him. He was asleep with most of his covers on the floor, so Nick covered him up and shut off the bedside lamp.

When he got upstairs, Sam was on the phone, apparently with Gonzo.

"We do have some threads, and we're pulling them. Carlucci and Dominguez are working on Lori's financials tonight, and we're looking at the church she belonged to. They protest at veterans' funerals, among other unsavory things. I'm going on TV with the chief tomorrow to talk about Springer, and I'll take advantage of the opportunity to direct the heat off you."

Nick lit the beach-scented candles, turned on the music they'd loved on their honeymoon in Bora Bora and shut off the overhead lights. He sat next to her on the foot of their double lounge chair, put his arm around her and kissed her neck. He was fine with starting without her. She'd catch up. She always did.

She leaned into him. "I know," she said to Gonzo. "It totally sucks that people are saying that, but the people who matter know the truth. Just remember that. I'll check in tomorrow, and I'll keep you posted. Try to get some sleep." She ended the call, then tossed her phone aside. "Sorry about that."

"No problem. I managed to entertain myself."

Laughing, Sam began tugging at his shirt.

He put his arms behind him so he could watch her push up the shirt she'd bought him to replace the ratty one she hated. "What's this about TV?"

"Oh. You heard that, huh?"

"Yep. What gives?"

"So, things with the chief are bad. The press is doing a number on him. I suggested he go out there and tell his side of the story." When Nick pulled the T-shirt over his head, she trailed her finger from his neck to the waistband of his jeans, sending all the blood in his body to his cock, which surged against his zipper.

"How'd you get roped into it?"

Sam bent to kiss the same path. "I might've offered to use my, you know…" She waved her hand. "What do you call it?"

"Your stature as the wife of the vice president of the United States?"

"Yeah, that."

Laughing, Nick fell back on the bed. "You are so funny, you know that?"

"How am I funny?"

"You don't even know how to play the game, do you?"

"What game?"

"The *fame* game. You're *famous*, Samantha. Everyone in this country knows who you are now. Go out there and use that to square things away for your chief."

"Use it." She bit her lip the way she did when she was thinking. "Isn't that kind of…unethical?"

"Not at all. It would be unethical if you asked me to get involved behind the scenes to make it go away. If you go on TV and take advantage of the interest in us to change the conversation then that's not at all unethical."

"It feels icky."

"Welcome to politics, babe."

She unbuttoned and unzipped his jeans. "I don't want to talk about politics."

Twirling a lock of her hair around his finger, he said, "What do you want to talk about?"

"I want to talk about how sexy my husband, the vice president, is and how every woman in America would like to be me right now."

"Sure, they would."

"Speaking of not knowing how to play the game."

"I don't want to play this particular game with anyone other than my beautiful wife."

"Spoken like a true politician."

"Or a smart husband."

"That too," Sam said with a laugh. She kissed a path from his belly to his chest, ending at his lips.

He wrapped his arms around her to keep her there, losing himself to her kiss and the way she made him feel. Her mouth opened and her tongue tangled with his. God, he could kiss her forever and never get tired of it. As he kissed her, he pulled at her clothes impatiently, breaking the kiss only to tug her top over her head. The scent of lavender and vanilla filled his senses and made him greedy for more of her.

Nick released the clasp on her bra and pushed the straps down, gasping at the exquisite feel of her breasts pressed against his chest. That was one of his top five favorite things in life. As he pushed her jeans down, he uncovered one of his other top five favorite things—her gorgeous ass. Truth be told, he loved every incredible inch of her, and the way she responded to him was a constant reminder of how damn lucky he was that she loved him.

And then she broke the kiss and reminded him all over again why he was so lucky. She pushed him onto his back and kissed a path straight down the front of him.

He drew in a sharp breath when she took him into her

mouth, sucking hard enough to make him see stars. *God-damn*, she was good at that. "*Samantha.*"

"Hmm?" She knew the vibration of her lips against his shaft made him crazy.

"You're going to end this before we get started."

"Let me have my fun."

Her idea of fun was his idea of heaven. He gathered her hair so he could watch, which was almost as sexy as what she was doing with her lips and tongue. Then she took him into her throat and nearly finished him off with the tight squeeze. "*Sam.*"

She released him slowly, taking her time and circling her tongue over the head.

He reached for her and pulled her up to him, their mouths coming together in a clash of tongues and teeth and lips. He couldn't wait one more second to be inside her, so he turned them and plunged into her. Surrounded by her heat, her scent, her arms wrapped around his neck and her legs around his hips, Nick took a moment to enjoy the sheer bliss he found with her every damn time.

Then she began to move beneath him, needing more. He raised his head to look down at her swollen lips, the clear blue eyes that looked up at him with love and desire and the hint of vulnerability that she saved only for him. She let herself go with him, and he loved that she gave him that.

"What's wrong?" she asked after a long moment of quiet during which he pressed deeper into her, but made no move to speed things up.

"Not one damn thing is wrong." He framed her face with his hands and kissed her softly. His Samantha liked it hard and fast, but tonight he wanted to take his time. He wanted to savor her. He started with her neck, kissing and nibbling while she squirmed beneath him, trying to break his control.

Cupping her breasts, he sucked on her left nipple, drawing it into his mouth and running his tongue over the tip.

She grabbed a fistful of his hair and tugged as she tightened her legs around his hips. Her internal muscles rippled and squeezed his cock, testing his resolve to go slow.

"I know what you're doing," he said.

"What am I doing?"

"You're trying to take control."

"I'm trying to get you to *move*."

"I will. When I'm good and ready to." He laughed at the frustrated face she made at him. "You may be the boss at work, but here," he said, knowing he'd probably make her mad, "I'm the boss."

"Says who?"

"Says me."

"I never agreed to that."

He withdrew from her so quickly, she gasped.

"What the hell?"

"Turn over. I want you on all fours, head down."

"Nick."

"Do it, Samantha." He got up from the lounge. "You're not in charge right now."

Nick caught the glare she directed his way, but she did as he told her to do. Taking direction was a challenge for his wife, but he was determined to do this his way. He crossed the room to get what he needed and returned to the lounge and the incredible sight of his wife's delicious ass raised in the air.

"Spread your legs some more."

Hesitantly, or so it seemed to him, she did as he asked.

"What're you doing?" she asked.

"No talking."

Her deep sigh was so filled with annoyance that he had to hold back a laugh. She was adorable and he loved her madly, even when she was willful and determined to get her way all the time, even in bed.

"I love you like this," he said, cupping her buttocks and squeezing.

"I thought we weren't allowed to talk?"

"You're not. I am."

"Not fair."

He bit his lip to keep from laughing. "Shhh. Just relax and let me love you."

"But I want to—"

He silenced her with a spank, a quick pop of his palm against her cheek that made her shudder. Discovering that his sexy, gorgeous, willful wife enjoyed being spanked had been one of the highlights in a year of incredible discoveries. Always careful to keep the focus on pleasure and not pain, he did it again and again and again, until her bottom was pink and her moans were all he could hear.

He spread her cheeks apart and bent to lick from her anus to her clit, sucking on the tight bundle of nerves as he sank two fingers into her. She came instantly, crying out from the force of her release. It was all he could do to hold back his own need to come as she let go so completely.

Taking himself in hand, he removed his fingers and replaced them with his cock, pumping into her and catching the end of her orgasm. Damn, she was amazing and tight and hot and so wet. He picked up the tube he'd placed next to him and squeezed out a dollop of lube that he spread over her back entrance.

She reacted immediately, gripping him with her internal muscles and gasping as he pressed two fingers past the tight ring of muscles. With his other hand he reached around to her clit.

"Jesus," she whispered, making him smile with the knowledge that he'd succeeded in emptying her mind of everything other than what was happening right here and now. He gave her his fingers and his cock, alternating so she was filled at all times while he pressed rhythmically against her clit. He loved her like this, completely at his mercy and accepting the pleasure she deserved.

The only thing that would make this better was if he could see her face, which he knew would be flushed and rosy from desire. He picked up the pace, hammering into her until he felt her come hard, her entire body seizing from the release that took him with her, surging into her until he was completely drained.

He withdrew his fingers and wrapped his arms around her, his face pressed against her back.

Sam's arms gave out and she slid to the mattress.

He went with her, still buried deep inside, feeling her muscles twitch in the aftermath of her release.

"You should not still be hard after that," she said after a long moment of silence.

Chuckling, he said, "I can't help it if once is never enough with you."

"You almost killed me with that one. Not sure I've got a second round in me tonight."

"I bet I can change your mind."

"I have no doubt that you can and will change my mind."

He cupped her breasts and toyed with her nipples.

"That was incredible, babe," she said softly.

"For me too."

She grasped one of the hands he had under her. "I love you."

He hugged her tightly. "I love you too."

FIFTEEN

ENSCONCED IN HIS parents' guest room with Christina, Gonzo was wide awake. He stood at the window and stared out at the light snowfall that had covered the yard. Alex would be excited to wake up to snow in the morning. Gonzo's parents had insisted on setting up the portable crib in their room so they could get up with him in the morning.

"Sleep in," they'd told him and Christina, knowing they were upset and afraid.

Sleep in. Right. How was he expected to sleep at all when he was so churned up over Lori's death and the suspicion that had focused on him—and Christina. They'd both had motive, the opportunity and the desire to see Lori permanently removed from their son's life, said one of the talking heads on cable news, which had gleefully picked up on the salacious stories coming from the Washington, D.C., Metropolitan Police Department.

Except neither he nor Christina would ever kill anyone, least of all the woman who'd given birth to Alex. Sure, he didn't like her very much, but she'd given them good reason not to like her. Starting with the day they'd met Alex when he was a couple of months old and found out she hadn't bothered to give his son a name.

Lori certainly hadn't endeared herself to his family, friends and colleagues when she came to the hospital after he was shot to stake her claim on Alex. Thankfully, he'd anticipated that possibility and had taken legal steps to ensure she couldn't take his son away from Christina and his parents if he were ever injured on the job.

Standing in front of the window, wearing only a pair of flannel pajama pants, he was cold, but he couldn't bring himself to go back to bed, where he would only lie there and spin.

"Tommy," Christina said, her voice sleepy and sweet.

"I'm here."

"What're you doing?"

"Looking at the snow."

"Come back to bed."

He'd rather stay up and pace all night, but that wouldn't help anything, so he joined her in bed.

"You're freezing! How long have you been up?"

"I don't know. Awhile."

She held out her arms to him, and he snuggled up to her.

Shivering, she said, "It's like snuggling with a polar bear."

"Sorry."

"I'm not. I love snuggling with you, even when you're freezing."

She was trying to take his mind off his worries. He knew that, but it wasn't working.

"You know what the worst part of all this is?" he asked.

"What?"

"All these years I've spent doing the right thing, chasing down criminals, taking scumbags off the street, earning promotions and commendations and getting shot in the neck and nearly dying not all that long ago. And it's like none of that ever happened. They just automatically assume, because I've had a beef with her, that I must've killed her."

"I know, baby."

"They just throw my name out there like it makes no

difference whatsoever that it's untrue. That all the good stuff I've spent my whole career doing doesn't matter."

"Would you consider talking to Darren? He was good to you after the shooting."

"That would be risky with so many people pointing the finger at me."

"So go on the record and say you had no reason to kill her. If your goal was to keep your son, that certainly wouldn't be the way to do it. You could also say how insulting it is to have your decorated career as a police officer swept aside in a sea of accusations and innuendo when there's no proof whatsoever that you had anything at all to do with Lori's death."

"You know, sometimes it's very convenient to be sleeping with a political operative."

Christina released the low, sexy laugh that he adored.

He wouldn't have expected to smile, but she always made him feel better.

"I take that to mean you like the idea?"

"Yeah, I do. I want to talk to Andy first, and make sure I won't be making anything worse."

"You need to talk to a criminal defense attorney, not a family law attorney. Maybe Bill Springer will take your case."

"Ha! Very funny. Can you imagine if I called him up and asked him to represent me?"

"It would give the reporters something else to talk about."

"No defense lawyers, for now anyway. The one thing I know for sure after all my years in Homicide is that the minute you lawyer up, everyone thinks you've got something to hide. I'll see what Andy says about talking to Darren and go from there."

"Do you feel any better?"

"Yeah," he said, "surprisingly I do."

"I find it always helps to have a plan."

"I find it always helps to have you. I don't know how I ever would've gotten through everything that's happened this year without you."

"And I couldn't have gotten through it without you."

He caressed her face and kissed her. "We really ought to get married one of these days."

"Any day you want."

"Yeah?"

"Yep."

"You don't want the big white deal?"

"I just want to be married to you. I couldn't care less about the big deal."

"Let's get past all this, and then we'll get serious about making that happen."

She rubbed soothing circles on his back. "I'm very sad about Lori. I wouldn't have wished this outcome on her, no matter how much trouble she might've caused for us. But we both know the truth—that we had nothing to do with it—so we can't let it suck the life out of us, you know? It's a challenge we have to get through, but it's not like when you were shot, and I didn't know if you were going to live. That was something else altogether."

"I know, honey. And you're right. I need to calm the hell down. All the accusations in the world don't change the truth."

"No, they don't. And tomorrow you can talk to Andy and maybe Darren and set the record straight."

"I just hope it doesn't do more harm than good."

"So do I."

SAM'S DAY BEGAN with a call from Lindsey at six. "Are you awake?" Lindsey asked, sounding chipper.

"Mmm, yeah."

"Sam. Wake up."

"I'm awake." Sam opened her eyes, looked around at the loft and realized she was alone under the comforter. "What's up?"

"I got DNA results for the semen found in Lori Phillips's vagina. We've got a match for your guy Hughes, but there was a second profile. I'm running that one now against the database. Thought you'd want to know there was a second guy."

"She had a busy last day, that's for sure. Booze and coke and two guys."

"Are you getting any closer to figuring this one out?"

"We've got a few leads to pursue today. We should know more by the end of the day."

"The morning papers have banner headlines, tying her to Gonzo and rehashing the custody case."

"Fantastic," Sam said. "That's just what we need."

"At least they aren't leading with Springer versus Farnsworth today."

"There is that. Thanks for the heads-up. I'll check in when I get to HQ."

"Tell your husband I said to have a good first day in the West Wing. Terry was up at four thirty because he was too excited to sleep. Thus my early arrival today."

"I'll tell him. See you later." She ended the call feeling guilty that she'd almost forgotten this would be Nick's first official day at the White House. It was probably more that she'd blocked it out. If she didn't think about it, it wasn't happening, right?

She'd no sooner had that thought when the vice president himself came up the stairs looking gorgeous and sexy in a dark suit with a white shirt and a red and blue striped tie. He was showered and shaved and breathtaking. A pang of fear struck her in the breastbone. Every woman in America would want him when they saw him on the news later in the day, because surely his first day would be big news.

For now, for this moment, he was all hers, and he came bearing her robe and a steaming cup of coffee. Sam sat up and let the comforter fall to her waist. She ran her fingers through her hair, straightening it. "You look good," she said, letting her gaze roam from his face down the front of him.

"You look *amazing*," he replied, his gaze fixed on her bare breasts. He sat on the edge of the lounge and leaned in to kiss her. "Morning."

"Morning." She took the mug of coffee from him and took a sip. "What time is it?"

He kissed her neck and made her squirm. "Six."

"You're leaving already?"

"Soon." He cupped her breasts and toyed with her nipples until they tightened. "I might be enticed to going in a little later though."

"You're all spiffy. I wouldn't want to mess you up."

He cupped her cheek and ran his thumb over her lips. "I love being messed up by you."

She offered a weak smile in return.

"What's wrong?"

"Nothing, why?"

"I know that look. Something is on your mind."

She ran her hand over the silky length of his tie. "Other than the fact that every female in America is going to be lusting after my sexy husband today?"

"Stop it. They will not."

"Nick, honey, trust me. They will."

Bending his head, he went to work on her neck, kissing and nibbling, not hard enough to leave a mark but just enough to make her squirm. "What about all the guys who'll be lusting after my sexy wife when she goes on TV this morning?"

"You smell so good."

"Is that your way of dodging the question?"

She shrugged.

"Do I have anything to worry about where you're concerned?"

"No," she said forcefully, surprised he would ask such a thing.

"Neither do you. You have absolutely nothing to be worried about. Every woman in the world could throw themselves at me, and the only one I'd want is the one I was lucky enough to marry."

Touched by his words, Sam took his hand and spun the wedding ring around on his finger, remembering the matching inscriptions on their rings that hadn't been planned. "I was pretty lucky that day too."

"We both were and we continue to be." He nuzzled her neck some more, setting off a surge of desire they had no time to accommodate. "Last night was so hot, babe. I'll be thinking about that all day today."

"You've got more important things to think about today," she said even as a heated flush overtook her face when she thought of the things they'd done.

"God, I love when you blush. It's the hottest thing ever. Well, second only to the sight of your sweet pink ass—"

Sam kissed him to make him stop talking.

He came up for air laughing. "What? Am I not allowed to talk about—"

She kissed him again. "Shut up about it or it'll never happen again."

"Oh, it'll happen again. As soon as possible, in fact."

"Don't you have a country to run? Go away and leave me alone, you sex-crazed beast."

He kissed the end of her nose and then her lips again. "To be continued. Don't you have somewhere to be at seven?"

Sam groaned at the reminder of her TV date with the chief. "Me and my big mouth."

"I *love* your big mouth."

"Somehow I don't think we're talking about the same thing here."

"I could show you what I'm thinking about."

"I don't have time for one of your demonstrations."

"All right, if you're going to be that way and send me off to my first day at the White House with an embarrassing hard-on."

"You did that to yourself."

"Um, I believe your bare-breasted hair thing did it to me."

"What bare-breasted hair thing?"

"You sat there, bare-breasted, and gathered your hair into a thing." He spun his hand around.

"A bun?"

"Yeah that. Again, with the bare breasts. That's really all it takes. In fact, thinking about that later will have the same effect."

"Are you really thirty-seven or seventeen?"

"A little of both when it comes to you." Seeming resigned to his fate, he stood and held her robe for her.

"If I get up, all bare breasted and whatnot, is that going to lead to other things we don't have time for?"

"You'll have to do it and see what happens."

Sam placed the mug on the table next to the lounge and got up slowly. Though her body ached in quite a few places, she felt languid and satisfied overall. She loved watching his gaze heat as she stood naked before him. Then she turned and he wrapped the robe and his arms around her.

"You're a sexy vixen."

She laughed. "I like that word."

"You dazzle me."

"Right back atcha, Mr. VP."

"We need to do something awesome for our anniversary."

"What do you have in mind?"

"I'm not sure yet. Let me think about it and get back to you."

"I'll await your reply."

"Plan to take that week off, okay?"

"Can you do that?" she asked.

"I have no idea, but I'm doing it." He pushed his hard cock against her bottom. "And doing it, and doing it and doing it for a whole week."

"Nick?"

"Yeah, baby?"

"Sometimes I still can't believe I get to have this— you—every day for the rest of my life."

He hugged her tighter and nuzzled his face in her hair. "Neither can I. I look at you and think, damn, I'm the luckiest guy in the history of the world."

"I never thought anyone would feel that way about me. You may not know this, but I'm kind of a pain in the ass."

"No! I had no idea."

She pressed her elbow teasingly into his belly. "Hope you have an awesome first day at the White House."

"It's already an awesome day, no matter what else happens." He held her for another minute or maybe it was two before he let her go.

Sam tied the robe around her waist, picked up the mug

of coffee and took his outstretched hand. "You had to clean up all the clothes from last night, huh?"

"Of course I did. Do you know me at all?"

"You're an anal-retentive freakazoid."

"I'm neat. There's a difference."

"Freakazoid."

"Speaking of anal…"

"Do not speak of anal. We have to go to work."

"I want to speak of it."

"No! There're Secret Service agents at the bottom of the stairs and a boy sleeping in his room who'd be scarred for life if he overheard that. Now be quiet and behave like the second most important man in the free world, will you please?"

"I don't like having to behave."

She gave him a gentle shove toward the stairs. "Move it. I need to hit the shower and make myself presentable."

"We're going to talk about the *A* word later. I have needs," he said with a teasing glint in his eye.

Needs that had been met in the past by someone else, not that he'd ever come right out and said that. He'd shrugged when she asked him if he'd done that before, and it had nagged at her ever since that he'd done it with someone else and not her.

He escorted her downstairs, past the agent outside Scotty's door and into their bedroom, closing the door behind him. "Why did you just go silent on me?"

"Perhaps it was because you were attempting to have an inappropriate conversation that could be overheard by all the wrong people?"

"How is that conversation inappropriate? You went quiet. I want to know why."

She turned to face him. "Because! It drives me crazy that you've done that with someone else and not me. But I don't even know if I want to. I just know that I don't want you to have anything with someone else that you haven't had with me."

He stared at her, an incredulous expression on his handsome face. "Samantha, for the love of God, I have never had *anything* with anyone else that could *ever* be compared to what I have with you."

"You had that."

"So what? Do you think I spend one second of my life thinking about people who never mattered to me a fraction as much as you do?"

"I don't know. Do you?"

"Look at me, babe."

It was easier to have this conversation with her back to him, but she did as he asked.

He looked her straight in the eye. "I don't think about anyone but you. I think about you so much there's no room for thoughts of anyone else."

"But still, you want that."

"I want that with *you*, because I think you'd love it, *not* because I've done it before and dream about the good old days."

"I hate that you've done stuff with other people that you haven't done with me."

"Samantha! Baby, listen to me, I've never had anything like this before. Not even close."

"You said you have needs."

"I was *joking* because I love the way you get all redfaced when we talk about any kind of kinky sex." With his hands on her hips, he tugged her into his embrace. "I can't bear the thought of something like this bothering you so much."

"It doesn't bother me a lot," Sam said, beginning to feel foolish for making an issue of it. "Just a little."

"Please don't let it bother you at all. If we get there, we get there. If we don't, we don't. You can't possibly think that I find anything lacking in our sex life. For God's sake, Sam, we're like bunnies. There can't be a more sexually satisfied husband in all of America than I am."

She couldn't help but chuckle at the emphatic way he said that.

With his hands on her face he gazed at her with those incredible hazel eyes that saw right through her. "You have nothing, and I do mean *nothing* to be insecure about where I'm concerned. I'm your slave, babe."

Sam slipped her arms inside his suit coat and clung to him.

He wrapped his arms around her. "Please tell me you know that."

"I do. Of course I do, and it's silly of me to be worried about ancient history."

"Yes, it is silly. How could you think I'm not entirely thrilled with every single thing about our life together? Well, except for the parts where you get shot at or pistol-whipped or run off the road. I could live without that shit."

She smiled up at him. "So could I."

Looking down at her, he said, "I don't like knowing you have these insecurities. What'll we do about that?"

"They're not insecurities so much as a desire to experience everything there is to experience with you."

"That we can do, as long as it's not tied to some misbegotten notion that you have to live up to some expectations that I don't have."

"Okay."

He held her for another minute. "Are we good?"

"We're great. We're incredible."

"Yes, we are. We're incredible exactly the way we are, and don't you ever forget it."

"I won't." She went up on tiptoes to kiss him. "Now go run the country while I get ready for TV."

"I'll see you tonight."

"Yes, you will."

"I love you so much, Samantha. I wish I had the words to tell you how much."

"You just did a pretty good job. And PS, I love you just as much."

He kissed her again and then let her go. "Be careful out there today."

"Always am. Got far too much to live for to screw up, so don't worry."

"That's like telling me not to breathe."

"Be gone with you. I have to beautify."

His phone chimed with a text that he glanced at. "Crap, it's from Shelby. She's sick and not able to work today."

"No word about why she was at the ER?"

"No, that's all she said."

"Well, damn, that changes the day."

"Not really. The agents can get Scotty to and from school, and they'll be here with him when he gets home."

"So now we're relying on them to babysit?"

"He hardly needs babysitting. He's thirteen."

"Still, how warm and fuzzy to come home to his Secret Service detail."

"Tell you what, I'll suggest he go to Skip and Celia's after school, and I'll give her a heads-up that he'll be coming if it's okay with them."

"That'll work. I'll check in with them too. I just hope Shelby's okay. I'll try to get a chance to call her."

"Sounds good. I'll get him up, and I'll see you later at the reception if you can make it."

Sam would never admit that she'd forgotten all about the reception. "Good luck today."

"Thanks, you too." He stole one more kiss on the way out the door.

Sam headed for the shower, her mind swirling after their conversation. It never failed to amaze her how different her second marriage was from her first. She and Peter hadn't talked about the things she and Nick covered so effortlessly. Everything was on the table with Nick, and she loved that about their marriage.

She hurried through a shower, took the time to blow-dry and straighten her hair and chose a black suit with a cranberry silk blouse under it for TV. She shoved jeans, a sweater and her trusty hiking boots into a backpack to change into later. From the bedside table, she withdrew her service weapon, which she tucked into the waistband of her skirt, as well as her badge, cuffs and notebook, which she put in the backpack.

When she got downstairs, Scotty was finishing a bowl of cereal while watching *Sports Center* on Nick's iPad.

"Wow, you look nice," he said. "Why are you all dressed up?"

"Going on TV this morning with Chief Farnsworth."

"Oh, hey, that's cool. How come?"

"There's been a lot of crap flying around since the Springer investigation, and we're going to tell our side of it. Or try to anyway."

"That's a good idea."

She ran her fingers through his hair. "It was *my* idea."

"It's a good one."

"Unless of course it blows up in our faces."

"Don't let that happen."

If only it were that simple. She downed a piece of peanut butter toast, then went back upstairs to brush her teeth and check her appearance one last time. In deference to her TV appearance, she slipped on her engagement ring and the diamond key necklace. She released a deep breath. Being on TV always made her incredibly nervous, but she was glad to do anything that might help take some of the heat off the chief.

Sam went downstairs where Scotty was putting the lunch Nick had made for him into his backpack.

"Nick told you Shelby is out today, so you'll be coming home with the agents and going to Skip's if it's okay with them?"

"Yeah, he said he'll text me after he talks to them."

"Sounds like a plan then."

"Is Shelby okay?"

"I think so. She didn't say what was wrong, but I'm sure she'd be happy to hear from you if you text her later."

"I'll do that. Are we going to Nick's reception at the White House? He ironed my work clothes for me."

As Sam wondered what the heck time her husband had gotten up—or if his insomnia had kept him up all night—she hugged her son. "I hope to be able to go. I'll let you know."

"Okay."

"Have a good day, buddy. I love you."

"Love you too." He paused before he said, "Hey, Sam?"

"Yeah?"

"Last night I told Nick that at some point, when it feels right, I'd like to call him Dad. Would it be okay if I did the same with you?"

The request hit her like a ton of bricks to the chest. "You wanna call me Dad?" she asked, making light of it so she wouldn't bawl her head off.

"Sam," he said impatiently. "You know what I mean."

She went to him, because how could she not? "Yes, I know what you mean, and nothing would make me happier in the entire world than for you to call me Dad. I mean Mom."

Scotty laughed. "You're such a dork."

"You're a bigger dork."

"Doubtful."

"We'll continue this conversation later, my friend. I've got TV people waiting for me."

"I've got algebra waiting for me. I'd rather be you."

"I'd rather be me too."

Debra, one of Scotty's agents, came into the kitchen. "Ready to roll?"

"Ready," he said. "See ya, Sam."

"I'll walk you out."

SIXTEEN

AFTER BATTLING TRAFFIC, she arrived at the CBC studios on Connecticut Avenue, stressing out about how close she was calling it. In full uniform, the chief greeted her in the reception area.

"Was I supposed to wear the uniform?" she asked.

"No, you look great. I just thought it would be appropriate for me to wear it today."

"And you wear it well. Don't let anyone ever tell you otherwise."

"I appreciate you doing this. I know it's not something you'd do for just anyone."

"If I have to put up with all the interest, I may as well take advantage of it when it suits my purposes."

"Was Nick okay with it?"

"He was all for it. He agrees with me. He informed me last night that I'm *famous* now, and I may as well make the most of it."

"Famous," the chief said with a snicker. "You were infamous before he was ever vice president."

"I know, right?"

He shook his head at her snappy comeback. "Any word on the Phillips investigation this morning?"

"Just that she was with two guys before she died, one of them Mr. Hughes from Baltimore. Lindsey is trying to identify the second profile, if he's in the system. We're going to dig in to the church she belonged to today, among other leads."

"And Sergeant Gonzales?"

"Safely out of town at his parents' place in Harper's Ferry for the time being, where he's about to spontaneously combust."

"Let's take the opportunity today to mention he's not a suspect."

"We're on the same page there."

The producer came out to get them and led them through winding corridors filled with cages and wires and all sorts of other junk that Sam wanted to stop to take a closer look at. They were deposited into a waiting room where coffee and donuts were available to guests.

"I'll be back to get you in a few minutes," the producer said.

"Thank you," the chief said. To Sam, he said, "Coffee? Donut?"

"You go ahead. I'm all set." She was too nervous to risk more coffee making her stomach ache during the interview. A TV mounted in the corner showed the on-air anchors delivering the morning's headlines, including an update about the mother of Detective Sergeant Gonzales's son being found dead days after she went public with the conflict of interest in their custody case. Of course there was no mention of how seriously injured he'd recently been in the line of duty.

"It's infuriating," the chief said quietly.

"For him too. All those years of decorated service disregarded like they mean nothing."

"Say that today. As often as you can."

"It won't look like I'm defending my friend?"

"So what if it does? It's true."

"You're feisty today," she said, smiling at him.

"I'm pissed off with the way my department is being portrayed in the media lately."

"Do the Public Affairs people know they're sending out a pissed-off chief today?"

He winked at her. "We'll let that be our little secret."

Laughing, she said, "Until you take it to the airwaves."

Farnsworth shrugged. "What can they do? Smear me in the news? Check. Already done."

"Have you heard from the mayor?"

"She's called a couple of times. I might've forgotten to call her back."

Sam snorted. "See why I love you so much? You're awesome."

"I could say the same about you, Lieutenant. No one has made me look better during my tenure as chief than the firebrand who runs my Homicide Division and also happens to be my niece."

Though she was touched through and through by the compliment, she nudged him with her elbow. "Stop being so schmoopy. Next they'll be saying we're having an affair the way Stahl used to."

"*Stahl* said *that*?"

"All the time. How else could I possibly get the chief to do whatever I wanted him to?"

"I hate that bastard. I'm so glad he's gone for good."

"Is he?" Sam asked.

"He can't come back from assaulting you outside your own home. There's no way he gets out of that with the Secret Service agents prepared to testify to witnessing it."

"Speaking of witnessing things, Sanborn's trial starts this week."

"How's McBride handling that?"

"She's handling it. Sort of."

"I hate that she has to relive that nightmare in open court."

"So do I, but it was way too much to hope for that Sanborn would take a plea deal and spare her having to testify. I worry that it's going to set her back to day one."

"Do whatever you need to as her commander to get her through it."

"I will, thank you." Her phone dinged with a text from Captain Malone. Peter Gibson rented another apartment near the old one and was in Florida for the holiday. Cross him off the list. He'd included Peter's new address for Sam's information.

She breathed a sigh of relief to know that whatever was going on, it had nothing to do with her ex-husband. Thanks, she wrote back to the captain. Now about Stahl.

Still looking for him.

Farnsworth checked his watch. "What the hell is taking so long? They told us to be here at seven and it's seven twenty."

"I'm sure we'll be on soon. How many do we have after this one?"

"Four."

"*Four?*"

He shrugged. "Can I help it that everyone wanted us when they heard you were coming?"

"Shit fuck damn hell."

"Language, Lieutenant."

"I'd apologize except I meant every word. Don't they know I have a murderer to catch?"

"Oh, they know, but according to the Public Affairs people they were, and I quote, 'Creaming their jeans' when they heard you were part of the package."

"That's just nasty."

"Don't kill the messenger." He was still laughing at his own joke when the producer returned to lead them onto the set, which was like half of a fancy living room. The other side was filled with cameras and wires and people wearing headphones. A young, extremely thin Asian woman fitted them with wireless microphones.

"It's super cool to meet you, Mrs. Cappuano," she said after she clipped the mike onto Sam's lapel.

"Thanks, you too." She caught the chief's glance and noted he was trying not to laugh. He was in an awfully jolly mood for a guy who'd been skewered on a daily basis for weeks now. And hey, if her notoriety helped to ease some of his tension, she was happy to be the butt of his jokes.

During a commercial break they were shown to the sofa. Monica Taylor, one of the bottle blondes from the media scrum that covered the police department, shook hands with both of them, welcoming them like they were old friends. "I can't tell you what an honor it is to have our nation's second lady joining us this morning."

"I'm here as Lieutenant Holland," Sam said, wishing now she'd thought to clip her badge to her jacket before she left the house. "Not as the second lady."

"Yes, of course." Monica flashed a blinding white smile that had Sam wondering if she gargled bleach to make that happen.

"We're live in five, four, three..."

"Welcome back to *Good Morning D.C.*, I'm Monica Taylor, and we're delighted today to welcome two very special guests, Metropolitan Police Chief Joseph Farnsworth and Lieutenant Cappuano."

"Holland," Sam said with a glare at Monica. "Lieutenant Holland."

"Oh, yes, of course. My bad."

Right, Sam wanted to say. *Sure it was.*

"It's just that we're all so excited about our new second family, and naturally there's curiosity—"

"Is that why we're here? To talk about the curiosity

about my family? I thought we were here to talk about the baseless accusations Bill Springer has been making about the chief and the department since his sons were killed in November."

"That's what I thought too," the chief said.

Visibly rattled, Monica said, "Yes, of course, we want to talk about all of that." Thankfully, she seemed to get that grilling Sam about being the vice president's wife was a no-go. "Let's talk about the accusations Bill Springer has made and give you a chance to respond to some of them. Let's start with his claim that his older son, Billy, is dead today because of you."

"I know Mr. Springer would like to be able to blame it all on me," Farnsworth said. "If I were in his shoes, I'd be looking for someone to blame too. I mean, how does a man deal with the knowledge that a child he brought into this world is capable of murdering his own brother and eight other innocents? How do parents ever accept that their son was a big-time drug dealer who'd been on our radar for more than a year before he was killed? Do I regret that Billy Springer died at the hands of my officers? Of course I do, but do I blame anyone but Billy Springer for creating a situation in which it was necessary for my officers to shoot him? No, I don't."

"Lieutenant, how do you feel about Mr. Springer's allegation?"

"Like the chief said, I believe he's looking for someone to blame, because without that, he's forced to accept that his son was a murderer."

"Mr. Springer blames you, directly, Chief, for his son's death because you put the homicide investigation on hold so your officers could complete the narcotics investigation. Does he have a point there?"

"He is correct in stating that I put the homicide investigation on hold—briefly—in order to give my Vice detectives, who'd been undercover with Billy Springer, twelve hours to complete a six-month investigation. He is incorrect in placing the blame for Billy's death on me. It was Billy Springer's decision to take his grandmother and cousins hostage that day. It was Billy Springer's decision to shoot at my officers, gravely wounding one of them. If neither of those things had happened, Billy would still be alive today and we wouldn't be having this conversation."

"Do you concur, Lieutenant?"

"Absolutely," Sam said. "Billy Springer almost killed Detective Sergeant Gonzales, who was shot in the neck and would've bled out if not for the quick action of his partner, Detective Arnold. Mr. Springer doesn't seem to want to talk about how Sergeant Gonzales was wounded so seriously. He doesn't want to talk about the eyewitness we have who was able to identify Billy as the person who killed Hugo Springer as well as the other eight young people in the Springers' basement. None of that seems to matter to Mr. Springer. He would put all the blame on the police who responded to an active hostage situation and acted appropriately in light of Billy's decision to shoot at us."

"What I don't understand," Monica said tentatively, "is how Billy found out that you were looking at him for the murders of his brother and the other young people?"

"We'd like to know that too," Farnsworth said. "We're conducting an internal investigation to determine if any of our people were involved in conveying that information to Billy the night before he was killed. To our knowledge, none of the undercover detectives who'd gotten close to Billy saw him between the time I put the homicide investigation on hold and the time he took his grandmother and cousins hostage in Friendship Heights. We're working on establishing a timeline and trying to determine the chain of events. When we have answers, we'll make them public. Until then, all we can say is we don't know how he found out, but we'd like to know as much as everyone else."

"Lieutenant, your niece was assaulted at the party at the Springer home. Can you tell us how she is doing today?"

Pissed off by the question, Sam said, "She's doing very well and completing her senior year of high school."

"You mentioned Sergeant Gonzales, and I'd like to follow up on that by asking about his possible involvement in the death of his son's mother, Lori Phillips."

"Sergeant Gonzales had nothing to do with the death of Lori Phillips," Farnsworth said sternly, "and it's irresponsible for the media to be tossing accusations around without any proof to back them up."

"Well, it's true that Ms. Phillips has been making waves recently, going public with the sergeant's connection to the judge who heard their custody case."

"There's a huge difference between being at odds with someone and killing them," Sam said defiantly. "Sergeant Gonzales is one of the best and most capable police officers I've ever worked with. He's a valuable member of my team, and he was nearly killed not that long ago in service to this city. I find it appalling that anyone would insinuate he was capable of murder a few short weeks after you were all calling him a hero. It's disgusting."

"It's a natural assumption," Monica said, her cool blond perfection beginning to curdle as it became clear to her that she was seriously outmatched.

"We don't work on assumptions, Ms. Taylor," Sam said. "We work on facts and evidence, and there's not a single iota of evidence that ties Sergeant Gonzales to the murder of Lori Phillips, and to imply otherwise is to open yourself and your employer to massive litigation."

"There's no need to get hostile, Lieutenant."

"There's every need to get hostile, Ms. Taylor. This is a man's life and reputation you all are playing with. It's nothing to you to report he's a suspect when he is absolutely *not* a suspect. Does it occur to you that you're ruining someone's life when you toss around words like *suspect* and *ax to grind* or some of the other things we've heard in the last twenty-four hours?"

"It looks like we're out of time. I want to thank our guests for joining me today, and we'll be right back after this check of the weather and traffic."

Sam stood and pulled the microphone off, tossing it on the sofa behind her. "Your journalism professors must be rolling in their graves."

"I didn't go to journalism school," Monica said testily.

"Oh, really? I couldn't tell. If Sergeant Gonzales chooses to file suit against you and others for implying he was guilty of murder, and I wouldn't blame him if he did, I'll back him up with everything I've got."

"We're done here," Monica said. "Thanks for coming in."

Farnsworth took Sam by the arm before she could tear the bitch's head off, and half-dragged her out of there. "That was fucking awesome," he said as soon as they cleared the shell-shocked set. Producers, directors and camera people stopped what they were doing to watch them go by.

"Language, Chief," Sam said, even though she was amused by his assessment. "She's a stupid bitch. The minute she dragged my niece into the discussion, the gloves came off."

"You were awesome. If I'm ever truly in trouble, I want you to defend me."

"Ha! You'll go up the river for life."

"Nah, the jurors would be too afraid of you to convict me."

"You were pretty damn good yourself," she said.

"Why, thank you. I paled in comparison to the second lady."

"Bite me. Do we really get to do this four more times?"

"Yep."

"Something tells me this day isn't going to suck as bad as I thought it was."

Their euphoria lasted until they emerged from the TV station to find Deputy Chief Conklin waiting for them. "Bill Springer was found dead this morning."

SHELBY AWOKE SORE and disoriented. She was supposed to be somewhere. Scotty. He was back to school today. And Nick. His first day at the White House. She needed to be there.

And then she remembered what had happened the day before and sagged back into the pillows. Avery's pillows. She was in his bed, in his room, in his house, even after he'd confessed to having had feelings for Sam.

Despite all his efforts to make it right, Shelby still felt sick over what three people she considered close friends, three people she loved, had kept from her.

And yes, she loved all of them—or she had before yesterday. Now she wasn't sure how she felt about any of them.

Snippets of conversation and odd moments ran through her mind, punishing her with the realization that the signs of something afoot had been there all along. However, she'd chosen not to dig in to them. Like the time she'd asked Sam why Nick didn't like Avery.

"Who knows?" Sam had said. "Guys are so weird."

But she'd known why. Everyone had known why—except her. Did Scotty know too? Wouldn't that make it all perfect?

At some point she'd have to talk to Sam and Nick about

this, and the thought of that conversation made her nauseated. How did you bring up such a topic with your employers who were also your friends?

She shifted to find a more comfortable position, and her knees burned from the movement. She wasn't sure which hurt more—her knees or her heart.

Avery came into the room wearing a D.C. Federals T-shirt and black sweats. It wasn't fair that he looked as sexy in sweats as he did in a three-thousand-dollar suit. He carried a steaming mug that he deposited on the bedside table.

"What've you got there?"

"That lemon tea you like. You can still have that, right?"

"Yeah, it's decaf." She didn't want to be touched by his thoughtful gesture, but she could see he was trying. Reaching for the mug, she took a sip and felt the heat travel through her.

"How did you sleep?" he asked.

"Okay. You?"

"Not so great." He tucked a strand of hair behind her ear. "I hate that I hurt you, Shelby. That's the last thing I'd ever want to do."

"I want to believe that. You have no idea how badly I want to believe that."

"You *can* believe it." He hesitated before he continued. "I was in a bad place when you and I met. I won't deny that. But you and I, we've built something here. Or at least I thought we had."

"I thought so too." Trying to keep her emotions in check, Shelby took another sip of her tea. "I'm almost forty-three, Avery. I'm pregnant with what will probably be my only child. For years, I put on weddings for happy couples and all the while I wondered if I would ever get my fairy tale. And then I met you, and I started to entertain the possibility that it *was* going to happen for me after all. Until I found out you were actually in love with my friend."

He took her hand and brought it to his lips, a move that would've made her swoon two days ago. "I never had anything with her. I've had everything with you. There's no comparison."

Okay, that was a good thing for him to say. He was charming. She'd give him that.

"And before you think I'm saying what you need to hear, ask yourself why I'd do that if I didn't want to protect what I have with you? If I wasn't invested, why would I bother to try to fix this?" As he spoke, he gently stroked her cheek with his index finger.

Electrified by his touch, Shelby looked up to find his golden eyes looking at her with everything she'd hoped to one day find in a partner. "I guess you wouldn't bother."

"No, I wouldn't, and yet all I thought about during a sleepless night was how I could fix it. I thought about how lonely I'd be without you and your pink perfection, and I didn't like how that felt. I didn't like it at all. So you see, Shelby, you have to forgive me because you wouldn't want me to be lonely and sad without you, would you?"

Laughing as she wiped away tears, she said, "You're fighting dirty, Agent Hill."

"I'm fighting for you, Shelby Faircloth. Will you please find it in your heart to forgive me for keeping something from you that I absolutely should've told you a long time ago? Will you try to put this in the past where it belongs so we can focus together on the future?"

The sweet Southern cadence of his speech was enough on its own to make her want to beg *him* for forgiveness. "I'll try because I want very much to focus on the future with you. But I need a little time to process it all. And I need to talk to Sam in particular and possibly Nick too."

"You do whatever you need to do, sweetheart. I'll be right here waiting for you to tell me we're okay again." With his finger on her chin, he tipped her face up to receive his kiss.

Shelby loved kissing him. She loved everything with him. More than anything, she loved that he'd apologized and took responsibility for causing her pain. That, right there, made him different from any other man she'd ever spent time with.

He took the tea from her and put it back on the table.

Shelby put her arms around his neck and drew him close to her, breathing in the sexy masculine scent that she'd become addicted to.

When he nuzzled her neck, she turned her head ever so slightly, putting her lips in line with his. He gazed into her eyes for a long, breathless moment before he took her mouth in a desperate kiss.

Shelby gave in to the desire he stirred in her every time he held her and kissed her this way. As always, she was powerless to resist him, even knowing she probably should.

SEVENTEEN

"WHAT'VE WE GOT?" Sam asked when she walked into Bill Springer's Georgetown office.

Officer Peterson, a patrolman, consulted his notes. "Bill Springer, age sixty-three, was found by his assistant, Pamela Desjardens, when she arrived for work at seven thirty-five. The office lights were on, Mr. Springer was on the floor and there was no sign of a struggle."

The result of a struggle could be cleaned up in the aftermath, Sam thought. "Forced entry?"

"Not that we were able to ascertain."

"Have you touched him?"

"Only to check for a pulse."

Sam squatted to take a closer look at the body. Like Lori Phillips, he had ligature marks around his neck that were indicative of manual strangling.

"Where's the admin?"

"Across the hall at one of the other offices. She was freaking out, and she has a friend over there. I thought it would be okay for her to wait there to speak to you."

"Good call, Peterson."

"Oh, thanks."

"Let's get Crime Scene here and do a canvas of the other offices in the building to see if anyone heard anything. You've called the ME?"

"On her way."

Sam turned to the chief, who stood in the hallway looking down at the man who'd caused him endless grief in the last few weeks. Farnsworth's face had taken on that grayish hue again after hearing the news about Bill Springer. Beside him, Deputy Chief Conklin took in the scene.

"What're you thinking, Lieutenant?" Conklin asked.

"That someone is trying to make trouble for the MPD. Big trouble." She went over to Springer's desk, where a planner sat open. She pulled on a pair of gloves and flipped through the last few days, noting the lack of anything written on the most recent pages. Either he'd stopped writing down his appointments or he'd stopped taking them. "I'd like to talk to the admin."

"Sure, right this way." Peterson led them across the hall to where a young blonde sat on a sofa, being comforted by another woman. "Ms. Desjardens, this is Lieutenant Holland, Chief Farnsworth and Deputy Chief Conklin. They'd like to talk to you about what happened this morning."

She nodded and wiped tears from her face. "I... I got to work early and...and Bill...he was on the floor. I went to him, and he was cold. So cold."

"Ms. Desjardens, do you know of anyone who might've wanted to harm Mr. Springer?"

She shook her head. "He hadn't been working much lately. After everything with his sons..."

"How long have you worked for him?"

"About two years now?"

"And were you *only* his employee?" Sam asked, playing a hunch.

She looked up at Sam, her tear-ravaged face red and swollen. "What?"

"Were you involved with Mr. Springer in any other way than professionally?"

"We were friends, if that's what you're asking."

"It's not what I'm asking, as we all know."

"You don't have to answer that, Pam," the other woman said with a scowl for Sam.

"Um, yeah, she does have to answer."

The air around them vibrated with anticipation.

"He'd been through a lot lately. It was a really upsetting time."

"Uh-huh," Sam said as her patience ran out. "Were you sleeping with him, Pam?"

She dropped her head into her hands, her shoulders heaving with sobs.

The other woman rubbed her back while continuing to glare at Sam. "Don't you have any compassion?"

"Lots of it, but I've also got a dead body across the hall, and I'm trying to figure out what happened to him."

"You should ask your chief. He had a good reason to see Mr. Springer dead."

"Except he didn't kill him, so you might want to watch out for lobbing baseless accusations at innocent people. Pamela, I need you to answer the question, or we'll have to transport you to HQ to discuss this further."

"You're going to arrest me?"

"Only if you don't cooperate."

"Yes! I slept with him. Are you happy now?"

"Not particularly. Lot of paperwork involved with dead bodies. Makes for a complicated day. How long had you been banging him?"

"Awhile," she said through gritted teeth.

"How long?"

"I don't know."

"Every woman knows the exact date she first had sex with the guy in her life. So how long are we talking? A week? A month? A year?"

"A year," she said softly, so softly Sam almost didn't hear her.

"That's a long time. So this was about more than comforting him after his tragic losses then, huh?"

"I loved him! He loved me! He was going to leave his
wife, and then Hugo was killed and Billy."

"Anyone in your life unhappy that you were getting busy
with a guy old enough to be your father? Like your own
father? An ex-boyfriend or a protective older brother?"

She shook her head. "No one knew."

"No one at all? You didn't tell a girlfriend or the woman
who worked across the hall from you?" She eyed the
friend. "No one?"

"I didn't tell anyone. Bill said… He said we had to keep
it quiet until he got divorced or she'd take him for everything he had. We were going to move to Florida." All at
once it seemed to dawn on her that she wouldn't be moving
to Florida or anywhere else with Bill Springer. She broke
down into heartbroken sobs, leaning into her friend, who
kept an arm around her.

"Do you have a way to get home?" Sam asked.

"I'll take her," the friend said.

"I'll need both of you to write down your names and
phone numbers in case we have follow-up questions." Sam
handed her notebook to the friend and then turned to Farnsworth and Conklin. They'd tried to talk the chief out of
coming here, but he'd insisted. "What do you make of it?"

"I have no idea what to make of it," Farnsworth said.
"We need to notify Springer's wife and family."

"I'll do it," Sam said, though she had no desire to be the
one to bring more bad news to Mrs. Springer. "You should
get out of here before the media catches wind."

"I agree, Chief," Conklin said. "You shouldn't be here."

"Fine, let's go," Farnsworth said. "You'll keep me
posted?"

"Of course." After they left, Sam retrieved her notebook from the women. "Stay local in case we need to reach you."

Pamela nodded as she stared vacantly at the far wall of her friend's office. "What am I supposed to do now? I don't know what I'm supposed to do."

"Let's get you home, Pam," the friend said.

Sam walked out of the office to find Peterson in the hallway. "Anything on the canvas?"

"Not yet. We haven't found anyone who was here last night."

Lindsey McNamara came through the door from the stairwell, carrying her field case. "Morning," she said.

"Morning, Doc." Sam gestured for Lindsey to follow her into Springer's office. "Keep me posted, Peterson."

"Yes, ma'am."

"This is going to be another shitstorm, huh?" Lindsey asked when they were alone with Springer's body. She secured her long red hair into a ponytail before getting to work assessing the victim.

"Yeah." Sam removed her suit jacket and tossed it over a chair. "Can you give me an estimated time of death?"

"Based on the temperature and the rigor, I'd say sometime before midnight, but I can't give you anything exact until I get him back to the lab."

"Roll with me for a second here."

"Sure."

"First we have the woman who accused Gonzo of conspiring with the judge to screw her out of custody of their kid. Then we have the lawyer who's been all over the chief about the botched investigation. Call me crazy, but this feels like a deliberate effort to undermine the department."

"I can see why you'd think so, but is it possible that neither murder had anything to do with the department?"

"Of course it's *possible*, but the murders of two people

who were causing trouble for us in two days feels too calculated to be random."

"So what're you thinking?"

"I'm not sure yet."

"Saw you on TV. You guys rocked it. I was cracking up laughing in pity for poor Monica."

"She was a boob. Five seconds before she referred to me as Lieutenant Cappuano, I'd told her I was not there as the vice president's wife."

"You certainly did a good job of reminding people not to jump to conclusions."

"Imagine the conclusions they'll jump to when this hits the news."

"Gonna be ugly," Lindsey said bluntly.

Sam waited for the Crime Scene detectives to arrive and for Lindsey's team to remove Springer's body. People from other offices stood in the hallway to watch the proceedings. She figured she had a matter of minutes to get to Mrs. Springer before the news hit Twitter or Facebook.

As she drove to the MacArthur Boulevard home of Marissa Springer, Sam called Freddie.

"Hey," he said softly. "What's up?"

"Someone killed Springer."

"Seriously? Oh my God. Hang on just a second." When he came back, he spoke in a normal tone. "What the hell is going on?"

"I have no freaking clue, but we're going to need to get one fast before our department gets dragged through the mud even worse than we have been lately."

"I was watching the news this morning. You and the chief killed it on CBC."

"For all the good it did us. The second the news about Springer hits, people will forget all about that."

"What can I do?"

"Are you working today?"

"Elin is still in the hospital."

"Oh, damn, really? How come?"

"The punch broke bones in her face. They kept her for observation. I'm not sure when they're going to let her out."

"You should be with her. Take a personal day."

"You need me. With Gonzo out—"

"We're okay. Take care of her and check in with me later."

"She'll probably be going home later, and I can work from home. Hit me up if I can help."

"I will. Tell Elin I hope she feels better."

"Will do."

Sam ended the call with her partner, and placed a second call, her stomach clenching as she pressed Send.

Hill answered on the second ring. "Good morning, Lieutenant."

"Yeah, hey, so I need your help."

"Really. Did it pain you to say those words?"

"More than you know. Bill Springer was found murdered in his office this morning."

"Seriously? *Fuck.*"

"You said it. I need you, Avery. I need someone outside the department making sure we aren't going to get totally screwed by this."

"I'm not working today. Terrell is available."

"I need *you*, not your deputy. You."

"I have a situation on the home front. I need to be here."

"What kind of situation does a single guy with no kids have on the home front?"

"A badly injured girlfriend."

Sam sighed with frustration about the case and empathy for her friend. "So she's badly injured? I though Cruz said she only skinned her knees. It's not the baby, is it?"

"The baby is fine. She's just… I can't leave."

"What aren't you telling me, Hill?"

His deep sigh set off a whole new wave of anxiety within Sam. "She found out about the thing, between us, back when we first met."

"There was no *thing* between us! What the hell?"

"The one-sided thing."

"You fucking *told* her that? Is this why she called in sick today? She's pissed with *us*?"

"She called in sick today because her knees and hands are a mess and the ER docs advised her to take it easy for a few days."

"And because she's pissed."

"Maybe a little."

"A little. Right. Thanks a lot for this. I can't tell you how much I appreciate you sharing something like that with her."

"I like her, Sam. It was way past time to be honest with her."

"So now she thinks you're dating her to get closer to me."

"I assured her that is not the case."

"Way to go, Hill. Seriously, great job." Sam thought about when Shelby and Avery were first dating and how she'd told Shelby to keep him far, far away from them— Nick in particular. Now Shelby knew why and was hurt. Excellent. "This is just what we needed with Nick starting the new job and me dealing with someone who has a beef with my colleagues."

"I'm sorry if the timing was inconvenient for you, Lieutenant."

"Forget I called. I don't need your help with this or anything else." She hung up on him and threw the phone into the passenger seat. "Motherfucker!"

Her mind reeled with the implications of Shelby finding out about Avery's so-called crush. What Shelby must be thinking! *Ugh*. As Sam pulled onto MacArthur Boulevard, she took a call from Gonzo.

"Hey, how's it going?" she asked.

"Never better. What's the latest?"

"Well, Springer's admin found him dead on the floor of his office this morning. Also manually strangled."

"Shut. The. Fuck. Up. Are you serious?"

"Unfortunately, I am." She heard Gonzo conveying the news to Christina.

"This is unbelievable."

"Starting to feel like a vendetta."

"No kidding."

"So I'm at MacArthur now. I got the short straw and have to tell Marissa Springer. Just looking at the place where Brooke was attacked gives me hives."

"You should get someone else to do it."

"No time. People know. It'll be all over social media if it's not already."

"Shit, Sam. What the hell is this?"

"I wish I knew, but I don't like it. And with all my best people dealing with other shit."

"Where's Cruz?"

"Elin is in the hospital with broken facial bones from an incident at the gym yesterday."

"Shit. What about Hill? Shouldn't we call in the Feds since this is all about us in some way?"

"He's sent his deputy because he's dealing with a personal issue with my assistant, who's pissed off at him, me and Nick because none of us told her about Hill's thing with me."

"What thing with you?"

"You honestly don't know?"

"No idea. Don't tell me you and him… You met him after you were with Nick."

"There was nothing between him and me, except for in his dreams. And now Shelby knows that."

"Hill had a *thing* for *you*? Seriously? Does he have a death wish? And how did I miss this?"

"I don't know. He was pretty fucking obvious about it. Nick hates his guts."

"*That* I had noticed, and I wondered why since Nick likes everyone. It all makes sense now."

"And it's the last fucking thing I need right now with him starting the new job and someone targeting my department. Now I've got a wounded assistant and friend who thinks I pushed her toward her boyfriend to get his attention away from me."

"Did you?"

"No! But if that happened, I wasn't going to be sad about it."

"I'm coming back to work. Enough of this sitting around shit. With Cruz out and the trial starting for Jeannie tomorrow, you need me."

"I can't let you come back until you've been medically cleared, Gonzo. You know that."

"Fuck that. I'm coming back. I'll work for free. I'll call you when I get to the city."

"Gonzo."

"See you shortly."

Sam stashed the phone in her suit coat pocket and got out of the car, dreading what she had to tell Marissa Springer, but secretly relieved to know she'd have Gonzo's help. It was too soon for him to come back, but she'd take all the help she could get to figure this out before more damage was done to the department and the people she cared about.

As she approached the door to the house where her niece's life was changed forever, Sam felt queasy reliving the horror of that night and the days that followed. Brooke was doing better. She was back to school in Virginia and trying to repair her life with the help of intense counseling. But she would never be the same person who'd walked into Hugo Springer's house that night.

Sam rang the doorbell and heard it echo through the three-story townhouse. Several minutes passed before the inside door swung open to reveal the Springers' housekeeper, Edna Chan, who'd been the one to discover the bodies of Hugo and eight of his friends in the basement.

"Help you?" the woman asked, though Sam had no doubt Edna recognized her.

Sam showed her badge. "May I please speak to Mrs. Springer?"

Edna's brows narrowed. "How come?"

"I need to speak to her." Sam could almost see the woman's internal debate as she tried to decide what she should do.

Finally, she pushed open the storm door and indicated for Sam to follow her to the front living room. "Have a seat. I'll get her."

"Thank you."

Sam was frankly surprised the Springers were still living in the house where one of their sons killed the other. If, God forbid, something like that ever happened in her home, she'd never be able to step foot in there again.

The woman who came into the room a few minutes later barely resembled the Marissa Springer she'd met during the earlier investigation. Her blond hair was stringy and greasy looking, her face pale and puffy. She wore sweatpants and a dirty sweatshirt.

Sam, who'd remained standing while she waited, had

to make an effort to hide her shock at the woman's disheveled appearance.

"Why are you here?" she asked in a dull, flat tone.

"I need to speak to you. About your husband."

"What about him?"

"Can you come have a seat?" Sam gestured to the sofa. Marissa eyed her suspiciously but did as she asked.

Sam joined her. "I'm very sorry to have to tell you your husband was found dead in his office this morning."

"Did the tart he was screwing find him?"

Taken aback by the woman's venomous words, Sam wasn't sure how to respond.

"You're surprised I knew?" Marissa said with a harsh laugh. "I knew everything that stupid, worthless man did because I've had him followed for years. He thought he was going to get rid of me and run away with a woman younger than his daughters? Not on my watch."

This had not gone at all like Sam had expected it to, so she recalibrated. "Mrs. Springer, where were you last night?"

"Right here. I hated his guts, but I didn't kill him."

"Were you here by yourself?"

"Edna was with me. We ordered in Chinese and watched a movie. I went to bed at ten."

"The investigator who followed your husband, could you please give me his name and number if you know it?"

"I know it. I've called it every day for five years." She wrote the information in Sam's notebook.

"What made you decide to start having him followed?"

"A combination of things. I knew Billy was up to no good and Bill kept blowing it off as a 'boys will be boys' thing, which infuriated me. Then I found out Bill was profiting from Billy's illegal activities."

"Profiting how?" Sam asked, feeling the buzz that she lived for as a homicide investigator.

"He… He knew Billy was a dealer and provided legal advice to him and his colleagues in drug dealing. I blame *him* for what happened to Hugo and his friends, not Billy. He could've put a stop to it years ago, but he chose to support him instead. It's *his* fault my babies are dead."

"Did your husband know you blamed him for the deaths of your sons?" Sam asked as she tried to process what Marissa was telling her.

"You bet your life he knew. I kicked him out of here the day after Billy's funeral, and I haven't seen him since."

"The guy you had following him, I assume you didn't call him off after you kicked him out?"

"Oh, hell no. He's been reporting in every day."

Sam really wanted to talk to him—like right now. "Mrs. Springer."

"Please, call me Marissa. Mrs. Springer reminds me of the man I was married to."

"Marissa, I can't help but notice you seem unwell." *Dirty, unkempt* and *disheveled* were more accurate words.

"I know you've been through an awful time."

"I hope you never know the kind of pain I'm in, Lieutenant," she said softly. "I wouldn't wish it on anyone."

"Have you spoken to a doctor?"

She shook her head. "That would take more energy than I can seem to muster these days. I'm not sleeping. I can't eat. It's just…" And then tears were spilling down her cheeks. "That my son could've killed his brother and all those other kids. It haunts me, you know?"

Sam couldn't begin to imagine how it must feel to have given birth to a man who was capable of what Billy Springer had done. "I have a good friend who's a doctor.

Would you like me to call him and ask him if he'd stop by to see you?"

"I... I, yes, that would be very kind of you. Thank you." She paused before she added, "Bill hated you—and your husband."

"Oh. Well..."

"It was only because he wanted someone to blame for what Billy did. But he—and Billy—were the ones to blame. He knew all along it was going to lead back to Billy. I asked him. That first night after we got that horrible call, I asked him if it was Billy, and he told me to shut up, that he'd kill me if I ever said that to anyone." She wiped away more tears. "He knew it was Billy."

Sam thought about the confrontation Springer had with Chief Farnsworth, when Sam had stopped him from punching the chief in the face. He'd been so angry about the homicide investigation leading to his son.

"Do you know how Bill and Billy found out that the homicide investigation was closing in on them?"

"They were here, both of them. Billy got a phone call and started screaming at the person on the other end. He ran out of here, and the next time I saw him was at the morgue."

"You don't know who called him?"

She shook her head.

"About what time was it when he received that call?"

"Around eight."

"I really appreciate your help, and I'm sorry again for your losses."

"Thank you for that and all you did to get justice for Hugo and the others."

"I'll have my friend Dr. Harry Flynn stop by to see you."

"That's nice of you."

"The media is going to descend again once the word gets out about Bill. If there's somewhere else you can go, this might be a good time to get out of town."

"I'll go to the house in Aspen. Tomorrow."

"Could you please write down your phone number in case I need to reach you again?"

She took the notebook from Sam as Edna appeared in the doorway looking nervous and undone.

"Edna?" Marissa asked. "What is it?"

"They call from Mr. Bill's office building. They say he's dead."

"Yes, he is. That's what Lieutenant Holland has come to tell me."

"It's too much," Edna said, shaking her head in dismay. "It's all too much."

"Can you tell me where Mrs. Springer was last night from around ten o'clock until this morning?"

"She was here. We got food from the China Express and we watched one of those silly TV movies. What was it called?"

"*Her Secret Stalker*," Marissa replied.

"Yes, that's it."

"And neither of you left all evening?"

"No," Edna said. "We stay home."

Marissa sent her housekeeper a warm smile. "Edna has been my savior through all of this. I couldn't have managed without her."

"Thank you for your time, Marissa. I can see myself out."

EIGHTEEN

SAM WAS ON the phone before she reached her car. "The wife was having him followed," Sam told Farnsworth when she got him on the line. "I'm going to track down the investigator now."

"Wow, that could be a big break."

"I know. I nearly jumped out of my skin when she told me. So get this—she also said Bill Springer was well aware of his son's illegal activities and was complicit in many of them."

"Why am I not surprised?"

"Marissa said something else about the night before Billy was killed. He and Bill were at the house on MacArthur and Billy got a phone call right around eight. He apparently went ballistic and ran out of there. The next time she saw him was in the morgue. I think that was the call where he found out we were closing in on him for murder."

"We've gone through all his phone records."

"We should go through them again. We're missing something, and now we're able to isolate when Billy Springer received the tip."

"I'll pass that on to McDonald."

"I'm having a thought."

"Are you planning to share it?"

"Stahl."

"Sam, come on. I know you've had a beef with the guy—"

"Is that what you'd call him coming to my house and

trying to kill me? A beef? It's been much more than that. Think about how many leaks we've had in the last year since you replaced him with me in Homicide. Think about how many times he's tried to haul me before the rat squad only to have you intervene. Remember the phone call to the media we caught him making from HQ during the Vasquez case?"

"I remember all of it. So what's your point?"

"He's going down on the assault charges. There's almost no chance that he won't do some time with Secret Service agents as witnesses to what happened at my house and members of the department planning to testify to the hard-on he's had for me since I took over his command."

"Gross choice of words, but okay, so?"

"Believe me, everything about him is gross to me too. Anyway, Malone and I went to his house last night. No sign of him."

"I'll ask Patrol to look for him."

"Keep this between us for now. It's only a hunch."

"It's a hunch worth looking into."

"Can you send me to the pit?"

"Hang on a second." The phone clicked onto Hold and that awful music. She needed to talk to him about that. "McBride."

"Hey, it's Holland."

"Morning, Lieutenant. Saw you on the news. You were awesome."

"Thanks. That Monica what's her name is a bimbo."

"You made her your bitch."

Sam laughed. "So listen, I need some info on a private investigator named James Donlon."

"Let me see what I can find."

Sam stayed parked outside the Springer home on Mac-Arthur while Jeannie clicked away on the computer.

"He has an office on Rhode Island Avenue. I'll text you the details."

"Thanks. Tell Arnold I need the info from Lori's text messages and the rest of the data dumped from her phone ASAP."

"Got it, will do."

"So, tomorrow…"

"Yes, tomorrow."

"I'll be there at some point."

"You've got other stuff to do."

"I want to be there to support you."

"I appreciate that, but Michael and my mother will be with me, so do what you need to until you have to testify."

"I'll be there. Anything new to report?"

"Tyrone and I are going to talk to the people at Lori's church this morning. I'll let you know what we find out."

"I'll be in after a while, and I hear Gonzo's coming back today because he can't bear to sit on the sidelines for another minute."

"Did he get medically cleared?"

"Nope, but a little detail like that isn't going to stop him."

"I can't say I blame him. If I were being accused of the things people are saying about him, I'd want to do something too."

"Same. Just don't let on I said that. I can't act like I approve of him coming back without the okay."

"My lips are sealed. I'll call you after we leave the church."

"Sounds good." She hung up with Jeannie and placed a call to Harry while she drove to Rhode Island Avenue.

"To what do I owe the pleasure, Mrs. C?" Harry asked.

"I need a favor."

"Anything for you."

Sam told him about Marissa Springer and asked if he'd be willing to stop by to see her.

"I can get there tonight."

"I'm not sure what she needs, but she looks like hell. I don't think she's been sleeping since everything happened with her sons. And today, her husband was found dead, not that she'll be shedding any tears over that. Apparently they were estranged."

"Bill Springer is dead?"

"Yep, but that's not for public consumption yet."

"I won't say anything. Damn. What happened to him?"

"I can't say."

"I understand. I'll take care of her. Will I see you at the White House thing later?"

"I hope so."

"Can you believe your husband went to work at the *White House* this morning?"

"He did? I somehow managed to block that out."

His guffaw echoed through the phone. "You're too funny, Sam. See you later."

"Thanks again, Harry."

"Anytime."

The office of James Donlon, private investigator, was located in a run-down strip mall. On one side of the office was a pizza and sub shop, on the other a massage "studio." The word made her laugh as she imagined what kind of massages went on in a storefront that had curtains pulled tight over the windows. On any other day, she'd want to take a closer look. Today, she didn't have time.

She walked into Donlon's office like she owned the place and came face-to-face with one of her favorite things—a receptionist.

"Help you?" the woman asked.

"I'd like to speak with Mr. Donlon."

"Do you have an appointment?"

Sam placed her badge on the counter above the receptionist's desk. "I don't need an appointment."

"One moment please." She got up and walked to the back of the space and into a room with a door that closed behind her.

Sam tapped her fingers on the counter. She was giving him one minute to show his face before she went back there. Dropping her hand to her side, she checked her service weapon, which was exactly where it was supposed to be. Maybe she shouldn't have come here alone.

The receptionist came out just as Sam's deadline was about to kick in. "Right this way," she said.

Sam walked to the back of the narrow office and into James Donlon's paneled office. It looked a lot like Jim Rockford's office in *The Rockford Files*. In other words, right out of the seventies. Donlon himself, however, was right out of the nineties. He was about thirty, with shaggy blond hair that needed to be cut and several days' worth of stubble on his jaw.

"I know who you are," he said, his brown eyes big with recognition and perhaps a bit of hero worship.

"Thanks," Sam said to the receptionist, dismissing her. Thankfully, the young woman got the hint and left the room. "Talk to me about Bill Springer."

Donlon's expression changed immediately, indicating he had zero poker face. "His wife hired me to keep an eye on him."

"So I've heard, and I'm sure you're well aware of why I'm here."

"I didn't kill him, if that's what you're asking. I would've had no good reason to kill him. His wife has been keeping me flush for years now."

"What do you know about who did kill him?"

"I didn't actually see it happen. I was outside in my car, keeping an eye on the building. I couldn't get much closer to him without blowing my cover."

"Did you see anyone go into the building after nine p.m. last night?"

"This is where it gets messy."

"How so?"

"I fell asleep. I didn't see anything after eight thirty. I woke up at twelve thirty, saw that Springer's car was still in the lot and went home. I heard about what happened after his wife called me to tell me he was dead. I feel awful that I didn't see anything that can help."

Sam felt awful too as a promising lead fizzled in the face of his incompetence.

"I had an all-night stakeout for another client the night before, so I was beat."

"Can you tell me if you've seen anyone around Springer in the last few weeks who might've been suspicious or if you witnessed any arguments he had with anyone?"

"Only with his wife. She hates his guts. I mean, seriously, I might never get married after watching those two in action."

"How do you mean?"

"She blames him for what happened to Hugo and Billy. She says her babies are dead because of *him*, even though he wasn't the one who did the killing. He may as well have, she would say. You ever see that movie about the chick who boiled the guy's bunny?"

"*Fatal Attraction*?"

"Yeah, that's it. She reminds me of that chick. Scary mean."

"Did you ever see her strike her husband or try to harm him in any way?"

"No, nothing like that. She did her best work with her

words. I have surveillance equipment in his office, and the stuff I witnessed—"

"Wait, you have surveillance equipment in his office?"

"Yeah, why?"

"That's where he was killed. Can you call up the video from last night?"

"I was just about to do that when you came in. I only got the call from Mrs. S about ten minutes ago."

Sam wanted to tell him to shut up and start clicking, but she didn't want to piss him off when he had access to information she needed. Without being invited, she got up and went around his desk to watch over his shoulder.

"So why don't you have Secret Service?"

"Because I don't need them."

"It's not required?"

"Only for the president, vice president, president-elect and VP-elect. Everyone else can decline it." She'd answered that question no more than five hundred times since Nick became the vice president.

"That's cool. So you got to keep your job."

"Yep."

"Huh, well that's odd."

"What's odd?" Sam asked with a sinking feeling in her belly.

He did some more furious clicking of images on his screen that showed the hallway and reception area. And then the screen went gray. "What the fuck?" More furious clicking and more blank screens. "Someone fucked with my cameras."

Sam should've known it was too good to be true. "Who else knew they were there?"

"Besides me? Only Mrs. S."

"You've been very helpful. Thank you."

"What the hell could've happened to my cameras?"

"I'll leave you to figure that out." Sam walked out of his office and strolled past the receptionist, nodding to the woman.

"Excuse me. Mrs. Cappuano?"

Sam gritted her teeth, bit back the nasty retort and had to remind herself that she was, in fact, Mrs. Cappuano, even if she'd prefer to be Lieutenant Holland on the job. "Yes?"

"Do you think I could have your autograph? My friends are never going to believe I met you."

The only thing that could've made this better was if Freddie had been there to laugh about it with her afterward. "Um." In that moment she thought of Nick and how much he did to support her career. Would it kill her to do something to support his? It might. It truly might. "Sure. What's your name?"

"Destiny."

"Of course it is." Sam took the piece of paper and pen that Destiny provided and wrote, "To Destiny, it was nice to meet you. Samantha Cappuano." She handed it over to Destiny, who'd withdrawn her phone from her purse. Sam drew the line at selfies. "Take it easy." She was out the door before the request could be made. On the way to her car, she took a call from Marissa Springer.

"I was wondering if you might stop by again. I thought of a few more things that might be useful to the investigation."

Since she had a few more questions for Marissa after interviewing Donlon, Sam said, "Sure, I'll come by in a few."

"Thank you so much."

She got into her car and called Harry, grimacing when his voice mail picked up. "Hey, it's Sam again. If you get this message, never mind about Marissa Springer. I've changed my mind about her deserving Dr. Flynn's brand of TLC. See you at the White House."

At a red light, she took advantage of the opportunity to reply to a text with a photo from Nick. *It's surreal that this is my office now. How's the day going? Will you be able to make the reception?*

Before him, before *them*, she never would've left an investigation as hot as this one was getting to attend a party. But how many times would he start a new job in the White freaking House? She was going to that reception.

I'll be there with bells on, she wrote. *Will they let me in?*

He wrote right back. *They'd better. You're the second lady!*

Do they know that? Haha!

Come with Scotty and his detail. That will make everything easier. The SS showed me to my office today. I wouldn't have had a clue where it was without them.

Got a few things to do before I head home. Will see you at the WH. Love you, Mr. VP.

Love you too, babe. Hope you're being careful out there. I'm always careful.

The light turned and she hit the gas, anxious to tie up some loose ends so she could get to the party. This would be her first official duty as second lady. Hopefully she wouldn't fuck it up in some massive way that would give the White House press corps something to talk about forever.

She never had changed out of the suit she'd worn for the TV appearance. Hopefully, that would be good enough for the White freaking House too. Sam drove back the way she'd come and turned on to MacArthur Boulevard a few minutes later. After she turned off the car, she glanced at her phone to see if Nick had texted again. There was nothing from him, but there was one from Gonzo.

I'm back in town. What can I do LT?

I've got one quick thing to do and then I'll be back at the house. Will see you then.

Sounds good.

Sam tossed her phone into the passenger seat, got out of the car and headed up the sidewalk to Marissa Springer's home. After she asked Marissa if she had monitored the cameras in her husband's office the night before and heard whatever it was Marissa needed to tell her, she'd be on her way to HQ to reconnect with her team before she had to leave for the party.

She was eager to hear what had come of McBride and Tyrone's trip to Lori Phillips's church, and she wanted to know if Arnold had found anything more in the text messages from Lori's phone.

The doorbell chimed inside the house while Sam waited on the stoop. She was about to ring the bell again when Edna opened the door. "Hello again."

"Mrs. Springer asked me to stop by again. Could I speak to her, please?"

Edna glanced nervously over her shoulder. "Um, yes, come in."

"Is everything all right?"

"Yes." Edna stepped back, still holding the door, so Sam could walk into the house.

As she crossed the threshold, Sam was hit by one of her gut feelings. *I shouldn't be here by myself. I didn't tell anyone where I was going. I've broken all my own rules.*

The click of a gun engaging only cemented her suspicions.

"Close the door, Edna, and lock it," Marissa said. "Right now."

Edna began to cry. "Miss Marissa, don't do this. You don't want to do this."

Marissa put a bullet between the eyes of Edna Chan, who fell to the floor.

Her ears ringing from the blast, Sam had to leap out of the way or Edna would've taken her down with her. "What the fuck?"

"Put your gun on the floor and kick it over here."

Furious with herself for fucking this up so royally, Sam stared down the other woman, looking for a hint of fear or nerves or anxiety. All she saw was calm, cool resolve. This was not good. Due to the TV appearance first thing, Sam had failed to wear her clutch piece on her leg the way she usually did while working a case, so she'd be completely disarmed if she handed over her gun. "What's going on here, Marissa?"

"You're done asking questions. I'm in charge now. Kick your gun over here or I'll shoot your knee. You've got five seconds. Four, three, two..."

"Fine." Sam withdrew her gun from the back of her skirt and thought for a second about trying to get a shot off. But even with the safety disengaged as it was whenever she was on duty, she'd be dead in the time it took to pull her weapon. Instead, she put it on the floor and kicked it in Marissa's direction. "What happened between the last time I was here and now?"

"Nothing. You did exactly what we expected you to

do. You went to talk to James and then you came back here when I asked you to. This time we're ready for you."

"Who's *we*?"

"You'll find out soon enough. Come with me."

This was ridiculous, Sam thought as she walked toward Marissa. She could kick this woman's ass, and Marissa was actually holding *her* hostage? Did she dare try to kick the gun out of her hand? The thing that stopped her was the way Marissa had dropped Edna with a perfect shot. That indicated a certain level of expertise.

"What do you want with me?"

"Enough with the questions."

"Um, you're holding a gun on me, and I'm not supposed to ask why?"

"You know why."

"If I knew, I wouldn't be asking."

The look Marissa gave her was positively venomous. "I blame *you* for my son's death."

"Which one?"

"*Billy!* Your incompetence led to my son's death, and you're going to pay for that."

"So let me get this straight. You're taking me hostage because I built a case against your son that went bad when *he* took hostages?"

Marissa leaned in closer to her. "No, I'm going to *kill* you because you and your band of incompetents ruined my life."

In that moment, the shock seemed to pass and reality set in. Unless someone missed her and figured out where she was, she was going to die in this house where so many others had already died.

Shit fuck damn hell.

Marissa marched her down the basement stairs. Sam immediately noticed the pool table, where they'd found drug paraphernalia and empty vodka bottles the night of the murders, had been removed. The bloodstained carpet remained, however, and every surface was still smudged with the fingerprint powder Crime Scene detectives had left behind. Sam wondered how Marissa could bear to live in the house with all these reminders of her son's violent death.

"Sit." Marissa gestured with the gun to a wooden chair in the middle of the room.

Keeping a wary eye on the gun, Sam did as directed. "So what's the plan, Marissa? How long are you planning to keep someone the entire police department will be looking for in a matter of minutes?"

"I told you to shut up, and I meant it."

"You have to know they'll be looking for me."

"You're so *arrogant*. Prancing around town like you own this city. Your husband is vice president, and you forgo Secret Service because you don't think you'll need it. How funny is that now? Taken hostage by a housewife. I wonder what your husband would pay to get you back?"

All the money in the world, Sam thought, saddened at the thought of him hearing she was in danger when there was nothing she could do to reassure him. She couldn't think of him—or Scotty or the rest of her family—or she'd lose her composure. She needed to stay focused on Marissa and the gun and trying to figure out what she hoped to accomplish.

Sam had far too much to live for to let a frustrated housewife be the end of her.

When Sam was seated in the wooden chair, Marissa pulled a phone from her pocket and made a call. "I got her to come back," Marissa said while Sam tried to figure out who she was talking to. "Get over here. Now." She ended the call and returned the phone to her pocket.

Then she began to pace back and forth in the space where the pool table used to be. She never took her eyes off Sam, who sat perfectly still while watching Marissa's every move. How had she misjudged this woman and this situation so completely? Sam had made a career out of trusting her instincts and following her gut. Both had let her down in this situation. She'd gotten no sense of violent tendencies during her initial visit with Marissa, but she should've taken what James told her about Marissa to heart before coming back here alone. She'd been in too big of a rush to think it all the way through, and she was paying for that now.

"Could I use the bathroom?" Sam asked.

"No."

"So I should just pee right here?"

"If that's what you've got to do."

Sam hadn't really had to go, but once she was told she couldn't, she needed to go urgently. She chalked that up to nerves. She was in a bad spot. No two ways around it, but she'd been in bad spots before, such as the time she'd walked in on a robbery in progress at a convenience store and managed to neutralize the shooter and save a few lives—including her own.

Then there was the time her malicious ex-husband had gotten the big idea to bomb her car—and Nick's. When hers had detonated, she'd been hurled against the brick-front townhouse where Nick had lived then. He'd been hit by flying glass, but they'd both survived. They'd been run off the road by some gangbangers, looking to use them to score initiation points. He'd broken ribs and she'd had a severe concussion, but they'd both walked away.

The week of her wedding, a perp had shot at her from a second floor window. Freddie had anticipated the shot, jumped on her and got her out of the way of the bullets, but not before her head connected with a huge rock, giving her yet another concussion.

Thinking about all the times she'd been through worse than this and come through fine boosted her confidence in this situation. What was one slightly crazy woman with a gun against a seasoned cop who'd overcome all that? If only she knew who Marissa had called and what they were planning. Did they want to take the vice president's wife hostage to make headlines? She immediately dismissed that angle because Marissa had indicated this was about revenge for Billy's death. It was about discrediting the department—and her.

"Did you kill Lori Phillips?"

"Do I have to shoot you to shut you up?"

Before Sam could answer, the upstairs door opened and closed.

"Down here," Marissa called up the stairs.

Sam held her breath, waiting to see what would happen next and looking—always—for a way out. But Marissa never took her eyes or the gun off her.

Heavy footsteps on the stairs took Sam's anxiety level into the red zone. She saw the belly first and had to smother the urge to gasp when Stahl appeared in the basement, his beady eyes alight with pleasure at the sight of her on the other end of Marissa's gun.

"Well, well, *well*, lookie here." He rubbed his hands together with glee, which made Sam's stomach turn with dread and nausea.

"Stop celebrating and tie her up," Marissa said.

"Don't snap at me, bitch. I've waited a long time for this moment. You need to let me enjoy it."

"Do your enjoying after you tie her up."

As Stahl approached her, it took all the self-control Sam possessed to keep from blinking or flinching or doing anything else that would only add to his satisfaction. No matter what happened here, she wouldn't give him anything more than she had to.

"What's a matter? Cat got your tongue, Lieutenant?"

She stared at him, unblinking.

He slapped her hard across the face, making her see stars. Then he grabbed a handful of her hair and yanked—hard. "When I ask you something, you'd better answer me."

Sam spit in his face.

NINETEEN

STAHL'S COMPLEXION TURNED that unattractive shade of purple she was so used to seeing. He used his sleeve to wipe the spit from his face and then delivered a punch to the same spot he'd slapped.

Sam fought through the darkness that descended upon her after the initial blast of pain, trying to stay conscious. Whatever happened, she had to keep her wits about her.

Stahl pulled a length of rope from his back pocket and moved to the back of the chair. He went for maximum pain as he tied her wrists and ankles to the chair. The one bit of solace she took was if she were tied like this, he couldn't rape her. She figured she could get through just about anything but that.

"The stupid bitch at CBC took the bait," Stahl said. "They're reporting that the FBI is talking to Farnsworth about his whereabouts when your asshole husband was killed."

"Very good," Marissa said with a satisfied smile.

To Sam, he said, "I also heard that your fuck toy Cruz did exactly what we expected him to do and went into the jail last night to tune up Elliott."

Sam processed that information, her foggy brain racing to keep up after the brutal punch. Cruz had gone into the jail to deal with the guy who'd hurt Elin. Had that been another setup?

Stahl cinched the ropes in tight around her wrist, so tight that her fingers immediately tingled from the lack of blood. He leaned in close to her. "You and your boys are going down."

Sam blinked back the tears that filled her eyes from the pain shooting through her skull. She refused to give him the pleasure of seeing her break down. The fact that they were tying her up rather than shooting her was a small consolation. It meant there was something they wanted before they took her out.

Her people would be looking for her. At least she hoped they would. Nick would look for her when she didn't show up at the reception. She just had to stay calm—and alive—until the cavalry arrived.

GONZO GOT TO HQ around four o'clock to find the pit deserted. He tried Sam on her phone, but it went to voice mail after it rang four times.

"Hey, it's Sam Holland. Leave a message and I'll get back to you as soon as I can."

"It's Gonzo. I'm at HQ. Where are you?" He ended the call and went to his cubicle, which had been cleaned and organized in his absence, mostly likely by his partner, Detective Arnold.

Speak of the devil. Arnold came into the pit carrying a stack of paper and a large coffee. He stopped short at the sight of Gonzo, his eyes bugging. "What're you doing here?"

"The world has gone mad, so I figured I'd come do what I can to help."

"It's so good to see you here."

"Thanks," Gonzo said to the young man who'd saved his life by applying pressure to a wound that surely would've killed him without Arnold's quick action.

"Did the doc say it was okay to come back?"

Gonzo picked up his ball of elastics and squeezed the

tight rubber object. His strength still wasn't what it used to be, but it was getting better every day. "Nope."

"So, um, should you be here?"

"Probably not."

"Gonzo."

"Don't start on me. I've already heard an earful from Christina all the way back to town from Harper's Ferry. I need to be here. I can't sit at home watching the media tear my life apart. Besides, something stinks to high heaven around here."

"We were just talking about that in the cafeteria. Two people who'd made trouble for the department suddenly murdered in the span of two days? That feels calculated, you know?"

"Not to mention, how did Lori find out about my connection to the judge? How did Billy Springer know we were coming after him for the murder of his brother?"

Arnold took a look around the deserted pit, lowering his voice. "You think it's an inside thing?"

"I don't know what to think. Do you know where the LT is?"

"She was going to tell Springer's wife and then coming back here last I heard."

"How long ago was that?"

Arnold checked his watch. "A while ago now."

"Is Cruz with her?"

Arnold shook his head. "He's out today. Elin is still in the hospital."

"So who's with Sam?"

"No one."

Tugging Arnold's portable radio off his belt, Gonzo tried to reach Sam but got no answer. He got up too quickly and a dizzy spell had him grasping the cubicle wall.

"Are you okay?" Arnold asked.

"Yeah, I'm fine. Just moved too fast."

"I'd hate to see you screw up your recovery by coming back too soon."

"I'm not going to screw up anything. And while it's just us here, I want to say, you know, thanks for what you did that day. I don't remember much of anything that happened after we got to Friendship Heights, but from what I'm told, you saved my life. I just want you to know I'm grateful. I've been meaning to tell you that for a while now, but there always seems to be other people around when we're together."

The young detective looked like he might cry but then pulled himself together. "It was nothing you wouldn't have done for me. Or at least I hope you would."

Gonzo laughed. "If you're stupid enough to get shot in the neck like I was, I'd do the same for you."

"That's comforting, Sarge. Thanks."

"What's with all the papers?" Gonzo asked.

"Lori's phone records. Slow going."

"I'll let you get back to it. I'm going to find Malone and see if he knows where Sam is."

"Keep me posted on what you hear."

"Will do."

Gonzo left the pit and went in search of the captain, who he found in a conversation with Farnsworth outside the chief's office.

"Sergeant Gonzales," Farnsworth said. "You're back."

"So it seems," Gonzo replied.

Malone gave him a shrewd once-over. "Funny, I don't recall seeing your return-to-work form."

"It's in the mail," Gonzo said. "I'm good as new."

"At the most, light duty, Sergeant," Farnsworth said sternly.

"Absolutely." Gonzo breathed a sigh of relief when he

realized they weren't going to send him home. "Does anyone know where Lieutenant Holland is? I tried to get her on the radio and on her cell and got her voice mail. She told me she had one quick thing to do and would meet me here, but that was more than an hour ago. Last Arnold knew, she was going to inform Marissa Springer."

"That was hours ago," Farnsworth said, his brows furrowing. "She was going there when Conklin and I parted company with her around eleven. She called me about seeing an investigator Mrs. Springer had hired to follow her husband but that didn't pan out. No one's heard from her since?"

Malone pulled his phone from his pocket and placed a call, frowning when he apparently got her voice mail. He then sent a text and watched his screen intently. "It delivered but it wasn't read."

"Let me try Cruz and see if he's spoken to her," Gonzo said with a growing sense of alarm. More than an hour off the grid. That wasn't like her. At all. "Hey, Freddie."

"What's up? Where are you?"

"At HQ with Malone and the chief. We're wondering if you've spoken to Sam recently?"

"Not since this morning when she called about Springer. Why?"

Gonzo shook his head and watched Malone and Farnsworth exchanged concerned glances. "We haven't heard from her in a while, and we're just trying to see if anyone else has."

"Did you call Nick? She usually keeps in touch with him all day, but today may be different since it's his first day at the White House. I can call Shelby too. She's probably talked to Sam."

"Let me know, will you?"

"Yeah, will do."

"How's Elin?"

"Sore but better. They're sending her home soon."

"What the hell happened?"

Freddie told him about the guy who'd been hassling her at the gym and the fight that had led to her injuries.

"Do we need to have a conversation with this guy?"

"Already done."

Gonzo turned his back to the chief and captain and walked a short distance away. "What'd you do, Cruz?"

"I took care of it. That's all you need to know."

"Took care of it how?"

"I'm going to call around to try to find Sam. I'll get back to you when I hear something. You do the same?"

"Yeah, but we're going to talk about the other thing later."

"Fine, see you."

The line went dead and Gonzo was left with yet another uneasy feeling. He placed calls to all of the Homicide detectives, none of whom had heard from Sam in the last hour.

"What're you hearing, Sarge?" Malone asked.

"Nothing. Nothing at all."

"Should we call Nick?" Malone asked. "If anyone's heard from her, he has."

"What if he hasn't, though? He'll be in a panic. I'd prefer to wait a bit on making that call."

Malone went to a house phone on the wall and dialed a number. "Archie, it's Malone. I need you to put a trace on Lieutenant Holland's phone. Do you have the number?" He paused and then groaned. "So it doesn't have GPS capability?" After another pause, Malone said, "She's getting a new phone. Immediately. Thanks anyway, Archie." He slammed down the receiver.

"I'm going to the Springer house since that was the last place we knew she was," Gonzo said.

"I'm going with you," Malone said.

"Me too," Farnsworth replied.

As they left HQ and headed for MacArthur Boulevard, Gonzo's chest tightened. He had a bad feeling about this.

NICK'S FIRST DAY at the White House passed in a blur of meetings and briefings on everything from national security to the latest situation in Iraq and Syria to an update on the Ebola outbreak in Africa and the efforts being made by the Centers for Disease Control to keep the disease from further encroaching on U.S. borders. Within the West Wing, a fierce debate was under way about sending ground troops to Africa to help contain the virus and offer aid.

He could see both sides of the debate. Containing the disease was in the U.S.'s best interest, but he could also understand the military's resistance to send troops into such a hot zone.

At quarter to five, Terry knocked on his door and came in. As he took a seat on the other side of Nick's desk, he looked energized and invigorated by the day they'd put in. "So."

"So?" Nick asked.

"So far, so good?"

"Yeah, I'd say that. Pretty intense day."

"I'd venture to guess most days around here are intense."

"I thought I'd see Nelson at some point."

"You're having lunch with him on Friday, and I'm sure he'll pop in to the reception if he's able to."

"Sure, whatever." Nick aligned the wedding photo of him and Sam on the corner of his desk. That and Scotty's recent school photo were the only pictures on his desk.

"What's up?" Terry asked.

"Nothing's up other than the first day on a new job."

"Why do you seem, I don't know, out of sorts maybe?"

Nick shrugged. "I guess I'm sort of hoping I haven't made a huge mistake."

"How do you mean?"

"Everything today... It sort of feels like..."

"Like what?"

"Busywork. Stuff they're throwing at me to keep me involved but on the periphery."

Terry thought about that for a minute. "They might be easing you in."

"Maybe."

"But you don't think so?"

"It occurs to me that Nelson has already gotten what he needed most from me."

"A boost in poll numbers," Terry said, nodding. The numbers showed the American people very much approved of the president's choice of a new vice president.

"Bingo." Nick held a pen between his index and middle fingers, letting it dangle. "He used me, Terry."

"You don't know that for sure."

Nick raised a brow. "Don't I? I haven't heard a single word from him or any member of his team, except Derek, who I talk to regularly anyway, since the day I was sworn in six weeks ago. Not one word."

"It was the holidays. Everyone was out of town from Thanksgiving to New Year's. You know how this city works."

"We still have a country to run. Are you going to tell me Nelson didn't work—at all—for six weeks? And why did they encourage me to wait until after the first of the year to officially start work?"

"Because they knew you needed time to put a team in place?"

"Six weeks, Terry. That's a long time for radio silence between the country's top two leaders."

"You should talk to Derek about it. Get his feel."

"You think he'd tell me if Nelson was purposely leaving me out of things?"

"I think you guys have been friends a long time, and if he can tell you anything, he will."

"True." While he agreed with Terry, Nick still hated to put Derek in the middle of potential issues between his boss and his longtime friend.

"I wouldn't worry too much about it—yet. It's early days. It'll all shake out in the next couple of weeks."

"I don't want to be bored. I want to be busy."

"Then we'll keep you busy. To start with, you have a slew of interview requests. They want you everywhere— all the Sunday shows and most of the news magazines are clamoring for you."

"Sure, I'll do them. Let's make the rounds. Do we need to clear it with Nelson's people first?"

"I don't see why. He asked you because you're popular, so it's safe to assume he'd approve of you capitalizing on your popularity."

"I don't like that word."

"Which word? Popularity?"

"No, *assume*," Nick said with a chuckle. "It gets people, even vice presidential people, in trouble. Let's clear it with his team before we do anything. I don't want to start off on the wrong foot."

"Yes, sir, Mr. Vice President."

Nick scowled at his friend. "Can it."

"So I wanted to share a bit of personal news with you."

"What's that?"

"I asked Lindsey to marry me on New Year's Eve and for some strange reason she actually said yes."

Nick laughed at his choice of words and his befuddled expression. "Congratulations, Terry. I couldn't be happier for both of you."

"Thanks. I'm pretty happy too. A year ago, I never could've imagined the life I've got now."

"Right there with you." Nick's personal cell phone rang and he took the call from his friend Andy. "Hey there."

"How's life in the White House?"

"The jury's still out. Anything new?"

"I met the guy this morning. Scotty looks like him." That news had Nick's heart sinking. He enjoyed thinking that Scotty looked a little like *him*. "I told him I represented his adoptive parents and asked if he'd be willing to sign away his parental rights so that Scotty could be adopted by a loving family."

Nick felt like his heart was going to stop while he waited for the other shoe to drop. "And?"

"He had no idea he has a son. His shock was quite genuine. He'd like to meet him before he signs anything."

"Ugh," Nick said with a groan. "And how do we do that without him finding out who Scotty's adoptive parents are?"

"I believe the Secret Service detail might be a give-away."

"Damn it, Andy. What do we do? Can we offer him money?"

"You're getting way ahead of the game worrying about that. And besides, no matter what happens, I wouldn't do that. It can come back to bite you in the ass in a number of unpleasant ways."

"If you're talking politically, I don't care about that."

"I mean legally. The court frowns on money changing hands in custody situations."

"Son of a bitch," Nick whispered. "What if he doesn't want to meet his real father?"

"I don't think he has a choice if he wants the adoption to go through. The other option is to continue to be his legal guardian without formally adopting him. If his father doesn't file for custody, then there'd be nothing preventing him from living with you until he's legally an adult."

"I don't like that option. I want him to be my son legally and every other way. It's what he wants too."

"Then we have to go through the motions, I'm afraid."

"I want to know everything there is to know about this guy."

"My investigator is working on a report. I'll get it to you as soon as I have it. In the meantime, why don't you talk to Scotty and see what he has to say about it?"

The thought of talking to Scotty about this topic made Nick queasy. Just when the boy was starting to feel comfortable in his new home and life, this was going to rock the foundation of that new life. "I'll do that and get back to you."

"Sounds good. I know this is a tough situation, but if we do it by the book, we shouldn't have any trouble."

"I don't like that word—*shouldn't*."

"There're never any guarantees, but I'll do everything I can to get you all the outcome you want."

"Thanks, Andy. I'll talk to you soon." He ended the call and tossed his phone on the desk.

"That sounds worrisome," Terry said.

"It is. His biological father didn't know about him and wants to meet him before he'll sign away his parental rights."

"Damn."

A knock on the door preceded Lauren, one of the receptionists from his Senate staff who had come with them to the White House. "Are you available for a Mr. Scott Cappuano, sir?"

"Always," Nick said, his smile wide even though his heart ached from what he needed to tell Scotty. "Send him in."

"This is so freaking cool," Scotty said when he came into the office wearing his "work clothes," as he referred to the navy blazer, light blue dress shirt and blue and red striped tie that matched Nick's. The khaki pants were new since he'd grown out of the others.

"I believe 'freaking' is on Mrs. Littlefield's swear list," Nick said as he got up to hug his son.

"Sam says it's not a swear."

"Do *not* take her advice on swearing, buddy. You'll end up in detention."

Terry laughed. "I gotta say your dad makes a good point."

"She does have a potty mouth," Scotty said.

"Speaking of my lovely wife, is she with you?"

Scotty shook his head. "My detail brought me over."

"So she wasn't home yet when you left?"

"Nope."

To Terry, Nick said, "Sam was worried about being able to get in here if she wasn't able to come with Scotty and his detail. Is there someone we need to tell at the gate?"

"I'll go check on that."

"Thank you. Please tell them to make sure the second lady gets in when she arrives or there'll be hell to pay."

Smiling, Terry said, "Will do." He left the office, closing the door behind him.

"I can't believe you actually work here now," Scotty said. "It's so, *so* cool."

"I'm glad you think so."

"The kids at school think so too. They treat me different now."

Immediately on alert, Nick said, "Different how?"

"Like I'm super cool because my dad is the vice president. Don't worry. It's a good kind of different."

"Oh," Nick said, relieved to hear that. "Okay. You'd tell me if something bad was going on at school, right?"

"Sure, I would. But I don't want to talk about school now. I want a tour of the White House! Can we walk around?"

"We can take a walk." Amused by Scotty's enthusiasm, Nick put his hand on the boy's shoulder. "Before we do, though, there's something I wanted to talk to you about." He'd promised to be honest with Scotty about the adoption proceedings, so he knew he couldn't delay in telling him the news.

"Is it bad?"

"It's not bad so much as it's kind of a weird situation."

"What is?"

"So you know that as part of your adoption, we had to make an effort to find your biological father so he could sign away his rights to you."

"Yeah. Did you find him?"

"Yes."

"Oh. So what does that mean?"

"You know my friend Andy, who is handling the adoption for us?"

Scotty nodded.

"He went to New Jersey this week to meet him. Your father."

"He's not my father! *You* are. You're the only father I've ever had and the only one I want." Scotty's chin trembled and his brown eyes glistened with unshed tears. "You can't let him take me away from you and Sam. You *can't*."

Nick felt like he'd been sucker punched both by what Scotty had said and how undone he was. He hugged him.

Scotty wrapped his arms around Nick and held on tight.

Nick ran his hand over the boy's back. "No one is going to take you away from us, buddy. No matter what happens, you're old enough to tell a judge where you want to live, and that will matter more than anything, if it comes to that."

"What do you mean, if it comes to that? What's going to happen?"

Nick stepped back from Scotty, but kept a hand on his shoulder as he led him to one of the sofas that made up the small sitting area in his office. "He says he didn't know about you. He wants to meet you before he signs the document we need that will relinquish his rights to you."

"What does that word mean? Relinquish."

"Give up."

"How is it possible that he didn't know about me?"

"Well, sometimes women don't tell the father about a baby."

"Why would they do that?"

"Sometimes it's because they don't want the man in their child's life. Other times, the couple breaks up before they find out about the baby, and the mother chooses not to tell the father."

"That doesn't seem fair to the dad."

"It's not, but it happens."

"He really wants to meet me?"

"He does. How do you feel about that?"

"I've always sort of wondered about him."

"Of course you have. That's totally normal."

"Where is he?"

"In New Jersey. In a place called Atlantic City."

"They have casinos there. I saw a commercial."

"That's right and there's a really cool boardwalk that runs along the beach too."

"Will we go there to meet him?"

"I think we'll have to if we want him to sign the paper. Would you be okay with that?"

Scotty was quiet for a long moment as he thought about it. "If we went there, the Secret Service would have to go with us, right?"

"Where we go, they go. And just think, we'd have to ride on Air Force Two to get there."

"That'd be cool," Scotty said with an uncharacteristic lack of enthusiasm. "So he'd know who you are."

"He'd probably figure it out. Yes."

"What if he's not a nice guy? What if he tries to get money from you before he'll sign the paper?"

Nick was impressed by Scotty's grasp of the possibilities. "That could happen, I suppose. If it does, we'll deal with it then."

"How will we deal with it? Will you give him money to get him to sign the paper?"

"I'd give him anything he asked for if it meant clearing the way for your adoption. However, Andy has advised me that it's not a good idea to let money change hands in these situations. The court tends to frown upon it."

"Because it's skeevy."

"Right," Nick said with a laugh. "Exactly." He rested a hand on Scotty's shoulder. "Listen to me. Are you listening?"

Scotty looked at him with those big brown eyes and nodded.

"There is nothing and I do mean *nothing* Sam and I wouldn't do to keep you exactly where you belong. I don't want you to be worried about this or sick over it or stressed out or anything else. It's all going to be fine. We'll go up there, we'll meet him, he'll sign the paper and we'll get a judge to finalize your adoption."

"It may not be that simple."

"Maybe not," Nick conceded, "but the end result will be the same. You're ours. We're yours. That's not going to change. No matter what."

"You're telling me everything, right?"

"I promised you I would, and I always will. You can count on that."

"He's *not* my father," Scotty said fiercely. "You are. I don't want anyone to call him that."

"You're going to make me cry, buddy."

"Men don't cry."

"They do when a boy they love with all their heart says something so sweet." He reached for Scotty and enveloped him in another hug. "It's all going to be okay. I swear to you."

"I hope you're right."

"I'm always right."

Scotty snorted with laughter. "Now you sound like Sam."

Laughing, Nick released him and stood. "Let's go do our tour before the party starts."

"Hey, Nick?"

"Yeah?"

"I love you too. You and Sam, you're the best parents ever, and I feel really lucky that you want me so much."

"We're the lucky ones. We say that every day." As he followed Scotty out of the office, he silently vowed to protect him and the family that meant so much to him with everything he had.

TWENTY

SAM WATCHED STAHL as he made a dozen or more trips from the garage into the family room, carrying items that had clearly been placed there in anticipation of this situation.

Even though she was still berating herself for the stupidity that had put her here, she took tremendous satisfaction from his pronounced limp, which had resulted from the time he attacked her on her own front stoop. He'd left that confrontation with a broken kneecap and a ruptured testicle. That was probably why he had such a hard-on for her, a thought that turned her stomach.

Sam honestly believed she could get through anything he had in store for her as long as he didn't touch her that way. The thought of being assaulted by him... *No. Don't go there. Do not go there. Think about Nick and Scotty. Think about being with Nick in the loft and in Bora Bora. Think about the love and the joy and the life we have together. Don't give him one second of any time you have left. And don't think like that either. That's not going to help anything.*

Watching Stahl unzip a bag that contained a semiautomatic weapon, Sam had to acknowledge the possibility that this wasn't going to end well for her. He had her tied so tightly she couldn't do a thing to help herself. She was completely at his mercy, just the way he wanted her.

She wanted to know how he and Marissa had come together to form this unholy alliance. She wanted to ask what he hoped to gain by taking her hostage. He had to know the entire police department would be looking for her. Maybe that's what he was counting on, and judging from the arsenal laid out in front of her, he was ready for the entire department.

She shifted in the chair, trying to find a comfortable position, which only reminded her of how badly she needed to pee. She absolutely refused to give him the satisfaction of watching her wet her pants. Her bladder could explode before that would happen. The movement sent a shaft of pain through her face and skull, making her see tiny dots of light that often meant the onset of a migraine. She moved her jaw, painfully, trying to determine if it was broken. Didn't seem to be.

Were they looking for her yet? Freddie and Hill weren't working today, which meant two of her closest colleagues wouldn't know she was missing. Gonzo would wonder where she was when she didn't meet him as planned at HQ. He'd begin to ask questions.

Would he call Nick?

God, Nick, I'm so sorry for doing this to you, my love. If he kills me, I hope you know I was thinking of you and Scotty and my family. But mostly you.

To pass the time and to give her something else to think about besides whatever unpleasantness Stahl had planned for her and how badly she needed to pee, Sam let her mind wander from the moment she first met Nick on a deck at a party, to the next time she saw him in John O'Connor's apartment after his boss and best friend had been murdered. She'd tried to resist him in the midst of the politically charged investigation, the first one she'd been on after the Johnson case had ended in disaster.

Truth be told, she'd actually done a horrible job of resisting him. The night she'd gone to his place in Arlington, they'd been so hot for each other, they'd practically done it standing up against his door the minute she walked into the house. They'd done it against a wall the very first time, she recalled. The night they'd met seven years ago. At the time, it had been the hottest sex of her life, but he'd topped himself many times since then in the year they'd been back together.

She smiled to herself, and then winced in pain, when she recalled the bet she'd made with him—that he couldn't make her come three times in thirty minutes. Not surprisingly, he'd won the bet and set their wedding date for six short weeks later.

Their wedding, which had been the most incredible day of her life. Nick's mother had shown up uninvited, but Sam had gotten rid of her before she could ruin anything for him. They'd had the same words, "You're my home," inscribed on the inside of their wedding bands. Despite the ropes tied tightly around her wrists, she could reach her ring with her thumb, rubbing back and forth against the cool metal reminder of all she had to live for.

Her mind drifted to the blissful days and nights they'd spent in Bora Bora on their honeymoon. She wanted to ask him if they could go back again this year to celebrate their first anniversary. What was the first anniversary gift again? Paper. That's right. She would write him a letter and tell him how much she loved him and wanted to spend the next fifty or sixty years with him.

Fifty or sixty years. Right now she'd be perfectly satisfied with fifty or sixty more hours with him.

That all his greatest fears for her safety could've led to *this* broke her heart into a million pieces, imagining him getting the news that she was missing and maybe dead.

Tears made her eyes burn, so she closed them tightly to keep the tears from escaping. She wouldn't give Stahl the satisfaction of seeing her bawl either. But oh, how she wanted to bawl when she imagined how Nick would suffer over losing her. And there was no way Stahl would let her out of here alive. Not when he'd already tried to kill her once.

It occurred to her, as she contemplated the possible end of her life, that she'd been extremely lucky up to now. She'd gotten through situations that should've killed or badly injured her. And she'd managed to steer clear of her many enemies.

Until now.

As Stahl readied for battle, Sam prepared for the worst. If her life ended today at his hands, she could only hope that Nick would know that her last thoughts had been of him.

CAPTAIN MALONE DROVE Gonzo and Farnsworth to MacArthur Boulevard. Gonzo breathed a sigh of relief when he saw Sam's car parked at the curb.

"Thank God," Farnsworth said, the first words any of them had spoken since they left HQ. "Let's get SWAT out here."

"All due respect, sir," Malone said, "I'd like to know what we're dealing with before we decide what we need."

"I want her out of there," Farnsworth snapped back.

"We all do, Joe. But we've got to do this right. We've got to protect her and the rest of our team."

"Let's go take a look."

Gonzo got out of the car and followed them up the sidewalk, glancing around at the other nearby houses. Ever since he'd been shot, he was constantly worried about it happening again. You never knew who was aiming for you.

On the Springers' stoop, they glanced inside through the glass windows that framed the black door.

"Oh, Jesus." Malone pointed to the feet and pool of

blood they could see on the foyer floor. He stood up taller, tipping his head down trying to get a better look. "It's the maid."

"Have you seen what you need to see?" Farnsworth asked.

"Make the call," Malone said to Gonzo.

They went down the stairs and tried to see in the basement windows, which were covered by blinds.

"Someone needs to tell Nick," Farnsworth said grimly as they returned to the car.

"I'll call Christina," Gonzo said. "She'll know how to get through to him."

"Do you think she's already dead in there?" Farnsworth asked, seeming older and more defeated than Gonzo had ever seen him.

He'd watched Sam grow up. Something like this would hit him even harder than the rest of them. And then Gonzo thought of Sam's father and had to swallow a growing lump of fear that settled in his throat. What would any of them do without Sam Holland at the center of their lives?

Before he could let the panic get the better of him, he made the call to Dispatch asking for SWAT. Then he called Christina. "Hey, baby. I need a favor."

"Sure, what's up?" He tried not to notice the unusually chilly tone of her voice. She was mad at him for going back to work before the doctor said it was okay.

"I need you to get in touch with Nick for me. Sam's in trouble."

"What kind of trouble?"

"We believe she's being held hostage at the Springers' house."

"Where all the kids were killed?"

"Same place."

"Oh my God, Tommy. Is she…"

"We don't know anything yet. Her car is parked outside, the maid is dead on the floor inside and no one has heard from Sam in more than an hour. We're operating under the assumption that she's in there and being held against her will."

"What am I supposed to tell him?"

"I would just say we're not sure yet what's going on, but we think she's being held hostage."

"He'll want to come there."

"The Secret Service won't let him anywhere near here."

"He'll lose his mind when he hears this. There's nothing else you can tell me?"

"We're doing everything we can. That's all I can tell you right now."

"I'll make the call. Keep me posted? Please?"

"I'll try."

"Tommy."

"What, baby?"

"Please don't get hurt again. I don't think I could take it."

"I won't. Love you." Gonzo didn't care that his captain and chief could hear him. He'd recently learned a hard lesson on how easily and quickly his life could be taken from him. He'd never again worry about such trivial things as his superiors hearing him tell his fiancée he loved her.

"I love you too."

Gonzo ended that call and placed another to Cruz. "You need to get over to the Springers' house on MacArthur," Gonzo said when Freddie took the call. "They've got Sam in there."

"Who does?"

"We're not really sure yet, but the maid is dead on the floor inside the front door, and Sam's car is parked at the curb. No one has heard from her in more than an hour."

"*Shit*." Since Cruz rarely swore, that said it all. "How do you know she's in there?"

"We don't know for sure, but we're operating under that assumption."

"I'll be right there."

"Call the rest of the squad, will you? I don't want to put it on the radio."

"Yeah, I will. Gonzo…"

"I don't know, man. I don't know anything."

"I'm coming."

MARISSA PULLED BACK the blinds to peek outside. "There're cops out there, Leonard."

"Close the blinds and come away from the window," Stahl said.

"I just want to see what they're doing."

"Marissa, do what I tell you to!"

"Don't snap at me. You wouldn't even be here if I hadn't called you, and you certainly wouldn't have *her* without me."

"Shut your mouth and come away from that window. I'm in charge now."

"The hell you are! This is *my* house and *my* plan."

With speed and dexterity Sam wouldn't have thought him capable of, Stahl raised a nine-millimeter handgun and shot her in the gut.

Marissa gasped as she went down, a look of shock on her face as a gurgling sound came from her mouth. The gut shot had been intentional. He didn't want to kill her instantly. He wanted to make her suffer. She whimpered pathetically, but Sam didn't have an ounce of sympathy for her. That's what happened when you got in bed with the devil.

The blast, occurring three feet from Sam's head, was

deafening. Her ears rang and the spots before her eyes became brighter. She shook off the shock to take note of what Stahl was doing.

He pulled a roll of something that looked like wire from a duffel bag. Then he grabbed a pair of work gloves and put them on. Carrying the spool of wire, he approached Sam.

She curbed her natural impulse to shy away from him. In fact, she refused to look at him, even when he grabbed her chin and tried to force her to.

"You know what I hate most about you?" he asked, his breath hot and moist against her face.

Sam stayed focused on a picture of what looked like the Rocky Mountains that hung on the wall.

He grabbed a handful of her hair and pulled hard. "Look at me when I talk to you!"

She remained stubbornly focused on the picture.

He pulled her hair until tears came to her eyes, but she never looked away from the picture as she imagined cool mountain air, crunchy snow beneath her feet and Nick on skis. Did he like to ski? She wasn't sure, and she hated that she didn't know, that they'd never gotten around to talking about skiing.

She'd sucked at it the two times she'd tried it.

"*Are you listening to me?*" Stahl roared as he slapped her hard across the other side of her face. "I fucking hate you because you think you're better than everyone else."

I am better. I'm better than you ever dreamed of being.

"You showed up right out of the academy acting like a hotshot because of who your father was—and don't get me started on him. He had his dick so far up Farnsworth's ass, and *everybody* knew it. How else do you think he made it to deputy chief? Someone must've been seriously pissed about that to shoot him."

Sam wanted to ask him if he was that someone, but again, she wasn't going to play his game. Not now or ever.

As he ranted about her father, he began wrapping the wire around her. Her heart skipped a beat and a bead of sweat ran down her back when she glanced down to discover it was razor wire.

"And then they give you *my* command. Tell me something. How long have you been fucking the chief? Has it been since you were a kid? Is that why he looks at you like you hung the moon? Do you have a magic pussy or something? I wish I had the time or the desire to find out, but the thought of fucking you makes me want to puke."

Right back atcha.

She almost sighed—audibly—with relief to know that particular atrocity wasn't in his plans, but she maintained her silence, which she could tell was getting to him. He'd expected her to be her usual mouthy self, and he didn't know what to do with silent Sam. *Silent Sam.* If she weren't tied to a chair and being wrapped in razor wire that was already poking through her clothes to puncture her skin, she'd find that funny. When was she *ever* silent?

The razor wire hurt, especially when he pulled it tight against her neck. If she so much as moved, her jugular could be punctured. So she remained very, very still, even when he brought his face right down in front of hers.

She closed her eyes, refusing to look at him.

"You can play your little games, Holland. But we'll see who wins this round."

She kept her eyes closed and thought about Nick, imagining the scent of his cologne, the scent of home, and finding comfort in him.

SCOTTY STAYED CLOSE to Nick's side during the reception, almost as if he was afraid to let Nick out of his sight. The poor kid had been through so much at an early age, and just when things were beginning to settle for him, a new challenge arose. Nick had hated telling him the news about his biological father.

He'd also hated the spark of curiosity he'd seen in Scotty, as well as the spike of jealousy he'd experienced at realizing the boy was interested in the man who'd fathered him. Of course he was. Anyone would be. But Nick didn't want him to be interested in any other father but him. Petty much? Yeah, he knew it was, but he couldn't help the way he felt.

Maybe Scotty wouldn't like the guy and would see him once and be done with him. But what if he liked him? What if he wanted to see him again? How would Nick be able to stand turning him over to his *other* father on any kind of regular basis? He'd loved being the first father the boy had ever had. He wanted to be his only father.

"What do you think, Nick?" Graham O'Connor asked, stirring Nick from his musings.

"About what?"

"I told you he was spacing out," Scotty said with a laugh.

"Sorry," Nick said with a sheepish grin for them.

"I was wondering what you thought of the West Wing so far."

"One day in, and so far, so good." He wasn't ready yet to share his concerns about Nelson's motivations with anyone other than Terry, even Terry's father. "Still trying to figure out where everything is and what I'm supposed to be doing, but I suppose I'll work that out eventually." At least he hoped so. No sign yet of Nelson, his chief of staff Tom Hanigan or Derek Kavanaugh at the reception.

The first chance he got, he planned to ask his good friend Derek if the chill he was feeling from the Oval Office was intentional. He'd hate to think he'd been so wrong about someone, but he'd expected better from Nelson, especially after the way he'd wooed him and waged political war to get him confirmed.

Out of the corner of his eye, he saw Terry take a phone call and then head into his office and close the door. Probably Lindsey. Nick was thrilled for them both. They made a great couple, and he couldn't be happier for his chief of staff after the road he'd traveled in the last year to turn his life around.

While Nick chatted with Graham, Laine and staffers who'd come from the Senate with him as well as those who'd recently joined his White House team, he saw Terry come out of his office and head straight for him. He couldn't help but notice the odd look on his face.

"A moment please, Mr. Vice President."

"Excuse me," Nick said.

"Duty calls," Graham said gleefully. No one was happier about Nick's new job than Graham.

When Scotty started to follow them, Terry said, "Scotty, will you go see if my mom needs a refill for me?"

"Sure." Scotty dashed off to tend to Laine O'Connor, one of his favorite new friends.

When Terry headed for Nick's office, he followed him, closing the door. "What's going on?"

"Christina called."

"I thought she might be here. We invited her, right?"

Terry nodded and rubbed a hand over the late-day stubble on his jaw. "I… I wish I didn't have to tell you…"

Nick's entire body went cold with fear. "Tell me what?"

"Sam's in some sort of trouble. Gonzo asked Christina to track you down. They believe Sam is being held hostage at the Springer home on MacArthur Boulevard."

"They *believe*?" Somehow he was able to force the

words out despite the fear that gripped him. "They don't *know?*"

"Not for sure. Her car is parked out front, and no one has heard from her for quite some time. They haven't yet tried to gain access to the house. Christina said Gonzo told her they're still assessing the situation."

When Nick pulled his personal cell phone from his suit coat pocket, his hands trembled as he checked to see when the most recent message from his wife had arrived. More than five hours ago. *Five hours.* Jesus.

"I need to go there."

"The Secret Service will never allow you to go to a possibly active crime scene."

At the words *possibly active crime scene*, Nick's chest began to ache along with his stomach. "Will you get Brant in here, please?"

"Nick."

"Do it, Terry. Please."

Terry walked out the door, leaving Nick in a state of stunned disbelief. Was she already dead and no one wanted to tell him? No. If she were dead, he'd know it. He'd *feel* it.

Agent John Brantley Junior came into the room, closing the door behind him. "You asked to see me, sir."

"My wife is involved in a situation at work. I need to go to her."

"Where is she?"

"From what I'm told, it's believed she's being held hostage in a townhouse on MacArthur Boulevard."

Brant was shaking his head from the word *hostage* forward. "I can't take you there, sir."

"Let me be clear—I'm going to her, and I don't give a flying fuck if you come with me or not. But I am going. It's up to you as to whether you'll be joining me."

The young agent with the close-cropped blond hair and

the chiseled jaw stared at him with unblinking blue eyes.
"My job is to protect you, sir. I can't do that if you put
yourself into dangerous situations."

"My job is to protect *her*. I'm *going*." Nick knew what
Sam would have to say to him taking responsibility for her
safety, but right then he didn't care. He could only hope
he'd get the chance to tell her he'd said it.

"Give me one minute to put something together."

"Just you and me, one car, no motorcade. One minute.
That's all I'm giving you, and it's sixty seconds longer
than I want to give you."

"Scotty?"

"Stays here with the O'Connors."

With a brisk nod, Brant left the room.

Nick ran shaking hands through his hair, forcing air to
his lungs. The thought of her in danger always made him
crazy, but knowing for sure that she was in some sort of
trouble made him tremble with fear. Nothing had ever
scared him more than the possibility of losing her suddenly.

The door opened and Terry came in. "What did Brant
say?"

"He's working it out so the two of us can go."

"I'm surprised he went for it."

"He didn't."

Terry offered a small smile that he intended to be reas-
suring, but Nick could see the concern in his aide's eyes.
"I'm sure she's fine, Nick. She's always fine."

"I wish I could be so sure. Do me a favor—keep Scotty
here with your folks. I don't want him to worry before we
know what's going on."

"Of course. We'll take care of him."

"Thanks." Nick stared at the door, willing it to open.
"Make my excuses at the reception?"

"Yes, I will."

"I feel like I'm going to be sick." Nick bent at the waist, propped his hands on his knees and forced himself to breathe, knowing he wouldn't be any good to Sam if he lost his composure. Somehow he also had to walk through a room full of people who'd be focused on him and leave his son without worrying him. *Get it together, man.*

Brant came back into the office. "Mr. Vice President? I'm ready for you, sir."

Filled with dread and anxiety, Nick stood upright and forced himself to take a step forward and then another.

"Keep me posted," Terry said.

Nick nodded as he walked past him into the room where the party was going on. He went to Scotty. "Hey, bud, I need to step out for a bit to take care of something. You're going to stay here with the O'Connors, okay?"

"Where're you going?"

"Something came up, but I'll be back before you miss me." God, he hoped that was true.

"Don't worry about him," Laine said, her hands on Scotty's shoulders she looked at Nick with concern. No doubt she was able to tell something was wrong with him. She was scary perceptive that way. "We'll go home with him and his detail and make sure he gets his homework done."

Scotty scowled at the dreaded word. "I thought we were friends."

Laine laughed. "We are friends, and that's why I want you to do your homework, so you can grow up to be just like your dad."

"That'd be cool."

Nick leaned in to give Scotty a quick hug. "I'll see you at home, okay?"

"Okay. Nothing's wrong, right?"

For the first—and hopefully the last—time, Nick looked

him in the eye and lied. "Yeah, it's all good. I'll see you later."

Brant ushered him out of the office.

Behind him, Nick heard Terry explaining that the vice president had been called away unexpectedly but wanted everyone to enjoy the party.

"This goes against every protocol we have in place," Brant said tightly as they walked through the halls of the West Wing on their way out.

"I'm sorry to put you in this position. I'll take the full blame if the shit hits the fan."

"*If?* The shit is probably already hitting the fan. The rest of your detail is most likely reporting the breach to Headquarters as we speak."

"Then let's get the hell out of here before someone tries to stop us."

TWENTY-ONE

"YOU WERE OUR FRIEND, Leonard," Marissa said softly from the floor. Blood flowed from her mouth and formed puddles under her head and midsection. Judging from the reek filling the room, she'd also lost control of her bowels. "You told us they were going to arrest Billy. You tried to help us. Why would you do this to me?"

At least Sam now knew how the Springers had found out about their plans to arrest Billy. What she still didn't know was who had told Stahl. If she ever got out of here, finding that out would be one of her first orders of business.

"Because you'd outlived your usefulness." He grunted as he tightened the razor wire around Sam's body. A drop of his sweat landed on her forehead, making her gag as it ran straight down her face. She sealed her lips to stop it from going in her mouth. The burn of vomit in her throat had her swallowing frantically to keep it from coming up any further.

She hurt everywhere from the cuts that marked her entire body. The warm, persistent flow of blood from her neck to her chest concerned her. Had she nicked a major artery? How long would it take to bleed out? Was that what he wanted? For her to have a slow, painful, drawn-out demise?

The idea of that scared her far more than a bullet to the brain did. At least that would be quick and over before the pain could register. This was torture. Her lower abdomen was on fire from the need to urinate that became more insistent with every passing moment. Part of her wanted to pee all over the place. But she couldn't make herself do it.

Once he had her totally trussed up in the razor wire, he went back to the garage and returned with a can of gasoline.

Sam knew a moment of sheer panic when she realized his intentions. He planned to burn her alive. He'd made it so she couldn't move without slicing herself open, and he was going to start a fire that she'd be unable to defend herself against. What a way to go.

Where the fuck were her people? And what the fuck was taking so long to get her out of here?

"TALK TO ME," Malone said to the team gathered before him. MPD's SWAT and tactical response teams were on-site, as was FBI Special Agent George Terrell, who'd informed him that Agent Hill was en route. "What's our plan?"

Freddie Cruz came running up to him, breathless and white faced. "What's the latest?"

"We're trying to figure that out right now, but we know there's been at least one shot fired since we've been on the scene." Malone spread out the architectural drawings of the townhouse that had been procured from the development's main office. "From what I can tell, there are three ways in." He pointed to a deck off the master bedroom, the front door and the garage.

"The garage leads into the basement family room," Cruz said.

"I recommend we hit all three points of egress and every window in the house at the same time," SWAT Captain Nickelson said. "Coordinated attack."

"I agree," Farnsworth said. "Let's hit it hard and fast."

"Shouldn't we try to establish contact first?" Gonzo asked, concerned about skipping steps in their haste to rescue Sam.

"We have no idea how long she's been in there," Farnsworth said. "I hate to waste any more time when she could be injured."

The possibility that she was worse than injured was left unsaid, but everyone was thinking it.

"The sergeant's right, sir," Malone said softly, painfully aware of Farnsworth's personal connection to Holland. Hell, he was personally connected to her himself and couldn't picture the department or his life without the brash lieutenant raising hell every chance she got. "We need to at least try to establish contact."

"Someone get me the landline number for the Springers," Farnsworth said.

"I've got it in my notes from the investigation," Cruz said, consulting his phone. "Here it is."

"Call it," Malone said. "Put it on speaker so we can all hear."

The phone rang five times before it was answered. "Well, hello there," a familiar voice said. "Took you long enough to get your act together, but I'm not at all surprised."

"Is that *Stahl*?" Gonzo whispered.

"Fuck," the chief muttered.

The entire group deflated when they realized what they were up against—or rather *who* they were up against—someone who had nothing to lose and a very big ax to grind against Holland and the rest of them.

Malone felt like he was having a heart attack.

"What do you want?" Farnsworth barked.

"Ahh, is that you, Chief? How you doing? I've missed seeing you around the house since you kicked me out for making a phone call. I've got your little girl Holland here, but don't worry. I'm taking very good care of her."

"Let me talk to her."

"She's kind of…tied up at the moment."

"Whatever you want, you're not getting it until we know she's alive."

"She's alive. For now anyway."

A gasp from behind them had them all turning to see Nick Cappuano accompanied by an extremely unhappy-looking Secret Service agent.

"If you harm one hair on her head," Farnsworth said, "I'll kill you myself, you worthle—"

Malone grabbed the phone from the chief and shook his head. Antagonizing Stahl wouldn't do a thing to help Sam, which the chief certainly knew. But this was personal for him. For all of them.

"Where'd you go, Chief?" Stahl asked. "It was just starting to get interesting."

"It's Malone. What do you want?"

"Captain! How nice to hear from you. It's just like old times around here. Hmmm, what do I want? Let me see. I'd like my old command back, for one thing."

"You're already facing felony charges for the attack on Lieutenant Holland. You know we can't allow you back into the department as long as that is ongoing."

"What is it you guys see in her anyway? Is she fucking the whole lot of you?"

"She's extremely good at her job, as you well know," Malone said through gritted teeth. God, he'd hated Stahl from the first minute the cheeky bastard had graduated from the academy and come to work under his command when Malone had been the lieutenant in charge of the Patrol Division. He'd been a pain in Malone's ass ever since.

But this… Taking Holland hostage and doing God knows what to Mrs. Springer and her maid.

"Good at her job. Of course she is. She's sucking all your dicks so she can run wild and do whatever she wants. Right now, she can't do much of anything."

"Have you hurt her?"

"Define *hurt*."

"Is she injured?"

"Let me see. Yes, I think you could say she's injured. For sure."

"Let her go and we can work this out, Len. I can't help you at all if you harm her. You know that."

"Now I'm Len, huh? What happened to Fat Fuck? Oh, you didn't know that I knew you called me that behind my back?"

"What does that have to do with Holland?"

"She's made my life a living hell, and now I'm going to do the same to her."

"Let me get you out of there and find you some help—"

Stahl's loud laugh startled everyone. "Now you want to 'help' me. Seems to me you took great pleasure in arresting me not that long ago. Now I'm going to take great pleasure in killing your golden girl. Good to catch up, Captain. Give everyone my regards, but I've got work to do. Gotta go."

"Don't hang up."

The line went dead.

"Motherfucker," Malone muttered under his breath.

"You have to go in there and get her," Nick said. "He said she's injured."

Malone felt for the guy. He truly did. The two of them were crazy in love. Anyone could see that. But he couldn't risk his people without having a solid plan in place, and solid plans took time they didn't have. He glanced at the chief. "What do you want to do?"

"I want to kill him with my bare hands," Farnsworth growled.

"What's your second thought?" Malone asked.

Hill came running up to them, looking frazzled. "What's going on?"

"Stahl has Lieutenant Holland," Malone said. "He says she's injured but he won't say in what way."

"Are you going in?" Hill asked, hands on hips, eyes intense and focused.

"We were just discussing our limited options when you joined us. Nickelson, what do you think?"

"I still say we hit it hard and fast through every window and every door."

"He'll be ready for us," Malone said. "He's no fool, and he's a well-trained police officer. He knows what we'll do."

"So let's play right into his hand," Gonzo said.

"How so?" Hill asked.

"Let's give him exactly what he expects. We give him his big moment and let him go out in his blaze of glory. That's what this is. There's no way he'll survive in prison, and he knows that."

"What about Sam?" Nick asked. "If you go in there with guns blazing, he's apt to take her with him."

"If we don't go in there," Malone said, keying in to where Gonzo was heading, "he's going to take her with him anyway."

"Exactly," Gonzo said.

"Chief?" Malone looked to his longtime friend. "It's your call."

Farnsworth looked at the house for a long moment while everyone waited for him to decide. He never blinked when he said, "Do it."

THE SMELL OF gas was overwhelming and made Sam's eyes burn. He dumped it around her in a big circle.

"You've lost your mind," Marissa croaked from the floor.

Stahl crossed the room to dump some of the gas on her.

She screamed from the pain of the gas connecting with her wound.

"I'm so fucking sick of women who think they should have an *opinion*. Shut your fucking mouths and do what you were put on this earth to do—spread your legs and breed. Lori Phillips understood that. When I offered her cocaine in exchange for a lay, she spread her legs *wide* open."

"You're a pig," Marissa said.

Sam couldn't have said it better herself. Her legs would have to be wide open to accommodate him.

"Worst thing they ever did was let bitches into the police department. Ruined everything."

Listening to his rant, Sam felt vindicated for the nearly visceral reaction she'd had the first time she ever met him. Her gut had let her know he was no good, and nothing she'd seen of him in the ensuing years had changed that first impression. But to hear his true thoughts about women in general and women on the job, in particular, was illuminating.

Speaking of illuminating... He pulled a box of matches from his pocket and shook it in front of her face. "Ready to roast?"

As she had all along, Sam pretended she couldn't hear him and tried to remain calm despite the pervasive stench of gasoline and the maniac with the matches. During her years on the job, she'd imagined a number of different ways her life might suddenly end. Most of the scenarios she'd imagined found her on the wrong end of a gun. She certainly hadn't considered the possibility that one of her fellow officers would wrap her in razor wire and set her on fire. And here she'd thought she had such a good imagination.

If it weren't so fucking sad, she'd laugh her ass off at the sheer lunacy of her life ending at the hands of Leonard Stahl, of all people.

She was scared. She'd never deny that. The idea of burning to death wasn't something she relished. But rather than obsess about what was about to happen and how she couldn't do a thing to stop it, she chose to think about her gorgeous husband, her handsome son, her sisters, her beloved dad, her nieces and nephews, her friends and colleagues at work and the amazing life she'd been privileged to lead. Sam thought about the mother from whom she was estranged and knew a moment of regret. She should've fixed things with her. If by some miracle she made it out of here, she'd take care of mending those fences.

She was loved, admired, respected and feared on the job, which brought her tremendous pleasure. She'd loved every second of her life and her career and especially her marriage to the most amazing man on the planet. Her adorable, wonderful Scotty had made her a mother, and he was everything she could ever hope for in a son. She had no regrets. She would've liked a little more time. She would've loved the opportunity to be pregnant with Nick's child, but overall, no regrets.

Stahl struck a match and flashed an evil grin as the flame ignited.

While Sam held her breath waiting for him to drop it into the gas he'd spread around the room, he looked at her and smiled maniacally, his eyes sparkling with pleasure. He'd truly lost what was left of his mind if he thought he was going to get out of here alive. And then it occurred to her in a moment of clarity that he planned to go with her.

Cops didn't do well in prison, and one with his snarky personality would be in for a particularly rough time of it.

Her spirits sank even further, if that was possible. *Just do it already, and be done with it.* But no, he wanted to drag out his moment of glory, so he blew out that match and reached for another. She could so see him going through the entire box before he dropped the last one into the gas.

Good, let him dick around for a while. That gave her people time to figure out where she was and how to get her out of there.

As long as he didn't accidentally drop one of those matches.

Sam directed her gaze to where Marissa lay on the floor by the windows. She'd stopped making noise shortly after Stahl had doused her with gas, and Sam wondered if she was dead. Not that she cared about Marissa, who'd played her for a fool and led her into hell. Normally she felt compassion for murder victims. Not this time. She'd made a deal with a sadistic asshole and had gotten exactly what she deserved.

Stahl continued to work his way through the box of matches.

Sam wondered how many were left before he was down to the last one, and the moment of truth would be upon them.

He'd just lit another one when the windows exploded and SWAT officers swarmed into the basement.

Fucking finally, Sam thought, expelling a sigh of relief that was short-lived when she saw Stahl calmly drop the lit match into the pool of gasoline that surrounded her. Motherfucker. Flames erupted only a few feet from her, the heat searing her face and other areas of exposed skin.

Two of the SWAT officers, wearing full riot gear, fell onto the flame, dousing it before it went any further. Three others jumped on Stahl, taking him down quickly as he screamed obscenities.

Sam watched it all happen with a detached sense of relief and disbelief. Was she actually going to survive after all?

"Is she alive?" a male voice Sam recognized in her heart and soul screamed from outside.

"I'm alive," she yelled back, wanting to keep her promise to let him know as soon as she could that she was all right.

"Thank fucking God."

For the first time in hours, Sam had reason to smile. "Don't touch me," she said to the SWAT officer who approached her. "Razor wire."

"Holy fuck," he uttered when he took in the sight of her tied to the chair and wrapped in razor wire. Into the radio transmitter he wore on his shoulder, he said, "We need some wire cutters in here. Stat."

Smoke hung in the air, mixing with the smell of gasoline.

"Close call, Lieutenant," Captain Nickelson said as he took in her predicament.

"Not the best day I ever had," Sam replied. "Get me out of here, will you?" She had things to do and people to see.

"Hang tight. You're bleeding like crazy and your face is unrecognizable. You've got a trip to the hospital in your immediate future."

"I want to see my husband."

"Not until we get you out of here."

"Well, hurry up about it, will you? I've got to pee like a racehorse."

Into his radio, Nickelson said, "She's fine. Full of *piss* and vinegar." He smiled at her as he said that. "Get EMS in here right away for her and one other vic."

Outside, a loud cheer went up that she assumed came from her MPD colleagues. "Aww, they love me."

"For some strange reason they do."

"I'm touched." In truth, she was elated and giddy and light-headed with relief—and probably blood loss, but why let that get in the way of a happy ending? She took great pleasure in watching the SWAT officers haul Stahl out of the room, kicking and screaming and squealing like the pig he was. While part of her wished they'd killed him, the other part of her took perverse pleasure in knowing what awaited him in prison. And this time, after he'd committed murder and taken a police officer hostage, there was no way in hell he'd be granted bail.

Farnsworth, Malone, Gonzo, Cruz and Hill came down the basement stairs. Freddie pulled on a pair of heavy gloves and produced a pair of wire cutters that he used to cut her free from the razor wire while the others stood back and watched, their expressions grim.

"Where's Nick?"

"The Secret Service agent wouldn't let him come in here. He's waiting—very impatiently—for you outside," Malone said.

"Why do you all look like you've lost your best friend?"

"Because we nearly did," Freddie replied.

"I'm fine. It's over. Nothing to worry about."

Hill stood back from the others, hands on his hips, golden eyes trained intently on her.

Sam looked away from him, uncomfortable as always by the way he looked at her.

"Um, you should see what you look like," Gonzo said. "If you could, you wouldn't be saying you were fine. He tuned you up pretty good, huh?"

Sam would've shrugged, but there was the matter of the razor wire. "He tried, but I didn't give him one ounce of satisfaction. I didn't say a single word to him the entire time, but I did spit in his face. That was fun."

Farnsworth turned away, his head bent.

Sam looked at Malone and nodded at him to see to the chief. "Did someone call my dad?"

"Nick did," Freddie said. "He was relieved to hear you're all right and glad he didn't know you were being held all this time."

Gonzo cut the last of the wires that surrounded her and grasped the edges to pull them apart. The wire strands fell into a pile on the floor. Next he went to work on the tight bindings on her hands and legs. When her hands were freed and the blood began to flow again, she gasped from the intense pain. "Fuck, that hurts."

EMTs came into the room, carrying equipment and two gurneys.

"See to her first," Sam said, nodding to Marissa. "He gut shot her a while ago. I don't think she's alive anymore, but I'm not sure."

"What happened to the maid?" Hill asked.

"Marissa shot her when Edna questioned what she was doing taking me hostage."

"So Marissa took you hostage?" Gonzo asked.

"She was in on it with Stahl. From what I could gather, they teamed up to discredit the department."

"Christ," Malone said. "What a partnership. So why'd he shoot her?"

"He said she outlived her usefulness. Is Jeannie here?"

"Yeah, she's outside," Freddie said.

"Tell her to come in here."

He made the call on his radio and Detective McBride came rushing in a minute later.

"Lieutenant, oh my God," Jeannie said, her eyes wet with unshed tears, "I'm so glad you're all right."

"I need your help."

"Of course. Whatever I can do."

"I need to pee—urgently—and my hands and legs are useless."

"Aw jeez," Gonzo said. "I coulda gone my whole life without knowing that."

Thankfully, Jeannie sprang into action, moving to Sam's side.

"Wait," one of the EMTs said. "Don't move her until we assess her injuries."

"I'm fine," Sam assured her. "Surface stuff. You aren't going to make me wet myself in front of my brass, are you?"

The EMT hesitated before gesturing for Jeannie to go ahead.

Jeannie lifted her right out of the chair and carried her to the bathroom.

"I had no idea you were so freakishly strong."

"I'm running on adrenaline after the last couple of hours." She put Sam down, waited for her to find her legs and then helped with her pants.

"This is kinda embarrassing," Sam said.

"We've been through worse," Jeannie said with a meaningful look.

"Yes, we have."

"This has been the second worst day of my life." Jeannie helped her onto the toilet, where Sam took the single most satisfying pee of her life. "Wow, you weren't kidding."

Her lower body ached from the relief and the pain of holding it for so long. "Had to go the whole freaking time and there was no way I was going to piss myself in front of that asshole. I was all about denying him satisfaction today."

"Good for you." Jeannie hesitated before she said, "He didn't try to, you know…"

"Thank God, no."

Jeannie blew out a sharp, deep breath. "Thank God is right. Nick is out of his mind."

"I can imagine. I need to see him."

Jeannie handed her some toilet paper. "Can you do this part yourself?"

"I hope so." Though she had very little feeling in her hands, she operated on rote, going through the motions and hoping she'd done a good enough job. What did it matter? She was going to need the world's biggest shower after this day.

Jeannie helped her up and smoothed the skirt that had been shredded by the razor wire. "Can you walk?"

"I think so. I don't want the press getting pictures of me like this. What can we do?"

"I'll take care of it."

She walked with her arm around Sam back into the family room, where a second team of paramedics waited for her. Marissa had been removed. "Is she dead?"

"Not quite but close."

They got Sam settled on the gurney and began assessing her. At the sight of a large needle heading for her hand, Sam said, "Whoa, what's that for?"

"An IV. We need to get some fluid into you."

"Get me a bottle of water. No IVs."

"Sam," Malone said in his no-nonsense voice. "Let them take care of you."

"No IVs." She fucking hated needles.

The paramedic shook his head at her insolence. "Whatever you say, Lieutenant."

"Get me out of here. I want to see my husband."

"Give us a second to clear the street of media," Malone said.

"Hurry up about it."

"Is she giving me orders?" Malone asked Gonzo and Cruz, who both seemed relieved to see that her day with Stahl hadn't done a thing to curb her sauciness.

"It sounds like that to me, sir." Freddie said the words in his best suck-up voice even if he seemed like he was about to lose his composure.

"You guys, look at Stahl for Lori's murder, Bill Springer's murder and Elin's assault."

"What?" Freddie said, his face flat with shock. "What did he have to do with that?"

"He put the guy up to it so you'd go into the jail and do exactly what you did. He was after my inner circle."

Freddie took an uncomfortable glance at Malone and Farnsworth.

"What exactly did you do, Detective Cruz?" Malone asked.

"I had a conversation with the man who assaulted my girlfriend."

"By conversation, do you mean…"

"I made sure he understood that she's off-limits to him, and it's in his best interest to leave her alone."

"I see," Malone said. "I suppose any of us would've done the same in your shoes."

"Yes, sir, I'm sure you would have if you could see what he did to her," Freddie said.

"So this whole thing—Lori's murder, Springer's murder, Elin's assault—it was all done to discredit the department?" Farnsworth asked.

"Yes," Sam said, "and he was also the one who told the

Springers that we were looking at Billy for the murders of Hugo and the others."

"How did he know that?" Gonzo asked. "He'd been relieved of duty before the Springer investigation."

"He must've had help from within," Malone concluded. "Someone told him and he told the Springers. That's how they knew."

"Look at Ramsey," Sam said. "He hates me for some unknown reason and would love to see me go down in flames like I nearly did today."

"It's a good place to start," Farnsworth said.

"Can you please get me the fuck out of here?" Sam asked the EMTs.

"Yeah," one of them said, "let's roll."

"Is the street clear of all reporters?" Jeannie asked.

"Let me check." Freddie ran ahead of the paramedics who planned to take her out through the garage. "Good to go," he reported a minute later.

The EMTs rolled her out of the house into the gloriously cold air. After more than an hour of breathing gasoline fumes, she'd never been happier to get a lungful of fresh air.

Nick and Brant were standing at the end of the driveway. Brant had his hand on Nick's arm as if he were physically holding her husband back. When Nick saw her coming, he shook off the agent and ran to her.

Sam held out her arms to him and finally broke down when he wrapped her up in his tight embrace.

"Tell me you're all right," he whispered in her ear.

"I am now."

"God, Sam."

"I know. I'm so sorry to put you through this."

"Not your fault."

"We'd like to get her to the ER," one of the EMTs said. "Sir."

Nick released his tight hold and grasped her hand. "I'm going with her."

Brant cleared his throat. "Um, Mr. Vice President—"

"Right now I'm Mr. Cappuano, and this is my wife. I'm going with her."

"You're going to get me fired," Brant muttered.

"You probably ought to get used to it," Malone said, speaking from experience. "That's how they roll."

"Awesome," Brant said sarcastically, making the others laugh. "I'll be right behind you. Don't step foot out of the ambulance until I'm there."

"I suppose I can live with that," Nick said.

The paramedics wheeled her to the ambulance and got her settled. Nick followed her into the back of the bone wagon.

"How bad do I look?"

"On a scale of bomb to pistol-whipped, you're more in the pistol-whip end of things."

Relieved that his sense of humor was intact despite what had to have been an awful ordeal for him, she took hold of his left hand and rubbed her thumb over his wedding ring. "You were all I thought about in there—you and Scotty and the last year. I relived every minute."

He hung his head and brought her hand to his lips. "He didn't, you know, try to... I can't even say it."

"No."

"Thank God." He continued to kiss her hand, but now she felt dampness on his face.

"Come closer. You're too far away over there."

Since she'd refused all needles, the EMT got busy consulting his phone.

Nick moved over to sit on Sam's gurney. He propped a hand on either side of her head and leaned in to kiss her.

"Why do you smell like gas?"

"Because Stahl dumped it all over the floor and was playing with matches when the SWAT guys busted in on his party."

Nick shuddered at the realization of what could've happened. "What was he doing out of jail after he attacked you the first time?"

"He made bail," Sam said. "I suspect Marissa Springer gave him the money. Between that and his long record of service to the department, his lawyer was able to make a case for bail. He won't get out again after this. That's for sure."

"If we're looking at the bright side, one less enemy to contend with."

"I have to say, you're rolling with all of this better than I expected. Dare I say you might be getting used to the insanity that goes along with being married to me?"

He shook his head. "I'll never get used to you being in this kind of danger. Never. When I got that call from Christina that you were missing and had possibly been taken hostage, my heart about stopped."

"You didn't tell Scotty, did you?"

He shook his head, but the grim set to his mouth worried her.

She traced a finger over his lips. "What's that about?"

"We'll talk later." He glanced at the EMT. "When we're alone."

"I don't like the sound of that."

"It's no big deal. It's nothing compared to what could've happened today." He dropped his head onto her chest.

Sam ran her fingers through his silky dark hair.

"Why are you all cut up?"

"He wrapped me in razor wire so I couldn't move."

"Fucking hell," he whispered.

They kept their voices down so their conversation wouldn't be overheard. Thankfully the loud sirens made it easy to keep their words private.

"I was surprised you were out there when I heard your voice. Afterward. I didn't think the Secret Service would let you come there."

"They didn't. I'm on Brant's shit list big-time."

Sam chuckled, imagining the scene he must've made. "So you laid down the law, huh?"

"There was swearing involved."

"You never swear!"

"I do when my precious, beloved wife is in danger and someone is trying to keep me from going to her."

She reached up to touch his hair and then his face. "Thinking of you was the only thing that kept me from losing my shit in there. I thought about you constantly."

He burrowed into the space between her head and shoulder, and despite the lingering pain in her stiff muscles and the burn from the cuts, Sam wrapped her arms around him.

"I'm sorry to have put you through this."

"Not your fault, babe, so don't go there."

"It was my fault. I went in there by myself with no one knowing where I was. It was stupid and not like me at all. But I didn't get any alarm bells from Marissa when I was there earlier. She really played me, and now I'm questioning everything. If Freddie had done something like this, I'd be ripping him a new one right now."

"From what I heard, you were shorthanded today and were working the case like you were supposed to. Don't beat yourself up."

"I could've gotten myself killed." She had to fight to swallow over the lump in her throat. "I thought for sure I was going to die. I even thought about my mother and how I should've made things right with her when I had the chance."

"Wow."

"I know, right? I was really scared this time in a way I never have been before."

"We'll have plenty of time to talk it all through after the docs do their thing."

"They better not come at me with needles."

He raised his head to meet her gaze. "Do what they tell you to do so you can come home where you belong."

"You called my dad?"

Nodding, he said, "I talked to him and Celia."

"I haven't even asked you about your first day at the White House."

He cracked up laughing. "Who the fuck cares about the goddamn White House?"

"What's happened to you? You're swearing like I do."

He lowered his head so he was speaking directly into her ear. "*You* happened to me. You make me crazy and frantic and out of my mind with fear and desire all in the same day."

Sam smiled with pleasure and gratitude for him, for the second chance she'd been given and all the blessings in her life. "I do what I can."

"I love you so much," he whispered. "So fucking much."

"Love you just as much. Maybe even more."

"No way."

"Yes way."

He looked down at her for a long moment, smiling softly before he kissed her.

They were giving the EMT one hell of a show, but Sam couldn't be bothered worrying about it. She was back in Nick's arms, and she didn't care about anything else but him.

TWENTY-TWO

THEY CAME AT her with needles—lots of them. The cut on her neck and two on her legs required stitches, which in turn required several shots. After a couple of predictable jokes about punching her frequent-flyer card, Dr. Anderson got down to business, insisting on an IV to get antibiotics into her to prevent infection. And then there was the tetanus shot he'd given her because God only knew what kind of germs were on the razor wire.

By the time they were done with her, Sam felt like a tired, sore, cranky pincushion. Nick never left her side for a minute, holding her hand through each needle stick, wiping her tears when the pain became too intense. Once the tears started, she couldn't seem to stop them as it came down on her how much worse this day could've been.

Though she desperately wanted to go home to her own bed, Anderson insisted on admitting her for observation.

"We need to call Scotty," Sam said once she was settled in her room and the tears had stopped—for now.

"I already called him and told him something happened today at work and you were hurt but you'll be fine. He said to tell you he hopes you feel better, and he'll come see you tomorrow. Graham and Laine are staying with him tonight. Everything is all set."

"You're sure you told him it was nothing to worry about?"

"I did." He brushed the hair back from her forehead, tucked it behind her ear and wiped away more tears with the sweep of his thumb over her cheek. She wanted to purr from the sweet pleasure of his touch. Even with everything hurting, she couldn't get enough of him.

"Come closer."

He'd removed his suit coat and tie hours ago and had rolled up the sleeves of his dress shirt. "How much closer?"

"All the way up here with me."

"We'll start a scandal if they catch me in your bed."

"Since when do we care about scandals?"

"True." He worked his way around the IV tube and onto the bed next to her. Somehow he managed to get one arm under her neck and another around her middle without causing her a second of pain. He was just that good.

Sam settled into his embrace and breathed in the scent of him greedily. "God, you smell so good. You always smell so good. Have I ever told you that?"

"I think you have."

"Do I still smell like gas?" The nurses had helped her to take a shower but the hospital soap hadn't been scented and wasn't able to do much against the pungent odor of gasoline.

"A little."

"I need my stuff from home."

"We'll worry about that tomorrow."

"I don't like smelling like gas," Sam said as new tears filled her eyes. She didn't like being a weepy female either, but in light of what she'd been through that day, she'd decided to give herself one day to wallow in it before she got on with her life.

"It's okay, baby. Everything is okay now. Why don't you try to sleep?"

"I don't want to sleep. I want to lie here with you and smell you and talk to you and touch you."

"Samantha, sweetheart, you're so tired. It's okay to sleep. I won't leave you for a second."

"You must be hungry."

"No way could I eat. Not yet."

"Your reception at the White House! I totally forgot. I'm such an awful second lady."

Laughter made his chest rumble. "Stop it. You're exactly what I want, just the way you are."

"I was going to be there. I swear I was."

"I know that."

"I want to see your new office as soon as possible."

"We'll do that. We'll do everything you want."

"I want to go back to Bora Bora for our anniversary."

"I already scheduled the plane."

"Damn, that's right. We've got our own plane now. Maybe this new job of yours won't totally suck."

"Maybe not."

"Do you like to ski?"

"Do I like to *ski*? What does that have to do with anything?"

"When I was in that basement, I was thinking about all the things I don't know about you. Skiing was one of them."

"I love to ski. I don't get to do it as often as I used to when I lived in New England, but we can go sometime if you want to."

"I suck at it."

"I'll teach you all the tricks."

"So what happened with Scotty that you said you'd tell me later?"

"We can talk about it tomorrow when you're feeling better."

"I'll never sleep worrying about whatever it is."

His deep sigh put her immediately on alert. Then he told

her about Andy's investigator finding Scotty's biological father and how the man hadn't known he had a son. "He wants to meet him before he'll sign away his rights."

"That can't happen! If he meets him, he'll want him. Anyone would!"

"Babe, settle down. You don't want to tear open your stitches and have to go through that again." He settled her back against the pillow. "As I told Scotty when we talked about it earlier, he's old enough to tell the court what he wants. And he wants to be with us. He was quite adamant about that. But he also wants to meet his biological father. I answered a lot of questions about how it's possible a man could not know he fathered a child."

"I hate that he has to deal with this after everything he's already been through."

"I do too." He caressed her arm, his fingers moving lightly over her skin, setting her entire body on fire for him, as if she hadn't withstood a major trauma that day. It didn't matter. If he was close to her, she wanted him. "He got quite upset when I made the mistake of referring to the guy as his father. '*You* are my father,' he said. He almost made me cry."

"That's so sweet," Sam said, blinking back tears. "He chose you as much as you chose him. Don't ever forget that."

"It makes me crazy to think of him having another father," he confessed. "Which makes me feel like a jealous child."

"I don't blame you for feeling that way. I do too. I don't want any other parents in his life either, but we're going to have to take him to meet this guy, aren't we?"

"Yeah. Andy said the other option would be to continue as his legal guardians without formally adopting him."

"That's not an option. I want it legal."

"So do I and Scotty does, as well. Besides, now the guy knows about him. We don't want him making trouble for us later. Better to deal with it now on our terms rather than later on his."

"He can't take him away from us, can he?"

"Not with Scotty wanting to be with us. Andy was very clear that the courts listen to kids his age on these things. I'll tell you what he told me—try not to worry. This is procedural stuff and we have to deal with it to get what we want. We've got a great lawyer looking out for us."

"So you're not worried?"

He paused, long enough to tell her his true feelings. "I don't want to be, but I am. A little."

"Me too."

Nick's phone buzzed with a text message. He pulled the phone from his pocket to read it. "Your dad, sisters and entire squad are here waiting to see you. Can they come in?"

"My dad is *here*? He hasn't left the house in weeks!"

"His baby girl was taken hostage. Where else would he be?"

Goddamn tears! She swiped at them and then regretted it when her bruised face protested. "My dad and the girls can come in. Ask the squad to come back tomorrow. And tell them thanks for everything today."

He typed the message and returned his phone to his pocket. When he started to get up, Sam stopped him.

"Stay right here."

"Your dad is coming in."

"He knows we sleep together."

"But does he want to *see* it?"

"I don't care. I need you right here."

"Then I'll stay right here."

The whir of her dad's wheelchair was audible through the closed door. Sam would know that sound anywhere after three years of listening for it. They could hear her family members speaking to Brant before Tracy came in first, took one look at Sam and burst into tears.

"Oh my God, Sam!"

Angela was right behind her and held the door for Skip.

"Goddamn," Angela said, covering her mouth with her hand when she saw Sam in the bed.

"Do I look *that* bad?"

"Worse than the pistol-whip," Tracy said bluntly.

"Much worse," Skip added after taking a shrewd, assessing look at her. "Stahl did this to you?"

"Dad…"

"Don't Dad me. Tell me what happened."

"You've already heard."

"Not from you."

Knowing she'd have to do it again for the record probably tomorrow, Sam took them through the whole thing, beginning with Lori Phillips's murder and culminating with her return trip to Marissa Springer's house. "I'm so freaking pissed with myself," she concluded. "I did everything wrong today."

"How so?" Angela asked.

"She never should've gone back there without telling someone where she was going, and she shouldn't have gone in there alone—once, let alone twice, knowing the beef the Springers have had with the department," Skip said.

Sam shrank into the bed, hating that she had disappointed him.

"That said," Skip continued, "it happens. We get short-handed with a hot case to contend with, and we do what's got to be done. And that's what you were doing today. Working the case. Doing your job. Trying to help to free your colleagues from the veil of suspicion. You did what anyone would've done."

"I didn't get any hint of anything to be worried about with Marissa the first time," Sam said.

"That was probably part of their plan—play the part of the wounded mother and lure you back there on the guise of something that would help the case. I could fucking murder that bastard Stahl for this."

"Someone else will take care of that for us when he gets to prison," Sam said.

"That's a small comfort when I look at your bruised face and smell the gas he planned to burn you with."

Sam shuddered at the reminder as both her sisters sniffled.

"Close call today, baby girl. You're going to need to take some time to process what happened and deal with it before you go back to the job. You won't be any good to anyone if you go back too soon."

"I know," Sam said with a sigh.

"So you're actually going to take time off and not argue about it?" Tracy asked, incredulous.

"Yeah, I am. I've got some things to take care of and Dad's right. If I've lost my edge, even temporarily, I'll be no good to anyone." She could only hope her edge would come back at some point or she'd be totally fucked on the job. "Gonzo is coming back. He can cover for me for a while." She looked at Nick. "Tell them about Scotty's biological father."

"What about him?" Skip asked. He and Scotty had become close pals and the alarm in her father's voice wasn't lost on her.

Nick filled them in on what was going on.

"He can't take him away from you," Skip said.

"We won't let him," Nick assured him. "Andy says everything is on our side here, especially the fact that Scotty wants to be with us."

"Does he know?" Tracy asked.

"Yeah, I talked to him earlier. He was upset but determined to do what's necessary to finalize the adoption."

"I can't believe his father didn't know he existed," Angela said. "Imagine what a shock that must be to find out about a kid that way."

"We have to hope he'll be satisfied to meet him once and let that be that," Nick said.

"What if he isn't satisfied?" Tracy asked.

"I guess we'll cross that bridge when we come to it," Nick replied grimly.

Sam didn't even want to think about that possibility.

"On another note," Nick said, "I made some calls today and found out about a spinal cord research study that's underway at the NIH. They've had some breakthroughs with spinal cord patients who experience painful sensation in their limbs. I told them about you," he said to his father-in-law, "and they're very interested in seeing you."

"Are they?" Skip said.

"Dad, that's amazing," Angela said. "They might be able to help you."

"Thank you so much, Nick," Celia said.

"Yes, thank you," Sam added with a warm smile for her husband.

"They want you to come in next week. Is that possible?"

Everyone watched Skip expectantly. "Yes, that's possible. Thank you, Nick. Even if nothing comes of it, it's nice of you to try."

"Something will come of it," Sam said. The alternative was unacceptable.

THEY LET SAM leave the hospital late the next afternoon and by dinnertime, she was settled on the sofa at home, surrounded by family, friends and colleagues. The abduction and rescue of the nation's second lady had dominated local and national news all day. Unfortunately, it had also drawn unwanted attention to the fact that she had chosen to forgo Secret Service protection.

"It shouldn't be up to her," one pundit declared. "This is a national security issue. Once the crackpots hear that the vice president's wife is unprotected, she's going to be a target for every lunatic who has a beef with the United States."

"Turn it off," Nick said. "I've heard more than enough."

"Wait, I want to know more about how I'm a national security issue."

"Samantha."

"Fine." She hit the power button on the clicker. "He ruins all my fun."

Nick scowled at her playfully, trying to hide that he was deeply concerned about all the same things the newspeople were talking about. Before yesterday, no one had paid much attention to the fact that she had declined protection. Now everyone was interested, including the Secret Service and Nelson's team, which had been more involved with and interested in their new vice president—and his wife—in the last twelve hours than in the last six weeks combined.

The thought of the crackpots taking an interest in his Samantha was making Nick crazy. That his new job could've opened her up to that kind of exposure was something he hadn't fully considered beforehand—and that made him doubly crazy. That he'd thought they'd somehow go on like before. How could he have been so naïve?

Unsettled by the disturbing thoughts circling through his mind, he got up from the sofa and went into the kitchen, looking for a drink.

Christina was right behind him. "How you doing?"

"Fantastic. Never better." He poured two fingers of bourbon and held up the bottle.

She shook her head. "No, thanks."

"Want wine or something else?"

"I'm good. I'm worried about you though."

"And I'm worried about her, as usual."

"I can't believe it was someone from her own department who did this to her."

"He's had it in for her for a long time. We failed to have the imagination to suspect he'd be capable of something like this, although after he tried to kill her once, we should've known he wouldn't stop at that."

"You had no way to know that, Nick. Most people, when they're arrested on a charge of attempted murder, are scared and chastened."

"Stahl isn't most people. He's a fucking lunatic, and she's known that for a while now."

"Still, you can't blame yourself for what someone else did."

"It eats at me to know I can't protect her."

"I feel the same way every time Tommy leaves for work. It's an awful feeling."

"You understand it better than most people do."

"So how's the new job?"

"It sucks."

"Really? I didn't expect you to say that."

"I didn't expect Nelson to basically ignore me until something happened to my wife. Now he's all up in my grill."

"What do you mean about him ignoring you?"

"He has no intention of using me for anything other than a boost in the polls. Derek says he hasn't heard anything to that effect, but they wouldn't tell him. They know we're friends."

"If they're going to ignore you, then it seems to me that perhaps you should set your own agenda, and if they don't like it, you could say you assumed they wouldn't care."

"I like the way you think. You're sure you want to stay retired?"

"For now, but I'm always available to you. I hope you know that."

"I do. Thank you, and I like your idea. A lot."

Brant came into the kitchen. "Pardon the interruption, Mr. Vice President, but Director Pierce is on the phone and would appreciate a word with you."

"Sorry," Nick said to Christina.

"No worries."

"Tell Sam I'll be right out."

"Will do."

After the door swung closed behind her, Brant handed the phone to Nick and then left the room.

"Director Pierce."

"Mr. Vice President, I hope you'll excuse the bother when I'm sure you have other things on your mind today."

"Not a problem. What can I do for you?"

"I was hoping we might get together tomorrow or perhaps the next day at the latest to discuss your wife's situation and how we might be of assistance."

"Is this coming from you or above you?"

"This is coming straight from the top."

"Sure, we can talk if you'd like to, but I don't expect anything to change."

"Mr. Vice President, with all due respect, *everything* has changed."

"Not from where I'm sitting. Sam has a job to do, and she can't do it with a detail in tow. It's that simple."

"It's hardly that simple. This has become a matter of national security."

"Why? Because the media is saying it is?"

"I would think, after what happened yesterday, that you'd want to protect her—"

"Don't talk to me about protecting my wife, Ambrose. You're so far out of line with that insinuation it's not even funny."

"Again, all due respect, sir, but protecting you and your family is my job. I'm trying to do the job the people hired me to do."

"My wife is not and will not be protected by the Secret Service, so that means she's not your job. I made that very clear before I accepted this position."

"Then I'm afraid we have a problem, and you're going to need to consult with President Nelson. He's very upset about what happened to her and the attention it has called to her lack of protection."

"I'll take it up with him as soon as I'm able to, but the only possible thing that's going to change is who his vice president is. Thanks for the call, Ambrose. I appreciate your concern."

"Thank you, sir."

Nick hit the end button and put Brant's phone on the counter. He was hardly surprised by the call or the concern from the administration. They had a valid point. He'd never deny that. However, they'd made a deal, and he was going to force them to adhere to it, even if he agreed with them.

He wanted Sam to have protection after what'd happened. He believed she would be at far greater risk than she'd ever been before now that the whole world knew she didn't have protection. But he could never ask that of her. He couldn't and he wouldn't. He'd resign before he'd take away the career that meant so much to her.

Scotty came into the kitchen, skidding to a halt in front of Nick. "Sam is looking for you."

"I'll be right there, buddy."

"Everything okay?"

"Yeah, it's all good."

He eyed Nick skeptically. "You said that same thing to me yesterday when it wasn't good. It wasn't good at all."

"I didn't want you to worry."

"I know that, but still." He bit his lip and glanced at Nick almost shyly, which reminded him of when they first met.

"What do you want to say? Whatever it is, it's okay to say it."

"We're a family now, right?"

"You bet we are."

"I want to know what's going on. I'm not a little kid, and I don't want you to treat me like one. It scared me more to hear about what happened to Sam from the O'Connors than it would have to hear it from you. When they told me, I thought maybe it was because something had happened to you too."

Nick winced. "You're absolutely right, and I'm sorry. I know you're not a little kid, and I didn't mean to treat you like one. I didn't know for sure what was going on with Sam when I left the office yesterday, and I didn't want to say anything until I knew more. But I should've told you what I knew, and I will if anything like that ever happens again."

"Let's hope it doesn't. That guy is freaking nuts."

"He sure is." Nick put his hand on Scotty's shoulder. "I'm sorry, okay?"

"Yeah, it's cool. I don't mean to make a big thing out of it, but I want to know what's going on."

"Fair enough."

"I think she's tired but she doesn't want to tell everyone to leave."

"We can do that for her."

Scotty smiled at him. "They brought a ton of awesome food, so we need to be nice about it."

Laughing, he said, "Yes, we do." Nick followed Scotty into the living room, where most of Sam's squad and her entire family, less her niece Brooke who was in school in Virginia, were gathered around her. He took a close look at his wife and saw that Scotty was right—she was fading fast. "Hey, guys, I think the patient needs a nap."

"No, I don't," Sam said.

"Yes, you do."

"He thinks he's the boss of me."

"Someone needs to be," Malone quipped.

"Ain't nobody the boss of her," Gonzo said to much laughter.

"Bite me, Gonzo."

"I prefer my bites sweeter," he said, slipping an arm around Christina, who gave him an elbow to the ribs.

"We should let you get some rest," Lindsey said. "We're all so damn relieved you're okay."

"Thanks, Lindsey. And thank you all for coming over and for bringing enough food to feed an army."

"That's the best part," Scotty said.

"I made the brownies you love," Angela told him.

"That's why you're my favorite aunt."

"Hey!" Tracy put him into a playful headlock. "You better take it back, mister!"

Laughing, Scotty said, "You're tied for first."

"Look at him," Terry said. "Already a diplomatic politician."

"He's a chip off the old block," Graham said. "We'll leave you all to get some rest. Sam, honey, don't scare us like that again, you hear?"

"I'll try not to, but something tells me…"

"Don't finish that thought," Nick said.

The private smile she sent his way lit up her battered face and made him melt on the inside. She was his kryptonite. There was nothing he wouldn't do or give up to make her happy. Seeing her alive and well and acting like herself was all he needed to be happy.

"Hey, Jeannie," Sam said.

Jeannie took Sam's outstretched hand.

"I'm so sorry to hear about the continuance. Goddamn defense attorneys."

Jeannie shrugged but the haunted look in her eyes belied the casual gesture. "What's six more weeks after all this time?"

"An interminable delay," Sam said. "But don't worry. We'll get him, and he'll spend the rest of his life behind bars where he belongs."

Jeannie leaned in to hug Sam. "Thanks. I'll see you tomorrow."

"I'll be here."

After the last of their friends left, Sam held out her arms to Scotty, who crawled into her embrace like he'd been doing it all his life. "How's my best boy?"

"Good. How are you?"

"Much better now that I can hug and kiss on you."

Scotty made a face but he put up with her need to love him. "I'm glad you're okay and back to being annoying."

"Annoying?" She tugged playfully on a tuft of his hair. "*Annoying?*"

"Tell her, Nick. She's annoying when she wants to kiss my whole face."

"I sorta like it when she kisses my whole face."

"Ewww, gross. I need a shower." He got up from the sofa. "I'm outta here."

"Is all your homework done?" Sam asked him.

"Yep. They go easy on us the first week back after vacation."

"We'll be up to tuck you in," Nick said.

"I don't need to be tucked in," he said as he did every night.

"Yeah, yeah," Sam said. "*We* need it."

Nick sat on the edge of the sofa and propped an arm on the back. "How you doing, babe?"

"A little tired, a lot sore, but otherwise, I'm okay. I'm glad he seems okay too."

"He's resilient like his mother." Nick leaned in to kiss her and rubbed his nose against hers. "Ready for a lift upstairs?"

"I can walk."

"Why would you want to walk when I love to carry you?"

"Because I have plans for your back that don't include it being thrown out from carrying me?"

"Plans? What are these plans of which you speak?"

She reached out to caress his face and then ran her fingers through his hair.

"What?" he asked, after she'd studied him for a long silent moment.

"I like to look at you and touch you. Because I can."

"Anytime you want." He kissed her again. "Let's get you comfortable upstairs." Sliding his arms under her, he lifted her and headed for the stairs.

She curled her arms around his neck and dropped her head to his shoulder. "My hero."

"Hardly."

"What does that mean?"

"I wasn't able to save you. They wouldn't let me go near the place until it was totally safe. Made me feel like... I don't even know how to describe how that made me feel. Like my safety was more important than yours."

"I hate to say it because it'll make you mad, but your safety *is* more important than mine and just about anyone's." In a whisper, she added, "You're the *vice president*."

"It's not funny, Sam. It made me feel useless, and I hate that."

"You're extremely useful to me and don't ever forget that."

"I'm not talking about sex."

"Who said anything about sex?"

He raised a brow and tried to scowl at her, but failed miserably because he was so damn grateful to be arguing with her. "You think you're so funny."

"I know I am. You laugh at most of my jokes and so does Freddie, except for the ones that are at his expense. Which is almost all of them."

Nick set her down gently on the bed and settled her under the covers.

"Brant was looking for you earlier. What did he want?"

"Nothing."

"Must've been something. He had that intense look he gets when something's up."

"Are you checking out my detail now?"

"Hardly. I pay attention, though, and he seemed stressed out."

"Let's talk about it tomorrow."

"Aha! So it is something."

"A little something."

"They want me to have protection, don't they?"

"Sam."

"Just answer the question."

"Yeah, they do, and it's coming from Nelson."

"What do you have to say about it?"

"I told Ambrose Pierce that if Nelson is going to insist on you having protection, he's going to need to get himself a new vice president."

"You really said that? To the Secret Service director?"

"I really said that. And I meant it."

"Even though you probably want me to have protection more than anyone. You still said that."

"I did, so what about it?"

"Do you know what I love best about you?"

"Did you suffer a head injury that hasn't been diagnosed?"

Sam laughed, a deep guffaw that had her gripping her stomach. "No, I did not suffer a head injury. Now answer the question."

"I suspect what you love best about me is what goes on right here in this bed."

"Nope."

"I'm wounded and more than slightly offended."

"Oh, shut up. You know I dig the sex big-time. But what I love most about you is that you *know* me. You really, really know me. You get me, and even though you'd love nothing more than to let them push you into pushing me to have protection, because you'd breathe a hell of a lot easier if I had it, you'd never, *ever* do that to me."

"No, I wouldn't."

"Because you know me."

"I know you." He kissed her softly, not wanting to cause her any more pain than she was already dealing with. "And I love everything I know about you, even the stuff that makes me crazy and gives me nightmares."

"Did you really tell them you'd quit if they push the matter?"

"I really did."

"And would you? Really?"

"I really would." He tucked her hair back behind her ear. "When are you going to figure out that all I truly need are you and Scotty? The rest of it—the job, the White House, the attention… It could all go away in a heartbeat, and I wouldn't miss it in the least. But you… If you went away, I'd never be the same. My life would be completely ruined in ways that could never be fixed. So yeah, if it came to that, I'd quit in a heartbeat."

She reached for him, and he went willingly into her arms. "I love you so much. I thought I knew how much until it was possible I might never see you again. And then I realized it's a million, billion, *trillion* times more than I thought it was."

"Me too, baby. Quadrillion."

She thumped him on the back. "Of course you know what comes after trillion!"

Laughing softly, he said, "Only because I'm keeping an eye on the federal deficit." He held on tight to her, overwhelmed with love for her and gratitude that she was safely back in his arms where she belonged.

TWENTY-THREE

SAM KNEW SHE was dreaming. It had happened this way before, after the disaster at the crack house the night Quentin Johnson had died in his father's arms. The nightmares had been relentless. Now there was a new nightmare. She was back in the Springers' basement, tied to the chair, at the mercy of a madman who was playing with matches.

The stench of gasoline burned her nose and made her eyes water.

Stahl lit a match and waved it around in front of her face.

Sam watched the flame dance before her eyes, the strong scent of sulfur overpowering the gasoline for a second. Then he looked directly at her and dropped the match into the puddle of gas at her feet. As the flames exploded around her, Sam screamed.

"Baby, wake up. You're dreaming."

Sam came awake sweating and crying and gasping for air. "Nick."

"I'm here. I'm right here." He held her tight and stroked her back while she sobbed helplessly. "You're safe."

How would she ever feel truly safe again? How would she ever trust the instincts that had guided her career up until now but had failed her so spectacularly in this case? Stahl had played her—and the people around her—like a well-tuned fiddle.

She pushed those disturbing thoughts from her mind, determined to focus on her loved ones and not give that animal one more second of her mental energy. He'd already gotten far more than he'd ever deserved.

Sam squirmed against Nick, trying to get closer to him.

He gasped at the press of her pelvis against his. "Sa-mantha."

"Need you."

"Baby, you need to rest and recover."

"I need *you* more than I need anything else." With her face nestled in the curve between his neck and shoulder, she took a deep breath of his endlessly appealing scent and then bit the tendon at the base of his neck.

Nick sucked in a sharp, deep breath. "Christ, you ruin me."

"No, I don't want to ruin you. I just want to love you."

"You're hurt, honey. I can't."

"Yes, you can. Please, Nick." Her mouth found his in the dark, the kiss frenzied—and painful, thanks to the punch Stahl had delivered to her face. But Sam didn't care. She needed the connection to him more than she needed her next breath.

"Easy," he whispered. "Nice and easy."

She wanted fast and furious but would settle for whatever he was willing to give her.

He kissed her gently, his tongue soft and undemanding against her bruised lower lip.

Sam strained to get closer to him. She couldn't seem to get close enough.

His big hand cupped her bottom as he slid his leg between both of hers. For the longest time he only kissed her while holding her as close as he could. Then his hand moved from her bottom up her side to cup her breast.

Breaking the kiss, Sam drew in a greedy deep breath.

Easing her onto her back, Nick pulled her T-shirt up and over her head and her panties off.

The stitches on her right thigh tugged painfully, but she paid no mind to the pain, preferring to focus on the pleasure of his mouth, hot and tight around her nipple. She grasped a handful of his hair to keep him anchored to her chest as he drove her crazy with his tongue and the light bite of his teeth.

He kissed his way down the front of her, softly, gently, reverently.

For hours the day before she'd wondered if she'd ever see him again, let alone make love with him. This felt like the first time all over again, as if she'd been reborn and given a second precious chance.

Settling between her legs, he opened her to his tongue and drove her crazy with the way he licked and sucked and worshiped every sensitive inch of her. When he drove two fingers into her, she came with a startled cry that had him shushing her, reminding her that they didn't have the house to themselves.

Sam pressed her own hand to her mouth to contain the cries that wanted out. Nothing had ever felt the way he made her feel, every damn time. Then he was above her, pressing into her, moving above her in the dance that had become as familiar as anything in her life. He dazzled her with the all-consuming way he loved her, and this time was no different. In fact, it was better than ever as the powerful emotions of the last couple of days fired their passion.

She held on to him and let him take her away from it all, swept away in a sea of the combustible desire they generated together.

"Samantha." The single word, whispered against her ear, sent a tingle of sensation all the way through her, landing in the place where they were joined.

Running her hands over his muscular back, she cupped

his ass and pulled him deeper into her. She couldn't get him deep enough.

He held on tight to her as they came together, something she'd never experienced until she'd loved him. Like every other time they made love, Sam harbored a secret hope that maybe this might be the time they created a new life together.

She held on tighter than ever to him in the aftermath, feeling him deep inside her as he pulsed and throbbed, his body hard and heavy above her.

"I'm crushing you," he muttered after a long moment of contented silence.

"I love when you crush me."

His deep chuckle rumbled in her chest.

"Thanks for this."

"It was a terrible hardship, but I'm always happy to serve you, my love."

Now it was Sam's turn to laugh. "Sorry I woke you up."

"I wasn't asleep."

She caressed his back, from the base of his neck all the way down to his hips. "Insomnia?"

"Yeah."

"Is it because you're worried about me?"

"Could be. But you know how it is. It's never predictable."

"How about a back rub from your favorite wife?"

He raised his head to kiss her. "My favorite wife needs to go to sleep."

"I've got plenty of time to sleep. Let me take care of you for a change."

"You take care of me all the time."

"Um, no, I really don't."

"You just did."

"Oh, so we're talking about sex again?"

"Aren't we always?"

Sam laughed and pushed at his shoulders. "Off me, you oaf, and onto your belly."

"Sam, really. I'm fine."

"Do what you're told."

Sighing dramatically, he withdrew from her and flopped onto his belly. "There. Happy now?"

"Yeah, I'm really happy."

He took her hand and kissed her palm. "Me too."

Sam got up, slowly and painfully, and went to retrieve the massage oil from the bathroom. She returned to the bed and straddled his hips.

"If this is supposed to settle me down enough to sleep, you're going about it all wrong."

The gruff tenor of his voice made her laugh as she spread the massage oil on his back, digging her fingers into the stress knots at the base of his neck. His deep moan let her know he was enjoying her efforts. She moved down, digging her thumbs into the grooves under his scapula.

"God, that feels so good, babe."

"Shhh, you're supposed to be relaxing."

"Um, news flash—I'm never going to sleep with you naked and straddling my back."

She bent over him, letting her breasts rub against his back.

"Not helping."

Laughing, she sat up and finished the massage by giving his perfectly perfect ass some attention before moving off him to settle next to him in bed. He'd been quiet at the end, leading her to believe he might be dozing. Then he turned over and reached for her.

"Nick! You're supposed to be sleeping!"

He took hold of her hand and brought it to the erection

that pulsed hard and thick against her palm. "How am I supposed to sleep with this?"

"Does he want a massage too?"

"Don't make me beg."

She reached for the bottle of massage oil and squirted some into the hand she then wrapped around him.

"Yes," he said through gritted teeth. "Sam… God… This is going to be fast."

She loved knowing that she had this kind of power over such a strong, controlled man. She loved that only she could break that legendary control and make him let go so completely. She loved that she was the only one who would ever again know him like this—hot and full and all hers.

He came hard, gasping as she tightened her grip for maximum effect. Closing his hand over hers, he stopped her from moving. "Can't take anymore," he said between deep breaths.

She kissed his chest and got up again to find a towel to clean him up. Then she got back in bed, crawled into his arms and held on tight to him. "Do you think you can sleep now?"

"Yeah."

"Nick?"

"Hmm?"

"Remember what you said to me when I had the dream? That you were right here and everything was okay?"

"Mmm."

"Same thing. I'm right here and everything is okay. It's safe to go to sleep."

He drew her in even closer to him, pressed his lips to her forehead and seemed to drift off.

Sam was awake for a long time, lost in the simple pleasure of being close to him, listening to his heartbeat, breathing in the familiar scent of home and knowing that for now, right this minute, everything really was okay.

AVERY TOOK SAM'S statement during a three-hour marathon that took place in her living room with her on the sofa under a blanket and him in a straight-back chair. He recorded the session and took notes, but mostly he listened, letting her take him through the sequence of events. She spoke in a cool, detached tone, but every so often he heard the underlying emotion—and the fear—in her voice.

For the first time in his life, he felt capable of committing murder. Every cell in his body was on fire with rage and disbelief over what she'd been made to endure.

"Then the windows burst open, and there you all were," she concluded. "The SWAT guys threw themselves on the fire before it could really ignite, and they neutralized Stahl. I've never been so happy to see anyone in my life."

"I bet."

"That's the whole thing."

"And you believe he was also behind the killings of Lori Phillips and Bill Springer?"

"Yes, as well as the orchestration of the assault on Cruz's girlfriend. He wanted him out of the way when he came at me. And he also knew Cruz would go into the jail to tune up the guy who hit Elin. I'm sure the plan was for Elliott to go to the media about police brutality the minute he was released from jail."

"He had it all planned out."

"Yes, and lucky me. I was the big prize."

"How do you suppose Marissa Springer went from being a housewife to a killer?"

"Rage," Sam said simply. "She was fueled by rage, and Stahl gave her a chance to get even with the cops who'd killed her precious Billy."

He could see that she was starting to tire, so he turned off the recorder. "Thank you for taking the time. I'll write up the report and run it by you before I submit it."

"Okay."

Avery unplugged the recorder and stashed it in his bag. "How's Shelby?"

"She's okay. Her knees and hands are a mess from a fall."

"And she's furious with all of us."

"That too."

"I don't know what the hell would've possessed you to tell her what you did."

"I care about her, and we're building something together—something that could be lasting. We can't have a secret like that between us if we're going to make this work."

"Is she ever going to talk to me again?"

"Yes, I believe she's hoping to check on you in the next day or two."

"Great. I'll do what I can to fix the damage you've inflicted."

"I know you're pissed and you have good reason to be, but I'm not sorry I told her."

"As long as it's all good for you."

"Sam."

She shook her head. "I told you once and I'll tell you again—this shit needs to stop. There's never going to be anything between us except collegial friendship. Unless you want my husband to have you transferred to Siberia, you need it to let it go."

"Siberia, huh?"

"Unless he can find somewhere farther away from here."

"I understand, and I'm sorry to have caused you any trouble."

"You've caused more trouble for yourself than you have for me. You've got a wonderful woman who is crazy about you. Go home to her, Avery."

"I'm going as soon as I can."

After twenty-four hours on duty, handling the paperwork on the resolution of Sam's kidnapping and assault, Avery drove home the next morning, exhausted and spent. He'd volunteered the FBI's services on the case since Stahl had deep ties to the MPD and none of them wanted conflicts of interest to derail their slam-dunk case against the disgraced lieutenant.

Stahl had been disgustingly unrepentant in the wake of his arrest, refusing to answer questions until his lawyer was present and even then, stonewalling them every step of the way. Didn't matter. Sam had lived to testify, and Marissa Springer, while in grave condition, was expected to live as well, so Stahl was screwed every which way to Tuesday and he knew it.

Sam.

Though he'd tried valiantly to hold on to his professional demeanor, the fact that Stahl had slapped and punched and terrorized her made Avery insanely angry.

He wanted to beat Stahl's portly face to a bloody pulp for daring to lay a hand on her. And yes, he knew it was wildly inappropriate for him to be so fucking furious over what had happened to her.

Once again he had to remind himself he had no right to feel that way about her. None at all. She was home with her husband, and he had Shelby waiting for him at home, possibly pregnant with his child.

The rage had no place in his life, he reminded himself as he pulled up to his house and killed the engine, taking a moment to calm down before he went inside. Before he could use his key in the door it swung open, revealing the tiny sprite of a woman who'd become so important to him.

"You're home."

Avery closed the door and leaned against it, exhausted all the way down to his bone marrow. "So I am."

"Is everything okay? Is Sam…" Her chin quivered. "She's really okay, right? You'd tell me if she wasn't?"

"She's had better days, but she'll be fine."

"And you. You're so tired."

"I could sleep."

Shelby bit her bottom lip and glanced up at him. "You look kind of bad through the eyes."

"It was tough to hear what happened to her."

Shelby stared at him for a long moment before she took a deep breath. "I'm not sure about this, Avery. I want you. In fact, I probably even love you. But I'm not willing to share you with anyone else, even a woman you want but can't have." She took another deep breath. "I need some time to figure out what happens next."

"How much time?" He stood up straight, suddenly frightened that she was leaving him.

She shouldered her large pink purse. "I don't know. But I'll be in touch."

"Don't do this, Shelby. I've had a hard few hours at work. Don't hold that against me."

"I'm not. I promise you I'm not. This is about me, not you. I need to get my head on straight after everything that's happened this week. And I need to see Sam. I'll call a cab."

"I can take you to her if you want."

"That's all right. Thank you for everything, especially the last couple of days. You were really nice to me."

"Shelby, God, you're breaking my heart. What about the baby?"

She wiped away tears. "We have plenty of time to figure that out."

"I want to be a father to your child, no matter what."

"I know, and I love you for that. I really do." She went up on the very tips of her toes to kiss his cheek. "Take care, Avery."

He hugged her close for a minute, breathing in the sweet scent of her. "I'll be waiting to hear from you." Avery moved aside so she could walk out the door and then shut it behind her. Closing his eyes, he leaned against the door, filled with regret and anger at himself and the situation in general.

How could his feelings for a woman who'd never been his—and would never be his—totally screw up his life this way? It was time to get his own head on straight and to fix this, once and for all, before he lost the best thing to ever happen to him.

SHELBY MANAGED TO hold on to her composure as she walked away from Avery's house. She kept it together while she hailed a cab and gave the driver Sam and Nick's Capitol Hill address. But once the car was moving toward the home of her employers, tears began to slide down her cheeks regardless of her efforts to hold them in.

She hadn't planned to say all that to him when he came home, but she'd seen the agony in his eyes and on his face. What had happened to Sam had set him back, and she couldn't stay there and hope that one day he'd feel that way about her. He either did or he didn't.

She'd waited a long time to find someone she wanted to spend the rest of her life with, but she'd meant what she'd said to him. She was not going to share him with anyone else—even if that someone else was a woman he loved from afar.

And now she had to deal with Sam and Nick and what they'd kept from her and how she felt about that. The thought of confronting them, especially in light of what they'd been through the last few days, made her sick.

The cab pulled up to the Secret Service checkpoint at the top of Ninth Street.

"I'll get out here," she said to the driver as she handed him cash for the fare.

Recognizing her, the Secret Service agents on duty waved her through. As she walked up the ramp to the front door, her heart pounded in her chest and anxiety coursed through her body. During the six months she'd worked for them, and even before when she'd planned their magical wedding, they'd come to matter greatly to her, and she didn't want to lose their friendship—or the job she loved.

But this conversation had to happen before she could make any decisions.

The Secret Service agent at the door nodded to her and let her in. "Morning."

"Morning," she said.

With Scotty long gone to school, she found Sam and Nick in the kitchen, enjoying a leisurely breakfast and the morning paper that was full of headlines about her abduction and the controversy over her lack of protection. Shelby had already read it while she waited for Avery to come home.

"Hey," Sam said when she came into the kitchen, "you're back! Are you feeling better?"

Staring at Sam's egregiously bruised face, Shelby tried to find the words, but all she could manage was a small nod.

"What's wrong?" Nick asked.

There could be no putting this off. She simply couldn't move forward without talking to them about it. But first things first. "You're doing okay?" she asked Sam. Her face was purple with bruises, but her startling blue eyes were clear and as sharply focused as ever.

"Better today, thanks."

"You gave us one heck of a scare."

"Sorry. We've missed you around here."

"About that." Shelby took a deep breath. "Could I talk to you guys about something?"

"Of course." Nick stood and held a chair for her.

"Is it the baby?" Sam asked.

"You heard about that, huh?"

"I did and I'm so happy for you. I know how much you've wanted a child."

"I do. I want him or her so much."

Sam reached out and took her hand. "We owe you an apology."

"We do?" Nick asked.

"Because of Avery," Sam said.

Nick immediately went tense, and this time Shelby knew why. "What about him?" Nick asked. "Things are going well with you guys, right?"

"They were. Before I found out he had feelings for Sam that no one told me about."

The silence between the three of them was as discomforting as anything Shelby had ever experienced.

"There was never anything between him and me," Sam said, probably as much for Nick's sake as Shelby's.

His face was set in a stony expression Shelby had seen at other times when Avery was around or his name was mentioned.

"I've done nothing at all to encourage any feelings he might have for me," Sam said.

"But you were aware he had them?"

Sam glanced at Nick, who still hadn't blinked. "Yes."

"Both of you knew. This is why Nick hates him, and I could never figure out why. I feel like such a fool that all of you knew this and I didn't."

"What would you have had us say?" Sam asked. "You were clearly taken with him, and I'd never do anything to ruin that for you. Whatever feelings he had for me were his alone. It had nothing to do with me."

"You should've told me."

"Shelby." Sam waited until Shelby looked at her before she continued. "There has never been nor will there ever be anything between him and me other than collegiate friendship. I'm happily married, and he knows that. Why in the world would I want to ruin my friend's happiness by telling her the guy she adores used to be into me?"

"I don't think it's as past tense as you'd like to believe."

"What does that mean?" Nick asked.

"He's not as over you as we'd all like him to be."

"How do you know?" he asked. "Did he tell you that?"

"He didn't have to. If you could've seen him when he got home from taking your statement, you'd know what I mean."

"Son of a bitch," Nick muttered.

"I love you guys," Shelby said tearfully. "You're more than my employers. You and Scotty are like family to me. It hurt me so much to know that you'd kept this from me."

"We love you, Shelby, and I promise we never intended to hurt you," Sam said. "It's not something we like to talk about around here. His *feelings* have caused a few problems for us too."

Shelby glanced at Nick. "When you encouraged me to go out with him it was to keep him away from Sam, not because you thought he'd be good for me."

"I'm guilty as charged on that, and I apologize," Nick said sincerely. "I shouldn't have done that."

"I know this is the worst possible timing with your new job starting and everything that happened this week, but I'd like to take some vacation days if that's all right. I need to get out of town for a while and figure things out."

"Of course," Nick said. "Take as much time as you need."

"You aren't going to quit, are you?" Sam asked.

"No. I'm not going to quit, but I hope you understand why I needed to talk to you guys about this."

"Yes, we understand," Sam said as Nick nodded. "We were shitty friends to you on this issue, and we could've done better."

Satisfied by their apologies and relieved to have cleared the air, Shelby got up and wrapped her fluffy pink scarf around her neck. "I'll be back in a couple of weeks. You'll let Scotty know that I'm on vacation and I'll text him?"

"We will." Sam got up, moving slower than usual, and hugged Shelby. "Let us know how you're doing, okay?"

"You do the same. I'm sorry for all you went through this week. I hope they're going to put that guy where he belongs this time."

"He's going away for a long time."

"Good. I'll see you soon." Shelby left their house and walked to the corner to grab a cab home. She had a vacation to plan.

"I WANT THAT guy sent to Timbukfuckingtu," Nick said the minute the front door closed behind Shelby.

"He's not our problem," Sam reminded him. "Whatever he thinks or feels, it has nothing to do with us."

"How can you say that when she just basically told us she thinks he's still in love with you?"

"I'd much rather focus on the fact that our actions—or our failure to act—hurt someone we care about."

"It wasn't like we set out to intentionally harm her. How were we supposed to broach that subject with her when she was gone over the guy?"

"I don't know, but we should've tried."

"Maybe so," he conceded. "But I still want him out of our lives."

"Nick, I'm telling you right now, if you fuck with his career, I'll withhold sex for a year."

"You wouldn't last a week," he said dismissively.

"Wanna make a bet?" She stared at him until he blinked.

"No, not really."

"Promise me you won't do anything to mess with him."

He replied with the stony look he got whenever Hill's name came up.

"*Nick.*"

"Fine! I promise. Are you satisfied?"

"Yes, extremely, and you will be too over the next year. Now let's change the subject."

"What do you want to talk about?"

"Since I missed the reception the other day, I'd like to see your new office. Can we do that today?"

"I don't know about going over there today when they're all hot on this issue of you having protection."

"I'm not worried about that. My husband threatened to quit his job if they push that subject, so there's no reason to stay away."

"You really want to go to the White House?"

"Well, no, not really, but I'd love to see your new office."

He smiled at her reply and said, "All right then. That's what we'll do."

TWENTY-FOUR

SHE TURNED HIS picture frames upside down and knocked the neat stacks of files on his desk out of alignment. On the paper calendar he kept on the desktop, she drew little hearts around the words Sam loves Nick.

He stood back and let her have her fun, the way she always did whenever she got a chance to mess with what she called his anal-retentive freakazoidisms. After the events of this past week, he didn't care if she made a total disaster of the place. As long as she was alive and able to mess with him, that was all that mattered.

"Seen enough yet?"

"What's in there?" she asked, pointing to a door.

"A bathroom."

"You've got your own bathroom?"

"I'm the vice president, babe. I have my own *plane*."

She rolled her eyes at him. "Don't let it go to your head, big shot." Getting up from his desk, she wandered over to take a look at the bathroom. "Wow, you've even got a shower in there, so when I come over for nooners, we can clean up after. Good to know."

"Samantha…"

His low growl had her turning to smile innocently at him. "Yes?"

"How am I supposed to work here when all I'll be thinking about is bending you over my desk?"

She returned to the desk, placed her palms in the center

and gave him a come-hither look. "Why imagine it when you can have the real thing?"

"That's not happening here." He pointed to the camera in the corner of the room.

"Oh, snap. That could've been embarrassing."

"You think?" he asked with a bark of laughter. "You're a danger to my career."

"As I recall, I tried to tell you that way back when you were talking me into 'just a year' in the Senate to complete John's term. And look at us now."

"Indeed. Look at us now." He held out a hand to her and she came around the desk to take it. "Let's get out of here before they make me work today when I told them I was taking the day off to take care of my injured wife."

"My injuries do require your constant care."

"Mmm, I feel a nap coming on before the boy gets home from school."

Sam grabbed her purse from the desk. "Let's go."

They were on their way to a clean getaway when the president's chief of staff, Tom Hanigan, stopped them. "Mr. Vice President, Mrs. Cappuano, it's good to see you. You're looking well."

"No, I'm really not," Sam said with a laugh, "but it's nice of you to say that."

"We're glad you're all right."

"Did you need something, Tom?" Nick asked.

"The president would like a word if you have a minute."

"Do we have a minute?" Nick asked Sam.

"I suppose we could make some time for the president." The sheer lunacy of the statement wasn't lost on her.

"Oh, um, he was hoping for a minute alone with you, sir. I could see Mrs. Cappuano back to your office if you'd like."

"Since we both know he wants to talk to me about her, there's no reason she can't be there."

"As you wish, sir."

As they followed him through the halls of the West Wing, Sam looked up at Nick and mouthed the word *hot*, rubbing her knuckles over her chest.

He mouthed the word *stop*, pointing again to cameras mounted in the hallway.

Sam muffled a laugh with her hand over her mouth while he shook his head at her irreverence.

Tom went straight to the Oval Office and knocked on the door before continuing inside.

Sam's eyes got very big as she followed both men into the most famous office in the world.

Nelson stood and came around his desk to greet them. "Nick, it's so good to see you, and Mrs. Cappuano."

"Please call me Sam, and don't bother to say I look well, sir. We all know that's a lie."

Nelson laughed at her cheekiness. "We're happy to see you alive. That's all that matters."

"Indeed," Sam said as she tried to take in—and memorize—every detail of the Oval Office. She wanted to pinch herself to believe she was actually standing in the room she'd heard about all her life.

"Have a seat," Nelson said, gesturing to the gathering of chairs and love seats in the middle of the room.

Sam and Nick sat together on one of the love seats, while Nelson and Hanigan took easy chairs.

"I understand you spoke to Ambrose yesterday," Nelson said, cutting to the chase.

"I did." Nick hesitated for a moment before he continued. "I want you to know, sir, that I appreciate the amazing opportunity you've given me. However, my wife and family will always come first. I cannot and I will not ask her to be anything other than who and what she is."

Sam's heart swelled with love for him, and despite her intense dislike of PDA, she took hold of his hand and linked their fingers.

"We understand where you're coming from, Nick. We really do. However, this is a much bigger issue now. You have to know that."

"I do. We both do." His Adam's apple bobbed in his throat, betraying his true feelings even as he stuck to his guns with the president. "And it's a risk we're willing to take so Sam can continue the career she loves. I won't ask her to give that up, and we all know she'd have to if she had protection."

"I have to be honest with you," Nelson said. "It makes me extremely uncomfortable that the whole world now knows the vice president's wife is unprotected."

"I understand. Trust me, it makes me extremely uncomfortable too."

"But you're unwilling to bend on this?"

Nick glanced at Sam before he replied. "I'm unwilling to bend. If you'd like me to resign, say the word and you'll have my letter by the end of the day."

"That's the last thing any of us want."

"Then I'm afraid we're at an impasse."

"So it seems, but I do appreciate your candor. I'd like to consult with my national security team before we make any decisions. Mrs. Cappuano… Sam. I hope you know our concerns are in no way a reflection of you or your abilities as a police officer."

"I understand." In their shoes, she'd be doing the same thing.

Nelson stood to signal the conversation was over. He shook hands with both of them. "Tom will see you out.

Thanks for coming by and I hope you feel back to normal very soon."

"Thank you, sir."

Holding hands, Sam and Nick walked out of the White House to the SUV the Secret Service had waiting for them.

"Thank you for that," she said when they were in the car.

Nick leaned over to kiss her. "Anything for you."

EPILOGUE

SHELBY CHOSE BERMUDA because it was a short plane ride and because it was beautiful and tranquil and one of her friends had a house there that she was happy to lend to Shelby on short notice.

Her vacation came together rather well given that she hadn't planned it months in advance the way she always planned everything. For all the good that had done her. Wearing a pink floral maxi-dress, she walked along the water's edge at sunset on her fourth day in paradise, her hand curved protectively over her abdomen.

She couldn't wait to be fat and round with pregnancy. She'd be forty-three when the baby was born, and she felt like she'd waited a lifetime for this moment. Nothing, not even the possible end to a promising romance, could detract from her joy at realizing her long-held dream of becoming a mother.

If it were just going to be the two of them, they'd be the happiest twosome in the history of the world. She'd take her baby with her everywhere she went, and she'd devote her life to giving her son or daughter the best possible childhood. Just knowing the baby was growing inside her made Shelby feel less alone.

She walked until the sun began to dip beneath the horizon and then turned back. Trudging along the water's edge, she enjoyed the gentle lap of the water against her feet and ankles.

With the darkness descending quicker than she'd expected, she picked up the pace and was breathing hard by the time she cut up the beach to the stairs that led to her friend's beachfront home.

As she approached the stairs, she stopped short, gasping at the sight of a broad-shouldered man sitting on the stairs.

"Is this beach taken?" he asked in that honeyed Southern accent that had made her weak-kneed from the first time she ever heard it.

When she recovered her breath, she said, "What're you doing here?"

"I came for you."

I came for you. Do not swoon, Shelby Lynn. Do. Not.

"How did you find me?"

He scoffed. "I'm an FBI special agent, darlin'. I find things—and people—for a living."

"What do you mean, you came for me?"

"Just what I said. The second you walked away, I knew I'd made a huge mistake letting you leave." He reached out and took hold of her hand, drawing her down to the step next to him. "I love what we have together, Shelby. I love who I am with you and how I want to be worthy of you and your baby. Our baby."

"It might not be our baby."

"I want that baby to be ours, and I don't care in the least if I actually fathered him or her."

"You don't? Really?"

"I don't care. All I care about is that you and the baby are healthy and safe and in my life to stay."

"The other day, when you came home…"

"I was messed up after having to hear what that bastard Stahl put my friend Sam through during a hellacious afternoon and evening. I was upset and concerned and sad that it had happened to her. I'm sorry if I didn't properly convey that to you. For what it's worth, I was looking forward to going home to you, knowing you were waiting for me."

Damn hormones had her teary-eyed as his sweet words seeped into her broken heart, filling the cracks and mending the wounds. "Don't say all this if you don't really mean it."

"I never would."

"I have to ask, because I'd like to believe I'm not a total fool. What about Sam?"

His lips tightened with what might've been displeasure, but Shelby refused to back down from the question that needed an answer. "Sam is my colleague and my friend. I probably don't have to tell you that she's a pretty amazing person. I admire her, and I'm more than a little intimidated by her at times, but please don't tell her I said that. She'll be insufferable. I'll never deny I was dazzled by her and at times I continue to be dazzled by the way she does her job, but I'm not in love with her."

"You're not?"

He shook his head. "I'm not in love with her, but I am in love with you."

"Avery, please don't say what you think I need to hear. Please tell me the truth."

"I came here because you deserved the truth, and it's long overdue." He linked their fingers and brought their joined hands to cover his heart. "You told me once you'd waited a long time to meet someone you liked enough to spend the rest of your life with. I have too. I'm almost forty. I'm settled in my career, and I'm ready to take the next step with you and the baby. If you'll have me."

"What're you saying?"

He got up from the step and dropped to his knees in front of her.

Shelby gasped and stopped trying to keep the tears from streaming down her face.

"Shelby Lynn Faircloth, I love you, I'll love our baby. Would you please do me the enormous honor of becoming my wife?"

"Yes," she said on a sob as she hurled herself into his arms. "*Yes*, Avery. I love you too. Yes, I'll marry you."

"I'll make you happy, Shelby. I promise."

Since she knew she couldn't ask for anything more, she decided to let him do just that.

ON SATURDAY, SAM, Nick and Scotty boarded Air Force Two for the short flight from Andrews Air Force Base to Newark, New Jersey. Aware of his carbon footprint and how much bigger it had gotten lately, Nick had wanted to drive, but the request had been declined by the Secret Service for reasons that hadn't been shared with him. It seemed wasteful to take the big plane on a thirty-minute flight, but because of the way Brant had bent all the rules for him when Sam was in trouble, Nick ceded to Brant's wishes this time.

Andy had gone up the day before to meet with the lawyer for Tony D'Alessandro to make sure everything was set for today. They were meeting Tony and his lawyer at a restaurant two blocks from the boardwalk. Nick had suggested Italian food because it was Scotty's favorite.

The investigator had uncovered a perfectly ordinary life. Tony had worked as a waiter in a number of the fine dining establishments in the casinos. He had no criminal record and was divorced with no children. Nick had no idea what to expect from this meeting, and he wouldn't be able to breathe comfortably until they were on their way home with a signed release of parental rights.

"This is so cool," Scotty said, taking in the sitting room

and office space that made up the vice president's quarters located in the front portion of the modified Boeing 757. He went to sit behind the desk and tried to look vice presidential as he took a pretend phone call on the line that was hooked in to the White House.

"Don't push any buttons," Nick told him. "You don't want to start a war or something."

"Could I really do that from here?"

"I don't think so, but I'm not a hundred percent sure."

"Shouldn't you know that?"

"Look into it for me, will you?"

"I'll get right on that."

Nick was happy to see Scotty excited about the plane rather than upset about the reason for the trip, which had kept him quiet and withdrawn for most of the week. Sam and Nick had been so concerned about Scotty that Nick had made a call to Mrs. Littlefield, Scotty's former guardian at the state home for children. She'd assured him that Scotty was processing the latest development in his own way and would bounce back the way he always did once the meeting was behind them.

Nick was counting on that. He hated to see his son worried or out of sorts.

It had been an odd week with Sam at home on sick leave while she recovered, Shelby off on her spontaneous vacation and Scotty stressed out about meeting his biological father—all while Nick went to work every day and waited to hear whether Nelson was going to accept his offer to resign. At his lunch yesterday with Nelson, the president had been cordial and welcoming and there had been no talk of Nick's resignation. Nor had there been any talk of what purpose Nelson would like his vice president to serve within the administration.

In light of that, Nick planned to take Christina's advice

and forge his own path, separate from the president's, since that seemed to be what Nelson preferred. If the president didn't like Nick's show of independence, so what? It wasn't as if Nelson was going to fire the guy who was boosting his numbers so spectacularly.

A knock preceded a steward into the cabin. "Mr. Vice President, Mrs. Cappuano, Master Cappuano, welcome aboard Air Force Two. I'm Jeffrey, and I'll be taking care of you today. Could I get you something to eat or drink?"

"Could I please have a cola?" Scotty asked, glancing at his parents to see if they would shoot down the request. They didn't. Not today.

"Absolutely," Jeffrey said. "Sir, madame?"

"Water would be great for me," Sam said.

"Make it a double," Nick said.

"Coming right up," Jeffrey said when he departed the cabin. The back half of the plane, which normally housed members of the White House press corps, was empty today. Nick had been adamant that this was a personal matter, and even though he was flying on the government's airplane he was not on official business.

To his knowledge, no one knew where they were going or why except for Brant. Nick had asked for the agent's discretion in arranging the security for the trip and to keep the motorcade as small as possible. The best Brant had been able to do was three SUVs—one for Nick and his family and two others, one to lead and another to follow.

While Scotty pretended to work at the desk, Nick took a seat on the sofa next to Sam. "How you holding up, babe?"

"I'll be much better when this is done."

"I was just thinking the same thing."

"What if he refuses to sign? I mean, look at him. Who wouldn't want him for a son?"

Sitting in the big leather desk chair, Scotty had his feet

on the desk, the phone tucked into his shoulder and was gesturing the way Nick did when he was on the phone. "Is he making fun of me?" Nick asked, a grin stretching across his face.

"No, he wants to *be* you. He watches your every move and follows your lead in all things. He loves us both, but you're his touchstone. He'll never let you go."

"And he admires you so much. You have no idea how much."

They shared a warm smile and then turned their gaze back to Scotty, who seemed to be negotiating peace in the Middle East.

A short time later, they landed in Newark, where they were met by more agents and the caravan of black SUVs. They were loaded up and transported with incredible efficiency and dispatch. Nick had to admit it was rather convenient to have other people figuring out the logistics for him.

Brant had agreed to keep the detail in the restaurant to one agent for him and one for Scotty. The others would remain outside.

Nick knew it was far too much to hope that Tony wouldn't recognize him or figure out who he was doing business with. At Nick's instruction, Andy had withheld that information up until now, but his cover was about to be blown, and the possibility of his position somehow messing this up made Nick incredibly nervous.

The closer they got to their destination, the quieter Scotty became. He'd worn new jeans with a Red Sox sweatshirt under the new ski jacket they'd given him for Christmas. He stared out the window, watching the beachfront neighborhoods go by with a spark of interest and curiosity mixed into the nerves Nick could feel coming from him.

"Hey, bud," Nick said.

"Yeah?"

"You okay?"

"Uh-huh."

"We'll be right there with you, okay?"

Scotty nodded.

They'd asked him if he wanted them there for the meeting with his biological father, and he'd looked at them as if they were crazy when he said, "Well, *yeah*, I want you there. Where else would you be? You're my parents."

"Just making sure," Nick had said then. Every time he referred to them as his parents, the wallop of emotion hit Nick in the gut all over again.

They walked into the restaurant, saw Andy sitting with two other men and knew immediately which one was Scotty's father. He had the same dark mop of hair, the same set to his jaw, and when he looked their way, Nick saw that his dark brown eyes were almost an exact replica of Scotty's.

Tony stood and Nick knew the exact moment when he realized that Scotty was with the vice president of the United States and his wife.

"Well, I'll be damned," Tony whispered loud enough to be heard.

"*Damn* is a swear," Scotty told him. He, too, had already figured out which of the men they'd come to see.

"Is it?" Tony asked, seeming amused. "I always thought it was one of those words that could go either way."

"Definitely a swear," Scotty said.

Nick placed a hand on Scotty's shoulder and reached around him. "Nick Cappuano."

"Yes." Tony shook Nick's hand, still seeming somewhat speechless. "I know."

"This is my wife, Samantha."

Sam shook hands with him. "Nice to meet you."

"Likewise."

"How about we all have a seat," Andy said.

Nick sent his friend a grateful smile for his efforts to smooth the way. They sat at a round table, they met Tony's lawyer, they ordered drinks and then food and they attempted to make conversation that was awkward and stilted and painful in so many ways. More than once, Nick caught Scotty taking surreptitious looks at the man who'd fathered him.

"I know you have questions," Tony said after another long silence. "I don't have all the answers you need, but I assure you I had no idea you existed until a few days ago. I'm sorry if you've felt let down by me all this time."

"I wondered where you were," Scotty said haltingly. "My mother, she died when I was six, but she never told me anything about you."

"We were together a very short time and didn't keep in touch. I'm sorry you were left alone when your mother and grandfather died."

Scotty shrugged. "I was okay. Mrs. Littlefield, she was my guardian, she took good care of me for a long time until I met Nick and then Sam."

"How did you meet your…um, your parents?"

"Nick, my dad, he came to the home for a visit when he was a senator representing Virginia. We…" He glanced at Nick.

Smiling warmly at the boy he loved, Nick came to his rescue. "We hit it off immediately and became really great friends by bonding over our love of the Boston Red Sox."

"I won't hold that against you," Tony said with a teasing grin.

"Tell me you're not a New York fan," Scotty said with a scowl.

"Guilty."

"Ugh," Scotty groaned. "That's awful."

Tony laughed, seeming charmed by the boy, which was no surprise to Nick.

"We spent a lot of time together," Nick continued, "and over a period of months, the three of us became somewhat of a family. Scotty came to live with us permanently last summer, and now we're trying to make it official."

"Is he… Is he safe living with you?" Tony glanced at Sam. "What happened to you. It made the national news."

"He has his own detail that watches over him around the clock," Nick said.

"The kids at school think it's really cool that I have agents following me around," Scotty interjected, making the adults laugh.

"What grade are you in?" Tony asked.

"Seventh."

"What's your favorite subject?"

"Lunch and recess, which we only have on special occasions now that we're in middle school."

"He likes history too," Sam said.

"Next year I get to take Spanish," Scotty said, "but I also have to take harder algebra." The face he made indicated what he thought of that.

"Math was never my thing either." Tony looked at Scotty with a hint of longing that struck a pang of fear in the vicinity of Nick's heart.

Lunch was served, and Scotty dove in to his favorite meal of spaghetti and meatballs with the usual enthusiasm. He glanced up at Nick. "Hey, Dad, would you hand me the cheese?"

Nick felt like he'd been struck by lightning.

Sam's hand landed on his leg, giving him a squeeze that snapped him out of the state of shock.

Nick reached for the Parmesan cheese and handed it to Scotty, who smiled at him.

"Thank you."

Nick covered Sam's hand with his own, feeling battered by the variety of emotions swirling through him—fear, anxiety, determination and love. So much love for his son.

"My mom is a cop," Scotty told Tony. "She catches killers."

"That's very cool," Tony said.

While Sam and Nick pushed the food around on their plates without really eating much of anything, they listened to Scotty and Tony make small talk. After the waiter and busboy had cleared the plates, Tony asked if he might have a few minutes to speak to Scotty alone.

Nick wanted to say no, and judging from the way Sam tensed next to him, she did too.

"Is it okay with you?" Scotty asked them.

"Whatever you want," Nick forced himself to say.

"I guess it'd be okay."

On wooden legs, Nick got up, helped Sam up and walked away from the table with the two lawyers following them. They settled in another booth, Nick choosing a seat that kept Scotty in his direct line of vision. Tony's attorney excused himself to use the restroom.

"I feel like I'm going to lose it," Sam whispered as she clung to his hand.

"Stay calm," Andy said. "Just let it play out."

"What about the paper?" Sam asked.

"Tony has it, and he knows what we need him to do."

Since they had no choice, Nick let it play out. But he was playing to win, and he wasn't leaving here without his son.

SCOTTY WASN'T SURE what to say to the man who sat across from him. Why had he asked to talk to him alone? Was this when he was going to say he wanted him to come live here, in New Jersey, with him?

"Are you happy?" Tony asked him. "Living with your mom and dad?"

"Yeah. They're great."

"They seem really busy. Do they have time for you?"

"Oh, yeah, we do lots of fun stuff together. We go to baseball games, and I play in a hockey league. My dad is an incredible hockey player. He taught me how to skate, and he's helping me catch up with the other kids. And my grandpa Skip, that's my mom's dad, he lives right down the street from us, and I go see him every day after school. Shelby, she's like a nanny but not really because I don't need a nanny anymore, she comes every day and she's teaching me how to cook all sorts of cool stuff. I have aunts and uncles and cousins, one of them a new baby named Ella. My cousins Ethan and Abby—they fight a lot, and my aunt Tracy says I'm the only one who can get them to stop fighting. My dad's friends, Graham and Laine O'Connor, they're like his extra parents, they have this super-cool farm with horses and I'm learning how to ride. One time, Laine and I made ice cream from scratch. I thought it only came in a box."

Scotty stopped and took a deep breath. "I'm talking way too much. Sorry."

"Don't be. I like hearing about your life."

"Could I ask you something?"

"Sure. Whatever you want."

"Are you… Do you want to… Are you going to try to take me away from them?" Scotty held his breath while he waited to hear what Tony would say.

"I was really surprised to hear about you. I was shocked. And to be totally honest, I didn't believe it until you walked in here today and I saw myself at thirteen. I'm not going to take you away from them. I wouldn't do that to you when it's obvious you have a life with them that you love."

"I love *them*. They've given me everything—a home and a family and my own room and an Xbox and posters on the wall and *everything*."

"I'm not going to take you away from them, but I would like to know you, if that's okay with you."

"What do you mean?"

"Maybe we can email or text or talk on the phone once in a while and you can tell me how algebra is going and whether you like Spanish and if you scored a goal in hockey. Would that be possible?"

"If I say yes, would you sign the paper?"

"I'm going to sign the paper no matter what, but I'd really like to talk to you once in a while."

Hearing that Tony planned to sign the paper, Scotty was suddenly unable to breathe. He dropped his head into his hands, desperately trying not to cry in front of a man he'd just met.

And then Nick was there, his hand on Scotty's shoulder. "Everything all right?"

Nick sounded scared, and Nick never sounded scared—except for when Sam got herself into some sort of trouble.

Scotty looked up in time to see Tony pass the signed paper to Nick.

Nick took it from him and then shook Tony's hand. "Thank you so much." He sounded like he was going to cry, and Scotty could certainly relate.

"Thank you for coming all this way. I appreciate it."

When Nick squeezed his shoulder again, Scotty stood and reached out to shake Tony's hand. "Thank you."

"Sure."

"I, um, I'll need your phone number." Scotty withdrew his phone from his pocket and punched in the number

Tony recited. Then he looked across the table at him. "I'll call you."

"I'll look forward to hearing from you."

Nick led him over to where Sam pretended she wasn't crying. "Come on, Mom." Scotty extended a hand to her. "Let's go home."

* * * * *

Look for Sam and Nick's next adventure,
FATAL IDENTITY,
from Marie Force and HQN Books.
Read on for an exclusive sneak peek...

SAM PUSHED through the double doors and into cool, crisp winter air that smelled like snow. She'd had a conversation yesterday with her son, Scotty, about how air can smell like snow. Scotty said it wasn't possible to *smell* snow, even after she got him to take a few deep breaths to see what she meant. He remained skeptical, but she had a few more weeks of winter to prove her point.

"Mrs. Cappuano."

Sam turned toward the man who'd called to her. He was in his late twenties or early thirties, handsome with dark blond hair and brown eyes. The panic she saw in his expression put her immediately on alert. "That's me, although they don't call me that around here. And you are?"

"Josh Hamilton."

Sam shook his outstretched hand. "What can I do for you, Josh?"

"I need your help."

"Okay."

"Today I was bored at work, so I started surfing the web, you know, just clicking around aimlessly."

As a technophobe of the highest order, Sam didn't know because she'd never done that and certainly not at work, where she was usually too busy to pee, let alone surf.

Josh took a series of deep breaths, and Sam's anxiety ramped up a notch. "I saw this story about a baby who was kidnapped thirty years ago. They had this age-pro-

gression photo showing what he'd look like now, and..."
He gulped. "It was *me*."

"Wait. *What?*"

With trembling hands, Josh retrieved his cell phone from his pocket and called up a web page, zeroing in on a digitally produced photo that did, in fact, bear a striking resemblance to him.

"Those photos are produced by computers. They're not exact."

"*That's me!* And it explains why I've never felt at home or accepted in my family. What if they *took* me?"

"Hang on a minute. What evidence do you have to suspect that your parents participated in a criminal act to bring you into their family?"

He seemed to make an effort to calm down. "They're extremely accomplished people and so are my siblings. My brother is a board-certified neurosurgeon. He went to Harvard for undergrad and medical school. My sister is an attorney, also Harvard educated, Law Review, the whole nine yards. And then there's me. I barely made it out of state college after having spent most of my five years there on academic probation. After four years working for the federal government, I'm a GS-9 at Veterans Affairs, where I shuffle paper all day while counting the minutes until I can leave. The only reason I have that job is because my father, who has never approved of a thing I said or did, pulled strings to get me in. They're all Republicans while I'm a liberal Democrat who fully supports your husband. I hope he runs in four years, by the way."

"None of that proves your parents kidnapped you."

"Will you take my case? Please? I need to know for sure. This would explain so much of why I've felt like a square peg in my own family my entire life."

Sam held up a hand to stop him. "I'm a homicide cop,

not a private investigator, but if you really believe a crime has been committed, I can refer you to someone within the department—"

"No." He shook his head. "I want you. You're the best. Everyone says so."

"I'm honored you think so, but I'm on a leave of absence for the next few days, so I'm not able to take your case personally."

"It *has* to be you. You're the only one I'd trust to do it right."

"The Metro PD has plenty of very qualified detectives who could look into this for you and help determine whether a crime has been committed, Mr. Hamilton."

"You don't understand. It can't be any random detective. It can only be you."

"Are you going to tell me why?"

He took another series of deep breaths, appearing to summon the courage he needed to tell her why. "It's… He's… Well, my dad, you see… He's Troy Hamilton, the FBI director."

HOLY BOMBSHELL, BATMAN! Sam's mind raced with implications and scenarios and flat-out disbelief. "You can't honestly believe that your father, one of the top law enforcement officials in the country, *kidnapped* a child thirty years ago."

"I wouldn't put it past him," Josh said.

"He's one of the most respected men in our business. He's revered."

"Believe me, I know all about how *revered* he is. I hear about it on a regular basis." He looked at her beseechingly. "You have to help me. I don't know who else to turn to. Besides some of the people who work for my father, I don't know any other cops, and you're the best. And… I'm scared." The last two words were said on a faint whisper.

Sam wanted nothing to do with the snake pit this case could turn out to be, but the detective in her was far too intrigued to walk away. "How'd you get here?"

"I took the Metro."

She took a look around to see if anyone was watching, but the parking lot was deserted, and the usual band of reporters that stalked the MPD were taking the day off. They tended to do that when it was freezing. "Come with me." She led him to her car and gestured for Josh to get in the passenger side.

Though she had no idea what she planned to do with him or the information he'd dropped in her lap, she couldn't walk away from what he'd told her. "Tell me more about this website where you saw the photo."

"It's a blog run by parents of missing children."

"How did you end up there?"

"I read a story about a baby who was kidnapped from a hospital in Tennessee the day after he was born and how his parents have never stopped looking for him. The thirtieth anniversary of the abduction is coming up, so they've gotten some regional publicity. There was a link in the story that led to the blog where the age-progression photo was."

"So the photo hasn't been picked up by the media?"

"Not that I could tell, but I was too freaked out by what I was seeing to dig deeper, especially since my thirtieth birthday is next week. I told my boss I had an emergency. I left the office and came right to you."

"Why me?"

"Are you *serious*? After the inauguration, the whole country knows what an amazing cop you are. Who else would I go to with something like this?"

Blowing off the comment, she said, "You realize that accusing the FBI director of a capital felony is not something you do without stacks of proof that he was involved."

"That's where you come in. I need proof, and I need it fast before that picture gets picked up by the wires or social media and flung around the country. I need proof before he knows that *I* know."

Sam had to agree that time was of the essence before this thing blew up into a shitstorm of epic proportions. With that in mind, she started the car, pulled out of the MPD parking lot and into weekday afternoon traffic that clogged the District on the way toward Capitol Hill.

"Where are we going?"

"My house."

She glanced over at him and saw his eyes get big. "For real?"

"Yes, for real." She paused before she continued. "Look, if you want me to dig into this, I have to do it at home. I'm…off duty right now. I've gotta stay below the radar on this or my bosses will be all over me."

"No one will hear it from me."

After a slow crawl across the District, Sam pulled up to the Secret Service checkpoint on Ninth Street. Normally they waved her through, but she had to stop to clear her guest. "They'll need to see your ID."

Josh pulled his license from his wallet and handed it to her.

She gave it to the agent, who took a close look before returning it to her. "Thank you, ma'am. Have a nice day."

"You too."

"What's that like?" Josh asked. "Being surrounded by Secret Service all the time?"

"About as much fun as you'd expect it to be."

"Why don't you have a detail?"

"Because I don't need one. I can take care of myself."
Thankfully, he didn't mention the recent siege in Marissa
Springer's basement as an example of her inability to take
care of herself. Sam liked to think that was a onetime lapse
in judgment, never to be repeated.

Outside their home, her husband's motorcade lined the
street. What was he doing home so early?

She parked in her assigned spot—everyone who lived
on Ninth Street now had assigned parking spaces—and
headed up the ramp that led to their home.

"Why do you have a ramp?" Josh asked.

"My dad's a quadriplegic. He lives down the street.
My husband installed the ramp so he could come to visit."

"Oh, that's cool. Sorry about your dad, though."

"Thanks."

Nick's lead agent, John Brantley Jr., met her at the door.
"Lieutenant."

"Brant. What's he doing home so early?"

"The vice president isn't feeling well."

"Say what?"

ACKNOWLEDGMENTS

THANK YOU FOR reading *Fatal Scandal*. I hope you enjoyed it! I want to extend a special thanks to the readers who have embraced Sam and Nick's journey and are always asking for the next book. Your excitement and enthusiasm keeps me actively engaged in the Fatal Series, and I look forward to many more adventures with Sam and Nick. This book was especially challenging as Nick, Sam and I adjusted to his new role as vice president. I'm enjoying the addition of new characters to the landscape as well as the way this storyline forces me—and Nick—out of our comfort zones.

As always, an extra-special thanks to Captain Russ Hayes with the Newport, Rhode Island, Police Department, who serves as my consultant and sounding board during the writing of these books. Russ is always quick with an answer or an idea, and I can't thank him enough for his ongoing help in keeping the police aspects of the Fatal Series as close to reality as I can get them.

Thank you to "Jack's" team: Julie Cupp, Lisa Cafferty, Holly Sullivan, Isabel Sullivan, Nikki Colquhoun and Cheryl Serra for all your help and encouragement, and to my family, Dan, Emily and Jake, for their never-ending enthusiasm for my career.

Thanks to my agent, Kevan Lyon, my editor, Alissa Davis and Carina Press executive editor Angela James for all their support of the Fatal Series. A special thank-you this time around to Farah Mullick with Harlequin, who has championed the Fatal Series in print with such incredible results. Thank you, Farah, and the entire team at Harlequin and Carina.

If you enjoyed *Fatal Scandal*, consider leaving a review at Goodreads and/or the retailer of your choice. Your reviews help other readers to discover the Fatal Series, and I appreciate every one of them.

When you finish the book, dish about the details, with spoilers encouraged, in the Fatal Scandal Reader Group at www.facebook.com/groups/FatalSeries/.

Also, if you're not on my newsletter mailing list, you can join at marieforce.com for regular updates about new books and possible appearances in your area.

Thanks so much for reading!

xoxo

Marie

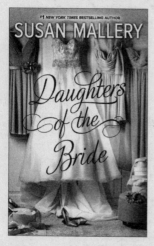

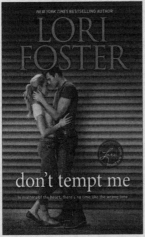

REQUEST YOUR FREE BOOKS!

2 FREE NOVELS
FROM THE ROMANCE COLLECTION
PLUS 2 FREE GIFTS!